# MEDIAN GRAY

# MEDIAN GRAY

Bill Mesce, Jr.

Between the Lines
PUBLISHING
"An Indie for Indies"

Copyright © 2020 Bill Mesce, Jr.

Cover Design by Suzanne Johnson

Willow River Press
Between the Lines Publishing
410 Caribou Trail
Lutsen, MN 55612
btwnthelines.com

First Published: 2020

Willow River Press is an imprint of Between the Lines Publishing.
The Willow River Press name and logo are trademarks of Between the Lines Publishing.

ISBN: 978-1-950502-27-1 (paperback)
Printed in the United States

Early praise for *Median Gray:*

"Equal parts Ed McBain, George V. Higgins, and *Barney Miller.* You can't go wrong." – author/screenwriter Nicholas Pileggi, *GoodFellas, Casino*

"Mesce conjures up wonderful, hard-boiled prose to tell a fast-paced urban story of crime, regret, pain, and redemption. The book is knowing and raw nerved." – David L. Robbins, *New York Times* bestselling author of *War of the Rats*

"It's the New York I remember from my days on the street in all its gritty, sooty, crazy glory." – Ret'd NYPD "French Connection" detective Sonny Grosso

"Mesce takes you on a blistering ride-along down mean New York streets with the most irreverent detectives this side of Richard Price. And with dialogue so true it feels wire-tapped; Price had better watch his back. This one's a winner." -- David Breckman, co-executive producer of TV's *Monk* and *The Good Cop*

"Smart, gritty, and authentic, *Median Gray* delivers a crackling tale complete with complex and damaged characters, and a keen eye for what cops know and think." – SFPD Sgt. Adam Plantinga, author of *400 Things Cops Know* and *Police Craft.*

"A masterful deep dive into the gritty New York City cop culture of the '80s. A page turner you won't be able to put down. Mesce keeps you guessing until the very end, tossing small grenades, injecting secrets, all the while keeping these characters human and relatable." – Suzanne Trauth, author, *Dodie O'Dell Mystery Series*

To Tom Kennedy and Ellen Akins who helped me
finally turn this into a real novel.

And to my Pop and the other Sages who gave me a
writing home when I most needed one.

*the city grows down into his open eyes*

*inverted and distorted. No. I mean*

*distorted and revealed,*

*if he sees it at all.*

Elizabeth Bishop, "Love Lies Sleeping"

*New York City, August 1963*

Meara has a foot post, three blocks along 11th Avenue in the 40s. The old hair-bags tell him, You walk your beat, you keep your eyes open, you listen, you *own* your three blocks, the people who live and work there are *yours.*

His uniform bought new for his first beat, still stiff and uncomfortable after two months, sticks to him in the already hammering morning heat, chafes at his neck. His scalp bakes under the peaked cap, his feet are dying in the heavy, rubber-soled shoes.

He complains to the old hair-bags, and they laugh and say, Hey, you wanted to be a cop? Welcome to being a cop.

He's surprised how quickly he learns the faces on his beat, learns their names, the names of their wives and kids and annoying brothers-in-law and the mother living in Florida. If he closes his eyes, he knows exactly where he is because of the sweet smell of Donatello's fruit and vegetable stand, the blood and sawdust smell of Ruffo's Butcher Shop, the smell of Old Spice and Vitalis from old man Donlin's barber shop, the stale smell of beer and cigarette smoke from Mickey's corner bar. He knows that for God knows what reason, the sewer at the corner of 11th and 44th stinks like no other sewer in the city and he wishes someone would get around to finding out what died down there.

He gets so fine-tuned to his three blocks he doesn't have to see or hear something to know when things are off. He can feel it. When he takes his post in the morning, and hands it off at end of his tour, he likes how savvy he feels trading info with the veterans who take the beat on the other shifts, like how when Donatello's wife wasn't in the shop he figured maybe Donatello beat her again, so he pulled that fat red-faced prick aside, held his nightstick under the grocer's double chin and told him if his old lady showed up with a shiner, he and the grocer were going to have a talk. He knows if he sees the MacAfee kid sitting on his stoop eating corn flakes dry out of a ten-pack box, his pop probably tied one on the night before, and now he's grumbling around the apartment hungover and looking for something to hit.

1

Sometimes the boy sits with the Cazale kid, a fat little girl with bad teeth whose mom makes ends meet by bringing home new boyfriends every night. Every so often, greasy-haired Feeney with the cigarette and magazine place has his pinky in a splint, and that means he's behind to the shylocks, and the other shifts tell him, Screw it, Feeney's a scumbag and a hump, he's got it coming, stay out of it.

Donlin gives him free haircuts. He doesn't ask for them, but Donlin comes out and says, Hey, Officer Jack, you're looking a little shaggy. Max with the Greek coffee shop and the daughter waitress who can't stop talking about how cute Trini Lopez is lets him use the bathroom, brings him in and sits him at the counter with a free coffee to get him out of the rain, a cold drink and a few minutes in the air conditioning when it's hot. He doesn't ask for these things, but they do them anyway. Donatello doesn't even like him and still he tells Meara he's gotten in a fresh batch of Rome apples from upstate that morning, he should take a few home.

That's how it's done, the old hair-bags tell him. That's what they do because they're yours, they belong to you and they know it, and what they expect for their tribute is you fuckin' A better take care of them in return.

Because this is what it is to be a cop.

He's 26 and he's two months out of training and still on probation, and these are his, these three blocks. He listens to the hair-bags, he makes himself know every crack in the sidewalk, where the curbside puddles will be when it rains, where the alleys are the truants slip through when they see him coming.

He walks his three blocks the same pace the same route each day so his citizens always know where he'll be if they need to find him. It takes him a half-hour to make his circuit, then he stops at his call box on the corner of 11th and 44th to make his "30 ring" – his every-30-minute check-in.

It's 10:30 on an August morning and it is hot, awfully goddamn hot. He was already feeling the scratch of the uniform shirt on his skin before he pulled it on that morning, felt it even while he was lying in bed fumbling to turn off the alarm before it woke up Mae. It's 10:30, it's hot as hell, and he's just locking up his callbox after making his 30 ring. He hears the slap of PF Flyers on the sidewalk, hears the kids panting even before he turns, hears something desperate in the way they're wheezing. He hears the MacAfee kid saying, "See? Here he is!"

They come up to him, the MacAfee kid, and some other boy he doesn't know.

"Tell him," the MacAfee kid gasps out. But the other kid freezes up, this isn't his cop, he's from someplace else, he's afraid bringing the bad, scary news, so the MacAfee kid says, "His dad told him to find you. He says somebody shot the other cop."

Meara's already unlocking the call box. "What other cop?"

McAfee pokes the other kid who finally blurts out, "Mr. McInerney. My dad, he says he heard the shot."

McInerney. Meara knows him, not well, but knows him; the other probie, sunny, smiley guy, still has pimples. He drew the foot post just south of Meara's. The old hair-bags are always busting McInerney's balls that he's too nice to be a cop. "They *eat* nice guys out there!" they say like they're telling spook stories to a little kid.

Meara gets an address out of the new boy that's down on 43rd, and now he has Dispatch on the horn. "Foot post 6-10, I've got a civilian reporting a 10-10," and he gives the address. "Reports shots fired, possible officer down, requesting 10-13 all units. Please advise."

It takes only a second before Dispatch comes back to him, but in that second the temperature seems to jump ten degrees and he's burning up in his scratchy blue, he has to take his cap off or his head'll explode. He picks at the places where his uniform is sticking to him in large, dark patches. The kids are looking up at him, MacAfee's friend looks like he's going to cry. Meara makes himself smile at the kids.

"Cover the door and wait for back-up, 6-10, do you copy?"

"Cover the door."

"And *wait!*" They remember he's a rookie. They'd never have to tell one of the hair-bags twice. "Understand? Do not enter the premises until back-up arrives."

He acknowledges this, tells the kids to stay by the callbox and if any other cops come by, point them to the scene.

He puts one hand over his holstered pistol, he doesn't draw it – that feels like too much just yet – and starts running, holding his cap in his other hand because it's still too goddamn hot to wear it, and now he is really burning up, he can feel it on his neck, on his ears, he's swimming in sweat and he knows it's not just the summer sun, he can feel the pounding in his chest, like a gorilla trying to break through his breast bone with a 20-pound sledge.

It's a two-block run and then he's standing at the base of the stoop of a five-story walk-up so dilapidated he wonders for a second if it's derelict. He sees scared eyes peeking out from behind ragged shades, hears a TV through the open windows, an old *I Love Lucy* repeat. There are people watching, keeping their distance, standing a few doors down on either side and across the street. If they didn't hear the shot, they heard the news, and they're waiting and watching to see what he's going to do; what he's going to do for their cop.

He can hear the wailing sirens. He climbs the steps to the top of the stoop. The outer and inner doors of the foyer are open and beyond them the hall is dark. It smells musty, damp. PRs have been moving into the neighborhood for years, but this dump is still Irish, he can smell that sewagey smell of boiling cabbage and potatoes.

"*Luuuuceeee!*" he hears a pissed-off Desi from one of the front apartments, "wha's goin' on here?"

Do not enter the premises they told him, and God knows he doesn't want to go down that dark hallway...

Then he hears him, McInerney. "Oh, God...Help me... Somebody help me..."

He wants to call out to him but if he does, then McInerney will know he's there and will ask him for help and he'll have to say, No, they told me to stay here, watch the door. Sorry.

"Oh, Jesus it hurts..." The way he says it – the feeble sobbing – reminds Meara of a whimpering puppy. "Help me..."

Meara sees that sunny face in his head. He remembers McInerney telling him about his wife, how the new baby is colicky and keeping them both up all night. He wishes he didn't know about the wife or that McInerney had ever shown him those fucking pictures of his fucking kids.

Lucy is wailing: *"Waaaahhhh!"* and the laugh track is in stitches.

He looks around at the people waiting, watching. They can hear McInerney, too.

"God, Jesus God, not like this..."

They teach you at the Academy, your Training Officer teaches you on the street, the old hair-bags tell you in the station house locker room, Don't be a hero; they say it over and over. You ain't Superman, no bullets are gonna bounce off you. Don't be a hero. Play it smart. Always, always, *always* wait for your backup.

He thinks of that sunny, pimply face and imagines it twisting in pain and the fear of dying, and he's thinking of McInerney's fucking wife and his fucking kids, and he's thinking maybe if McInerney just hears a voice, it'll help him hold on.

He calls out. "It's me! Meara!"

"Jack! Jack, God, Jack, I'm dying..."

The sirens are close, close enough, so Meara thinks it won't make a difference now if he stays or moves.

"Help me, Jack...Please don't let me die..."

Jesus, he had to say my fucking name! I don't know *his* first name, why's he know *mine?*

5

The civilians are still standing around, watching him, waiting.

Lucy is telling Ethel she has a plan for some goddamn thing, but they can't let Desi and Fred know what they're up to.

I got a wife, too, Meara says in his head to the gawking civilians, and I got a shitty little apartment in a shitty walk-up in Brooklyn and we talk about how once I'm through probation we're gonna start a family and get a house and they told me not to enter the fucking premises so what do you want from me?

They still watch and wait.

It's not like he's going to go hunting down those dark halls and stairways after the perp, that'd be stupid, that'd be fucking insane. He's just going to find McInerney, keep him company until the ambulance gets there, maybe he can do some First Aid; maybe he can do… something. Anything.

He unsnaps the restraining strap on his holster and pulls out the .38, and he's surprised at how light that pound and a half of steel feels, not tugging at his hand the way it does on the firing range at Rodman's Neck, but popping clear of the leather like it's on a spring because he's got so much adrenaline going through him he could spin a Mack truck on his finger.

He steps through the foyer and into the must-and-cabbage smell of the hallway. It's hot and close in there, he wonders why there are no fucking lights.

"I'm coming, Mac," he says moving slowly down the hall, straining his ears, trying to find shapes in the dark.

He can't hear Lucy anymore, but he can still hear the bubbling laugh track. Something's still funny.

There's a splash of yellow sunlight at the foot of a staircase halfway down the hall.

"Jack…" From the stairwell.

"I'm coming, Mac."

He hears the sirens, they sound like they're practically in the hallway with him, but he looks back and there are no cars on the street, no uniforms silhouetted in the front door, and he wonders what in God's name is taking them so fucking long? And he's so deep in sweat his uniform drags at him, won't let him open his chest to breathe.

Then he's reached the foot of the staircase, there's a window up over the between-floors landing, that's where the light's coming from, all bright yellow with morning, and sprawled on the landing is McInerney.

Meara already knows it's bad he's in the building, bad that he's all the way down the hall, and he knows it'd be *really* bad if he goes up those stairs.

"Jack…"

Meara whispers: "Where is he?"

"Help me, Jack…God, I'm dying, I know I'm dying…Tell her for me, Jack, tell her…"

The fucking wife, again.

Meara starts up the stairs, one slow step at a time, his pistol raised, his eyes looking up to the next floor.

Cars screech to a stop out front, the sirens fall into a dying moan, and now he feels ok, it's going to be ok.

He kneels by McInerney and he says that; how it's going to be ok, the troops are here.

He hears a shout upstairs, something panicky about cops out front, feet stumbling down the stairs. He gets up, turns as a figure hurtles around the second-floor landing and down the upper stairs of the first flight. He barely gets his gun up, hasn't even said anything when they collide, entangle, and there's one, brief, brilliant second of mental clarity – when he's swamped by just what an unbelievably fucking bad idea it was to come down that hall – and then that clarity collapses into panic as he and the figure grapple and try to untangle themselves, and then he feels himself losing his balance, falling backward, he reaches a foot back but there's nothing there and now he's on his back, his breath punched out of him as he skids down the stairs to the hallway floor.

He's still got his pistol in his hand but he's dazed, he can't get enough breath to move, and he looks up, sees the guy he just wrangled with standing on the landing over McInerney, silhouetted against the soot-streaked window, sees the guy's right arm coming up and he knows what that means, he fucking *knows,* and he feels everything from the pit of his stomach down to his groin turn to cold mush, he's trying to draw in some air, enough to get his own piece up –

There's a flash. Quick, bright, like lightning. In that flash, dark eyes look down on him, cold fucking hard eyes.

And with the flash...

There's a POP – a small noise, like a single clap of hands, but in the confines of the hall it sets his ears ringing…

The guy runs down the stairs, jumps over him, heading for the back door.

Meara tries to bring his pistol up but suddenly it feels heavy, like cement, a ton of cement, and when he tries to move, he can't.

He thinks about the flash and the pop and wonders if he's hit, thinks he must be hit, but there's no pain, just this heaviness, and now he doesn't feel hot anymore, there's a creeping cold, like he's lying naked on a winter sidewalk. He smells the warm, dusty wood of the hallway floor under him, hears the tick-tick-tick of claws out in the darkness drawn to the smell of blood. He can still hear muffled laughter down the hall, but he doesn't know why because he doesn't think anything about this is funny.

Somebody over him, standing, kneeling, he's not sure, the face seems a 100 miles away, he hears the shout echoing down the hall…

"Jesus, they're both down! We need a wagon!" Then, quietly, closer to him, "It's ok, kid, ya gotta hang on."

8

Another voice, another figure far away looking down on him. "Stupid-ass rookies, man."

Maybe he's losing consciousness, maybe the darkness of the hall is filling his eyes.

Or maybe he's dying.

But in that dark, he still sees the sudden flash and those eyes, those cold, hard eyes, hard fucking eyes…

*December 1982*

# one: the kid

*I got my pinball*

*my textbook*

*lead me to the station*

*I'm off to the Civil War.*

Pete Townsend, "Slip Kid"

"Ma'am, can I ask how you know this guy's gonna rape you?"

"He says he's a repairman. That's what *DeSalvo* used to say."

"All right," Ronnie said.

Apparently, the old lady – and Ronnie had known from her first, warbling tones that it was an old lady – could tell Ronnie still didn't know who she was talking about. *"Albert* DeSalvo! He *was* The Boston Strangler."

"You think your repairman's The Boston Strangler?"

"No, you silly goose! The Boston Strangler's *dead!* He died in prison *years* ago! You're a *policeman!* You should *know* that!"

The old lady was making Ronnie's head hurt. In the two weeks since he'd been assigned to the detective squad, he'd found his head hurting quite a lot. The headaches always started with a dull throb across the break in the bridge of his nose where it took a slight jig to the left, and then as the throbs increased they would radiate up into his forehead and out behind his eyes. Right now, the old lady had his left eye tearing and the right one wasn't far behind.

"Ma'am, tell you what. You keep your door locked and we'll send a car over to check this out for you, ok?"

"But I'm not home! I'm in a phone booth."

"What're you doing in a phone booth?"

"I had to use the phone, you silly goose! Mine's *broken!* Maybe *he* did something to it! So, he could pass himself off as a telephone repairman!"

The pain in Ronnie's head became blinding. He wondered if it was acceptable Proper Police Procedure for someone in the detective squad room to hang up on a caller deemed to be – in stationhouse jargon – CTS: Crazier Than Shit. "Ma'am, could you please hold on a second?" Ronnie punched the "hold" button and looked around the squad room for help.

Big Sid was standing over his desk taking a bag of bagels from a young woman in blues. "Hey, kid, how come you don't talk to this nice lady?"

"What nice—"

"How much is that, Teri?" Big Sid asked. "Cover that for me, wouldja, kid? We'll even up later." Before Sid tilted his 50-inch waistline toward the Mr. Coffee, he folded his massive, mocha face into a guiltless grin of felony perjury quality indicating Ronnie was going to get screwed on the bagels.

In the few months Ronnie had worked patrol in the precinct, he'd seen Teresa Ortiz more than a few times, enough to exchange a smile, a wave, a hello as they passed in the stationhouse halls. She had high cheekbones, canted, almond eyes, and straight dark hair cut to a practical shortness, all making her look more Asian than Puerto Rican, especially when her face crinkled in a shy smile. She was on the short side (one locker room wit had suggested she was the only cop in the house shorter than Ronnie), and the PAL sweat jacket she was wearing over her blues which, in turn, bulged over her Kevlar Second Chance vest, gave her the sweet, rounded look of a Renaissance cherub...albeit a cherub with a .38 on her hip.

Though Ronnie had never said more than six words to her, he'd begun to miss seeing her since his move off patrol. His right hand went to the peaks of his hairline to make sure his slightly-longer-than-regulation strands covered the base of the central peninsula. "How much did you say?" he asked Teresa Ortiz.

"Call it five," she said.

Ronnie fished around in his pocket. "I dunno if I got a five."

"I got change," she said.

"Well," Ronnie said, clearing his throat, fumbling out a ten. "I got this call," he said nodding at his phone. "Some nutcase, I think."

She shrugged.

"Same nuts like on patrol. Look..."

Her eyebrows went up expectantly.

"Ya know, maybe some time, um…"

"Sure."

"Right. I'll stick my head in downstairs one day. Maybe coffee or something."

She nodded, shrugged a last time, flicked her shy smile. Ronnie watched her walk out, liked the way the gear on her duty belt – holster, keys, baton, the rest of it – swayed this way and that, emphasizing the natural pendulum swing of her –

"Wow!" Big Sid bellowed from across the room and Ronnie shrunk in his seat. "What a *smoothie!*"

At that point, Ronnie would rather have crawled under his desk than beg Sid for help, but his alternatives were Dewey Berberick and a host of empty desks, and Dewey Berberick would've been slightly less helpful than a boil on his ass. Ronnie started waving at Sid.

"Problem, kid? With that kind of *smooooth* approach, you got a problem? What kind of advice could I give a *smooooth* operator like you?"

"Sid, would you please help me out here, please? *Please?*"

Big Sid parked a cream cheese-drenched marble twist bagel in his mouth while he off-loaded four spoons of sugar into a cup of black varnish from the Mr. Coffee, then ambled over to Ronnie's desk. "Tell Daddy the pwobwem."

Ronnie explained about the lady on hold.

Big Sid took the receiver. "You better *hope* she's nuts, kid. The Department frowns on putting rape victims on hold." Then he said into the receiver, "Detective Sergeant Leland speaking, can I help you? …Yes… Mmm…I see…Yeah, yeah, just like The Boston Strangler…" Big Sid eyed his bagel, said to the lady on the phone, "Tell you what, ma'am, cases like this, we got experts, skilled professionals. That's the best person for you to talk to. Hold on and I'll put you in direct contact with one of these specialists."

Dewey Berberick was short and round, had a sour bulldog face and a mood to match. His desk was jammed against the sooty front windows where someone had hung a wrinkled "Merry Christmas" banner, mangy where the old glitter had flaked off. Berberick grumbled all day every day about the glitter falling into his coffee.

"Hey, Berbs!" Big Sid called across the room. "Someone for you on Line One. I think it's your wife." Sid tossed the phone back to Ronnie and retreated to his own desk.

Ten seconds into the call, Dewey Berberick was extending a middle finger with an accompanying glare in Big Sid's direction. Sid responded with an offended 'who-me?' look and pointed a deflecting finger toward Ronnie. Ronnie took that as a cue to attend to business in the men's room.

He was crossing the head of the stairs just outside the squad room when he heard a politely repressed sneeze in the stairwell. "Bless you."

Rising from the stairwell was a thick mane of silver and black hair, deftly sculpted and lacquered into a TV anchorman's sweep. Then, the face, lined and just a little jowly, the long, straight nose glowing with influenza. Then, the London Fog overcoat, Italian leather briefcase, a glimpse of pinstriped suit pants, and, finally, a pair of Bostonians protectively sheathed in clunky Totes. Captain Victor Van Dyne, air wheezing painfully through his congested nose, paused for breath at the top of the stairs. There was a radio on downstairs, "Dominick the Christmas Donkey," and every time Lou Monte sang "Hee haw! Hee haw!" a couple of somebodies downstairs hee-haw-hee-haw-ed along. The hee-haws made Van Dyne close his eyes, shake his head, then his eyes opened, took in Ronnie in his layered look of thermal undershirt, YMCA cut-off sweatshirt, and thermal vest. One of his thick eyebrows raised in a mix of curiosity and dismay.

"You have an interesting interpretation of what 'plainclothes' duty means, Ron, if you don't mind my saying." Then Van Dyne noted the

18

motley collection of sweaters, insulated vests, and sweatshirts passing by in the hall. "Or is there a reason everyone is dressed for the next ice age? Some reason I probably don't want to know?"

"Something about the plumbing—"

Van Dyne held up a hand for silence, closed his eyes, and hung his head. "I *don't* want to know." After an appropriate amount of silent suffering, Van Dyne opened his eyes and looked in the squad room. The empty desks brought back the pained look.

"Cutler and Berman are on a call, jumper on the NYU library," Ronnie said. "And Murillo called in this morning, says he's still got the flu. Says he'll try for tomorrow."

"*I* have the flu!" Van Dyne said. "But *I'm* here!"

"Yessir."

Van Dyne took a deep breath and started across the squad room for his office.

"Oh, Captain, there's something from the Review Board about McQuillikan on your desk. Hey, how'd it go with the Chief of Detectives?"

"It went," and Van Dyne's office door closed behind him.

The heat missing from the rest of the station was in force in the confines of the second-floor men's room. A spidery little black guy in dirty Building Maintenance Division coveralls clanged at the radiator pipes with a wrench and the radiator hissed back at him.

"How's it goin?" Ronnie asked.

"It fuckin' *sucks* is how it's goin'," the Maintenance guy said through gritted teeth as he tried to budge a coupling that wouldn't uncouple.

"So, Doctor, any idea what the problem is?"

"The problem is – *umph!* – they don't wanna spend no fuckin' money – *c'mon, move, you mother* – to fix nothin' in this pile a brick –

*aaarrrgh!* – 'cause General Services says they're tearin' it down next year. *Fuck!*"

"Ya know, in the meantime, if you could get some of the heat in here out to the rest of us."

"Hey!" the Maintenance guy barked so sharply Ronnie jumped back, "do *I* tell *you* how to do *your* fuckin' job?"

Ronnie made some vaguely apologetic motions with his hands and the Maintenance guy went back to wrestling with the radiator. Ronnie went to the faded mirror over the stained sink and toyed with his hairline again, noting a few strands of gray at the temples. Two years on the job and look at that, he brooded, calculating he'd be all gray or all bald by the time he hit 30.

Ronnie had just moved to one of the urinals when the men's room door banged open.

"Where are you, ya little Jersey faggot!" Dewey Berberick stomped up to Ronnie and bellowed in his ear: "You suck moose cocks, ya little prick! You eat donkey dicks! Why don'tcha go back to Jersey 'n' suck on a fuckin' smokestack or somethin'!"

"What're you shouting at me for? It was *Sid!*"

"Fuck Sid, and fuck *you*—"

"Jeez, c'mon, it was a joke!"

"Yeah, real fuckin' *funny!* Ha ha! I'm bustin' a fuckin' *gut* over it! Ha ha ha!"

"I can't pee when you're shouting."

"You little cunt!"

"Hey now—"

"You little—"

"It was a *joke*, for Chrissakes!"

Realizing he would be unable to finish what he'd started, Ronnie zipped up and went to the rusty sink. He spun the taps. They made wheezing and groaning sounds before they spat out dashes of brown water. "Hey," he said to the Maintenance guy. "What's with the water?"

*"One fuckin' thing at a time, ok?"* The Maintenance guy looked ready to come after Ronnie with one of his wrenches.

"You keep cockin' around wit' Sid 'n' I'll see you back on a foot post for the rest a your miserable fuckin' life, ya little whore-bitin' bastid!" Berberick hissed. "Have you put on dog turd patrol, writin' up them old ladies what don't clean up after their little *shit*-soos, turd patrol for all fuckin' *eternity!*"

Ronnie was never one to be rude if he could help it. Besides, Berberick was technically his superior. Still, it seemed a good idea when he raised his wet hands from the sink to pretend to absently flick water into Berberick's eyes.

"You *fuck!*" Berberick screamed, frantically wiping at the brown water in his eyes. "I swear to *Christ!*"

Ronnie scooted by him back to the squad room. At his desk there was a non-regulation pink "While You Were Out Fucking Around" message slip wedged in the cradle of his phone. Something was scribbled in the message box, but Ronnie couldn't read it. He assumed the scribble belonged to Big Sid as Berberick never took messages for anybody ("I'm *nobody's* fuckin' seckaterry!").

Sid was on his phone, partly bored, partly exasperated: "I'm not saying it's right, mister, I'm just telling you it's not against the law...No, don't do that. That *is* against the law...Well, if you do *that*, I'm going to have to come over there and arrest *you*...I know, that's not right, either, but that *is* the law..."

Ronnie flagged Sid with the message slip, shrugging his shoulders in question. Sid covered up the mouthpiece of his phone and held the receiver away from his ear.

"What's this?" Ronnie waved the message slip.

"Call Lou."

"Who's Lou?"

"How the fuck *I* know? She's *your* sweetie," and he went back to his call.

Ronnie scooped up his phone and dialed the number Sid had scrawled on the message. A bear growled, "Yo, Diamon' Lil's."

"Yeah, hi, this is Officer Valerio at the Twelfth Precinct. I got a message to call somebody named, 'Lou'? Hello? *I'm supposed to call somebody named 'Lou'!*"

*"Who?"*

A jukebox in the background was *whump-whump-whumping* pretty loudly. *"LOU!"*

"Yo, stop *screamin'!* Jesus, I ain't deaf! Hold on."

Ronnie winced as the phone on the other end dropped with a clunk and rattle, followed by louder, unobstructed *WHUMP-WHUMP-WHUMPing.*

Somebody rapped on Ronnie's desk. Ronnie looked up at a tall, black cop wearing a ragged Cornell sweatshirt over his blues. The cop was waving some fax sheets at him. "Captain in?"

Ronnie nodded him toward Van Dyne's office.

There was another clunk and rattle in the earpiece as somebody picked up the phone. "Hello?"

"Hello, this is Ron Valerio at the—"

"Oh, yeah, right, Little Blue."

He flinched at the "little." "Excuse me?"

"Don't you 'member me, Blue?" It was a woman's voice, husky with a Spanish cadence. "Lourdes Bracero? Bartender down here at Lil's? Down on Canal? You helped me out last month, 'member? You left me your card? Took me to the hospital."

"Oh, yeah, yeah, yeah." He shifted in his seat, warming to the call. "What can I do for you, Miss Bracero?"

"I told you to call me, 'Lou,' 'member? You said I ever needed somethin', give you a call."

He waited.

"I'm givin' a call."

"Ok. So..."

"So... I don't think I should say on the phone. Can you meet me after work?"

"I'm off soon."

"I mean when *I* get off. 'Bout two."

*"A.M.?"*

She laughed, a cigarettes-and-whisky sound.

"Where you at?" he asked.

"Canal, like I said. Don't you 'member? South Side, just a block short a Chinatown? We got a sign. You sure you 'member me?"

"Sure. Lourdes. Lou."

"Lourdes what?"

"Lourdes –. Well, I never forget a face. Names, I gotta check my own name tag sometimes to remember who *I* am."

He was so pleased with his performance on the phone that he didn't immediately notice Big Sid standing over his desk.

"The Master beckons," Sid said, doing a little beckoning himself as he waved at Ronnie to follow him into Van Dyne's office.

Van Dyne was on the phone, waving at Sid to close the door behind him, then waving them to the cracked-vinyl sofa against the wall. Ronnie sat at one end; Sid dropped his bulk on the other. The impact brought a groan from the wooden frame.

"Eldon," Van Dyne was saying into the phone, "I've spent almost every day since your boss's case went down the toilet getting reamed. I've been reamed by experts. I've been reamed with power drills. The borough commander, a deputy commissioner or two, today it was the Chief of Detectives. Those gentlemen are all in my line of report, so I have to take it from them; I *don't* have to take it from *you.*"

As he spoke, Van Dyne, still in his London Fog coat, peeled off his Totes and swabbed at invisible scuffs on his spit-shined Bostonians with a Kleenex.

"Eldon, maybe the problem over there is failure of memory. I can tell you the exact date I memoed your boss, and if he's *still* foggy, I can send you over my copy of that very same memo in which I strongly advised – and those were my words, Eldon, '*strongly advised*' – the DA's office not to take this to trial; to hand it off to the US Attorney's office. I told you *then*: too many of my cops were involved, it was going to taint the case...Because, Eldon, you can't suspend 30 cops in the middle of a Mob investigation and not expect to have a credibility problem... Jurisdiction my ass, Eldon, he saw a big prize and he didn't want to give it up! You know it, I know it, the editorial pages of *The Post, The Daily News,* and *The Times* know it... So, fine, your boss got himself some headlines, and 12 days ago Anthony Maiella stood out in front of the courthouse tossing off one-liners for the press, not so subtly making the point that the NYPD and the DA's office could collectively kiss his ass as it went out the courthouse door..."

Ronnnie let his eyes wander around Van Dyne's office. Despite the walls being covered with the same dingy institutional paint as the rest of the station, and that it had the same scuffed and warped floorboards the other rooms had, along with the same grimy windows and scarred furniture, Van Dyne's office had always struck Ronnie as unexpectedly *classy.*

Van Dyne didn't have pictures of family, blow-ups of attempted vacation photographic artistry, official certificates, awards, and photo ops with departmental VIPs and passing-through celebrities cluttering up his walls. Instead, mounted in frames of glass and chrome, were a poster from the Spoleto Arts Festival, another from the New York Book Festival, and a print of Francis Bacon's *Study After Velázquez,* which looked to Ronnie like some screaming guy drowning in a downpour of orange and purple.

On Van Dyne's desk was a green baize blotter in a holder of engraved leather nicely squared in the center of his desk. A twin penholder of polished obsidian sat centered at the head of his desk just behind a mahogany nameplate reading, "Capt. V. Van Dyne." Folders were spread in neat fans for easy reference, but nicely angled off the central work area of his desktop. At his elbow was an ashtray from the Dorchester Hotel in London.

Behind the desk, Van Dyne was poised in a chair decidedly not Office Services standard issue. It was a high-backed swiveling throne of shiny black leather, polished dark wood, and gleaming brass studs.

On the wall behind Van Dyne, over his head between the dirt-streaked windows that flanked him, was a wooden plaque on which was carved:

*A policeman's lot is not a happy one.*
*Gilbert & Sullivan*

"As far as I'm concerned, Eldon," Van Dyne was saying, "this is between your boss and the Chief of Ds; not me! If I discuss this any further with you, I'm going to go into a tizzy, and I'm already well over my tizzy quota for December goodbye!" and he hung up. Ronnie thought it appropriate to stand and started struggling out of the sagging sofa, but Sid waved him back down.

Van Dyne had left his hand on the receiver, sighted on the phone through half-moon reading glasses parked far down on his nose, looking as if he expected an immediate ring-back. He gave a long, slow breath that was more simmer than sigh, and slowly withdrew his hand. He suddenly shuddered, rubbing his hands together. "Brrr."

"They're working on it, Captain," Ronnie said.

Van Dyne abruptly sneezed. "Perfect." He took another Kleenex from the little cellophane pack on his desk and dabbed neatly, gingerly at the red, chapped end of his nose.

"That the verdict on McQuillikan?" Big Sid asked, nodding at a manila folder open and centered on Van Dyne's desk.

"'Suspended pending further investigation yadda yadda,'" Van Dyne loosely quoted. Another long breath – this one an obvious and tired sigh – as he reached inside his coat and jacket and drew out a cigarette holder of dark wood, a silver cigarette case, and a matching silver lighter. He sprung open the case, took out a slim Paris Opal, carefully inserted it into the holder.

"So, we're down another head," Big Sid interpreted.

"We're down another head." Van Dyne clamped his teeth on the cigarette holder and flicked up a flame on his lighter.

"Should you be smoking when you're having problems breathing, Captain?" Ronnie asked.

Van Dyne fixed him with a glare that was enough for Ronnie to make never-mind motions with his hands. He fidgeted nervously on the sofa and the cracked vinyl made a sound Ronnie hoped no one would mistake for a fart.

Van Dyne wiped his nose again, leaned back in his leather-padded throne. He nodded at two pages of glossy fax paper on his desk. "One of those is from the Cape May County sheriff's department down in South Jersey. That's your part of the world, isn't it, Ron?"

"Depends. Cape May County's a pretty big—"

"Isn't it, Ron?"

"Yessir, I'm from down there."

Van Dyne pulled the fax within reading distance with his letter opener. "'Cape May County, yadda yadda,'" he read, "'In response to an anonymous 911 phone call night of 12-21...'"

"Last night," Ronnie said.

Van Dyne looked up. "Why, yes, Ron, that *was* last night! Ladies and gentlemen, a remarkable demonstration of the deductive skills which are the trademark of the NYPD. Bravo! May I continue?"

Ronnie sank a little deeper into the bottomless seat cushions.

Van Dyne read on: "'Salvatore Vincent Dell'Acqua aka Sally Dell'Acqua aka Kid Sally so on and so forth, found shot to death approx 13:30 hours –'" Van Dyne tapped the fax with the point of his letter opener. "Sidney, that name mean anything to you? Salvatore Dell'Acqua?"

"I know we've got him on our books for something."

"'For something.' Now I see where this young man – " a nod at Ronnie " – is getting his deductive expertise. Bookmaking, Sidney. He has a string of places in Soho. Well, *had*." Van Dyne turned back to the fax: "'Yadda yadda, automatic weapons fire.'" Van Dyne made an unhappy face. "'One assailant found dead, as yet unidentified... Please advise any pertinent information... Alfredo Francis Nardo, grandfather of deceased, being held at Cape May Regional Medical Center...'" Van Dyne made his unhappy face again and pushed the fax away.

"Ok," Sid said. "So, a bookie gets whacked out in the Jersey boonies."

"A *New York* bookie," Van Dyne clarified. "In fact, a bookie from *our* precinct. It may be nothing more than the product of a territorial dispute." Van Dyne held the other fax sheet up for Sid. "Seems they weren't even done working the crime scene in Jersey when somebody moved on Dell'Acqua's operations. Know that name?"

Sid squinted at the fax and made a sour face. "Juan Teixeira. Him I know."

"Still," and Van Dyne placed the second fax alongside the first, moving it a little this way and that to make a neat alignment, "under the present circumstances, I think it behooves us to take an interest."

"You want me to go down there?"

"You have correctly divined my gist, my dear Sidney. Take a car with you tonight, head straight down in the a.m. It'll be nice. It's Jersey. You'll see cows."

Sid made a face. "Send Berbs."

"I was considering it," Van Dyne said. "But depending on what gets turned, if anything, I'd prefer someone with a certain *savoir faire* to be there."

Van Dyne gave Sid a look, Sid gave Van Dyne a look back, then finally nodded glumly.

"Take *that* with you," Van Dyne said, nodding in Ronnie's direction.

"Me, Sir?" Ronnie asked.

"Yes, you, Sir. You're from down there, yes?"

"Like I was saying, Cape May, Sir, which is a good ways—"

"And your father was a cop down there."

"That was a long time ago, Sir, in Cape May—"

"I'll bet you even know where this hospital is."

"I was born there."

"See? You're the perfect ambassador."

"Well, that was a long time ago, too, Sir—"

"Still." It was not a rebuttal, but another way of saying, "Shut up." "Maybe having a native son in tow might grease the gears for Sergeant Leland, don't you think?"

"I guess, Sir, yessir."

"That's gonna leave you pretty short-handed," Sid observed.

"I'm already pretty short-handed. It's like Fort Zinderneuf out there. I'm going to have to prop up bodies in the windows."

Ronnie and Big Sid shook their heads.

"*Beau Geste,*" Van Dyne explained.

Ronnie and Big Sid shook their heads.

"Never mind. I'll pull another uniform or two upstairs to cover. They always think plainclothes work is a treat. But we know better, don't we Ron?"

Ronnie grinned but then wondered if Van Dyne was joking or not.

"This is not a boondoggle, Sidney. Hustle down there, talk to who you need to talk to, hustle back. Understand?"

Big Sid nodded, resigned.

"And Ron?"

"Yessir?"

"Before you leave; haircut."

"Yessir."

Ronnie opened the door to the squad room and there was Berman's lanky form folded behind his desk, his gray-templed face a little longer and sadder than usual. He was rolling a report form into his typewriter when he looked up at the sound of Van Dyne's office door.

"Hey," Big Sid said.

"Hey," Berman said without looking up.

"Where's Cutler?"

Berman shivered and reached for the coat he'd hung over the back of his chair. "Why's it so cold in here?"

"Cutler," Big Sid tried again.

Berman shrugged. "30th."

Ronnie felt a fleeting heaviness pass through the room. The morgue was on 30th Street.

"He went with the wagon to fill out the papers," Berman said.

Van Dyne appeared in his office doorway. "You're talking about your jumper? What happened?"

"How'd it go with the Chief of Ds?" Berman asked.

Van Dyne waved the question away. "What happened?"

Berman sat back in his chair, made a movement with his hand: up, over, then a long drop down, and a final spreading motion. "Raspberry jam."

Ronnie jogged south from the station house, down into the narrow streets of Greenwich Village. Whenever possible, he jogged home after his shift. He'd stop in the locker room, pull on some sweats, a blue NY Giants wool cap topped with a big red ball, sunshine yellow moose-hide mittens, and tuck his street clothes into a Day-Glo orange backpack. The first time Big Sid saw Ronnie in his running togs, he made a pained look and said, "Kid, I hope you run *fast*."

The winter twilight was coming on rapidly and just as quickly turning into night. The bistros and coffeehouses glowed with low, warm lights and Christmas colors. Between the collections of clubs and eateries, the streets were lined with four-, five- and six-story walk-ups. Each had a brick face painted a different, bright color – this one red, this one white, this one brown or orange – a scheme which found a playful resonance in the Christmas lights and electric menorahs blinking in apartment windows. Along the curbs, small, empty trees stood in little squares of bare earth.

There were other joggers on the street getting in their evening runs. Some huffed and sweated, others seemed to float easily down the streets leaving choo-choo train puffs of exhalation in the cold air. Some passed Ronnie exchanging a collegial nod, while others pounded by obliviously, Walkman headphones clamped to their heads.

Ronnie never wore a Walkman on his neighborhood runs. He liked the sounds of the street, the overheard conversations and music spilling from the clubs, even the horns from traffic-jammed cars.

This was a kind of music which reminded him every night how far from home he'd come.


Cape May is just about as far south as you can travel in New Jersey without winding up in the Atlantic Ocean. Isolated by tidal flats, woodlands, and inlets, it sits in a sedate part of the state below the Pine Barrens, an area most people don't conjure up when they think of New Jersey and start making Turnpike and landfill jokes.

Horse-drawn carriages trot along tree-lined streets bordered with the largest collection of Victorian-era architecture in the country, most of it converted into antique-filled bed-and-breakfasts. In the center of town is a cobblestoned open-air mall of quaint shops in clapboard buildings dating back a century or better. In winter, a robed choir moves from the stone Our Lady Star of the Sea church at one end of the mall to drift among the Christmas Victoriana and places selling antiques, hand-carved wooden toys and Save the Whale trinkets, Santa Claus sitting in front of a candy shop giving away free samples of hand-poured chocolate.

Ronnie's dad had been a cop in Cape May. That had never really inspired Ronnie since Cape May didn't require much heavy-duty policing. Most of the time, his dad might just as well have been driving a Mr. Softee truck up and down those shaded streets as a police cruiser.

But then came the call, some kids – probably not much older than Ronnie was at the time – drag-racing along the empty off-season streets, and his dad went chasing after them, lost control of his car on a patch of ice on the causeway leading out of town across the salt marshes, and skidded into a utility pole.

Years later, when Ronnie was undergoing routine psychological testing for the NYPD, the departmental examiner told him most people who honor the dead by taking up the deceased's profession were just trying find a way to keep the deceased alive. Ronnie asked him, "What's wrong with that?"

There was a jogger coming Ronnie's way, a young girl, and she had the smooth, untroubled gait of a veteran runner. She was hard to make out in the jigsaw pattern of streetlight coming through the branches of the sad, barren trees along the street. Ronnie could see enough, though: shining blonde hair tied back in a sashaying ponytail, breasts tussling under a Villanova sweatshirt.

He thought he saw her looking his way, so he picked up his pace, started vaulting over the garbage cans parked at the curb. Yeah, there we go! Get your fat ass over that, Sid! Ha! He leaped another garbage can, and another, trying to make it look effortless. He thought he saw her smiling his way. He smiled back and that was enough to lose his effortless rhythm and, instead of arcing neatly *over* a garbage can, he came down *in* it.

The can made a lot of noise when it went over. When the clatter stopped, Ronnie was sitting on the cold, slate sidewalk, holding a bruised and bleeding shin with one hand while he brushed coffee grounds off his sweats with the other. He could still see the swishing blonde ponytail bobbing off down the street. He could also see she was shaking her head from side to side. He was sure he could hear laughter.

Ronnie's building was a neat rectangle of brick painted sunlight yellow, not far from Washington Square, where he lived in a long, narrow fourth floor studio with a wooden floor which rolled like the ocean. There were two windows at the front overlooking the street, and at the other end of the apartment was a miniscule bathroom whose window opened on an airshaft. The kitchen area, such as it was, consisted of a sink, a stove not much bigger than a hot plate, and a refrigerator not much bigger than the stove. He had a futon and a TV he'd gotten at a discount through the Department's credit union, and a coffee table he'd found on the curb. There was a folding table and two folding chairs tucked behind the stove. There wasn't room for anything else. Ten paces took Ronnie from one end of his apartment to the other.

Ronnie locked the three locks on his door and slipped his anti-burglar bar into its notch. He flipped on the TV for company and dropped on the futon. He squirmed, trying to get comfortable, then pulled out the holster stuck in the back of his sweatpants and laid it on the banged-up coffee table next to an uncompleted model of a Sopwith Camel. There were simpler, completed model aircraft dotted around the apartment. Ronnie's effort on behalf of the Sopwith had stalled over the engine section which seemed composed of countless, near-microscopic parts that could only be handled with tweezers, infinite patience, and a couple of hand-steadying beers.

The answering machine on the floor by the futon was blinking with three messages. Ronnie's head hurt; he already knew who they were from. He steeled himself, then reached down to hit the playback on the answering machine, playing each message just long enough to recognize the voice – the same voice on all of them – and get the gist of the message before fast-forwarding through to the next.

It was his mother, and she began each message with, "This is your *mother,*" saying it like a declaration of war. Her voice was something between a goose's honk and an air horn, blaring about whether or not he was coming home for Christmas, why he hadn't returned her earlier calls, she'd been calling since last week, for all she knew he could be lying dead in the gutter somewhere and so on and so forth.

Ronnie erased the messages, then limped to the bathroom to clean and bandage himself and take a nice, soothing hot shower. He was stopped by a knock at the door. He closed his eyes. "Tamela?"

"Is that you, Ronnie?"

He hobbled to the door and undid the locks.

He had a quick glimpse of moussed, purple-tipped spikes of hair as Tamela brushed past heading straight for the stove. She had a casserole dish in her hands. "I brought you dinner."

Ronnie lifted the steamed-over glass cover and took a smell. The aroma made him think of dead ponds.

"What happened to your pants?" she asked.

"An accident."

"I can sew that up for you."

He ignored the offer. Ronnie wrinkled his nose at the casserole. "Ok, I'm stumped. What is this?"

"You don't eat right, Ronnie. All that poison in your fridge; I've seen it. Look at this!" She pointed at the shelf over his sink which served as a pantry. She started taking things down: a can of beef ravioli, a can of beef stew, a box of Rice-a-Roni, a box of mashed potato flakes, three boxes of generic macaroni and cheese. "Sodium, sodium,

sodium. Sodium and chemicals. Like, what's the use of all that exercise if you're going to absolutely poison yourself?"

"Ya know, a lot of this stuff isn't so bad—"

"The *chemicals*, Ronnie! That stuff'll turn you into a human toxic dump! You – Ooooh, what *happened?*" She had gotten around to noticing the spreading dark stain on his sweats. "Is that *blood?* Maybe I should have a look."

"No, it's fine. Just a bump."

"I could, like, kiss it and make it better."

"I don't think that's necessary." He noticed her footwear for the day: combat boots painted bright green. The day before it had been canvas sneakers painted hot pink.

She was a year or two younger than Ronnie, still in college (NYU probably, in some art program undoubtedly). Her mother and father were Korean and she had their wide, high cheeks and angled eyes. Tamela, however, had not been born in Korea, but in the moneyed part of Long Island and she showed that ancestry, too. Her straight, shiny black hair was kept short and spiky, and, over any period of time, sported a variety of hues. Conversely, her wardrobe – at least what Ronnie had seen of it – was strictly baggy things in black or white, or black-and-white with an occasional bright slash of gray. She wore matching rings on her thumbs.

Under the mousse and the baggy, glum clothes was a nice, petite shape and a swaying walk Ronnie's eyes enjoyed following. If that had been the entire package, Ronnie would've rather spent time with her – spiky tinted hair and all – than fiddling with his aggravating Sopwith Camel. And, indeed, they had tried an evening together once.

She'd asked him out not long after he'd moved in – a "Welcome to the Village" kind of thing she'd said – and they'd wound up in a cramped bunker of a place down by the Hudson jammed with people in sleeveless leather jackets and Stan Laurel haircuts. Afterward, she'd taken him to an all-night vegetarian eatery where she'd ordered for him, and the waitress presented Ronnie with a dish which looked and tasted like lawn cuttings. Ronnie had ended the night delivering a polite peck on her check to which she'd responded by stabbing her tongue so far into his mouth he'd almost choked. He'd been dodging her ever since.

"It's bean curd," she announced, pointing to white slabs floating in her casserole.

"What's that over there?" Ronnie asked, gesturing.

"Bean sprouts. I might be wrong. They might be, like, bamboo shoots or something. Bean sprouts or bamboo shoots. I forget. Oh, and that's shrimp over there."

"Ahhh, shrimp!" It was nice to see something recognizable, but it made Ronnie uncomfortable that the sprouts or shoots or whatever the hell they were looked like giant sperm.

"Try some of this." She held up one of the rubbery white slabs. "It's good for you."

"Ya know, I ate before I came home, Tam. I'm not really that hungry. Maybe later, huh? I'm really beat, and I need a shower and I just want to crash, see, because I gotta pull a late shift tonight."

"Oh." She looked at the casserole and Ronnie couldn't tell if she was disappointed or suspicious. "You can have it later, then, like, when you get home. It's just as good for breakfast as it is for dinner."

"I'm sure it is."

"And it's *good* for you. You *should* eat it. I *know* you don't eat right."

"I know. I will. I don't."

"Oh, before I go, what I really came over for? Was to, like, see what you're doing Thursday? Well, like, Thursday *night*, really. Like, this friend of mine? This guy from my Advanced Art Appreciation class? He's having this, like, Christmas party? Kind of a pre-Christmas Eve party?"

Ronnie flashed on a vision of Santa with purple-streaked hair and dressed in green gabardine and Ray-Bans. "I dunno. Maybe. If I'm not working. I don't know my schedule—"

"Great!" she beamed. "See you at ten!" She gave him a sloppy smack on the cheek and bounced out the door.

Ronnie stood there for a second, and it did feel nicely warm where she'd kissed him, but then he remembered that night down by the river and all those leather punks. He reset the anti-burglar bar and re-locked all the locks on his door. He turned to the casserole. The shrimp tasted gummy.

He clanged a pot on his little stove and reached for a box of macaroni and cheese.

*"Live!"* Don Pardo bellowed. "From *New York* – the most *dangerous* city in the world – it's *Saturday Night!"*

Don Pardo was lying. It wasn't Saturday night and after Ronnie blinked his eyes open and saw John Belushi on the TV, he realized the show wasn't live either. On cable, he thought, everybody lives forever.

It was a little after 11. When he felt mobile, he shuffled into the bathroom – his leg still hurt but he managed not to limp – and threw some water on his face. In the small, unevenly frosted mirror, he could see skin where he wanted to see hair. He fiddled with his hair, shifting it here and there, then almost turned out of the bathroom before he decided to give his teeth a quick brush and his breath a fast gargle.

He rummaged through his one, small closet until he found one of his newer pairs of jeans, something that still had a crease in it. Then he thought, well, if you're wearing the nice jeans, you should wear a nice shirt. And after the shirt he was back in the bathroom fussing with his hair again. Finally, he tucked his badge cover in a back pocket, clipped his holster to the back of his belt, bundled himself in parka, scarf, cap, and mittens, and went out.

The one-way street in front of Ronnie's building was full of cars, and the cars were full of angry people. Up ahead blocking the street was a garbage truck. All the pleading, swearing, fist-shaking and middle-finger waving going on behind it did nothing to speed up the slow, methodical pace of the garbage truck crew.

Somewhere at the back of the pack, someone started leaning on a horn. That, in turn, irritated a driver somewhere at the front of the pack who felt compelled to respond with some horn-honking of his or her own. Between the two of them, they managed to sufficiently antagonize the rest of the blocked cars until they were all beeping and blaring.

Ronnie was considering flashing his badge and trying to do something to quiet everybody down, when, from the sky, came a man's raw voice screaming, *"BEEP BEEP BEEP BEEP!"*

Ronnie looked up to see a young fellow in a beard and yarmulke hanging out a second story window. It seemed to do the trick; the cars quieted down. The young fellow looked down at Ronnie, quite proud of himself. "I fucking well told *them*, huh?"

It was pushing midnight and the knot of backed-up traffic in front of Ronnie's building notwithstanding, the streets were still. The clubs, restaurants, cafes, bistros, and shops that filled the Village were all quiet and dark, and apartment lights were winking off one by one. He saw the blue light of TVs in some windows and heard Johnny Carson, and passed another window where he saw the shadows of wildly gesticulating debaters flash back and forth across drawn curtains as they argued the direction of the world under the resurgence of Reagan's rah-rah nationalism. He heard New Age chimes from one building and passed through an invisible cloud fragrant with incense and marijuana. He turned onto Christopher Street and passed a few shaggy-haired NYU types still roaming in search of a last beer or slice of pizza before turning in, then a lesbian couple walking hand-in-hand as they escorted their German shepherd on its evening ablutions.

Ronnie flashed his badge to the TA man in the token booth at the Christopher Street station and the TA man waved him through the turnstiles. The station was empty, and Ronnie hopped the 9 Train downtown, sharing his car with a single passenger, a fretful old woman clutching her purse to her chest. She kept looking nervously over at Ronnie until she finally wobbled off through the rocking compartment into the next car.

He got out at Canal and came above ground close to Broadway. It was a rough neighborhood, old and battered, with hulking warehouses and wide, empty streets. He could see the few blocks down to the Hudson, the moon brittle and cold far out on the black water. The biting wind off the river made his eyes sting. He turned his back on the wind and headed east, toward Chinatown where Canal was flanked by electronic surplus shops, cut-rate jewelers, Army/Navy stores, and Chinese groceries, now all locked up tight behind scarred and graffiti-covered security gates.

He walked with maybe just a hint of a swagger. A guy screaming at honking cars, a walk down Canal Street after midnight, crazy old ladies who thought they were going to get raped by dead serial killers – to Ronnie, this was the edge where a cop should be. That was the job of the badge, to patrol that edge and to keep things tottering on the rim from falling in.

The night Ronnie had met Lourdes Bracero, it had been about 2:00 a.m. and Ronnie's partner, a 27-year-hairbag named Kesky, had just had them pull up to a 24-hour McDonald's on Canal because he needed to use the bathroom. Kesky had the radio mic in his hand to call in his 10-7 when a 415 crackled in: a disturbance. The address was just up the street but over their patrol border by a block, into the territory of the Fifth Precinct. From what Ronnie got over the radio, their unit was actually closer to the call by several blocks than the nearest Fifth unit, but Kesky squawked.

Nobody else would ride with Kesky, and if Ronnie hadn't been junior in the station and had had a choice, he wouldn't have ridden with him either. A jowly, pear-shaped, thin-haired grump, Kesky's idea of police work was anything that didn't involve him getting out of the car. He didn't arrest, he didn't investigate, he didn't even ticket. "That fat-assed Polack won't get outta the goddamn car unless it's on fire," they'd say in the stationhouse locker room.

"Keep 'em movin'," Kesky'd snarl at Ronnie which was his entire concept of law enforcement. "'At's all ya gotta do, kid, is keep 'em movin'."

"Keep *who* moving?"

"It don't matter *who!*" Kesky said. "Just keep 'em movin'! Whatever they're gonna do, make sure they do it somewheres else!"

The only occasions for which Kesky would haul himself out of the car was to go to the bathroom, and after 27 years of eating bad food on the run, he had to go to the bathroom a lot on a tour; so often the other One-Two-ers referred to him as Badge 10-7 (radio code for "out of service").

So there they were in front of the McD's and Kesky's attitude was fuck the call, he needed to use the shitter. "When the vic's family sues the City, what're you gonna say?" Ronnie said to Kesky. "I'm sorry but I had to take a crap?"

Ronnie threatened to leave Kesky at the McD's at which point Kesky, cursing the disrespectfulness of the young, climbed back into the car.

Ronnie zoomed up to Diamond Lil's, a hole in the wall topless bar jammed in among a row of low-rent electronics stores; he almost missed the small, blinking sign. Ronnie charged through the door. Kesky, cradling his grumbling lower regions, waddled along behind.

The "disturbance" came in the form of a young man, college age Ronnie guessed, and if he was, indeed, actually in college, it was probably on a full football scholarship. He was huge and not in a flabby, beer-sodden way, but in a slab-of-granite, weight-lifter way. The minute Ronnie looked up – *way* up – at the massive, square head sitting atop shoulders so wide they blotted out the bar's feeble lights, he thought maybe it might've been a better idea to have let Kesky take his crap.

What Ronnie got in the witness statements later was that The Tackle – and that's how Ronnie would always think of him – had been sitting quietly by himself off in a corner, downing one beer after another with an awesome, fast-paced regularity. Most of the patrons hadn't noticed him, their focus being on the chesty little thing wobbling and quivering on the bar's small stage. Most of them weren't aware The Tackle was on the move until he strode evenly through – not around, but *through* – the tables, chairs, and oglers around the stage. The Tackle marched up to the stage, clambered up and grabbed at the dancer.

At that, the bar's bouncer was over the bar, vastly overestimating his ability to handle a man half again as big as himself. The bouncer said, "Hey—" and before he got any further, The Tackle had laid him out with a single punch. Thereafter, The Tackle amused himself holding the struggling little dancer by his side while he growled and threw chairs at the other patrons.

Lourdes Bracero had been bartending. The second the bouncer hit the floor, she put a call into 911, then grabbed a fungo bat the bouncer kept stashed under the bar and which he had unwisely left behind. She skidded over the top of the bar and charged The Tackle.

The Tackle responded like a Rottweiler charged by a Pomeranian; he looked down at her from up on the stage, blinked his eyes curiously, not quite believing something so small would come at him. He reached down and set his free frying pan-sized hand on Lourdes Bracero's head, holding her at a safe distance, and laughed when she told him to get his fucking paws off her and off the dancer and get his drunken ass out. If he hadn't been laughing so hard, he might've seen the blow coming, but, as it was, Lourdes Bracero caught him unawares when she whacked him on his restraining forearm with the fungo bat.

The Tackle went, "Hey!" though he sounded more insulted than hurt. Lourdes Bracero didn't give his beer-addled mind time to gather its thoughts, and struck quickly a second time, taking a two-handed grip on the fungo bat and slamming it into one of his shins.

Now The Tackle was mad. He tossed the dancer away like a gum wrapper, jumped down onto the floor, pulled the fungo bat out of Lourdes Bracero's hands, and gave her a shove which sent her flying headfirst into a bar stool. When Ronnie and Kesky came charging into the bar (well, Ronnie charged; Kesky was moving carefully so as not to jar his distressed southern hemisphere), the patrons who hadn't run away were huddled in one corner, the dancer was crawling off to another, and the bouncer and Lourdes Bracero were stretched out on the floor.

Ronnie was in the lead and The Tackle focused on him, squinting like he was measuring how much force he'd need to send Ronnie's head flying out into Canal Street with the fungo bat. Ronnie saw no positives in meeting force with force. "Listen, fella," he began, opting for reasonableness, "Let's talk about it, ok?"

But while The Tackle's attention was on Ronnie, Kesky, with an expeditiousness spurred on by his building internal pressure, popped The Tackle behind the ear once sharply with his baton, delivering the blow with the deftness one would expect from a 27-year veteran, and then ran for the men's room before The Tackle hit the floor like a felled Sequoia.

Eventually, a unit from the Fifth did show up and Ronnie gave them the collar, it being their precinct, but he sat with Lourdes Bracero to take her statement. She held ice in a bar rag to the knot on her head, and Ronnie dabbed at the spider web of blood trails spreading across her face. She didn't want to go to the hospital, but she wasn't that steady on her feet and the blood kept coming, so Ronnie and Kesky ran her over to Gouverneur Diagnostic where the young resident on duty diagnosed "a pretty fair conk on the noggin." Ronnie kept her company while Kesky penguin-walked off and collared an internist to grill him on digestive tract problems.

In the flat white light of the treatment room, Ronnie got his first good look at Lourdes Bracero. It wasn't a particularly flattering light, but, even under the best circumstances, she wasn't someone whom one would necessarily label "pretty."

She was older than Ronnie had thought back in the bar, somewhere in her hard-looking early 30s. There was a small stippling of old, faded acne scars on her cheeks. There were lines around her eyes and the corners of her mouth, and a dusting of unabashed gray in her butch-styled shag. She had a narrow face with high cheeks, and stingy M&M eyes. Her nose most would have considered a touch large, and Ronnie recognized the bump and cant in it as membership in the same fraternity of the broken-beaked to which he belonged. She was small-breasted, her belly had an unfashionably detectable curve to it, and there were those who would, no doubt, have thought her jeans were just a little too snug in the hips by health spa standards.

But as Ronnie sat by the treatment table while an intern stitched the gash in her forehead together, all those pieces came together rather nicely in his eyes. He liked the lines on her face, the way they seasoned her, made her look lived-in and real in a way Tamela didn't. And, if her jeans were a hair tight across the hips, she still managed to walk with a nice swing, and not a young girl's *faux* coquette swing, but a brassy, cocky stride he found sexy (at least as much of it as he'd seen before she'd gotten woozy and had to be helped to the car).

It was that brass he liked, the fact she'd leapt over the bar to take on The Tackle with her itty-bitty fungo bat, the fact she could lay there on the treatment table, wincing against the pain, yet still give the stitching ER intern a running commentary along the lines of, "Hey, Doc, you wouldn't wanna hem my jeans while you're at it, huh?"

With each remark, she'd looked over at Ronnie and done this *thing*. Not a laugh, really; her mouth would open, and her little eyes would scrunch up and twinkle, but there'd be no sound. Like a mime's laugh.

She wouldn't agree to X-rays or staying overnight for observation, but she did let the intern talk her into resting for a bit before she headed home. Ronnie sat alone with her for a moment in the treatment room after the intern had left. He glanced at his watch and silently moaned. Reluctantly, he stood. "Well, look, Miss Bracero—"

"Hey, we been in combat together, Little Blue (which is what she'd dubbed him immediately: "Jesus, Little Blue, you were gonna take on *that* ape? Hell, *I* can take you!"). I think we can be a little more informal, dontcha think?" She held out her hand. "Lou."

"Ronnie," and he held out his.

Her grasp was firm, as tough as the rest of her, and Ronnie felt a flush when she pumped his hand in a comic shake.

"I gotta go, Lou," he told her. "I'll check in when I get off shift, see if you're still here, how you're getting along. You gonna be ok?"

"He only hit me in the head. Nothin' valuable there he could hurt."

He handed her a business card with the station's phone number. "You ever need anything, you call, ok? If you ever have any more trouble..." He shuffled on his feet, trying to make sure the offer sounded like legitimate police business. "I mean, I know you're in another precinct, but if, well, ya know, sometimes, like if, uh..."

"Sure," she said, and he thanked God she'd provided punctuation for him before he'd gotten to sound any dumber.

He mumbled some kind of good-bye and started to leave.

"Hey, Little Blue!"

He turned and found her suddenly sitting up on the examining table and before he knew what was happening, she'd leaned over and gave him a little peck on the cheek. "You're one a the good ones, Blue," she said, grinning when he turned red and his mouth moved with nothing coming out of it. "You can pass that on to your partner, too."

"I'll just shake his hand if that's all right with you."

He came back after his shift, but she'd already gone home.


The front of Diamond Lil's was marked by a blank metal door and a small window. In the window was a lit sign, flickering with a bad bulb, dim from a blanket of dust, which read, "Diamond Lil's – Live Entertainment." In acknowledgment of the holiday season, someone had draped a meager string of colored lights on the sign.

Ronnie went inside and stood by the door until his eyes adjusted to the gloom. There were a dozen banged-up tables with banged-up chairs crowded around a small, raised stage in the center of the high-ceilinged room. There was a single, small, fixed spotlight bolted to the ceiling and focused on the stage. A plastic disc revolved in front of the beam of light, changing it from red to green, blue to white. The audience was a few old men and some young ones, all looking as banged-up as the tables they were sitting at. They were all ignoring their drinks in favor of the black woman on the stage. She looked pretty banged-up too.

Her face was slack and tired. Her cellulite-dimpled legs looked even more cottage-cheesy in her red fishnet stockings. She wore a string top, G-string, garter belt, spike-heeled black boots and a red-with-white trim Santa Claus cap. The jukebox was playing "Three Times a Lady."

Whatever her physical shortcomings, the men in the bar seemed to like her well enough. When she dropped her string bra, they liked her even more.

Ronnie parked himself on a wobbly stool at the bar running along one side of the room. He saw Lourdes Bracero down at a far end of the bar pushing drinks.

"Hey, Little Blue!" she called out when she saw him.

He waved at her not to rush.

"That's why I don't wear no helmet," he heard somebody say nearby. "Man, when *I* go, I want it to be *fast!* I don't wanna wake up in no hospital bed all wired up or nothin'."

"I'm wit' you, my man."

They were sitting next to Ronnie at the bar. Biker types: denim, beer bellies, a lot of hair.

"Hell, somebody tells me I got, like, three months to live or somethin'? I'm gonna take 'er out on the road, like out on fuckin' Route 80, man, 'n' get 'er cranked as far as she'll crank, 'n' then take 'er over the high side, man. Fuck, man, I'll be leanin' over the fuckin' handlebars to make *sure* my melon hits square! *Boom!* Over 'n' out! Know what I'm sayin'?"

"I'm wit' you, my man! Take 'er out on the road, me 'n' a bottle of JD, right? Knockin' back my JD—"

"Hell, when I hit the fuckin' wall, man, just before, I'm gonna take me a mouthful so that's the last taste I got in my mouth! 'N' be buck naked!"

"Yeah! Buck naked 'n' swillin' Jack fuckin' Daniels—"

"'N' over the high side, my man!"

"Crank 'er up and *leap* into the fuckin' abyss, my man."

"So when I hit bottom, the only thing stickin' outta the ground is my bare ass!"

"Let 'em all kiss your ass, my man!"

"Yeah! The whole fuckin' *world* can just line up to kiss my ass goodbye!"

Then Lourdes Bracero was standing across the bar from him. "I almost didn't recognize you in your civvies!" she said.

He smiled at her, squinting to pick her out in the gloom behind the bar. He caught the glint of her little round eyes. "I recognized *you!*" he said.

"Bullshit artist," she teased.

"I told you; I never forget a face."

"You think this face is worth 'memberin'?"

"I even remember you changed your hair. You had it different then." It was still short, but now done in loose curls falling across her forehead.

"Yeah, well, I hadda make a few changes." She leaned forward, pushing her hair away from her forehead. Ronnie winced at the small, zipper-like scar where the stitches had been, still fresh and angry red. "They just took 'em out yesterday."

"Well," he said, "I like the hair. So. What can I do for you?"

"I figured we could talk after I got off, but you come early."

"Am I *that* early?" He tried to act surprised.

Her smile changed a bit; a wry, amused re-tuning which made him suspect she easily saw through him. "Maybe I can get off early," she said, "but it's gonna be another hour. I'll ask Kookie."

"Kookie?"

She nodded at the bear-like bulk of the bouncer/bartender hovering in the shadows at the other end of the bar. He was snapping toothpicks between his teeth.

"I don't remember him last time," Ronnie said.

"After that little dance you was here for, the owner figured we needed somebody a little more—. Well, just a little *more,* ya know?"

"Let's not provoke him. He looks like he bites. I'll just hang. Can I get a drink?"

"I thought you guys don't drink."

"Not on the job. I'm on *my* time now. How about a 7&7?"

"Well, we got Seven, but no Seven."

"Come again?"

"All we got is 7-Up, some near-beer—"

"What the hell is *that?*"

"Three-two beer. Like makin' love in a canoe! Fuckin' close to water!" She laughed her noiseless laugh. "We got some Perrier, some fruit juice—" She saw the puzzlement on his face. "After that last party with the, you know…" She pointed to the scar under her curls. "The guys who hand out the booze licenses? They say either the booze goes or the girls go." She poured him a 7-Up and set it on the bar. "Enjoy the show 'n' stay outta trouble. Keep both hands on the bar where I can see 'em." Then her face went soft for a moment. "Hey, Little Blue; thanks for comin'."

Ronnie held up his soda in salute, then let his eyes drop to her hips as she walked away to tend another customer. He thought it wouldn't do him any good to get caught with his eyes in that vicinity, so he swiveled around to watch the dancer. The girl gave him a listless, gap-toothed smile which looked sickly under the red, green, and blue light. Ronnie smiled politely back.

Contrary to the consensus in the room, Ronnie felt she would've looked better with more clothes *on*. Like, for starters, maybe a veil.

"Hungry?" Ronnie asked her.

"Little bit."

"I know a place. We can sit. Talk."

She nodded. She nuzzled up close to him. "You mind? I'm *really* cold." He saw her shivering inside her cheap cloth coat.

He slipped an arm around her. "Better?"

She nodded.

Ronnie's heart picked up a few beats over the feel of her hip moving along the top of his thigh.

There were still lights on up in Chinatown. Ronnie headed them up Canal, then down Mott Street to Bayard.

Just inside the door of the Kam Bo Rice Shop, Ronnie was buttonholed by an ancient, walnut-faced Asian in a blue serving jacket. "Hey, big time police commissioner!"

"Yo, Lee, how ya doing?"

The natural stern set of Lee's wrinkled face arranged itself into a series of happy horizontal lines as he pumped Ronnie's hand. "Been long time I see. Ah, and who's this very pretty friend, hm? New friend?"

"First visit," Ronnie said, trying to make it sound casual, hoping the tortured twisting of his face transmitted to Lee the message he should do likewise.

Lee led them to a corner table, then tugged Ronnie away by the elbow and whispered in his ear. "Zoot-zoot?" he asked, making poking motions with his finger and wagging his eyebrows at Lourdes Bracero.

"Behave," Ronnie said, looking past Lee's shoulder to make sure Lourdes hadn't seen the zoot-zooting.

Lee looked over at Lourdes, then his wrinkled face wrinkled a bit more thoughtfully. "Somehow, I think not too much luck for you, eh, Commissioner?"

"I appreciate your support, Lee, thanks."

Lee took him back to the table and yanked Lourdes' menu out of her hands. "You don't worry. I take care of the commissioner and his *friend.*" Ronnie winced; if Lee had said "friend" any more suggestively, Ronnie would've had to bust him for public indecency. Lee brought them tea and some fried noodles and duck sauce to occupy them while he toddled off into the kitchen.

"Charming guy," Lourdes said, obviously enjoying Ronnie's wincing. "He seems to know you pretty good."

"Lee and I have an understanding. I get good service and he doesn't get a ticket when he double parks his Rolls."

"Rolls?" She looked around the small dining room with its faux bamboo wall coverings and pseudo-Oriental polyester wall hangings. "As in Royce?" she said disbelievingly.

"I know. I thought the same thing. I wouldn'ta believed it myself, but I wrote the sucker up with my very own little summons book."

She tilted her head back to study the polyester hanging over their table. "Absorutry rovery," she said.

Ronnie picked up the corner of the hanging. "Made in Hoboken, New Jersey," he pretended to read.

She did her open-mouthed silent laugh.

"Ya know something, Blue, I almost didn't recognize you when you come in."

"You guys should get some lights in there."

"No, I mean, like, without the blue coat and everything? You practically don't look like you; know what I mean?"

"Get used to it. That's all I'm wearing these days."

"What? You quit or something?"

He tried a nonchalant shrug that didn't come off very nonchalantly. "They got me working with the detectives." Ronnie didn't mention the temporary nature of the assignment.

"No kiddin'? Hey, you movin' up fast there, Blue. I mean, you gotta be... What? 20s?" she mused, narrowing her eyes in study. "28, nine..."

Ronnie fidgeted. "Seven."

"That all?"

"The last time, you saw me in uniform. I think the blues add a few years."

"Lemme see you without that hat."

Ronnie had shrugged off his parka but the woolen cap was still on. "I'm gonna have hat-hair I take it off now."

"C'mon," she pushed.

He tugged the cap off with one hand, his other immediately charging in to fluff up the hair over the thin spots.

"Whoa, Blue, is that a little pink I see through there?"

"I told you; the hat does that."

She was enjoying this. "You look young enough, Blue, don't worry. Kinda nice, too."

49

He kept fluffing his hair. "Really?"

"You shouldn't worry about it. You're not a bad lookin' guy, Blue, I'm tellin' ya."

"Well. Thanks. Ya know, you—"

"You don't have to return the favor."

"Not a favor. I'm a trained observer. I calls 'em as I sees 'em."

"Good lookin' 'n' sweet, too. How long you been a cop, Blue? Can't be that long."

"Well, technically, going on two years." A year and a half was almost two years, he told himself.

"What's 'technically'?"

"They count from when you start training, so the first five and a half months you're in the Academy, then you got six months in an FTU – a Field Training Unit. That means you spend a lotta time walking a beat somewhere."

"After that, you're a real cop?"

"Believe me, you walk a beat, you're a real cop. I got my nose busted in my FTU. Then, after that, you're still on probation for a year, but all that time you're a real cop."

She smiled sadly. "Don't worry about trying to sound older, Blue. It'll come soon enough." She picked at a noodle, biting into it with a crunch. "Probation. Just like the bad guys."

She asked him about the broken nose. It was a story he rarely told as he found saying he'd gotten his nose broken on the job had significantly more drama to it than the actual story of *how* he'd gotten his nose broken on the job.

The borders of the 19th Precinct, where Ronnie had done his FTU stint, ran from Fifth Avenue to the East River, and from 59th Street to 96th. Newspaper columnists who were always writing paeans to The Working Man and whose header pictures always had them with their ties loosened and shirtsleeves rolled up disparagingly referred to the neighborhood as "a millionaires' ghetto." But millionaires' ghettos have their problems, too.

Ronnie'd been walking his beat when he'd been flagged by the liveried doorman of a luxury high rise. The doorman wanted him to do something about the homeless man who'd made camp in a flower planter in front of the building. The homeless man – whom it would later be ascertained was homeless because he was a delusional psychotic – was, at that moment, trying to quiet the voices in his head by pounding his cranium against the front of the building. When Ronnie tried to shoo him away, the homeless man thought Ronnie was another of his delusions and tried to quiet him by pounding his cranium against Ronnie's face.

The homeless man earned an ambulance ride to Bellevue where the doctors – mindful of an earlier case brought by the ACLU which established that crazy people have the constitutional right to be crazy – gave him a hot meal and a shower, stuck some gauze on his dented cranium, and sent him back out on the street.

Ronnie got a bumpy ride in a patrol car to New York Presbyterian where an unimpressed ER resident manhandled his nose more or less back into place, telling him to put some ice on it and take a few days off.

Lourdes Bracero smiled sympathetically at the story as she reached into her coat pocket, came out with a little plastic medicine bottle and tumbled a small pill into her palm. She popped the pill into her mouth and washed it down with some tea.

Ronnie picked up the bottle and read the prescription label. "Percocet? For...?" He pointed to the fresh scar hidden under her bangs. "That still bothering you?"

"A lotta things bother me, Blue. Say, this you-makin'-detective thing- "

"Well, I didn't actually make -- "

"That 'cause of all that mess I read about in the papers? About all those cops gettin' canned? Wasn't that your precinct?"

"We were one of them."

She was sorry she made him uncomfortable and reached across the table to pat his hand. "Take it any way you can get it, Blue. You don't get many shots. Trust me on that."

He almost didn't hear her. His attention was on his hand where she'd touched him.

Lee was back, setting down a sizzling skillet of iron steak swimming in brown sauce with baby corn, mushrooms and water chestnuts, a platter of orange chicken, and a side dish of pork chao fan.

"Jesus, Lee, it's only two of us!" Ronnie said.

Lee winked. "Leftover, you take home. Chao fan taste good cold. In the *morning*." He leaned over and lowered his voice. "Good *breakfast*. Enjoy!"

Lourdes twirled a wide chao fan noodle on her fork and slurped it off the tines with a mock suggestiveness. "Whaddaya think he meant by that, Blue? About breakfast?"

Ronnie scratched at his brow, hoping she didn't notice he was using the movement to mask dabbing at the sweat on his red face. "I, uh—"

She tried the orange chicken. "Mmmm. I see how this guy got his Rolls. Chao fan for breakfast. I gotta try that sometime. Maybe my guy'll like it."

Ronnie went cold. He looked down at the three plates of food just then and didn't want a bite of any of it. "Oh?"

"Ya know, he's a cop, too."

"No kidding." He tried to sound interested.

"Yeah. He's a detective. Manhattan South. He's coming up on his 20 years soon."

"No kidding." Ronnie forced a smile. "You, uh, been seeing this guy long? I mean, is this, uh..."

Her smile was sympathetic, and he could tell – in a way that made him want to crawl under the table – she'd read him all along.

"You mean are we serious?" She shrugged, not quite sure herself. "You should eat something, Blue."

What he'd like to eat, he thought, was that bottle of Percocets.

"You don't know my guy? Jack Meara?"

"I don't know anybody down there."

"I keep thinking all you know each other." She slurped down another noodle. "I think all cops are a little funny in the head. Ya gotta be a little funny in the head ya wanna be a cop."

"I think a lotta cops'd probably agree with you."

"He doesn't like to talk too much about what goes on in a day. He's got his moods. He comes over in a mood, you wonder what happened that day. And maybe you don't really wanna know 'cause a bad day on the street isn't like a bad day at the office, right? He works late, he works a double shift, he don't call. You don't hear, you worry. You wanna scream at him when he comes home 'cause you don't know what it means when you didn't hear from him. But, you don't scream and you live with it 'cause that's how it is. But…" She frowned.

"But?"

"But this is different."

"What's different?"

"Coupla days ago, Jack drops outta sight. I call his station; they say he's off duty for a while. I say, What's that mean? Off duty? He on vacation? Sick? What? They say it means off duty. I call his place, I go by, nobody's there. I got a key, ok? I go in. He hasn't been home. Not for a coupla days."

"Could be he's on something. A job. Undercover work, maybe."

"I thought a that, Blue. I even thought, maybe…"

"What?"

"Maybe he's seein' somebody, ya know?"

Ronnie had been thinking the same thing. Hoping, actually.

53

"But something else happened about the same time he drops outta sight," Lourdes said.

"Somebody started following you."

Her eyebrows went up, surprised and curious. "I think so. There's this guy hanging 'round, outside Lil's, outside my place. I *think* it's the same guy all the time."

"Young guy—"

"Yeah, maybe your age."

"—dark hair, dresses nice."

She noticed his eyes were looking past her shoulder. She started to turn.

"Don't," he said.

"He out there?"

"Some poor bastard is across the street freezing his ass off. If that's what your guy looks like, that's him."

She pushed one of the orange slice garnishes back and forth through the gooey sauce on the chicken platter. "Should I be worried?" No panic, not even concern. A straight, evaluative question.

"Let's do this. Lemme take you home. We'll see what happens with this guy, see if he follows."

She nodded. "We go now?"

He shook his head. "Thermometer's gonna hit 20 tonight. Five with the wind chill. Let's let this guy ice up a bit more. You gonna eat that orange?"

Ronnie took two of the orange slices and laid them over his teeth: orange rind dentures. He made a few gorilla grunts. That brought out Lourdes Bracero's silent open-mouthed laugh and he smiled behind his orange rinds.

They walked with their arms around each other, snuggled against the cold. When the wind shifted, Ronnie caught a sound from a few blocks away, a muffled mix of bass thumping and a noise like high-speed machinery tearing itself apart. One of the new Tamela-flavored punk clubs springing up downtown, he thought, a band trying to blow the walls out.

Ronnie didn't look for the long-coated man he'd seen across the street through the steamed-over windows of the Kam Bo. If there was anything to what Lourdes had told him, he could trust the man'd be somewhere behind them.

Checker cabs catapulted down the broad expanse of The Bowery ignoring Ronnie when he tried to flag one down.

"Down here," Lourdes explained, "after midnight, Christ himself could come down off his cross, no cab's gonna stop for him."

They walked for 15 minutes along The Bowery, then Lourdes turned onto a narrow side street, almost an alley, jigging between ranks of tall, gaunt tenements sagging like wet cardboard. The street looked derelict with ancient cobbles showing through holes in the asphalt, and pools of shadow beneath broken streetlights. Ronnie wondered how Lourdes got herself to walk down that street every night. He was carrying a gun and that street still gave him the willies.

She had a railroad flat five steep flights up in one of the tenements. There was a bathroom at the back, an eat-in kitchen in the middle, a room with a view of the street serving as living room and, as evidenced by the unfolded, unmade sofa bed, bedroom. The paint was dull, the walls bare, the plaster buckling. The scant furnishings in the few rooms made Ronnie think if he'd found Lourdes Bracero's furniture sitting at the curb next to his coffee table, he would've taken the coffee table and left everything else.

"Don't put the front light on," he said when they stepped inside.

She went to the kitchen and Ronnie walked to the front windows, standing off to the side, looking down on the street. He unzipped his parka. He could feel the chill in the apartment.

The kitchen light went on, he heard her stamp her foot: "Ya little fucker." Roaches. "Coffee?"

"I could really go for a hot chocolate you got any."

He heard her moving through the kitchen cabinets. "Believe it or not, yeah. I bet you didn't think I was a hot chocolate kinda person. I bet you think I'm a coffee person; black, hot, with all the caffeine you can stand. Well, I am. On the job. But there's something nice about hot chocolate on a night like this. All I got is the one with the little marshmallows."

"That's fine."

"I should break down 'n' get some real marshmallows. Who the hell knows what these things really are?" He heard a pot clang onto the stove, the scratch of a wooden match, the puff of the gas range igniting. Then another sound, the clink of glass on glass. "Cold?"

He turned. She was in the kitchen doorway, a water glass in her hand, but it wasn't water sloshing around in it.

"You should complain to the super about the heat," he said.

She shrugged and threw her coat toward the sofa bed. It missed. She held up her glass. The contents glowed amber in the light from the kitchen. "Want something to keep you warm?"

"That's what the hot chocolate's for. Hey, should you be having that with your pill?"

She leaned against the kitchen doorway, shrugging again. She took a sip from the glass, looked around the apartment. "It's not much, huh?"

He gave a diplomatic shrug. "A roof is a roof."

A kettle whistled in the kitchen. She turned for the stove. Before she turned off the gas, he heard the clink of bottle and glass again.

"It's right here," she said, setting a steaming mug down on the windowsill by him. She dropped on a chair covered with a frayed and faded Rockaway Beach towel and lit a cigarette. "That ever bother you?"

"What?" His hands were on his hips, pulling back his parka, revealing the holster on his belt.

She nodded at the gun. "That."

"I don't even think about it half the time," which was all lie. "C'mere."

She didn't look down to where he was looking. She looked across the street at a fire escape level with her apartment. Someone had placed a small, artificial Christmas tree on the fire escape, strung it with colored lights. "You decorate for Christmas, Blue?"

"I keep meaning to."

"I should. I should do *something* with this place." She took a sip from her glass.

He nodded down at the sidewalk across the street. "That him?"

She squinted at a dim figure in the shadows of the tenement across the street. "I think. I guess."

"You're not sure?"

"I'm no owl, Blue. I can't see him too good." She took another sip from her glass, a deep one.

He took the glass gently from her hand and handed her his cup of hot chocolate. "Better." He zipped up his parka.

"Where you goin'?" she asked.

"Get some air. I'll be back." He headed for the door.

"I don't want nobody gettin' hurt here, Blue."

"Nobody's gonna get hurt. What're you talking about getting hurt? I'm not gonna do anything."

"If you're not gonna do nothin', then where you goin'?"

"Anybody ever tell you you're a nag?"

"No."

"You're a nag." He gave her a grin he hoped said this was no big deal. She stood in the apartment doorway watching him go down the hall.

Out of her sight, in the ground floor hall, he stood for a long while since he really *didn't* know what he was going to do. He stepped outside counting on inspiration.

He stopped at the top of the stoop, took a moment to adjust to the cold. He took the same moment to pass a casual glance along the other side of the street. The man in the shadows was still there.

Ronnie headed down the block until he reached a dark stretch under one of the broken streetlights. He stepped deeper into the shadows along the building fronts and turned. He couldn't see the watching man and so assumed the watching man couldn't see him, either.

Departmental PPP was that if an off-duty cop came across something police-worthy, he or she should call it in, get some proper backup, and do the job right so as to minimize risk to lives and property.

But the more Ronnie thought about it, the more he was sure the Department would not think there was anything here qualifying as "probable cause" or "reasonable suspicion" or anything else requiring a call-in or any other kind of police action. All Ronnie had the authority to do was ask the guy to produce some identification. Anything else was going to make it more a case for the ACLU than for the DA.

Ronnie crossed the street and headed back toward Lourdes', this time on the same side of the street as the watching man. He stepped lightly. Drawing closer, he could make out the man in the shadows more clearly: moon-faced, head topped with short, spiky hair, shoes shiny and pointy, wearing a long, billowy, black-belted leather coat that seemed to be doing a damn poor job of keeping its occupant warm. The man kept shifting from one cold foot to the other and flexing his gloved hands. He either didn't notice Ronnie or didn't care, his eyes remaining fixed on Lourdes Bracero's building.

Ronnie stood there a few seconds trying to think of a way to engage the man in a way that wouldn't offend a Civilian Review Board. "Hey, got the time?"

"What?"

"The time. You got the time?"

The man's head started to bob; his voice sounded annoyed. Oh Christ, Ronnie thought getting a quick read on him, he's one of *those*. "No."

"You don't have a watch?"

The guy studied Ronnie for a second, probably trying to think of some smart-ass remark to chase him off. But then his head stopped bobbing, the guy clearly opting for the quickest way to get rid of Ronnie. He brought his arm up into the dim light and Ronnie saw a flash of gold band. "Half past three."

Ronnie cleared his throat. "I gotta tell ya..."

"Tell me *what?*"

"The lady upstairs—"

"*What* lady upstairs? I don't know what the fuck.... Look, buddy, take a fuckin' walk, huh?"

"You don't know what I'm talking about?"

"That's right." The head was bobbing, again, like a fighting cock's. "That's right. I don't know what the *fuck* you're talkin' about, so just—"

"The lady upstairs says you been following—"

"What're you, her *mother?* Look, missy, do yourself a big, fuckin' favor 'n' mind your own fuckin' business, awright?"

"Ok, look, show me some kind of identification."

It was the magic phrase. The guy's head stopped bobbing, and Ronnie could see the alarm bells going off behind those beady eyes. The guy turned slightly to his right, away from Ronnie, and Ronnie felt a tingle on the back of his neck; the old station hair-bags had told him that meant this prick was probably carrying, and carrying on his right side. "What for?"

Ronnie dug into his back pocket, which wasn't easy with his mittens, and pulled out his badge cover, flashed his tin. "Right now. I want to see—"

The instant his badge hit the open air, the guy bolted. He slammed into Ronnie and the badge cover went flying. So did the guy, off down the street.

"Hold it!" Ronnie called. "Police!" He fumbled around in the shadows for his badge. "Halt, goddammit!" He found the badge but didn't bother to pocket it as he ran off after the guy. "I said hold it, you stupid asshole!"

Ronnie's nightly jogs paid off. The guy in the coat was soon wheezing; Ronnie could hear it as he closed with him. Ronnie got his mitten into his flying coattails. The guy felt the tug and started to shrug the coat off his shoulders. Ronnie felt it loosening, let go the coat, flung off his mitten, picked up his speed enough to get his fingers inside the guy's shirt collar. The guy went into an epileptic dance trying to shuck the coat the rest of the way off and twist Ronnie's fingers loose from his collar in the process.

The guy's Italian leather shoes were not designed for sidewalk dancing; his hopping and sliding feet lost their grip on the frosty concrete and the two of them went down with Ronnie on top.

"Boy, are you *dumb!*" Ronnie seethed. "What the hell's the matter with you?"

"Fuck you!"

Ronnie had him spread eagle face down on the sidewalk and patted him down. He pulled a toy-sized chrome-plated .25 automatic out of the prick's belt (right side; one for the hair-bags). "And you just keep getting *dumber*, dontcha?"

"Oh, Sweeeetie! C'mon, Sweeeetie! Time to get up!"

Ronnie tossed in his near-sleep. "Still go' time, Ma. Too early. Fi' mo' minis."

Something flat, hard, and wide as a ping-pong paddle hit Ronnie square on his ass. He shot up, finding himself stretched out on an uncomfortable wooden bench in the hallway outside the detective squad room. The flat, hard paddle had been Big Sid's flat, hard hand.

Ronnie tried to get his eyes focused. "Hey," he grunted through a yawn.

The baggy set of gray sweats he was wearing under his overcoat coupled with his slack face made Sid look like he was melting with exhaustion inside his coat. He stuck out a thick wrist, shoving his watch in Ronnie's face. "You see the time?"

The dial was just a white blob floating in front of Ronnie's blinking eyes. "Not really."

"Fuck you, *I* can, and that's all that counts. Move your ass over before I crush you." Ronnie did and Big Sid dropped on to the bench, rubbing his sleep-puffy eyes. "You got no idea how *pissed* I am being up before the birds."

"Sorry."

"Ya know, the phone's on the missus's side of the bed. Phone rings middle of the night scares her half-shitless. Thinks somebody in the family died. Thinks her little girl wrapped her car around a phone pole. Turns out it's *you!* I'm telling you, kid, stay away from my house. She comes by the station, hide in the toilet, because how she's feeling right now, she gets hold of you, your own momma won't be able to identify the body, y'understand?"

"I mean it, Sid, I'm really—"

"Why are you even calling me? Why the fuck are you calling *anybody?*"

"I didn't know who else to call."

"*Nobody!* That's who you call! Don't you know how this works yet? You get your shield yesterday? You bust a guy, you walk him through booking, you show up in arraignment court. If it's a bullshit bust, the arraignment judge tears you a new one for wasting his time and wants to know when the Department started giving powers of arrest to mental defectives. Then the poor ADA who drew this shitwad, *he* tears you a new one for wasting *his* time. When they're done, the Boss tears you a new one for wasting *your* time on this horseshit instead of being down at the ass-end of Jersey with me like you're supposed to. You'll notice nowhere in this process you hear me say, 'And at this point, you call Sid in the middle of the fucking night and drag his ass out of a nice, warm bed and away from his nice warm wife.'" Sid glanced at his watch and groaned. "We're supposed to be on the road in just a coupla—"

"I know."

"You don't know dick."

"There's something hinky going on. You're the only guy with rank left in the squad. I thought if I bothered the captain, he'd probably skin me."

"And *I* won't?"

"My first day upstairs you said come to you if I had questions."

"I assumed you knew I meant during business hours." Sid waved at him to get on with it. "This better be good, kid. I got a gun."

Ronnie told him about Lourdes Bracero and Lourdes Bracero's missing boyfriend who worked Manhattan South, and the sullen-faced guy now sitting in the squad room's holding cage.

When Ronnie was done, Big Sid grunted to his feet, shuffled over to the doorway to the squad room for a look at the guy in the cage. "He got a name?"

"Ralph Zinni. He's got a Brooklyn address."

"He got a sheet?"

"I'm still waiting to hear back from BCI, but a prick like that, I'll bet he's got priors back to nursery school."

"What the fuck *you* lookin' at, fat-bag?" Ralph Zinni called to Big Sid.

Big Sid sat back down next to Ronnie. "Priors back to the fucking *womb*." He pursed his lips, seemed to be thinking something over, then turned to Ronnie and surprised him when his puffy, fatigue-sagging face pulled itself into a smile. "You dog!"

"What?"

"You fucking *hound!*"

"What the hell're you—"

"I didn't think you had it in you, kid. I'm impressed, y'understand. This broad's workin' a titty bar down in the Fifth, but you told her to call *you* if she had any trouble? That's *smooooth.*"

"I was just—"

"Yeah, I know, being a nice guy. And then she calls you, she says, 'Oooh, oooh, poor me, the boogy man is after me,' and you, because you're a nice guy, 'C'mon, we'll talk about it,' and you take her out for a late-night dinner? *Very* smooth."

"Sid—"

"And then a moonlight stroll? You fucking *dog* you!"

"Jesus, Sid, did you pay *any* attention to the *important* parts?"

"Those *were* the important parts."

"What the—"

"Because those are the only parts that *count.*"

Ronnie could feel his face growing warm though it was as much from aggravation as it was a blush. "Her boyfriend's a *cop,* Sid."

"Yeah, I got that, and, by the way, that part, a little disappointed in you. Pretty shitty, snaking a brother cop like that."

"He disappeared, Sid!"

"Maybe her suspicion is right. Maybe he's shacked up with another broad. Maybe *your* sweetie's the 'other broad,' and he went back to shack up with his wife. Maybe he's shacked up with some skank Green Point hooker because like a million other fucked-up cops he thinks she's the only person who understands him."

"Sid—"

"Maybe he's one of the guys who shot Kennedy and they discovered his true identity and he had to skip. Point is, it doesn't fucking *matter!*"

"So, it's just a coincidence her cop boyfriend drops out of sight, then this guy Zinni starts tailing her around."

"Maybe he's got the hots for her."

"He lives in Brooklyn. What's he doing outside her building at 3:30 in the morning in The Bowery?"

"*Serious* hots." Sid leaned over and gave Ronnie a painful poke in the ribs. "You know how that goes, right, kid?"

Ronnie was getting one of his headaches, a sharp throb at the break in his nose. "He *ran!*"

"3:30 in the morning down in The Bowery, you come up to me outta the dark, *I* woulda run! Even if it's some bleached-white motherfucker like you, I'm outta there a missile up my ass."

"Hey!" It was from the stairwell: a uniform with bleary graveyard shift eyes was standing there. "One a youse the guy popped the perp in the cage? There's some slick downstairs askin' about him."

"That's me, thanks," Ronnie said.

"Good lookin', too," the cop called on his way back down the stairs.

Ronnie pulled himself off the bench, started for the stairs. Sid grabbed him by the wrist. The big man's face was no longer tired, or caustic, or fed up. The puffy eyes were now clear...and curious.

"Zinni made his call?" Sid asked.

"Soon's we got to the house."

"When was that?"

"Around four, I think."

Sid looked at his watch and frowned.

"What is it?" Ronnie asked.

"Not even an hour. If it was me, I wouldn'ta been able to get my *wife* down here that fast this time of night. And I like to think she loves me." Sid pondered this for a second or two then nodded Ronnie toward the stairs. "It's your collar, kid." And then he smiled a this-is-gonna-be-fun smile that made Ronnie think twice about going down those stairs.

The woman standing at the front desk looked, to Ronnie, like one of those women he'd seen in magazine and TV stories on how women past 40 can still be sexy. She was trim, her face only slightly lined and graced with a golden tan which announced, I spend the winter where it's warm and sunny and cabana boys bring me mimosas all day while you pasty-faced schmucks are shoveling your cars out of snow drifts. She had dressed in a hurry: tying the late-night tangle of her frosted coiff up in a silk kerchief, pulling on jeans, a pullover, cowboy boots. But the jeans were designer, the pullover cashmere, the boots snakeskin, and, the whole package was lushly wrapped in a deep pile mink coat which looked as at home on her as her tan.

She had been standing at the front desk, coquettishly chatting with the blotchy-faced desk sergeant, then held up a polite just-one-second-please finger to the desk sergeant when Ronnie came down the stairs. She flashed a smile of stunningly even white teeth and Ronnie bet that even with the sun not quite up yet her breath probably smelled great.

"Good evening, Detective...?"

"Officer, actually," Ronnie said, flinching at how low on the totem pole that sounded. "Officer Valerio."

"I had just wagered your charming desk sergeant here—"

The desk sergeant – somebody Ronnie remembered as having all the charm of a rabid mutt – smiled.

"— that the next body down those stairs would be Mr. Zinni's arresting officer. I suspect I just won my bet."

"And you're?"

"Allison Kiernan."

She held out a gloved hand, barely let Ronnie touch it. Ronnie caught a whiff of something floral. Wow, he thought, she even remembered perfume.

"You're here for Mr. Zinni?" Big Sid asked.

Ronnie turned to see Sid sitting on the stairs.

"And you are...?"

"Just a neutral U.N. observer."

Allison Kiernan nodded at Ronnie. "They're taking them awfully young these days."

"Have to get 'em before they know better."

Kiernan smiled, Sid smiled, the desk sergeant smiled, and Ronnie wondered why everyone but him seemed plugged into some connecting circuit.

"I thought you had a strictly one-client practice," Sid said.

"I have one major client, yes. But I do take on some other work from time to time."

"Like this."

"Well, this is more on the order of a favor for a friend."

"A friend."

"A friend of a friend, actually."

"Right."

"Do we know each other?" Kiernan asked. "I have a pretty good head for faces and names, but I don't recall our ever meeting."

"We didn't, Ms. Kiernan. I recognized you from TV. Ya know, the cameras don't do you justice."

She nodded graciously. "How very kind of you to say. I'm hardly at my best right now."

"Oh, you're doing just fine, Ms. Kiernan. Whaddaya think, kid? She doing fine?"

"Um," Ronnie said.

"Well, Detective, I'm sorry, *Officer* Valerio. About Mr. Zinni."

"Yeah, well, there's some question about what he was doing so far from home at that hour of the night. See, he lives in Brooklyn, but he was—"

"Well, as I said, I'm just doing a favor for a friend."

"Yeah, I heard that, but—"

"I don't know Mr. Zinni personally, so I can't answer that. But then—" and she flashed those brilliant white teeth in a taunting smile "—I don't have to. And neither does Mr. Zinni since there's nothing criminal—"

"It looks like he was following someone, a woman, and she—"

"And she made a complaint?"

"Well, no, not exactly, but—"

"Well then."

"There is a possible gun charge," Ronnie said, feeling like he was playing a trump, but damned if that white smile didn't get a little wider.

"'Possible'?"

"Well, he was in possession of a firearm."

"There is no gun, Officer Valerio."

Ronnie looked from Kiernan to Sid to see what he was missing, but only got an irritating-as-hell smile in return. Ronnie turned back to Kiernan. "I'm afraid there *is* a gun, Ms.—"

"No, officer, there is no gun."

"Would you like me to bring it down and show it to you?"

"I think what would be a lot more fun, Officer, is for you to show it to the arraignment judge and have *him* tell you it doesn't exist." Kiernan looked past Ronnie to Sid. "What do they teach them in the academy these days?"

"It's a shame, isn't it?" Sid said.

"Ms. Kiernan—"

"There was nothing about Mr. Zinni's conduct remotely qualifying as Probable Cause, Officer."

"He was—"

"Standing on the street, late at night which, let's face it, in a city like this one, hardly constitutes suspicious behavior, and certainly nothing justifying an arrest. Are you acquainted with the phrase, 'fruit of the poison tree'?"

"The what of the what?"

"The bust was bogus, Officer, therefore any evidence derived therefrom..." She didn't have to finish. She also didn't have to say, "He's cute when he blushes," to Big Sid but she did. "But if it raises your comfort level about the weapon..." She went to the front desk where she'd left a large, leather shoulder bag, and made a big show of fishing around inside. "Did you know, Officer, that there are over 65,000 licenses to carry a concealed weapon in the New York metropolitan area?"

"I didn't."

"And my client happens to – now, where did that slide down to? – happens to hold – ah, here we go! – happens to hold one of them. And here are the registration papers for the gun as well." She held them out to Ronnie who frowned at them before he took them in his hand, then frowned at them some more.

"I wonder on what basis Mr. Zinni was able to justify a carry permit?" Sid asked.

"This from the neutral observer?" Kiernan said. "As I said, I don't know Mr. Zinni personally, so—"

"So you wouldn't know."

"I wouldn't know."

"And you just happened to be holding these for Mr. Zinni?"

"The friend of the friend had access to Mr. Zinni's residence. When Mr. Zinni called to say he'd forgotten them—"

Big Sid made a grave face. "That's a hell of a thing to forget."

Kiernan also made a grave face. "I agree. Nevertheless..."

"Nevertheless. Do you mind if Officer Valerio makes copies of those?"

"He wouldn't be doing his job otherwise."

"These look awful," Ronnie said, holding up the faded copies. He was at the Xerox machine at the end of the upstairs hallway.

Big Sid was behind him, walking in a little circle, his head hung low on his chest in thought. "Probably needs toner."

"I *know* it needs toner," Ronnie said. "The little 'add toner' thing is blinking. These goddamn night-shift guys, they just let it go. They don't clean the coffee pot either. I come in in the morning, I got to chisel that gunk off the bottom of the pot."

"When you rotate to nights, tell me *you* feel like adding toner," Big Sid said.

Ronnie fussed with the light/dark adjustment. "That was a lot of fun for you, wasn't it? I mean that mugging I got downstairs?"

"I had a perfectly good reason for letting her chew on you like that."

"To teach me not to wake you up in the middle of the night?"

"Ok, *two* good reasons. The other: experience is always the best teacher, and the best of the best is a completely humiliating experience. I don't think you're gonna fuck up like that again anytime soon, do you? Look, don't tear up Zinni's paperwork. Keep those copies with it. When we come back from Jersey, run 'em through Albany, make sure they check out." He stopped his circling and fixed a nasty look on the stairwell. "I'll bet your left nut she's got a drawer full of those things all filled in except the name. Somebody gets popped on a gun charge, she fills in the name—"

"Something turned you around on this," Ronnie said.

Sid went back to making his little circle. "Keep the gun, give Zinni his permit and registration, and bounce him. Tell him he can claim the piece after we check out his papers. We'll call him when he can come down. Don't stand there with that dumbass grin – Go!"

Ronnie headed into the squad room, grabbed the key ring from inside the doorway and headed for the holding cage. "C'mon, Ralphie, Santa came early for you."

Ronnie and Big Sid stood by one of the squad room windows, watching Kiernan and Zinni climb into a white Cadillac waiting for them at the curb in the predawn grayness.

"You said this broad from the titty bar, the one you got the hots for—"

"I don't—"

"She home? Without putting a scare into her, tell her keep her eyes open. And before you leave, flag Manhattan South. Let 'em know something might be going on with their boy. What's the name? This guy Meara."

"What's going on, Sid? What pushed the button for you?"

"You didn't recognize her?"

"Who, the lawyer?"

"No, your mother. Yes, the lawyer."

"I wish I did. She was pretty, dontcha think?"

"You belong in a cage."

"What're you talking about?"

"You seem like one of those nice kids, but here you are hitting on another cop's girl—"

"Don't start."

"—you string along that poor Teri girl from downstairs with your *smooooth*—"

"Sid—"

"—now you got a thing for this lawyer? How much is enough for you? You got some kinda compulsion or something?"

"I didn't recognize the lawyer, ok? Was I supposed to?"

Big Sid smiled pityingly. "Kid, brains like you got, it's amazing you can take a shit without help. Try watching the news for a change instead of Scooby-Doo. Tony Boy Maiella's trial. Every time you saw him, she was right there. Ms. Allison Kiernan there is Tony Boy's lawyer."

# two: dark side

*and if the band you're in starts playing different tunes*
*I'll see you on the dark side of the moon.*
Roger Waters, "Brain Damage"

From the top of the Driscoll Bridge, Ronnie could see down to where the Parkway broadened into a 20-lane-wide toll plaza packed with morning commuters cutting this way and that, like a field of bumper cars, as they fought for the slightest advance toward the toll gates.

"Sid!" Ronnie nudged the big man slouched against the passenger door. "Sid! Wake up! I need money for the toll!"

"You don' ha' a'y mo'ey?" Sid's eyes stayed closed; his lips barely moved.

"I used my last change at the Union toll."

"So gi' 'em a bill."

"I don't have anything small. I can't give a guy a ten for a 25-cent toll, Sid. They give you that look."

"Fu' the loo'."

"Sid!"

With something between a grunt and a growl, Sid dug into his overcoat pocket, pulled out a handful of change. "Don' bother me no more. 'N' make sure ya get a receipt."

Depending on where you sat in the unmarked Buick, the car either smelled of puke or pee, testifying to the condition of some of the persons who'd been carted away in it at one time or another. When they had been gassing up that morning, Sid had insisted on buying two extremely powerful air fresheners to hang from the rear-view mirror that were supposed to smell like bubble gum but reminded Ronnie of Pepto Bismol.

They were in the crawling mass of cars in the toll plaza now, oozing forward toward the gates with the rest of the morning traffic. "Jeez, lookit this guy," Ronnie said as he eased the car along. "What's he's got? Is this guy on a walkie/talkie?"

Big Sid opened one eye to look across Ronnie's front to the car next to them. "Issa portable phone," he said, letting his eye slide closed.

"Cost a zillion fuckin' dollars. Been seein' 'em aroun'. Didn't know many people had a zillion fuckin' dollars to burn."

"That's kinda cool, I guess," Ronnie said. "Lookit this guy. Gab gab gab. We got a radio in the car, we don't talk that much."

"Oh really?"

It was not restlessness or boredom that kept Ronnie poking at Big Sid. Something had been nagging at him all morning. He would start to ask, but some other part of his brain would chicken out and he'd find himself commenting on portable telephones.

The traffic eased up on the other side of the Raritan toll. Ronnie fidgeted. His mouth opened and closed a half-dozen times.

Somehow Big Sid sensed it. "What?"

"Nothing."

"Get it over with so I can get back to sleep."

"No, it's—"

"Say it before I hurt you."

"Ok. Something's not right about this."

"About what? About the way you keep irritating the shit out a guy with a gun, you already ruined his night's sleep? You oughta go see a departmental shrink about these suicidal tendencies you got, kid. You still thinking about Zinni?"

"Well, yeah…but that's not it."

Big Sid grunted impatiently.

"Ok," Ronnie said. "When we were in with the captain yesterday, when he was telling us we had to take this ride, you were wondering what business was it of ours. Remember?"

"So?"

"You were right, Sid."

"Oh, Lawdy, thank you! The mental defective thinks I'm right! Now I can sleep happy…if he'll let me."

"Sid, we've got no reason to go down there. We've got no jurisdiction. They have any questions about this guy's activities in New York, hell, that's a phone call. So..."

"So," Big Sid said through a yawn.

"I'm wondering why we're going. You and the captain, there was a part there where you two were saying something to each other...without actually saying it."

"Picked up on that, didja? Boy, nothing gets past you. Except that I want to be left alone."

"Sid, you wanted me to ask, I'm asking."

Sid finally opened his eyes and pulled himself upright. Sort of. "You're aware that over the last six months, 29 cops from our precinct and the precincts immediately adjacent have been suspended and are being investigated for being in the pay of various criminal enterprises."

"Sure."

"I just wanted to make sure since despite your keen eye for detail, it seems a lotta big news gets by you. Almost half those cops are from *our* house. Almost half of *them* are detectives. Maybe that sharp eye of yours noticed all those empty desks in the squad room?" And then Sid didn't say anything more.

Ronnie took his eyes off the road for a quick glance at the big man. Sid seemed to be waiting for something. Ronnie shrugged: what?

"You still don't get it, do you?" Sid said. "You musta flunked Connect the Dots in nursery school. A bookie used to operate in our precinct – the same precinct with a lot of these suspended cops – shows up in Jersey. Shot to death. By submachine guns. Which is kind of a heavy way for a lowlife bookie to get croaked."

"Ok."

Sid waited. Again. Then, "Kid, you scare me. Bookmaking, so you know, is a criminal enterprise that has been known to protect itself by paying off cops."

"And the captain thinks there's a connection between this dead bookie and our dirty cops?"

"No. The Boss is worried there *might* be a connection between this dead bookie and our dirty cops. If there is, it'd be better if we helped turn it and got out ahead of it, instead of the Jersey cops turning something and we're sitting back at the house with our thumbs up our ass and our heads in the sand. Get it now?" Big Sid tried to settle back down to sleep, but only fidgeted and humphed. "You fucked this up for me. You see a place where we can get some coffee, pull over."

They found a food-and-gas stop down around Tom's River. Big Sid headed for the men's room and pointed Ronnie to a coffee stall in the food court. "Make sure you get a receipt!"

Then they were sitting in uncomfortable plastic chairs at a plastic table in the food court. They were alone there.

Sid looked at the bagel Ronnie had gotten him bleeding cream cheese. "I thought I told you *extra* cream cheese."

"That *is* extra. Jesus, Sid, ya want them to put it on with a trowel?" He watched Sid work his way through the pile of sugar packets he'd brought back from the coffee stall, mixing one after another into his coffee. In response, Ronnie bobbed his teabag of decaf tea around in his cup of hot water. "When I was at the One-Nine, we had this guy, your age, a sergeant, too. He wasn't too careful about what he ate either. He took off after some perp on a foot chase, got a heart attack chasing him up some stairs."

"Nice story," Big Sid said, slurping at his coffee.

"You should think about your family. Your wife, your daughter. What happens to them if something happens to you?"

"They live happily ever after on my insurance."

"I mean if nothing else, just speaking aesthetically—"

"What?"

"You know; how it *looks*—"

76

Big Sid responded by biting into his bagel with exaggerated relish. "How's that colored water of yours? Good? I'm glad. Where's my receipt?"

"You worried you're gonna get dinged over a coffee, a tea and a bagel?"

"With extra cream cheese. Kid, you weren't around for Knapp. I was. I know what it's like when the shit comes down. With the shoo-flies halfway up the Boss's ass, half the detective squad on suspension, fucking A you get receipts for *everything*. You use a pay toilet; you make sure you get a receipt."

Ronnie looked around the food court, let out a long breath. Something else was on his mind.

"What?" Big Sid said, annoyed.

"I didn't say anything."

"You *think* awfully fucking loud."

"It's just I don't think I'm gonna be as much help to you as the captain thinks just because I'm from down there."

"I know. So does he."

"Just because I'm... Wait, what?"

Sid smiled the way a cruel older kid smiles when he enjoys telling younger kids there is no Santa Claus. "When he pulled you upstairs you musta thought it was because you were the *hottest* shit on patrol."

"No, I, uh, didn't—"

"No, I, uh, uh, duh duh," Big Sid mocked. "Fuck you, first day you showed up dressed for a funeral – I'll bet that's your only suit (Ronnie blushed; it was) – and your head was so big I don't know how you got through the door. Well, I don't want to piss on your parade, kid, but he brought you upstairs because you're still green on the vine." When it was obvious Ronnie still didn't understand, Big Sid rolled his eyes. "Jesus, you're dense. There's a million fucking eyes on those three houses where they found bad cops, including ours. You haven't been in the house long enough to get dirty, y'unnerstand? He brought you upstairs because he needed to know for sure at least one dude in that squad room was clean. That's why you're *here*. You're my chaperone, kid."

"The captain doesn't trust *you?*"

Big Sid smiled prosaically and took a bite of his bagel. "As much as he can, I guess. More than most of the guys. Lemme tell you something maybe you didn't know: the Boss did a year with Knapp and a year with IAB hunting dirty cops. After that, you don't trust *anybody.*"

"Pull over some place," Big Sid said.

"We're almost there. Maybe a half-hour."

"Fuck the half-hour, I gotta pee *now.*"

"It's all that sugar. Diabetics pee a lot. I'll bet you're diabetic. Or borderline diabetic."

"Thank you, Doctor Kildare, now will you pull over?"

The Parkway had narrowed to two lanes, and the morning commuter traffic had long since evaporated; they were alone in the Pine Barrens. Ronnie pulled over on the shoulder, Big Sid hauled himself out and trotted into the woods.

The air through the open door felt good after the long ride and Pepto Bismol reek of the deodorizers, and Ronnie climbed out to get more of it. He sucked the piney smell in deep. There was something to the fresh-scented silence, the endless, unbroken ranks of solemn evergreens rolling out for a million acres that hadn't meant anything to him when he'd lived in the area as a kid. Maybe the feeling came from him being close to home for the first time in a long time.

"Police work, if you haven't noticed, is goddamn stressful," Big Sid called over his shoulder from the woods. "Stress didn't bother me. I drank, I smoked, that took the edge off, I was happy as a fucking clam. Wife says, 'Sid, sweetie, I think you're drinking too much,' so I stopped drinking. Doctor says, 'Sid, ol' boy, I believe you're smoking too much,' so I stopped smoking. So I'm gonna eat my goddamn bagels with my extra goddamn cream cheese and drink my goddamn coffee with a goddamn ton of sugar because that's all I got left and I'm not gonna hear shit about it from you, y'unnerstand? Jesus fucking Christ, kid, most stress I get these days is from *you!*"

Big Sid came out of the trees zipping up his pants, then wrapping the flapping ends of his overcoat back around himself, shivering against the cold. He saw a pensive Ronnie leaning against the car and a pained look crossed his face. "God*damn*, kid, you're a broody sonofabitch today. What's on your mind *now?*"

Ronnie shifted on his feet, looked down at the sandy ground. "I didn't say anything!"

"Ok, good," Sid said, reaching by him for the door. "Then let's go."

"It's just—"

Sid shut the car door with a moan and propped himself against the car next to Ronnie.

"Just *what?*"

"I'm trying to…you know…understand…"

"Understand *what?*" Sid pushed impatiently.

"You knew some of those guys, didn't you? Some of those guys who got suspended."

Sid nodded, let out a long, resigned breath, looking as if he'd expected this. "I didn't 'knew,' kid. I *know*. All of them. Well, the dicks from our house, I know all of *them*. I know some of the uniforms, too. I even know some of the guys from the other houses."

"Did you know…?"

"What? They were on the pad?" He turned a hard stare on Ronnie. "Ya know, anybody else – like a Dewey Berberick – about now they'd drag you in the woods, strip you bare-assed, make sure you're not wearing a wire."

"I'm not wearing a wire, Sid."

"I know."

"It's just, well, 29 cops, that seems like a lot."

"If they're standing on your head, it's a lot. There's 35,000 cops on the force, kid; 29 isn't a lot."

"So…did you? Know?"

"Like in a courtroom kind of way?" Sid stood at attention, the prosecutor interrogating the witness. "'Sergeant Leland, you ever see anybody take money?'"

Emphatically: "'No, Sir!'

"'Did you ever hear anybody *talk* about taking money?'

"'No, Sir!'

"'Did you ever hear anybody talking about anybody *else* taking money?'

"'No, *Sir!*'" His right hand went up for the oath, his left mimed resting on the Bible. "'So help me God!'" Then he slumped back against the car, dragged at by the weight of it all: "But if you're any kind of cop… Who just bought a new car, who just put their kid in some fancy-ass private school, who just dropped a ton at the orthodontist for his kid's rabbit teeth, who's getting a built-in pool, who's taking the family to Disney World…and he's two pay grades *below* you… Meanwhile *you're* counting pennies the end of each month.

"You see who's *not* getting busted, you see which cases get flushed… A piece of evidence disappears, a surveillance gets blown… After a while, you kinda know."

"You ever…say anything to them?"

"Like what? Tsk-tsk, naughty-naughty?"

"I dunno. You never said anything to IAB? Or the captain?"

"Disappointed in me, kid? Boohoo for you. Not that simple. I know some of these guys back to the Academy. They're friends of mine, kid. *Still.* I've gone through the door with 'em. I've had their back. They've had mine. Y'unnerstand? No, you don't understand." Sid took a moment, pondering. "If you found out your momma was cheating on her taxes, would you rat her out to the feds? See? Not simple."

"So now they're busted for a coupla bucks."

Sid smiled and Ronnie knew he was being laughed at. "Like I told you; not simple, not always about money. Some woke up one day, suddenly hit 'em they've spent their whole grown-up life standing up to their ass in a cesspool trying to empty it with a teaspoon. They know it's not gonna matter two shits one way the other they shovel harder or slower. They wear out, kid, y'unnerstan? "

"You ever feel like that, Sid?"

"Get a few more years in, kid, and if you *don't* have days you feel like that, I'm gonna assume you really *are* a mental defective."

They were quiet for a moment, and Sid must've figured they were done as he started reaching for the car door.

"Did...?" Ronnie started, but he couldn't finish the question.

"We know how this goes. Eventually, it's gonna piss me off you leaving some question hanging in the air like this, you'll wind up asking me anyway, so let's skip to the chase. Did I take? They never asked me. Maybe some figured, 'Well, I know this dude, I don't think we should ask him.' Some the others, well, I know those pricks, I'm sure it was just they didn't want to share with a nigger. Ok?" He reached for the car door again.

"What if they had? Asked you?"

"Gonna keep you up nights wondering?"

"Maybe."

"Good!" Sid declared, reaching for the door. "Let's go."

"Hey, Sid?"

"*What?* "

"Who's Doctor Kildare?"

Ronnie and Big Sid were off the Parkway now, following the directions from Van Dyne that took them along county roads deep into the Pine Barrens, then onto an unpaved access road which would take them to Salvatore Dell'Acqua's house.

"I'm gonna lose a kidney, this fucking road," said Big Sid as the car bounced along the deeply rutted track. He looked out nervously at the passing woods. "Some howling wilderness you got here. Gives me the creeps."

"I think it's kinda nice."

"My ass, nice. Who the fuck would live out here? This is where chainsaw killers live. Cuts through your front door, chops you up into dog food, wears your scalp for a hat, who's gonna hear anything? Fuck this, get me back to the city."

After a few minutes, they came to a Cape May County sheriff's car pulled across the road. The driver stepped out, a tree of a man looking even bigger in his brown sheriff's department parka. As he came up on Ronnie's side, Ronnie saw a burst of flaming red hair from under the arctic cap, and a wide, thick-featured face beaten tough and ruddy by 20-odd winters spent on the rural patrol routes of Cape May County.

"You talk to him," Big Sid said to Ronnie. "He looks like he might bite."

The toughened, leathery face unexpectedly folded into a broad smile as Ronnie lowered his window. "Sergeant Leland? Officer Valerio?" The county cop pulled off a glove and shoved a bear paw into the car. "Lieutenant MacAlistair. Sheriff Willis's compliments. I was the shift commander the night it all came down so he figured I should do the honors. We're all probably better off. The sheriff's a bit distracted these days. He's down in Cape May shaking hands. Getting an early start on his re-election campaign for next year, you know. I'm afraid you're going to have to walk from here. A lot of the grounds are a secured crime scene."

"Tell me it's not a long walk," Big Sid said.

Ronnie got out of the car, noting he barely came up to the lieutenant's shoulder. Standing between him and Big Sid, Ronnie felt like a Smurf.

"I was a bit surprised they sent you all the way down here for this," MacAlistair said.

"Well, our boss is a no-stone-unturned kinda guy," Big Sid said, then flashed an I-had-to-tell-him-*something* look to an eye-rolling Ronnie.

"I hope they're paying you mileage," McAlistair said. "Sheriff Willis can be a little territorial about jurisdiction, but for myself? I'm glad you came. My last homicide investigation was three years ago: man took an axe to his wife for turning off the Super Bowl. That's the kind of thing we get. If it was up to me, I'd say take this case; you can have it."

"You don't have any men posted?" Sid observed.

"To keep who out?"

Sid looked into the pinewoods which ran off endlessly into shadows on either side of the access road. "I see what you mean."

MacAlistair turned to the paperwork on a clipboard he'd toted with him from his car. "I'm not sure where we should start. I guess we might as well start *here* since this is where we are. This way, gents." He noted Sid with his hands jammed deep in his overcoat pockets, his shoulders hunched up. "Cold, Sergeant?"

"I figured it'd be warmer this far south."

"It's just South Jersey. Hardly a trip to Florida." He pointed at Ronnie comfortable in his parka. "You should've been smart like him."

"Any time I want to be smart like him, I'll hit myself in the head with a mallet."

A few yards past the roadblock, MacAlistair pointed to a car-sized rectangle of crime scene ribbon staked out in the brush alongside the road. "We've got a car here; by the wheelbase, we're assuming a sedan." MacAlistair pointed to a line of crime scene ribbon tacked to a series of stakes leading from the rectangle to a position at the foot of the road bank near an opening in the trees leading into a clearing.

That opening was what passed for a drive leading down the embankment into a half-acre of open space. In the middle of the clearing sat a house: two stories, peaked roof, a lower shape – garage, probably – out back. The house was narrow, old, clapboard, not much of a place, made worse under its coat of dirty, peeling, battleship gray paint. A front porch ran the width of the house, a wooden lawn chair on the porch. Door to the left, picture window to the right. Except for a jagged frame around the edges, the glass in the picture window was gone.

"Two sets of footprints from the car to that point there," MacAlistair said, pointing to the spot near the drive. "The kind of sandy soil we have here takes a good imprint, particularly when it's got some moisture in it like it has now. We've got some nice, clean moulage impressions of the tire treads and footprints. They've all been sent off to the FBI, but it could be weeks before we get a report back.

"Anyway, you've got these two guys. One's a big guy. Going by impression depth, pressure release, typical height-foot size ratios, we peg him around six foot, 240. Looking at the way he set himself up in his firing position, he's a right-hander."

"You figure out which finger he picks his nose with?" Big Sid asked, impressed. "Considering you don't get much of this kinda thing... What're you, some kinda Indian scout or something?"

"Actually, I'm one-tenth Lenape Indian."

"Seriously?"

MacAlistair nodded with a smile. "But it's not like reading sign is genetic, Sergeant. I've been hunting these woods since I was a kid. You learn a few things about reading sign. Now, this big guy, he's the one who got away. They park here in the brush, sneak up to here. They both open up on the house together."

"How heavy were they carrying?"

"They were serious. Nine mm Smith & Wesson Model 76s."

"Yeah, I'd call that pretty serious."

"The Staties are trying to trace the one machine gun we recovered, but so far we've got nothing on it. Ok, so," and MacAlistair referred back to his clipboard, "one shooter leaves 36 casings; a clip's worth. This other guy, though, the heavy guy: almost 90 rounds."

Big Sid had moved off, following another line of crime scene ribbon marking footprints running off into the woods circling the house. "The gorilla stays put giving cover fire while this second guy heads out that way. Around to the back of the house?"

"Yeah. Those tracks stay with the trees, then cut to the back door."

"Any returned fire?"

"Let me show you what we've got inside," and MacAlistair led them toward the house.

"Wasn't exactly living in the lap of luxury, was he?" Big Sid said.

"The rental agent said the call was for something cheap and secluded. This is cheap and secluded."

As they crossed the field to the house, they saw two more rectangles of crime scene ribbon staked out in front of the house.

"What's that?" Big Sid asked.

"We'll come back to that. I want to show you inside first."

The front door opened into a small hallway that led to the kitchen at the rear of the house. Stairs to the left ran to the second floor. An archway to the right led to the living room.

Big Sid still shivered inside his coat. "Christ, it's just as cold in here as it was outside!"

"Didn't make any sense to keep the heat on with the window gone. At least you're out of the wind."

"Maybe I woulda noticed if I wasn't frozen numb."

In the middle of the front room, the outline of a splayed human figure was marked out with masking tape on the bare wood floor, a massive pool of blood dried black spreading out from the torso like butterfly wings. On the wall behind the tape silhouette, blood had been applied with a fire hose, crawling down toward the floor in long, dark tendrils.

Ronnie looked around at the scuffed floor, the few pieces of cheap and plain furniture: a TV, a sofa, an end table, a chair with a brick filling in for a missing leg. In that oppressively banal setting, the vehement spray of blood seemed obscenely out of place.

"Here's the crime scene photos," MacAlistair said and unclipped a sheaf of eight x tens from his clipboard. He glanced at the top photo, shook his head over the blood-spattered portrait of man's inhumanity to his fellow man, then handed them to Big Sid. Sid flipped quickly through them, offered them to Ronnie.

Ronnie nodded them away.

Referring to his clipboard notes, MacAlistair stood in front of the window, his feet where Dell'Acqua's had probably been before machinegun fire had carried him across the room. "The Staties sent us a CSU team to work the scene for us. Their ballistics guys put Dell'Acqua right about here when the machine guns open up. There was all broken glass on the floor around here. The CSU techs vacuumed that up when they worked the house. Dell'Acqua was hit six times, head and chest, variances in the bullet wound trajectories indicating he was hit from both guns simultaneously."

"So," Big Sid said, "they open up together and he goes down in the first burst." Sid pointed to a pistol-shaped tape figure by one of the body outline's outstretched arms, made a question of his face.

"Three-eighty auto," MacAlistair said and made a hold-on-a-second gesture. He went to the entry hall and pointed through the doorway to the kitchen and the back door, swinging open in the wind, the jamb splintered where it had been forced open.

Big Sid went into the kitchen, saw another tape outline on the back stairs. "This the second shooter?"

86

"Male Cauc, 30s-40s, no wallet, no ID. The Staties sent his prints to Trenton for an ASIS check, but nothing's kicked back yet. I've got more pictures."

Again, MacAlistair handed over photos to Big Sid, and, again, Ronnie nodded them away when offered.

"He comes around, he kicks in the door, and he's taken down with three shots." MacAlistair pointed to three chalk circles on the entry hall floor. "We recovered three .380 casings. It looks like the shooter was about here." MacAlistair pointed to some faint, dark smudges on the kitchen doorsill a few feet from the floor. "You've got powder residue and flash burns. I'm figuring..." He sat down behind the wall, planted his elbows on his bent knees, stretched out his two hands, cup-in-saucer, the "cup" hand index finger outstretched like a pistol barrel, and sighted on the back door. The height of MacAlistair's "gun" closely matched the smudges on the doorsill.

"That fits," Big Sid said.

"That means he didn't come running over here snapping off shots. He wasn't in a panic; he wasn't in a rush. He was *waiting* for this other guy to come through the back door. Do you mind?" He held out a hand and Big Sid helped him to his feet, which was good because Ronnie couldn't imagine how he would've pulled that big bulk off the floor.

Big Sid frowned at the powder residue marks, he frowned at the open back door, he frowned at the chalk circles marking where the spent casings had been found.

MacAlistair saw the look on Big Sid's face. "I know."

"What?" asked Ronnie and then Big Sid gave him that face he'd been giving him all morning: how big a dumbass can you be?

"It doesn't work," Big Sid said.

"What doesn't work?"

"Dell'Acqua went down in the first burst."

"Medical examiner says he was dead before he hit the floor," MacAlistair said. "And there's no GSR on his hands or sleeves."

"The piece by his hand was a drop," Sid judged. "So, who shot the guy who came through the back door?"

It seemed obvious as hell, so obvious even Ronnie began wondering if Sid was right; that he *was* incredibly dense. "These ejected casings—"

"They match the gun we found by Dell'Acqua," MacAlistair said, anticipating. "It's *his* gun. We pulled his prints off the clip, the ammo, these casings."

"But the outside of the gun was clean," Big Sid surmised.

MacAlistair nodded. "And not just the gun. This is a rental property. I thought we'd be taking elimination prints from this place until I was on Social Security. But there's hardly anything, not even Dell'Acqua's or his grandfather's."

"He wiped the place down before he left."

"He was thorough. All the places you'd look: banisters, glasses, light switches, the toilet… "

"The 911 call came from here?"

"Yeah, but the phone was clean, too. Something else. The guy on the back stairs. The different trajectories of the wounds indicate he took the second and third hits as he was falling. Yet, all three hits landed center target, and the spread was little bigger than this," and he set an open hand on the middle of his chest. "You add that to the way he positioned himself to take that guy out, his anticipation, the way he wiped down the gun and everything else… This was someone who knew what he was doing. Dell' Acqua was yours; do you know of anybody he might've known -- "

Big Sid was already shaking his head.

"No friends? Associates?"

"I don't think he knew anybody who'd even come down to say hello let alone get in a firefight for him. And as for handling themselves like this? Dell'Acqua was a shithead. All he knew was other shitheads. What about calls? You run his LUDs?"

"We're having a problem with the warrant. Dell'Acqua put everything in his grandfather's name: Nardo. It's an obvious front, but you've got a senior citizen, no living relatives, mentally incapacitated. They're being real cautious about the old man's rights. The county prosecutor is pretty sure the judge'll sign off in the end, it just won't be quick."

"You said the grandfather's 'mentally incapacitated'?" Ronnie asked. "He too far gone to—"

"He's too far gone to tie his own shoes," MacAlistair said. "Trust me, he didn't do this."

"Maybe he saw—"

MacAlistair was shaking his head, told them to follow him upstairs.

The second floor was two small bedrooms crimped by the angle of the roof. One had a sagging bed, knocked-around dresser. The other had a twin to the dresser but a hospital bed jammed into the cramped space. Ronnie could still smell a trace of disinfectant in the room.

"This is where we found Grandpa. He wasn't getting out of that bed under his own power. We have all their effects in our property room if you want to go through them, but there's nothing of interest. Mostly clothes, a ton of medications for the old man. Dell'Acqua wasn't much of a homemaker. Looked like they were both still living out of their suitcases. We've transferred the old man from Cape May Regional to a senior citizens facility not far from here. I'll take you over to see him later, you can see for yourself, but you won't get anything useful out of him. Half the time I'm not sure he knows his own name. If he did see anything…" The lieutenant shrugged helplessly. "If there's a lead, it's outside." He headed for the stairs.

"Outside?" Big Sid said unhappily.

"Outside."

MacAlistair led them to the two ribboned-off rectangles in front of the house. He pointed to one with its narrow end facing the missing front window. "I'm not much for the lottery, but I'll put up a few dollars that says this was Dell'Acqua's houseguest. These tire marks are older than the shooting team's, maybe by as much as a day. Going by the wheel-base and the depth of the impressions, I'm guessing a sedan, one of those fat old tanks, like from the 1970s, maybe even older. It's wearing out, too." He knelt by the ribbon, pointing to the forward part of the space where numbered wooden stakes had been driven into the ground marking recovered evidence. "He was parked nose to the house. You may not be able to see it but over here, under where the engine would be, the CSU guys found leaked oil, antifreeze, power steering fluid. Nothing big, nothing serious, but signs of the kind of wear and tear you'd expect from an old jalopy." He stood and led them around to the tail end, pointing to another numbered stake. "Over here, this would be the exhaust. They think at one point, going by the residue build-up, he was idling for quite a while, maybe as much as an hour. They're nowhere near finished their analysis, but from the composition of what they found, the CS guy's initial thinking is whatever this heap is, it's pre-catalytic converter."

Big Sid was staring down at a series of footprints running down the long side within the ribbon perimeter. "I think this dude is working hard trying to keep it running."

MacAlistair nodded. "You noticed that, too? Very little foot traffic in and out of the driver's side, but a lot of traffic back and forth from engine to trunk and back, like he kept going for tools to work on the engine. Look here in the sand, up at the front, the way his right footprint is smudged: that's him going up on his right to reach into the engine with his right hand."

"A rightie."

"Looks like. From these prints: average height, weight, wearing some kind of work boot."

"That's not much."

"No, but I've got my fingers crossed these guys can help us out," MacAlistair said, leading them over to the second ribboned rectangle. "From the wheelbase, a van, maybe a light truck. It got here around the same time as this car; well, within the same window of a couple of hours. If their stays overlapped at all, maybe these guys saw Dell'Acqua's visitor, or maybe they can at least give us a descrip on the car."

It had awed Ronnie – as well as irritated the hell out of him – the way MacAlistair and Big Sid had quickly fallen into synch with each other, speaking the same forensic language, looking at smudges on the wall, squidgy prints in the sand, and both knowing immediately what they meant, while Ronnie tagged along behind wondering how long you had to be on the job to develop those kinds of eyes…providing you *could* develop those kinds of eyes. His mind raced, trying to find some contribution to make. "Truck, van," he mulled aloud, then offered, "Deliveries?"

"We're checking with anyone we can think of: grocery stores, fuel oil, furniture, hospital supply companies for the grandfather… But I'm thinking repairmen are more likely. Look at the prints."

Naturally, I'm wrong, Ronnie thought.

"Two guys, but little traffic in and out of the cab," Big Sid said, studying the ground.

"But a lot of back and forth from the rear of the vehicle to the house," MacAlistair said. "Again, we're checking everybody: plumbers, electricians, furnace repair… If you guys can think of anything we haven't thought of, please feel free to throw something in the pot."

"Are we done out here?" It had come out in a tremolo as Big Sid was shaking violently. "Because if we are, my nuts are frozen to my left leg, so if you'll excuse me…" and Big Sid hurried off into the house.

MacAlistair and Ronnie shared an amused smile, then stood quietly together, looking out into the silent woods.

"I know it's not for everybody," MacAlistair said after a bit, "but *I* like it."

Ronnie nodded, understanding.

"I mean," MacAlistair went on, "I'd just as soon not have to poke around dead bodies *anywhere*. Still... Some kid holds up a liquor store, some guys at a bar have too much to drink and get into it... I like that that's an occasion instead of a daily routine."

"You sound like you've gone the big city route."

"Philadelphia. About 100 years ago. When my wife and I thought about starting a family, it seemed like time for a move. I never looked back. You thinking of relocating?"

"I already did. I'm originally from here. Well, over Cape May proper. My dad was a cop there."

"Valerio? I don't know the name."

"It was a long time ago. I was still a kid. He, um, he died."

"On the job?"

"Sort of. Car accident."

"Oh. Sorry."

"I guess bad things happen no matter where you go."

They each took a last whiff of the sweet pines and turned for the house.

Big Sid was sitting on the stairs to the second floor, buried as deep inside his overcoat as he could go.

"I have a thermos of coffee in the kitchen," MacAlistair offered. "I don't know if it's still warm, but—"

"Sounds good," Big Sid said, heading for the kitchen without hearing the rest.

Ronnie went into the front room, stood in front of the missing window as MacAlistair had done. He could hear the lieutenant and

Big Sid in the kitchen, the sound of the thermos unscrewing, the splash of something into a cup.

"Still hot?" he heard MacAlistair ask.

"Well, it's not cold," Big Sid said. "I'll settle for that."

"We've been backtracking Dell'Acqua's moves," MacAlistair said and Ronnie could hear the lieutenant flip through his clipboard paperwork. "It seems about a week and a half ago, he started calling realtors in the area trying to find –"

"Something cheap and secluded," Big Sid said through still chattering teeth.

"Right. He made the deal over the phone. Month-to-month."

"He wasn't counting on a long stay."

"Once he settled the rental for the house, he contacted some hospital supply outfits to arrange delivery of hardware he was going to need to take care of his grandfather. About a week ago, he pulled his father out of a retirement facility in Westchester in the morning and showed up here that afternoon to get the keys from the realtor. He paid the deposit and first month up front, in cash, took possession that day."

"That's a lotta cash," Big Sid said. "The realtor didn't think that was a little, you know, out of the ordinary?"

"She did, but this place isn't easy to unload even in-season –"

"Nice looking spread like this? Really?"

"So, someone wants to pay cash on the barrelhead in the off-season—"

"She wasn't gonna ask a lot of questions."

"I think you've got the picture. Once he moved in, seems Dell'Acqua pretty much kept to himself."

While MacAlistair and Big Sid went back and forth over the last days of the late and unlamented Salvatore Dell'Acqua, Ronnie stared out the window at the ribboned areas, ran his eyes along the trajectories the gunfire would've followed to account for the blood spray on the wall behind him. He was trying to learn, to teach his eyes to see the way the two veteran cops in the kitchen could see.

Looking out what was left of the front window, something tickled at the corner of Ronnie's eye, a brightness from the frame.

It was the window putty where the glass went into the frame.

What struck Ronnie was not just how brightly white the putty was, but its contrast with the dingy and cracked painted wood of the sill around it.

The sill had been painted countless times over the life of the house, the ridges in the frame and the sill smoothed and partially filled in by layer after layer of paint. But there was a crack in the paint, a seam cutting through the years of it all the way around the window.

And then he noticed the glass, what there was of it. It was clean, not a streak, not a water spot.

He went into the dining room behind him, to a window facing out from the side of the house. The putty around the glass was as dingy as the gray paint around it, paint piled up coat upon coat upon coat…without any breaks in the paint.

And the window glass was covered so heavily with water spots and zebra stripes of dirt from dripping rain that looking through it was like looking through a scrim.

He looked down at the windowsill and ran his bare finger along the surface, leaving a clear trail in the dust there.

"Hey, Lieutenant?" Ronnie called to MacAlistair. "You said something about oil deliveries, calling oil furnace repairmen?"

"Yeah."

"So, this place has oil heat?" He looked through the dining room doorway into the kitchen, held up his smudged fingertip for MacAlistair to see. "My mom's got oil heat. She's always complaining about the dust."

"My wife hates it, too. When you have the heat up in the winter, you dust one day, by the next you need to do it over. She's been getting on my back about converting to gas, but there's no gas lines out where we are."

Ronnie went back to the front room, ran a finger along the sill of the front window.

Clean.

"Where's this guy's garbage?"

"There's a can under the sink," MacAlistair asked.

"No, I mean when he had to take his garbage *out.*"

He didn't wait for MacAlistair's answer, hurrying by him in the kitchen and out the back door. He quickly spied a small hutch by the garage with two trashcans in it.

"When did this guy get his garbage picked up?" he called back to MacAlistair.

"He was outside any town limit. Usually, people like that hire a service." MacAlistair flipped through his paperwork. "Yeah, the realtor took care of that for him, put him with a service picking up once a week. You know, since Dell'Acqua was just signed on, I don't think that service has even made their first pick-up. Why?"

Ronnie was at the hutch, pulled out the first can, grabbed it by the handles and shook it. "So whatever's in these cans has only been here since Dell'Acqua moved in."

"Presumably."

Ronnie shook the second can, smiled at the jangle of broken glass. He lifted the lid, saw shards of plate glass mixed in with pieces of gray-painted wood. He turned to where a curious MacAlistair and an equally curious Big Sid were standing on the back stairs of the house. "I believe this rates an 'a-*ha!*'"

The two older cops still hadn't put it together and that made Ronnie's smile all that much wider. "Lieutenant, I think those repair guys you're looking for do window repairs." Ronnie took them back in the house and showed them what he'd found.

MacAlistair clapped one of his mammoth hands painfully down on Ronnie's shoulder. "God*damn* that's good, son! I'm going out to my car and get on the radio and get some of our people on this right now!"

A still-beaming Ronnie turned to Big Sid who seemed as surprised as he was impressed. Then Sid's wide, dark face started to twist into a slight smile, and he reached across and gave Ronnie a playful – if smarting – slap on the cheek. He nodded his head approvingly: "Not bad, kid. Regular Sherlock fucking Holmes."

Sid went back to the kitchen for more of the tepid coffee, leaving Ronnie standing at the missing window, listening to the wind whistle around the jagged edges of glass. He was still basking in the afterglow of "Sherlock fucking Holmes"…and then the glow began to fade. Something new tugged at him the way the white window putty had tugged at him.

The wooden chair on the porch…

He headed back through the kitchen – "Where you goin'?" Sid called after him -- and out the back door, back to the garbage cans. Inside the can with the broken glass, he took one of the pieces of wood, a hunk about a foot long, and used it to dig deeper finding still larger pieces which clearly resembled pieces of a chair like the one on the porch.

Then back through the kitchen, heading toward the front porch.

"What the hell's with you?" Sid called, this time following.

"There's a question we haven't asked yet," Ronnie said when Sid appeared in the broken window.

"Which is?"

Ronnie held the piece of wood next to the chair on the porch; the wood and paint were an exact match. "Which is how that window got broke in the first place. Here's what I'm thinking." He pointed with his piece of wood to the ribboned square that was Dell'Acqua's visitor's car. "He gets here late at night, maybe early in the morning. Comes up to the door, knock-knock, Dell'Acqua doesn't let him in."

"Shit, if *I* lived here, somebody knocking on my door middle of the night, *I* wouldn't let 'em in, either. Some fucking werewolf or something."

"This guy decides he's coming in whether Dell'Acqua wants him or not. And then it doesn't figure. Dell'Acqua's expecting trouble; he's got the gun. But he doesn't use it."

"*Having* a gun and *using* a gun, two different games, kid. Sallie was no shooter."

"Ok, maybe. But this guy is no Bad Guy. He doesn't whack Dell'Acqua out, and when the Bad Guys show up that night, he takes one down."

"Doesn't mean he was on Sallie's side. Maybe he was just stuck in the house with him."

Ronnie nodded another maybe. "But he makes the 911 call so the old man doesn't freeze to death. That doesn't sound like a Bad Guy." He turned to stare at the ribboned square again, the footprints going back and forth from engine to trunk and back, again and again. "Sid, the guy was here all damn day. He's here before sun-up, he's here when the shooters show up that night. He spends some time futzing with his car, but what the hell does he do here all day? He didn't bust the window to borrow a cup of sugar."

Big Sid paced one of his contemplative circles, coming back to the shattered window. "Remember what the lootenant said about the two of 'em living out of their suitcases? What if it wasn't that Sallie hadn't *unpacked...*"

"But instead he was packing?"

Sid nodded. "Our guy's here because he wants Sallie to go with him. Sallie doesn't want to go, so it takes our guy the day to persuade him."

MacAlistair was coming back from his car across the open ground in front of the house. "I have a call in. Our people are going through the phone book now. It shouldn't take long. In the meantime, I

97

thought maybe you fellas could use some lunch about now." Then he stopped, catching the ruminating looks on Ronnie and Big Sid. "Did I miss something?"

"Lootenant, anything in the ME's report that Dell'Acqua had any injuries *besides* gunshot wounds?" Sid asked.

MacAlistair paused for a moment, wondering where this was going, than began flipping through the documents on his clipboard. "'Numerous shallow lacerations about the face...'" he read. "They assumed that came from flying glass. Let's see, hm..." Then, reading again: "'Several mild to moderate contusions about the face and side of the head...' They figured that must've happened when Dell'Acqua hit the floor."

"And why," said Big Sid, "did they figure that's what *must've* happened."

MacAlistair shrugged. "How else could they have happened?"

Big Sid beckoned MacAlistair up onto the porch, reached through the missing glass for the lieutenant's clipboard and flipped to the crime scene photos. "Look. Dell'Acqua fell on his back. The blood under him wasn't disturbed; nobody turned him. That's how he fell; that's how he stayed. So how did his face get banged up?"

Ronnie saw it now: "By somebody 'persuading' him to start packing."

Big Sid nodded, turned and looked down at the taped outline on the living room floor and the wings of blood spread across the bare wood floor. "Bet you're wishing you made up your mind a little quicker, eh, Sallie?"

Ronnie and Big Sid decided they liked MacAlistair's idea about lunch and followed him across the clearing back to the road and their cars.

Then Ronnie had another nagging thought, laid a hand on Sid's arm to get him to lag back from the lieutenant. "Remember what you said about this was a pretty heavy way to whack out some low-rent bookie?" He said it quietly, not wanting it to carry to MacAlistair.

"What if – "

Sid was already nodding. "What if they weren't just here for Sallie."

"Dell'Acqua was here for a week, but they only showed up when this other guy did. You might want to call that a coincidence—"

Sid shook his head glumly. "Wasn't gonna call it that. I'd *like* to, but I can't say it. Ya know, kid, you're on a hot streak coming up with the right questions. I wish it included you coming up with some answers."

MacAlistair had Ronnie and Big Sid follow him from Dell'Acqua's house to a place just outside of Cumberland. MacAlistair started to slow in front of what Ronnie and Big Sid thought was an abandoned shack sitting alone in the woods, looking ready to collapse under the first strong wind. But then MacAlistair turned into a bare square of frozen mud alongside serving as a parking lot.

"It may not look like much," MacAlistair reassured, "but this guy's got the best cheese-steak sandwiches outside of Philadelphia."

It didn't look like much inside either. Peeling linoleum, barely room for three tables and a counter. a skeletal, one-eyed cook covered in tattoos working the flat-top behind the counter looking as ready to chop up the clientele as the meat crackling on the hot metal. Ronnie and Big Sid sat on tottering chairs and ate at a wobbling table while MacAlistair went back out to his car and his radio. It was toasty warm in the place, smelling deliciously of grilling steak strips, cooking grease, and fresh bread. After Ronnie and Big Sid took their first bites, they knew MacAlistair had been right about the sandwiches.

Big Sid grinned at the way Ronnie was energetically chomping at the juice-soaked bread. "I thought you're the guy always careful what he eats."

"I'm trying to be polite to the guy, Sid."

"Sure."

"He brings us here for these sandwiches, I should have a sandwich. I don't want to be rude. Besides, I got a Diet Coke with this."

"I got cheese fries. With gravy."

Ronnie started reaching for Sid's plate of fries. "Can I—"

"No."

A beaming MacAlistair came trotting back inside, got himself a cup of coffee at the counter and pulled up a third tottering chair.

"Well?" Big Sid asked.

"Bingo!"

"Grab yourself a sandwich and share the good news."

"Oh, just the coffee's fine. I can't eat those monsters. My doctor says I've got to watch my cholesterol. They're good, huh?" MacAlistair said it with a polite smile lost in a generally mournful look.

"Beats the hell out of bean curd," Ronnie said.

"So, what've you got?" Big Sid said, mopping up a puddle of grease and some strands of melted cheese with the edge of his bread.

MacAlistair turned his attention away from the plates of food with a silent sigh. "Once we knew what we were looking for, it only took about five minutes with a phone book to run it down. In these parts, you don't exactly get lost in a crowd. I've got people talking to two guys at their shop in Milmay right now. According to them, they got the call from Dell'Acqua that morning, first thing soon's they opened. They said it must've been some party; someone threw a porch chair through the window."

Big Sid started to open his mouth.

"And yes," MacAlistair eagerly jumped in, "they were there when Dell'Acqua had his mystery guest."

Ronnie started to open his mouth.

"But they didn't get much of a look at him. He kept to himself in the back of the house."

"The car," Big Sid jumped in before MacAlistair could preempt him again.

"We're really lucky there. They got a good look, and – better still – one of these guys is one of those types who knows his cars. He makes it a late '60s Chrysler, white, either a New Yorker or a Nieuport – they had the same body style."

"That squares with what you showed us at the house," Ronnie said.

MacAlistair nodded. His eyes had settled on Big Sid's dwindling pile of cheese fries with gravy. Big Sid nudged the plate closer to MacAlistair. "One's not gonna kill you, Lootenant."

MacAlistair wasn't sure he believed that, but shrugged, took one, then firmed himself up and pushed the plate back in front of Sid.

"I've got a call in to the Staties," MacAlistair went on, "see if they can't get hold of some old dealership catalogues. We'll put those in front of our brand-new witnesses and see if we can't get them to narrow down the make and year a bit more."

"They get a look at the plates?" Big Sid asked.

MacAlistair looked less enthusiastic, solaced himself with another gravy-soaked fry. "The best we got on the numbers is one of them said he thinks it might've had a one in it. But they *did* notice they were out-of-state plates," the lieutenant continued more hopefully. "Dark figures on a background of –" here MacAlistair read from his notebook, quoting " ' – kind of orangey-yellowy-ambery'. That's a new one for the Crayola box."

Big Sid immediately divined the pedigree: "New York plates."

"Probably," MacAlistair agreed. "Pennsylvania, possibly; the colors are somewhat similar. But considering Dell'Acqua's history, I'm putting my money on New York. We'll do the due diligence: we'll put the inquiry in to both Harrisburg and Albany, but any New York metro addresses that kick back, we'll shoot those straight off to you hoping you won't mind running 'em down for us. I think that's where we'll find our guy.

"My feeling is a car like that is no rental. And you wouldn't steal something that conspicuous. This is *his* car. We run it down, we'll know who he is, even if he ditches it."

Big Sid nodded in agreement, looking sadly down at his now empty plates. "Don't worry; I got a gut feeling he didn't ditch that car. He should've, but he didn't."

Which intrigued both Ronnie and MacAlistair.

"Had this heap, what? If you're right, 15 years, maybe more. He works keeping it on the road, carries his tools with him. It's not just his wheels. This guy's got an *attachment.*"


"That us in 60 years?" Ronnie nodded at the gray-haired people going by in the corridor off the solarium. They went by on canes, leaning on walkers, some in nurse-pushed wheelchairs hooked up to oxygen tanks hung behind.

"Who?" Big Sid was at the tall windows of the hospital solarium, his mouth full of Doritos he'd found on a foraging expedition to the vending machines down the hall. He looked at the old people and shook his head definitively. "That's *you* in 60 years. In 60 years, *I'm* gonna be daisy food, y'understand."

"Walk up and down a bit."

"What?"

"C'mon, just take a coupla steps. I want to see something."

"See what?"

"I'm not sure. C'mon."

Big Sid took a single step, then froze, turning warily to Ronnie. "See *what?*"

"Maybe it's just your pants."

*"What's* just my pants?"

"I dunno, Sid, but when you came back from the machines, I dunno, I never noticed it before—"

"Noticed *what?*" Big Sid looked down at his legs. "Don't tell me I ripped these fuckin…"

"No, no, it's just you look a little bow-legged."

"*What?*"

One of the nurses walking by the solarium shushed them.

"You're nuts!" Sid whispered, dropping into a chair alongside Ronnie. "Bow-legged?"

"No, really, it looks like you're getting bow-legged."

"You don't *get* bow-legged! That's something happens to you when you're a kid! Grown-ups don't *get* bow-legged."

"Cowboys get bow-legged."

"Oh, yeah, you see me riding a horse *all* the fucking time."

"Hey, gents?" It was MacAlistair standing with a youngish doctor with wire-rimmed glasses, wearing $90 Reeboks and a white medical coat over Jordache jeans. "Come meet Dr. Devane."

After introductions, they all sat together in the solarium.

The doctor frowned at the shirt buttons straining over Sid's belly, and then at the bag of Doritos. "The cafeteria's still open. We have a very nice salad bar."

Sid smiled in mock gratefulness. "The story on Grandpa Nardo?"

"I've been over his records from the facility he was at in Westchester. He's been deteriorating for some time, and it's been accelerating. A series of small 'mini-strokes,' they also suspect Alzheimer's. And the physical and emotional trauma of the last few days -- "

"Physical trauma?" said Ronnie. "I didn't know he'd been hit."

Devane shook his head. "He wasn't, but by the time the sheriff's people had gotten to the house, he was borderline hypothermic. In his degraded condition, that was enough to… Think of a house, and someone's going through it turning off the lights one room at a time. By the time his grandson pulled him out of the place in Westchester, a lot of the lights were already off. These last few shocks, though, they blew a fuse that sent a whole wing of the house dark."

"Can we see him?" Big Sid asked.

"Sure. I'm just telling you not to expect very much."

Ronnie and Big Sid followed Devane down the wide corridor, MacAlistair lagging. There were a few Christmas decorations on the wall: pictures of Santa Claus, toy-making elves, a flying reindeer-pulled sleigh, on a nurses' station a dwarf silver artificial Christmas tree decorated with red balls, none of which made the wide, antiseptic halls any merrier. Through the open doors on either side of the corridor Ronnie saw sallow-faced geriatrics stretched out on their beds. The conscious ones stared emptily back at their TVs. Not a lot of yuletide merriment there, either.

"In here." Devane stopped at a door guarded by a sheriff's deputy. "I'll be at the nurses' station," and the doctor left them.

"I'm going to pass if you fellas don't mind," MacAlistair said. "I can't take a second go-around with this gent. It gets frustrating."

The room was small and clean: a bed, a night table, a hospital tray. Some prints of summer landscapes on the walls, blinds pulled over the windows, the air in the room – smelling of disinfectant and medication, like the bedroom back at Dell'Acqua's place, only more pungent – turned up incubator hot.

Grandpa Nardo sat slack-faced in a wheelchair in front of a TV, evidently unimpressed by the ringing bells and flashing lights that went along with Bob Barker giving away washing machines and refrigerators to giggly middle-aged ladies in Day Glo-colored polyester pantsuits. Grandpa Nardo was bent and shriveled, blue veins visible in parchment skin. His white hair was thin, downy, his watery eyes unfocused behind Coke bottle glasses.

Ronnie and Big Sid looked at each other, then Big Sid stepped up to the old man.

"Mr. Nardo? Mr. Nardo, we'd like to talk to you about your grandson. Mr. Nardo? Mr. Nardo, we're from New York. Hey!" Big Sid waved a hand in front of the old man's face. The old man leaned to one side to see around the big man's hand. Sid turned to Ronnie and groaned, then sat on the edge of the bed shaking his head.

"Mr. Nardo?" Ronnie tried. "Mr. Nardo, I'd like to talk to you about your grandson. I want to ask you about Salvatore. Sal. Mr. Nardo?"

Big Sid dug into the bottom of his Doritos bags for a few last fragments. "You have better luck talking to the wall. Hello, wall! How are *you* today?"

Ronnie gave Sid an irritated look. Sid balled up the empty Doritos bag and tossed it at a corner wastepaper basket with a hook shot. He missed.

Ronnie knelt by the old man and put a hand on a bony arm. He closed his eyes and tried to remember the words he'd heard around the family table as a kid. "*Padrone...Padrone...*"

The old man's foggy eyes focused slightly behind his thick glasses.

"*Padrone,*" Ronnie said, "*Salvatore...è morto.*"

The old man turned his wavering head to Ronnie. "*Il mio...il mio Salvatore?*" he asked in a weak voice that sounded like rustling paper.

"*Si. È morto.*"

Tears formed in the rheumy eyes. "*Il mio Salvatore...*"

But then the old man turned back to the TV, blank-faced again, the tears forgotten half-way down his cheeks.

Ronnie stood. He wiped at his nose. For the first time he noticed how small the man looked, even in this little room. He picked up the balled Doritos bag and put it in the wastepaper basket. "I can't remember how to say, 'I'm sorry.'"

Aptly named, Point Pleasant is one of the northernmost of the Jersey shore towns. It has a tidy smallness which tends to keep the place, even at the height of the summer, less raucous than some of the other shore resorts. The teens go to Seaside to raise hell and hopefully get laid, the grownups go to Atlantic City to lose money. Point Pleasant gets families with small kids…and young single professionals raising a quiet kind of hell while hoping to get laid.

Most of the eating and drinking on the Point Pleasant boardwalk gets done at Jenkinson's Pavilion. Inside the building filling the pier there's a counter for ordering food down one side, a bar in the back. In the winter, while the rest of the boardwalk is tarped over or boarded up, Jenkinson's stays open. Barely. The bar is locked up, and only one of a dozen stations at the food counter is operating with one cook running between the flattop and pizza oven. It's a busy afternoon that sees more than a handful of people sitting in the chilly dining room.

From where Meara was sitting, he could see past the empty booths and tables of the dining room, out the side windows past the picnic tables on the patio, up the wide, white, empty beach to the Manasquan Inlet. Despite the threatening gray sky, someone was taking their sailboat down the channel out to sea, a 30-footer it looked like. The sails hadn't been unfurled yet, the boat chugging along on its auxiliary motor. Beyond the jetties of piled stone marking and sheltering the channel, the sea heaved and capped white, but it seemed to matter little to the slicker-clad man at the sailboat's helm, and he pushed steadfastly out onto the gray, rough water.

"It's pretty, isn't it?" she asked.

He moved his wooden stirrer around in his coffee. "If you like the water. I never liked the ocean. Too many things in all that deep water can eat you."

She laughed. "It's why I moved us down here," she said. "I like it. I like it better in the off-season, but still…"

She was pushing 40, a bit worn looking. She had once been pretty in a girly kind of way, but that kind of pretty is a fragile thing and hadn't taken the years very well.

"I appreciate your seeing me like this, Sara. I wasn't even sure you'd be home. I thought you might be working or something…if you *were* working…"

She smiled. She looked better when she smiled. "You were lucky. Where I work, we have a use-it-or-lose-it policy on vacations. I had all this time banked up, so I thought I'd burn it off over the holidays. It's worked out; I got to finish decorating the house, do some last-minute Christmas shopping…"

"That's nice."

"You could've come by the house."

"I didn't want to intrude. You might've had holiday stuff going on—"

"You could've stayed for dinner. The kids, they still remember you. Well, Josh is away, but Nikki's home for the holidays." She looked past his shoulder down the beach. Whatever she saw down there made her smile fleetingly, then she turned back to Meara. "I was surprised to hear from you. It's been, wow, how long?"

"A long time. But you still send me Christmas cards."

She reached across the table and patted his forearm. He saw her frowning at his bruised and scraped knuckles. "I never forgot what you did for us, Jack. I don't know how we would've gotten through it."

"You would've. You're a tough lady."

She laughed away the compliment. "I don't know about that." Her face grew ruminative. "I just figured, you know, you were living your life, we had ours, and that's why we didn't hear from you anymore. But I never forgot, and I wanted you to know that." She waved the seriousness away. "Jesus, Jack, it's just a Christmas card!"

"I always appreciated the gesture."

She shrugged a "You're welcome." Then she laughed. "I saw you still have that same tank of a car! I saw it at the curb and I recognized it right away, but I still couldn't believe it! That thing looks like it's been through the wars!" Then she stopped laughing, looked at him like she was saying, "So do you."

"It was a wedding gift to ourselves. My wife and I drove up to Lake George for our honeymoon in it."

"Do you ever hear from her?"

"No. She moved out of state." He shrugged; it was better that way.

"You know, sometimes I used to wonder... Well, when I heard you two broke up. If maybe because she thought, you know, all the time you were spending with us..."

"I never thought of that," and now he was surprised he hadn't. "I don't know. We had so many other problems I'm not sure it mattered. If you're worried, that wasn't why we broke up."

"Because that would've been a shame."

"I wanted to do it."

She nodded at his hand cupped around his coffee cup, the damaged knuckles. "What'd you do—"

"Ah, I was working on that damn car. I'm always working on that damn car. How do you think I keep that monster on the road?"

"Maybe it's time to think about getting a new car."

"Maybe."

She looked back down the beach, again, but not at anything; he could see some nagging thought in her eyes. "What I never understood... ," she began, "I hope you don't mind my asking. Well, you and my husband weren't even close, Jack. All these years, I've wanted to ask. I wanted to back then, but I was afraid it would sound ungrateful, you know?"

"So ask."

"Why? Why was it your job to take care of us? You hardly knew him."

"I knew him."

"Jack..." she pushed.

He looked down at the heavy wood table, years of piled scratches, scuffs, carvings of who loved who and fuck you's. "If I'd been a little faster or he'd been a little slower... If I'd walked my foot post a little different, I might've been closer, or if he'd walked his different he might've had further to go... What I'm saying is it could've turned out different."

"You mean you –"

"I mean it could've turned out different."

She nodded and a heaviness he didn't like settled over the table. He brightened: "How're the kids?"

She gratefully took up the change in subject. "Josh is in the Army now. He's a little lost, I think. Well, he's *been* a little lost. For a long time. There were a lot of years, the important years, there was no man in the house. I think that hurt him, you know?"

She took a sip of her coffee and he watched her left hand restlessly tracing the carvings in the tabletop. It surprised him he hadn't noticed the wedding band before.

"You got married again."

"You didn't know? Yeah. It's quite a while now. I guess that's how long it's been since we talked. Probably since I moved down here. That's got to be, what? 12, 13 years? Hal's good with the kids. You should stay for dinner; he'd like to meet you. I've told him enough about you."

"You started over. You moved away, you got married..."

"You sound like that bothers you."

"Jealous. How's Nikki?"

"Maybe because she was so young and didn't remember him, maybe it's because she's a girl and she still had her mother... I don't know, but it's gone a lot smoother for her."

"Maybe girls are just stronger."

"Maybe. She's a sophomore now, over at Glassboro. Environmental Science. I don't even know what that is."

The sailboat had cleared the channel and he could see the man in the slicker bringing up the sails. The strong wind quickly puffed out the white canvas. "How did *you* do it?"

"Do what?"

"You started over. You let it go."

"You never let it go. You know that, Jack. You just find a way to carry it with you." Her eyes fixed on him, studying, curious. "Why'd you want to see me? After all this time?"

"I wanted to let you know I'm gonna take your example. I'm gonna start over. As of next month, I've got my 20 in."

"You're retiring? Congratulations!"

"I'm gonna move away."

"Where?"

He took a moment; he didn't have an answer. He put on a false smile and grandly declared, "Anywhere."

"Way to go! Is there, um…"

"There's a girl."

"Even better."

"I just wanted to say…" The wind was taking the sailboat further out at a rapid clip, the sharp bow splitting the water easily. He didn't see anybody else helping the man in the yellow slicker. How do you do that? he wondered. How do you go out there like that by yourself? On the deep water? "I just wanted to say…"

"Goodbye?" She set her hand on his arm. "It's ok, Jack. I understand. It was sweet of you to come by. Let me know where you end up, I'll still send you your Christmas card every year. Maybe you could try sending one back once in a while."

"Well," he said, and he stood.

She stood and they hugged, standing together in the middle of the empty dining room.

"I just wanted to tell you it's gonna be ok," he said quietly in her ear. "Things are gonna be…ok."

He walked back alone to his car parked on the empty street running parallel to the boardwalk. Someone had drawn a finger through the built-up road grime on his car, "CLEAN ME!!"

"You guys look dilapidated," Berman said, amazed the two burnouts shuffling through the squad room door could still move under their own power.

"If that means we look like shit, then I *feel* dilapidated," Big Sid said as he dropped into his desk chair.

Ronnie plopped down at his own desk and let his head fall forward onto the blotter making it unanimous. He heard his phone ring and heard the other squad room phones ring. He hoped someone would pick them up. His head had been hurting before he'd gotten to the station house and all those jangling bells weren't making it any better.

It had been a long ride back from south Jersey, made more wearying by their managing to catch the evening rush hour clog as they'd neared the City. By the time they'd made it back to the precinct house, it was dark, Ronnie was stiff from hours in the car, hungry, cranky, wanting a shower, an aspirin, and a nap. He guessed Big Sid wasn't feeling much better, and all these goddamn unanswered ringing phones weren't helping his disposition any.

"Don't get comfortable," Berman said.

"He wants us?" Big Sid asked.

"Pronto, Seien Schnell, posthaste. Told me to tell you soon's you came in."

Ronnie and Big Sid pulled themselves out of their chairs. But then, with a belated awareness, Big Sid froze in the middle of the squad room, shook his head as if to clear it, and let his eyes wander around the empty desks. "Hey, what're you doing on?" he asked Berman. "I thought you didn't rotate nights 'til next week."

"Filling in," Berman said after telling a few callers to "Hold please."

"We *that* short?" Big Sid asked.

Berman nodded. "Murillo's on, too. He finally showed up. He's out on a call with a uniform. I don't know what offends his sensibilities more, climbing out of a sick bed, or going out on a call with a uniform. Present company excepted."

Ronnie acknowledged with a grunt.

"Cutler didn't come in today," Berman added with a certain measure of concern.

"He sick?"

"I don't know. He didn't call in."

They shook their heads, neither knowing what Cutler's unexplained absence meant but thinking it couldn't mean anything good, then Big Sid gave Ronnie – damned near asleep on his feet – a push toward Van Dyne's office.

The captain looked worse than he had the day before. All through Big Sid's recitation of the day's events, Van Dyne blew his nose, dropped Visine into his bleary eyes, sucked up Dristan, put his hand on the icy radiator as if he was trying to will up heat.

"Maybe you should go home, Captain," Ronnie offered.

"Maybe you should get that haircut I told you to get yesterday," Van Dyne said.

When Sid got to the part about Ronnie's Sherlock fucking Holmes coup re: the window repairmen, Ronnie looked to Van Dyne for some sort of salutary acknowledgment. But all Van Dyne did was briefly flick his eyes in Ronnie's direction and make a dismissive "Big deal" motion of his eyebrows.

When Sid finished, Van Dyne pursed his lips, seemed to be rerunning it all in his head. He focused his gun sight glasses on Sid: "So...?"

One of those unspoken bits of communication Ronnie had noted the day before went back and forth between Van Dyne and Big Sid, something – Ronnie gleaned – along the lines of Big Sid saying, "Boss, I told the kid everything so we don't have to be so coy," and Van Dyne responding with a sigh denoting, "Gee, I wish you hadn't done that," and then Big Sid turning to Ronnie with a glower that said, "See? Now the Boss is pissed and it's *your* fucking fault because you couldn't just drive and keep your yap shut!"

"So," Van Dyne began again, "you didn't turn anything connected to what's going on up here?"

"We didn't see anything," Big Sid said, but there was a hitch to his voice.

"But?"

"These dudes went in awfully heavy to take out a bookie. This wasn't just some disgruntled customer stiffed on a bet, y'understand. *Something*'s going on. I don't know it's tied to us, but those machine guns and somebody in that house could go head-to-head with the shooters got me not wanting to completely close the book."

Van Dyne seemed pained by the logic of that. "Well, Jersey's got the ball now. There's nothing we can move on until Albany turns something on the car, providing there's anything to—" Van Dyne's phone ringing cut the captain off. "Van Dyne... Hold on..." He turned to Ronnie and Big Sid sunk deep into his office sofa. "One of you bring in a Ralph Zinni last night?"

Ronnie tentatively put up his hand.

Van Dyne frowned, went back on the phone. "Yes..." Van Dyne started scribbling on a notepad. "When was this?...I've got it, thanks." He slowly hung up his phone and eased back in his chair, studying Ronnie through his gun sight eyeglasses. After a long moment, he started fitting a Paris Opal into his cigarette holder while he stared up at the ceiling and let out a long, unhappy breath. "Seems there's a problem with Mr. Zinni."

"Goddamit, I *knew* it!" Big Sid exploded. "Let me guess. False arrest? Harassment? I'll bet that vanilla bitch was doping out papers while she was still in the car."

113

Van Dyne turned his red-rimmed eyes toward Sid, his eyebrows raised in an officious-looking kind of curiosity. "Obviously, Sidney, there's a story I need to hear and you can tell it to me on the way." Van Dyne gave his nose one last toot into a tissue before he tiredly got to his feet and waved both Ronnie and Big Sid up.

"On the way where?" Big Sid asked.

Van Dyne shot his French cuffs, his lighter flashed as he lit his cigarette. "Call came in a few minutes ago. They found Mr. Zinni's body in a dumpster a block and a half from here."

Even trailing behind Van Dyne, Ronnie could hear the captain wheezing through his congested nose. But that didn't stop the captain puffing away on his cigarette or slow his express train pace along the sidewalk. In fact, the more of their story Ronnie and Big Sid spilled out as they hurried after the captain, the harder the captain's cigarette puffed and the faster his pace got.

When they finished their story, Van Dyne stopped so short they almost ran him down. "You boys are very lucky," the captain said. "You're lucky I'm not one of those petty sorts worried about appearances, because if I was, the body of a – as the papers will put it – 'known Mob figure' assassinated less than two blocks from a stationhouse already target of an Internal Affairs sweep might *piss me off!*" For a moment, Van Dyne's pasty face flamed red. He turned a hard glare on Big Sid and the end of his Paris Opal pulsed.

"Boss, I'm sorry, but like I said, we had no reason to hold him."

Van Dyne held up a finger. "Ah! Correction, Sidney! You had no *legal basis* to hold him, but you had *plenty* of *reasons*! I can't believe I'm saying this, but Junior here—" a nod at Ronnie "—had better instincts on this than *you!* I don't expect much from him, but Sidney, *you...!*" Van Dyne shook his head exasperatedly, and turned, storming off across the street, oblivious to traffic.

114

Big Sid turned to Ronnie with yet another of his now-familiar somehow-this-is-*your*-fucking fault looks.

They trotted off after Van Dyne, going a block east and then a half-block south of the stationhouse to an alley between a take-out Mexican place and a take-out Chinese place. There were two blue-and-whites parked in front of the alley next to a garbage truck. It was a little after seven, the temperature was a hair short of 28 degrees with a wind chill factor bringing it down to almost ten, yet there was a crowd.

"Jesus," Big Sid said, "Don't these people got some place to go?"

"*This* is it," Van Dyne said. "By tomorrow this'll be a stop on the tour."

A half-dozen or so uniforms were telling the crowd there was nothing to see, and that – paradoxically – they didn't want to see what there *was* to see, and would they please keep moving.

Van Dyne flashed his ID to pass the three of them through the cordon. Ronnie recognized the patrol sergeant coordinating the uniforms, a salt-and-pepper-haired, no-nonsense telephone pole named Troupe. Troupe came over to Van Dyne as soon as he saw him. He gave Ronnie an efficient half-wink of recognition before turning to the captain.

Ronnie's, "How goes it, Sarge?" got stepped on by Van Dyne's, "Who was first on-scene?"

"Burnette!" the sergeant called. Ronnie recognized the young, black patrolman who'd come up to the squad room the day before with the fax about Sal Dell'Acqua.

"What about a CSU?" Van Dyne asked Troupe.

"Flagged 'em as soon as the call came in, Captain."

"Find out where they are for me, would you, Sergeant?" Van Dyne turned to Burnette. "You were first on-scene?"

"I guess so, Sir."

"You guess?"

"Yessir, I was."

"Who found the body?" Van Dyne asked.

Burnette led him over to three black guys in coveralls who belonged to the garbage truck. They looked impatient to leave.

Van Dyne dabbed at his nose with a tissue he pulled from his coat pocket. "All right, Ron, think you can manage to take their statements?"

The three coveralled guys didn't have much to say. They worked for a non-residential private service which handled restaurants and hotels. They had backed their truck into the alley, one of them had gone to hook a tip cable to the dumpster there, saw the body, the end.

Ronnie read his notes back to the three men to make sure he'd gotten their story straight, checked with Burnette to make sure the patrolman had full names and addresses and phone numbers for them, and contact information for their company. About the time he wrapped it up, Troupe was giving Van Dyne more uncheering news.

"CSU is backed up, Captain. Sounds like a busy night. They won't be able to pop a unit free for another couple hours."

"Lovely," Van Dyne said. "All right, Officer Burnette, let's have a look at him."

Burnette led them down the alley to a green dumpster sitting against one of the alley walls. The four of them stood on a ledge around the bottom of the dumpster and looked in. The body was in a half-tucked position facing the far side of the dumpster, lying on a bed of trash about a third of the way down. Ronnie immediately recognized the billowy black leather coat.

"All right, Ron," Van Dyne said, nodding Ronnie into the dumpster.

"All right what, Sir?"

"He was your collar. You want to be a detective? Get in there and detect."

Burnette – with a better-you-than-me look of relief – reached into his back pocket, pulled out a pair of latex gloves and handed them to Ronnie along with his flashlight.

Even standing at the rim of the dumpster in 28 degree cold (not counting the wind chill), the smell of a rotting mix of Mexican and Chinese food from inside the dumpster was still stomach-churningly bad. Ronnie took a breath and climbed over the side, wishing he had Van Dyne's congested sinuses.

Van Dyne blinked at the smell and lit up a fresh Opal. "Try not to touch anything you shouldn't in there."

Ronnie waded through paper, cardboard, and sundry kitchen detritus. The more Ronnie churned around in the dumpster, the worse it smelled in there.

"Try not to disturb the crime scene so much," Van Dyne said.

Ronnie picked himself up from where he'd lost his footing and fallen in a mass of something green and sticky. He stumbled across the dumpster, knelt by the side of the body. He switched on the flashlight, got the beam on Zinni's head, glad the face was turned away toward the metal wall of the dumpster. "What am I looking for?"

"I believe they're referred to as 'clues,' Ron. Let's start with wounds."

"Doesn't look like they even *tried* to cover him," Big Sid said.

"They wanted him found," Van Dyne said.

"Calling card?"

"Maybe. Maybe a warning."

"There's some blood here on the back of his neck," Ronnie reported. "Not very much. I can't see a wound unless it's something small under the blood. There's no other blood any place I can see. Wait a second."

There were some shadowy marks on the marble skin of the dead man's jaw. Ronnie leaned over for a better look. The last time he'd seen those eyes they'd been following Ms. Kiernan, Esq. out the station house door, looking back at Ronnie with a gloating twinkle. Now, they were flat, and half closed as if on the verge of sleep. The mouth that had had a matching smirk was pulled back in a humorless rictus grin.

"What do you see?" Van Dyne asked.

"He seems to still be in rigor."

"This cold throws off the usual timeline. What else? You see something there?"

"Looks like some kinda bruises on his face, like finger marks but bigger."

"Gloves," Big Sid judged.

Van Dyne nodded. "Where?"

"The jaw. Four on this side."

"How much you wanna bet there's a thumb on the other side," Big Sid said to Van Dyne.

"No doubt," the captain said. "The blood on the neck; where on the neck?"

"At the top."

"Here." Ronnie looked up and saw Van Dyne tapping the base of his own skull. "Where the spinal column enters the cranium."

Ronnie nodded and turned back to the body and the blood spot on the neck. "Yeah. I can't see a wound, though. The blood's crusted up. I don't want to mess with it."

"Don't."

"So, either it's a real small hole, or something so small it closed right up. Not a bullet. Some kinda knife?" He looked to Van Dyne again.

Van Dyne mimed an action: one hand pretended to hold someone under the jaw while the other speared into the base of the imaginary skull. "Sidney? Weapon of choice?"

"Ice pick."

"Ok, Junior, come on out of there. This is the kind of thing usually referred to by the media as, 'a gangland-style execution.'"

Big Sid helped Ronnie back over the side of the dumpster. "Do yourself a favor, kid. Take a good, long bath tonight." Sid turned to Van Dyne. "They must've done him as soon as they turned the corner."

Ronnie was brushing himself off while Big Sid indicated he'd appreciate some distance between them. "Hey, Captain?" Ronnie said. "I don't know, maybe I'm just being paranoid, but if they took this guy out because he got caught following Lourdes Bracero, how safe is the girl?"

Van Dyne went still for a moment, then blew his nose into his tissue. The captain paced to the far end of the alley, then started back. "We don't know what the goal is here, we don't know what the interest in the girl is. What we do know is they're willing to kill one of their own out of hand because of it, and that Anthony Maiella seems tied in somehow. When you consider how much we *don't* know, and that the little we *do* know is all bad news, it's probably best we work from worst-case assumptions." Apparently unsure Ronnie and Big Sid had followed all that, Van Dyne added, "Better safe than sorry." He checked his watch. "Ron, it's a little after seven; where is she now?"

"I don't really know her that well, Captain."

"Puh-*leeeze*," Big Sid said. By way of explanation for Van Dyne, Sid beat out a passionate heartbeat on his chest and fluttered his eyelashes.

"Lovely," Van Dyne said. "And her another officer's girl. Tsk-tsk, Ron, tsk tsk."

As cold as it was in the alley, Ronnie felt his face grow hot. "Captain, I only met her twice! And one of those times was to take her to the hospital!" The more he spluttered on, the more entertained Van Dyne and Big Sid seemed to be, so Ronnie blundered his way back to business: "I'm just, you know, guessing because of the, you know, last night, but if I *had* to guess, she's either getting ready to go to work, or she's already there."

"Let's hope she's at the bar," Van Dyne said. "Fairly public, I wouldn't think they'd try anything there. But, just to be sure... I'll send an unmarked car by her building, see if they can sniff out if she's still home. I'll also send somebody in plainclothes to her bar—"

"I can do that," Ronnie said which spurred Big Sid to tap out more heartbeats on his chest. "Would you stop that?"

"Ron?" Van Dyne nodded at the dumpster behind them. "Have you forgotten Mr. Zinni? You've still got a crime scene to work. Wherever we find her, we'll sit on her, but, unless the other side makes a move, it'll be strictly observe-and-report. I don't want her knowing we're around. She might get nervous and do something that'll get the other side nervous and precipitate a move from them before we're ready. How long will she be at work?"

"If she works the same schedule she worked last night, she's on until they close at two," Ronnie said.

"A.M.?" Van Dyne shook his head, incredulous. "Credit her for stamina. That gives us some time to work with."

"Then what?" Big Sid said. "Ferry her home in a blue-and-white?"

"If we do, I'd like to ride with them," Ronnie said.

"I'll bet you would," Big Sid said.

"A blue-and-white won't be enough," Van Dyne said. "It won't scare them off. We know they're around, and that's good, but they know we know, and that's bad. They've had almost 15 hours to anticipate us and plot out a way around – or through – any security we set up around the girl. Between that head start and our current manpower limitations, the safe worst-case assumption is, if they want her, they'll get her."

"Isn't there something we can do?" Ronnie asked.

Van Dyne nodded. "Let them make their move."

"That sounds kinda dangerous," Ronnie said.

"It is," Van Dyne said, "For somebody."

There was a rumble from the clouds – invisible in the night sky – that seemed to have taken up permanent station over the City. It began to rain.

The rain rippled down the big, square windows of the diner in thick, ropey streams. The crawl of taillights on Route 3 glowed through the water, blurring together and slowing like clotting, iridescent blood. Meara looked in the other direction, at the westbound traffic, white headlights detaching themselves from the soft, white glow that marked the City, hidden behind the Jersey Palisades a few miles off.

"Somethin' else, hon?"

Meara pointed to the empty coffee cup in front of him without turning to the waitress. He heard her squeak off on her rubber soles, then she was back, coffee sloshed into his cup, and she squeaked off again. He held his right hand over the top of the cup and let the warm vapor curl around his stiff fingers.

There was a construction crew doing some damned thing on the westbound side of the highway across from the diner, squeezing three slow-moving lanes of traffic into two choked lanes. Between bursts from a pair of jackhammers, a backhoe clawed at the muddy exposed ground, a mini dozer shoved the piles of dirt this way and that. The work crew moved among the machines, hunched against the rain, bulky in their yellow hard hats and orange safety vests, lit by glaring work lamps and blinking yellow caution lights.

Meara downed half his coffee in one pull, then set the cup back down and put his hand, again, over the top. He flexed his fingers, felt the pain in his bruised knuckles, and under that, a duller, burning arthritic pang, and thought, *this is how you die; a little bit at a time.*

A siren caught his ear. He saw blue police flashers escorting a wrecker in a slow weave through the westbound traffic. The police siren whooped and warbled; the tow truck driver leaned on his horn.

The clogged lanes heaved and squirmed, but there was no room on the already squeezed road for the cars to move out of the way.

Ruby-red taillights and sparkling white headlights, work lights and blue police flashers, warning lights and the yellow flashers of the tow truck splashed across the watery diner windows, a much brighter, more colorful display than the thin strand of Christmas lights hung around the window frames.

He sat his empty cup back down on the saucer. The waitress squeaked up to his table, again.

"I wish they'd let 'em through," she said. "That racket's givin' me a headache. Anythin' else, hon?"

He looked at the unbroken, barely moving river of taillights heading east. It'd be a while before it made any sense to get back on the road.

He pointed to his cup and her rubber soles squeaked off for the coffee pot.


Van Dyne had gone back to the station to put out APBs on Alison Kiernan and her white Cadillac, to get her car's plate numbers from the DMV, and to get a warrant to search the car providing it wasn't already sitting on a river bottom or cut up in a scrap yard.

Big Sid and Troupe huddled out of the rain under the awning of the Mexican restaurant in a discussion concerning consent-to-search. They agreed they were going to have to knock on the doors of the buildings on either side of the alley to see who belonged to the alley and to the garbage in the alley. They'd have to get somebody to sign consent-to-search forms for the alley and the garbage cans but weren't sure about the dumpster containing Ralph Zinni. The dumpster was, technically, the scene of a crime and Big Sid didn't think they needed permission to go through the garbage in the dumpster, but Troupe wasn't sure.

"I think the *body* is ours," Troupe said, "but I don't know about the garbage *under* the body."

While Troupe delegated the uniforms to digging up consent signatures, Big Sid and Ronnie worked the crime scene. They did a slow walk-through finding what they'd expected, which was absolutely nothing. With a tape measure from one of the blue-and-whites, they measured distances between and dimensions of everything in the alley, and then Big Sid let Ronnie do the crime scene pencil sketch only to grouse when he saw Ronnie was going so far as to draw in the handles on the garbage cans.

"They're not gonna hang it in the fucking *Goo*-genheim!" the big man grumbled, his mood no doubt aggravated by being – by then – thoroughly soaked by the cold December rain.

About eight o'clock, a meat wagon showed up for the corpse but since the crime scene unit *still* hadn't arrived, the EMTs on the rig weren't allowed to touch the body.

By 9:00, the CSU still hadn't shown up and Big Sid and Ronnie had done all they could with the scene. They got take-out from one of the restaurants near the dumpster and sat eating out of cartons in the back of one of the blue-and-whites. Ronnie was eating a pint of beef Chao Fan with chopsticks while Big Sid spooned his way through a quart of vegetable fried rice.

"What's that smell?" Big Sid said without stopping the locomotive gyrations of his jaws.

Ronnie smelled it, too. He dipped his nose in his carton of Chao Fan.

"Smells like bad guacamole," Sid said. "Jesus, kid! It's *you!*"

Ronnie shrugged apologetically and cracked one of the car windows. "Sorry, Sid. I think I fell in it in that dumpster."

"On your way home, you wanna pick yourself up some shampoo with lemon. It'll get the stink out of your hair, y'understand. In the meantime, ya wanna move closer to that window?"

The crime scene crew finally showed up, Big Sid climbed out to touch base with them, then climbed back in the car to finish dinner. He leaned over to stare into Ronnie's carton. "Boy, for a guy always making noises about how good he eats…"

"What?"

"I was just wondering how you can eat that. I *never* order meat from these places. And I *like* meat. You know what you didn't see in that alley? Cats."

"Oh, brother."

"You got a Mexican place on one side, a Chinese place on the other."

"I'm ignoring you."

"You ever get Chinese food with that funny pork in it? Those little funny red bits of pork? C'mon, honestly, that look like pork to you? You ever see anything in a slice of bacon that looks like that?"

"I don't eat bacon."

"That's supposed to be beef, right? That look like any part of a cow you recognize?"

"Stop."

"They eat dogs in China, kid. That's a fact, y'understand. And in Korea, too, and a bunch of those gook places over there. Ask Berman when we get back. He's a fucking Whiz Kid, he'll tell you. Know why they eat dogs over there?"

"You're embarrassing yourself."

"'Cause they already went through all the cats." Then, "You're not impressing anybody with those." He meant Ronnie's chopsticks.

Outside, the CSU techs were done, and Ronnie could see the EMTs trying to wrestle Zinni's now-sodden corpse out of the dumpster to the open black plastic body bag they had stretched out on the alley floor.

"Where you going?" Big Sid asked but Ronnie didn't answer as he climbed out of the car.

He stood by Troupe, blinking against the rain, shivering with the cold, and watched the EMTs bag the body. There must've been something about the look on Ronnie's face – beyond being wet and cold -- because Troupe said, "C'mon, kid, it's not like this is your first stiff."

"I know, Sarge."

"Don't feel too bad about this shithead. Think of it as somebody saved the taxpayers a $10,000 trial with a $1.99 ice pick."

Meara crossed back into the City through the Holland Tunnel, rolled out onto Canal, his tires rumbling over the old paving stones, then turned uptown. The commuter crowd had finally cleared out, and the cold and the rain had emptied the sidewalks and streets of lower Manhattan of everything except Checker cabs trolling for fares.

The old factories and warehouses of Soho were being turned into pricey condos, but however chichi they may have looked on the inside, they still looked like old factories and warehouses on the outside. The rain pulled soot out of the air and left it in long, dark streaks on the sides of the buildings and in dirty watermarks on the large windows.

Oily water slithered between the paving stones, gathered in rainbow-tinted pools in potholes and at the street corners where the sewers were clogged with garbage the runoff had dragged along the curbs. The glowing neon from the new clubs and the new coffee bars and the new retro diners glowed in swaths on the wet streets, smeared and bright like a whore's makeup.

Just past 14th Street he turned into the Stuyvesant Town complex, a collection of tall, bland, red brick apartment buildings stitched together with parking lots and strips of dead earth and dying grass sparkling with broken glass.

He considered this a time for prudence, so he didn't park, as he usually did, in the lot in front of his building. Instead, he cruised through the lot slowly, looking for signs of surveillance: exhaust vapor from an idling engine, steamed-over car windows. Even though he saw nothing, he pulled around the back of his building, parked, entered through the door to the basement laundry room, then got the elevator up to the seventh floor and took the fire stairs a flight down to his floor.

He took a moment at his door, checking the lock for picklock scratches, then turned the key and pushed on the door very lightly with his fingertips, feeling for any tug or unusual weight on the door. With the door open just a crack, he ran his fingertips around the rim of the door. Clean.

He checked to make sure the hallway was empty then drew his pistol. He stood clear of the doorway and pushed the door open.

He waited.

Then he took a breath and stepped into the doorway, offering a clean, clear target. The blinds were open, that was a help – the apartment wasn't completely dark.

He waited.

He did a quick walk-through of the apartment – a few small rooms, some cheap, functional furniture, bare walls – then closed his front door, hooking the chain and throwing the dead bolt.

He pulled the blinds on his windows then sat tiredly on his sofa, holding his pistol in his lap. It was cold in the apartment – he'd turned the thermostat down before he'd left – but he found himself sweating, was suddenly aware of how hard his heart had been working, how juiced he'd been by adrenaline during the walk-through.

He slipped off his bombardier jacket, holstered his pistol, turned up the heat and shuffled tiredly into the kitchen. There wasn't much in the fridge; he plastered together a quick peanut butter and jelly sandwich with bread starting to go stale, washed it down with some flat Coke, sat in the living room eating in the dark.

He looked around the small, spare apartment. He felt tired, more than just from the ride, more than from the last few days. He felt 20 years tired.

It wouldn't be hard to leave, he thought. If he walked out the door that night and never came back, all it would take was the super throwing a fresh coat of paint on the walls and it'd be like he'd never been there. You go under in the deep water and you don't even leave a ripple, and that made him feel even more tired.

The heat was up now. He stripped off his clothes and after the days in the car it felt good to be out of them. He took a long, hot shower and felt even better. Afterward, in his bedroom, he set his alarm clock for 01:30. He slipped under his blankets, shivering until the cool sheets warmed under him, his holstered pistol on the nightstand near his head.

It was going on 9:00: the girl would already be at work. She got off at 2:00, so getting up at 1:30 would give him time to dress and get over to her place just as she was coming home. He thought that would make for a nice surprise.

Lil's had that same slightly desperate, slightly aimless air it'd had when Ronnie'd come in the night before. The jukebox was even still playing "Three Times a Lady."

The girl dancing was white and skinny enough for her ribs to show. While she had slightly better teeth than her colleague of the night before, she carried the same trademark look of mechanized Eros, her moves languid but thoughtless, her tongue flicking at her lips with sham sensuality.

The dancer peeled off her halter top, a rather sad and pointless exercise considering how little she had there to promote. She targeted a young, bespectacled collegiate type in a varsity jacket sitting close to the stage. She knelt by the edge of the stage, spread her knees wide apart, her crotch eye-level with the kid. She pulled aside the little concealing band of g-string and the kid's eyes went wide and he squirmed in his seat, his pimpled face shone with sweat. He was so engrossed in what was in front of him he missed catching the only genuine emotion on the girl's face – a brief mocking look.

Ronnie swung on his stool away from the stage. He watched Lourdes Bracero move up and down the bar. She was lost in a denim jacket sizes too big for her with an NYPD shoulder patch on the sleeve. Sometimes, while she'd be pouring a drink, a customer would bend his head toward her, she'd bend hers toward him, there'd be a little conversation and maybe even a shared laugh. Every time she had one of those little chats, Ronnie felt a small pang and wished he didn't.

He turned back to the dancer. She was standing now, her knees bent and her weight resting back on her wobbly high heels. She was holding her g-string aside while she ran a creased five-dollar bill up and down between puffy labia. Ronnie wondered if she ever got paper cuts.

"Boo!"

"Jesus!"

Lourdes Bracero made her silent laugh face. She nodded at the dancer. "Whatcha studyin' there, Little Blue? A little biology, maybe? Anatomy?"

Ronnie hoped it was too dark in the bar for her to see him blush.

"You keep hangin' 'round places like this 'n' you gonna get a reputation," she chuckled.

"Think I might get my name up on the ladies' room wall?"

"You ain't got that much class. So, what's this? You after another dinner date?"

"It *is* cold out tonight."

She reached into one of her jacket pockets for a pack of Pall Malls. "It's cold every night. It's winter. It happens like that. Ain't you heard?" She struck a match.

"Well, I'm thinking it's so cold, maybe I'll drive you home."

"*Drive* me home?" She spoke around the cigarette, not missing a beat as she touched the match to the tobacco.

"Got a chauffeur-driven limo waiting right outside."

He smiled. So did she. But her smile was different; hers meant she'd caught him.

"What is this, Blue?"

"I told you, it's cold—"

She expressed her opinion of his fiction by blowing a puff of smoke in his face.

"Ok," he coughed.

"Ok what?"

"Let's just say we're being cautious is all."

"Ok, let's say that. What're we bein' cautious *about?*" But while Ronnie mentally stumbled around for an answer, she seemed to come to it by herself, nodding her head and letting out an enlightened, "Ahhhh. This is about that dude you rousted outside my place last night."

"Could be."

"Somebody else followin' me?"

"Not that we know of," he said, "but we thought maybe we should be—"

"Yeah, cautious, I got that."

"We're probably overreacting."

She nodded, not agreeing, but appraising. She took the cigarette out of her mouth, studied the glowing red tip, shook the growing ash loose with a deft flick of her pinkie.

"Those are bad for your health, ya know," he said.

She took a deep drag on the cigarette and sent the smoke out in a long, controlled stream aimed at Ronnie's face. She held the cigarette in her teeth grinning when she was done. "Ok, Blue, we take a ride tonight." She looked at her watch. "You might as well relax and enjoy the show; I got some time yet. You want somethin' to drink?"

"Lemme try some of that Perrier stuff. I never had any of that."

She put the little green bottle and a glass of ice on the bar in front of him.

He took a sip. "It tastes like club soda."

She took a slice of lemon from a bar tray and squeezed it over his glass. "Suppose' to give it some zing."

"Mmmm. Tastes like club soda with a twist of lemon."

"You got no class, Blue, that's your problem. That's why you hang around places like this. Behave yourself; I gotta go back to work."

He wanted to say something – anything – that might keep her talking to him. He wanted to tell her he was sorry for all her troubles because she looked like somebody who'd sure as hell had had more than her fair share. But she was already off down the bar.

Last Call came and went. With the lights up, the dancers and customers gone, Lil's had the harsh, pitted look of an old combat bunker. Kookie the bouncer unplugged the juke, turned a radio behind the bar to a channel playing Chuck Mangione. He shuffled around the empty barroom, scooping up chairs one-handed and setting them down upended on the tables. Lourdes Bracero came out of a back room pushing a mop and bucket.

"Leave it," Kookie said. "You go on home."

"Sure?"

Kookie didn't say things twice. He took the mop out of her hands and swirled it through the litter on the floor.

She went in the back again, came out with her coat over her arm. She stopped behind the bar, poured herself a short shot of 7-Up. She dipped into her pocket and Ronnie recognized the vial of Percocet. She popped one in her mouth and washed it down with the soda. She hopped over the bar and Ronnie helped her pull her coat on over her denim jacket.

"I take that back 'bout you havin' no class," Lourdes said. "You're kind of a gentleman."

"It's because I'm from the South. We grow up learning the gentlemanly arts."

"What South?"

"South Jersey."

The silent laugh.

He took her by the elbow and led her toward the door...where he stopped. "One thing. Little thing."

"Oh-oh."

"When we go out..."

"Yeah?"

"The car's gonna be right there at the curb."

"Good." She turned for the door, but he stopped her again.

He cleared his throat, which was feeling pretty tight. "When you get to the car, go right for the back door. And whatever you see back there, just slide in. Ok?"

She was frowning now. "Ok." She reached for the door and he stopped her. Again. She looked peeved.

"Lemme go out first," he said.

"This is all that 'just bein' cautious' bullshit, right?"

He smiled weakly because he couldn't think of anything to say.

"Ok, Blue." She stood clear of the door and swept out her hand offering the right of way to him. "Do your duty."

He stepped outside. The rain had stopped. Puddles were already wearing a wrinkled glaze of ice. Except for a few Checkers jouncing down Canal, the street was empty. He took a step and hit ice. Lourdes grabbed him from the doorway and kept him from falling.

"Which one of us is supposed to protect who?" she said, and he was happy to see her grinning again.

Ronnie took her arm and rushed her toward the back door of the Buick at the curb. Big Sid was bent over the wheel, trying to get the engine started. Ronnie opened the back door, Lourdes started to climb in but froze half-way through.

"You're supposed to get right in, remember?" he said, pushing her.

"Who the hell—"

"Get in and I'll introduce you," Ronnie said. "And try not to step on her."

"Think you could take any longer?" Big Sid said. "I'm only half-fuckin'froze. Pardon my language, ladies."

"It's supposed to look normal, right?" Ronnie said, sliding in besides Lourdes, careful not to kick the figure on the floor crammed between the front and rear seats. "Well, this is when she normally leaves. Lou, let me introduce you to your escorts for the evening. Down there in the lounge is Officer Teresa Ortiz."

A bright, "Hi!" came up from the darkness between the seats.

"Hi," Lourdes Bracero said back. "You comfortable down there?"

"For your sake, I hope so," Ronnie said. "As soon as we turn the corner, I want you to trade places with her. If we ever get to the corner. What's going on, Sid?"

Big Sid was still bent over the wheel, turning the key, and pumping the gas pedal. The engine groaned and whined and coughed but didn't start. "Left me out here all night, now she's cold."

"I'm not zackly feelin' too safe with all this protection of yours," Lourdes said. "*Oyez*," she said to Teresa Ortiz, "*Ella es la unica aqui con una mente.*"

Teresa Ortiz laughed.

"Do I even want to know?" Ronnie asked Teresa Ortiz.

"She says the sister's probably the only one in this car with a brain."

The engine coughed a couple of times, then finally turned over.

"Let me introduce the man at the wheel," Ronnie said, "an automotive genius in his own right—"

"Fuck you, kid. Excuse me, again, ladies." Big Sid nursed the engine through a few more coughs and gags until it settled into a rough thrum. The car lurched into gear and immediately crashed through an enormous pothole.

"Umph!" Teresa Ortiz grunted. "I think I lost an ovary on that one."

"How do we look, Sid?" Ronnie asked.

Big Sid checked his side and rearview mirrors. "I don't see a tail. I think we cleared."

"Ok, Lou, here we go."

Big Sid rushed a yellow light and hit the turn from Canal onto The Bowery. Lourdes Bracero gracelessly slid onto the floor while Teresa Ortiz clawed her way up past Ronnie and onto the seat.

"Jeez, it smells like a toilet down here," Lourdes said, squirming to make herself comfortable. She came to rest against Ronnie's legs, one arm draped across his lap. Ronnie flash-fantasized it wasn't a totally meaningless gesture.

"Hey," Lourdes said, "Somethin' smells. I mean, like *garbage.*"

"I smell it, too," Teresa Ortiz said, sniffing the air. Her nose started to home in on Ronnie.

"Kinda like guacamole," Big Sid chuckled.

"It's just the car," Ronnie said.

"Gimme a hand with this, Ronnie," Teresa Ortiz said. She was wrestling with a wig that looked more like Lourdes' shorter, curlier hair then her own straight-ish shag cut. Ronnie helped tug the wig into place.

"Police work don't work out, you got a second line there," Lourdes said. "You'd be great in the beauty parlor."

"Yeah," Big Sid chimed in. "Mr. Ron's."

Which set the girls laughing although Ronnie didn't think it was that funny.

"Look, Lou, Officer Ortiz is gonna need your coat."

"She's gonna need my keys, too, right? Here. Better take my pocketbook, too."

Ronnie helped Lourdes wriggle out of her coat and then helped wrangle it on Teresa Ortiz. "She'll check out your place while we cruise around the block. When she turns on your lights, that'll be the all-clear, and that's it."

"We gotta do this every night?" Lourdes asked.

"Well, let's get through tonight, first. We're just—"

"You say 'just bein' cautious' one more time 'n' I'll bite you on the kneecap." She playfully gnawed on his kneecap.

Ronnie felt a flash of warmth run up from his knee, tingle through his groin, and then to his face.

"You tell her about the wire tap?" Big Sid asked.

"*What* wire tap?" Lourdes asked.

"We'll talk about it later," Ronnie said.

"*When* later?" She punched his kneecap, but it didn't feel playful at all.

"This is it," Big Sid said as the Buick pulled to a stop in front of Lourdes' building.

Ronnie climbed out of the car and opened the door on the other side for Teresa Ortiz.

"*Gracias, mija*" Lourdes said.

"It's just your tax dollars at work," Teresa Ortiz said and stepped out onto the pavement.

"I'll walk you to the door," Ronnie said. He saw her face was tight, and the streetlights made it pale. "It's as easy as walking across the street," and he slipped his arm around hers.

In the foyer of Lourdes' building, Teresa Ortiz fumbled through Lourdes' key chain. "I forgot to ask which key it was." She tried one then another while Ronnie stood by the outside door, looking up and down the street through the glass then checking the rooftops across the street.

He thought the keys were jangling quite a bit. "You ok?"

"Fine."

The interior door opened. He turned and stopped her with a hand on her shoulder. "I could go up with you."

She smiled. "I thought that wasn't the idea."

"To hell with the idea."

"It's supposed to look normal."

"Well, I went up with her once."

"Oh, really?"

"Well, I mean because she was worried about this guy following her, that's all. Do you want me to go up?"

She shook her head. "But thanks." She turned for the door.

"I owe you a dinner." It had bubbled up without his thinking.

She was smiling wider now. "Soon as this is over?"

It felt good to have said it, and having said it, more seemed to come easy: "The *minute* it's over. Oh, hey."

"What?"

"She always kisses me goodnight when I bring her home."

"I thought you only brought her home the once."

"Oh, yeah."

"Then I'm sure it was just a friendly kiss." She pecked him lightly on the cheek then stepped back, her nose wrinkling. "About that dinner? Shower first. Maybe a haircut, too."

She let the hallway door close between them.

"Be careful," he called through the window of the door.

She nodded at him and waved a hand to shoo him away.

Still, he waited until she disappeared up the stairs before he turned and left. He walked slowly back to the car, his eyes flashing up and down the street and along the roofs. He climbed into the front seat of the Buick.

"What the hell took you so long?" Big Sid asked.

"That's how long it took."

"What happens now?" Lourdes called from the floor behind them.

"We've got two back-up units cruising the other side of the block, so they won't get spotted," Ronnie said. "They can be here like –" and he snapped his fingers.

"I meant, what happens to *her?*"

"Nothing." Ronnie looked skyward as he said it because it was something like a prayer.

Meara reached out for the alarm clock without opening his eyes, knowing by habit exactly where to set his hand and switch off the alarm. After a few minutes he opened his eyes, stared at the diagonal stripes on his ceiling; bone-white light from the parking lot lamps coming through the window blinds. When he felt fully awake and his eyes were comfortable with the room's shadows, he sat up and swung his feet to the cold floor. He reached for the night table lamp, but the last few days reminded him these were not healthy times and he left the room dark.

He peed, threw some water on his face, dressed, was halfway out the front door before he was prodded with another reminder. He pulled a thread from the frayed hem of his jeans, tucked it into the crack of the door, hidden beneath the lower hinge, held it there while he closed the door to hold it in place. Then, he took the elevator to the basement and left by the same laundry room door he'd entered through.

Meara liked driving the streets late at night. He'd liked it all the way back to the days when he'd driven a beat car. There were no civilians out at this hour, in this part of town, just the lovely simplicity of "you" and "them;" you, and the kind of people that lived in the shadows. There was a rush that went with living in that kind of purity.

He turned onto Lourdes Bracero's street. There wasn't an open parking space on the block. He pulled up in front of her building. Her windows were dark. He checked his watch. She should be home. Maybe she was; maybe she'd gone straight to bed.

He left the Chrysler double-parked. Whomever he blocked in, he'd hear them honking in the morning. A flash of his badge and they'd work it out. As he stepped to the curb, he reached into his pocket for the key she'd given him.

Teresa Ortiz grew up poor, female, and Latina, which, in terms of finding some path out of Spanish Harlem, made for three strikes. Her badge was supposed to be her ticket out, and it had been... but not quite as far out as she'd hoped. The *pendajo* whites would tell you she got her badge because she was a spic, any man would tell you she got it because she was a woman, and the old hair-bags who remembered the days when women cops were still called policewomen and wore skirts still thought the only thing women cops were good for was filing and fetching coffee. So, when she lucked into this chance to get her head blown off, she took it because it seemed to be the only way anybody was ever going to think of her as anything more than a poor spic broad coasting on her gender and minority status.

She had no illusions: it was luck that had brought her the call (though as she walked down the main floor hallway leaving Ronnie behind her on the stoop, it was an open question about whether that luck was good or bad). She hadn't been offered the opportunity because of her experience because she didn't have much more than Ronnie, or out of favoritism because she doubted Captain Van Dyne even knew who the hell she was. She'd gotten the offer only because she could pass for Lourdes Bracero in the dark.

But, she'd matured early up there in Spanish Harlem, enough to know you don't get to pick your chances; you take them however they come. The thing was to make something of them. She'd do this right, by the book, by the numbers, and next time she got this kind of assignment, it wouldn't be because she resembled the target; it'd be because they knew she was good.

Of course that was all contingent on her not getting killed.

She stopped on the stairs, just short of the girl's floor. It had been a lot of stairs and she wanted her breath when she went through the door. She took a moment to clear her mind, to forget about Ronnie and that kiss on the stoop and dinner. Forget about being scared, she told herself, forget about messing up. Focus: by the book, by the numbers.

She leaned out of the stairwell to look up and down the hall, not sure what she was looking for.

Then she was moving down the hall, past the apartment doors covered with drab, cracked paint until she reached the girl's place. She reached inside the girl's coat and drew her .38 from the holster on her hip, then fumbled through the girl's key ring until she found the one for the apartment door.

In her few years on The Job, Teresa Ortiz had only ever drawn or used her weapon on the firing range. She didn't remember it feeling this heavy and awkward in her hand. She pulled off her right glove, thinking maybe that was the problem. It wasn't.

"Ok," she said, surprised it came out aloud. She turned the key, the bolt slid free with a heavy clunk she felt in her chest. She stepped clear of the doorway and pushed the door open.

She waited, she listened.

She crouched down, quickly peeked around the doorsill and pulled her head back just as quickly.

She shifted the pistol to her other hand for a moment so she could wipe her damp right palm dry on her jeans. Still staying low, she moved through the doorway quietly, moving fast to stay out of the light from the hall. In the darkness just inside the door, she waited, she stared hard into the gloom of the apartment. She listened.

The old coiled steam radiator clinked and hissed, the floorboards creaked under her, wind rattled the windows.

She waited for her eyes to adjust to the darkness. She could take in nearly all the apartment with a slight turn of her head.

She closed the door and pulled off the wig. It didn't fit quite right, and her scalp was itching. She shrugged off the coat, let it drop to the floor so she could move more freely.

Softly, slowly, she kept telling herself, fighting the adrenaline surge pumping through her as she checked the bathroom, the apartment's one closet, even under the kitchen table and the unfolded sofa bed.

When she had cleared the apartment, she found herself back in the front room. She didn't like those tall windows, too much exposure. Staying out of their sight lines, she drew the shades.

And that's it! she suddenly realized, laughing at the sweat she could now feel on her face, all over inside her clothes, the way her clammy hands – released from duty's discipline – now started to shake.

Her knees suddenly felt weak and she sat on the edge of the sofa bed, dabbing at her damp forehead with the back of her hand. She could breathe – only now realizing how tight her chest had been during the sweep – and she pulled in the cold air of the apartment in deep gulps.

Now, she thought, looking about in the dark, where was the light switch? Probably on the wall by the—

A key rattled in the door lock.

She got a cold and queasy feeling in her middle. She moved to one side of the door, cradled her .38 in her two hands and went into a firing crouch. Drop the sight on the target, she reminded herself, take a normal breath, let half out, line up rear sight, front sight, target, aim center mass, squeeze the trigger, don't jerk it…

The door swung open and a figure – broad-shouldered in a bombardier jacket – stepped into the room.

*Dios te salve, Maria,* she said to herself, *llena eres de gracia, el Senor es contigo…*

"Lay down on the floor! *Now!* Hands behind your head!" Her voice sounded more ragged to her than she would've liked.

The figure inside the door didn't flinch, but slowly moved his arms away from his sides. "You mind telling me who the hell *you* are first?"

"*You* first," Teresa Ortiz said, giving the back of the man's neck a poke with the muzzle of her pistol. "But *after* you hit the floor! *Move!*"

"Ok, I'm down. Now, do you mind identifying – Jesus! What the hell is *that?*" He batted at something furry on the floor. It was her wig.

She scooped the wig up protectively. "I'm a police officer." She stood over him, keeping her gun at his head with one hand while she patted him down with the other. She pulled a revolver out of his jacket pocket. "Whoever you are, this just put you on the bad side of things."

"Officer, do yourself a favor and look in my back-hip pocket. The right one."

She reached into his pocket and immediately recognized the leather sheaf by touch. She held the badge cover open in the light from the hall. "Oh, damn…"

"Meara," the man identified himself. "You can call Manhattan South and confirm it. Now that we got all that taken care of," he said climbing off the floor, "you mind telling me what the hell's going on? Where's Lou? The woman who lives here?"

"I'm not sure I'm supposed to tell you. I didn't know Manhattan South was in on this."

"In on *what?*"

"Tell you the truth, I'm not sure. All they told me—"

The phone ringing stopped her. The two of them stood staring for a moment at the phone sitting on a milk crate at one end of the sofa.

"I'm supposed to be her," she said. "I better take it." She picked up the receiver. "Hello?…Yeah, this is she…Ok, I'll hold."

The other cop, this Meara, was still standing by the lit doorway. She could see him studying the phone, his face moving in a mulling way. She thought maybe he was just curious about the call, so she gave him an I-don't-know-yet shrug.

Then his eyes went from the phone to the windows, and there was something about his face…

140

"Hello?" she said impatiently into the phone, and for a second – not even, less, only the briefest of moments – her attention slipped from the cop, this Meara, to the phone, and when she turned back to Meara it hit her like a brick between the eyes – *Maldita sea*, I screwed up – and she was pissed at herself because she should've known better, and pissed at herself because all the old hair-bags back at the stationhouse were going to go on and on about how this is what happens when you let a dumb spic broad handle things, and she was pissed at herself because this would probably kill her mother, and all of these things were exploding in her head all at once because when she'd turned back to this Meara guy he was coming at her with his arm outstretched and she knew she'd never get her weapon up in time and she was right because he grabbed her by her gun arm and started pulling her down, off her feet – *Maldita sea* and oh, *fuck* how I screwed up! – down to the floor…

And then there came a gust at her back of what she thought was wind but wasn't, and then there was a ripping, stuttering sound, and something hit her from behind and her breath was gone…


After Ronnie had climbed back in the car, sliding into the front seat, Big Sid had taken the car slowly around the block. As the car completed its first circuit, they both saw the lights were still out in the girl's apartment.

Ronnie thought it had been an awfully long time.

Big Sid must've seen it on his face because he said, "'S'ok, kid. Give her a few minutes to check the place out." Big Sid took them on another tour of the block.

"How you doing back there?" Ronnie asked Lourdes Bracero.

"Can I come up now? It really stinks down here."

"I guess." He turned to watch her climb up. She was brooding. "You ok?"

"That girl."

"She knows what she's doing. I hope."

They passed one of the other unmarked cars they had placed in a cruising pattern close by. Ronnie caught a glimpse of a bored Berman on the passenger side. There was a lazily waved hello.

They turned back onto Lourdes Bracero's street. Big Sid, his voice alarmed, started to say, "Hey, Ronnie –"

"Shit!" Ronnie said.

"Big old white—"

"What's goin' on?" Lourdes asked. She leaned forward and saw the white Chrysler double-parked in front of her building. "Hey, that's Jack's car."

*"Shit!"*

The two submachine guns that tore into the night together from a roof across from Lourdes' building made a continuous roar echoing up and down the street.

Big Sid popped his door open even as he was scooping up the radio mic and calling in the back-up units. "10-13 forthwith!" he yelled.

"You stay here!" Ronnie said to Lourdes, only afterward aware he was shouting. "Lock the doors and get behind the wheel! Anybody but us comes for you, take off!"

Big Sid was already out of the car and bouncing down the street, revolver out and moving faster than Ronnie thought possible. "Up there!" Sid called out, pointing at one of the roofs. "I saw the flashes!"

Ronnie was running for Lourdes' building. She called after him from the car, but he didn't hear it, then he was in the foyer, punching buzzers and banging on the inside door, shouting that he was the police and for somebody to open the goddamn door, and then, *Fuck it,* and he drove his parka-cushioned elbow through the door glass, reached in, unlocked the door and bolted for the stairs screaming *"Police! Police! Stand clear!"* as he charged past bathrobes and wide eyes.

142

His nightly jogs notwithstanding, he was gasping for air by the time he got to Lourdes' floor. There was a buzzing crowd around the open door of her apartment, and he could never remember a crowd in New York meaning anything good so, wheezing and staggering, he pushed through, flashing his badge. "C'mon c'mon c'mon, clear out! Police! Let's go! *Move!*"

The apartment was still dark. The shades over the windows had snapped open and the glass in both windows was gone, spread across the floor and open sofa bed, and lit up like ice from the hall light. Outside, he heard sirens clear and close.

In the dark, he almost tripped over Teresa Ortiz. She was sitting with her back against the wall, her left arm cradled across her front and resting on a sofa cushion. Her face was twisted in pain.

"Teri!" He knelt by her, but despite all the grimacing and wincing, she was nodding, saying she was ok.

Then she opened her screwed-shut eyes, looked past Ronnie, quickly swept the apartment. "Where is he?"

"Where's who?"

"The other guy. The cop."

# three: trail of tears

*...in my dream, I thought I heard*

*The Truth behind the spoken word*

*I thought I had something to believe in.*

*But all too soon the dream was gone...*

Robin Trower, "Twice Removed from Yesterday"

"How is Officer Ortiz?" Van Dyne asked, settling himself in his leather-backed throne. He pinched one nostril closed and was sucking air through the other one, trying to clear it.

"Nine mils don't have much of a punch, it didn't hit straight on, the vest held," said Ronnie. He was parked on one arm of the sagging sofa in the captain's office. "She's got a cracked shoulder blade from the impact, but the doctors say she'll be fine. Ya know, Captain, if Meara hadn't pulled her out of the way when he did—"

"Gotta give it to the guy, Boss," Big Sid said, sunk deep into the cushions at the other end of the sofa, his voice a scratchy grumble from another night without sleep. "He's got good instincts."

Van Dyne gave up on his nose. "Since he may be responsible for her having been in that situation, I'm not quite ready to shake the sonofabitch's hand in hearty gratitude if that's alright with you." He stood, massaged his lower back as he turned to the dark, empty street outside the windows behind his desk. The radiator under the window clanked and groaned. He set a hand on it, shook his head at its stubborn coldness. He shivered and Ronnie was unsettled by how, for just that flash of a moment, Van Dyne's gray-templed head no longer seemed regal but aged.

A gust of wind rattled the windows, and Ronnie was sure he could feel it pass through the old stationhouse walls in a chilling wave. Van Dyne sighed, yawned, then turned back to them, propping himself tiredly against the windowsill. "You both left the woman you were supposed to be protecting alone. Notably *un*protected, I might point out." His eyes flicked to the big man at one end of the couch. "Sidney?"

"They thought she was in the apartment; that's why they took the shot. So, I figured she'd be ok in the car. I went after the shooters. I kinda assumed that was part of what we were doing; hope they'd take a shot so maybe we could nail one of 'em, squeeze him to find out what the fuck is going on. Or was I wrong, Boss?"

Van Dyne closed his eyes and rubbed a small spot in the middle of his forehead, looking pained. "What about the shooters?"

"Like Dell'Acqua," Big Sid said. "Two machine guns, nine mils. I told Ballistics to redball the testing, told 'em what to look for. It'll still be a coupla days before we get a report, but doing a quick prelim on the shell casings, yeah, they were both S&W 76s. I got a call in to Jersey asking them to send us casings from Dell'Acqua's place, see if they match either of our shooters. I've also got Ballistics running back cases looking for ballistic matches and similar MOs."

Van Dyne nodded but it was neither approval nor satisfaction, only automatic acknowledgement. "Officer Valerio. You left the subject alone in the car as well."

Ronnie cleared his throat. "I, uh, was worried about Teri. Um, Officer Ortiz."

Van Dyne opened his eyes, his gaze lost in the cracks in the ceiling. "I have a complaint here from the building super. I'll probably be hearing from the landlord this morning. Was it absolutely necessary to break that door glass, Officer Valerio?"

"Uh… I'll pay for the glass, Captain."

"No you won't. I just want to hear it from you that—"

"It was, Boss," Big Sid said. "Absolutely."

Van Dyne's chest heaved and settled as he fixed both with a look over his eyeglasses. "The girl identified Meara's car. The car fits the description of the car you think was at Dell'Acqua's place in Jersey. And yet despite that, Meara manages to walk out of a crime scene, climb in that identified vehicle, and put-put-put away. I'm having a problem understanding how that happened."

"A lotta stuff was popping at once, Boss," Big Sid said.

"You had four men assigned to you as backup."

"We planned for a possible hit, y'unnerstand. Meara showing up, something nobody—" and here it was Big Sid turning on the hard glare, giving it right back to Van Dyne – "—*nobody* anticipated. The

148

backups didn't know about the car, none of us had a descrip on Meara. Wild card."

"A wild card." Van Dyne chewed on it. "So. You went after the shooters. And?"

"Those buildings there, on that block, they're shoulder to shoulder," Sid said. "They could've skipped roof-to-roof and come down somewhere around the corner by the time I got up there. Maybe if we'd had more men—"

"We don't have more men!" and Van Dyne no longer sounded tired, sick, or fragile. He might just as well have been banging out the message on his desk with an iron bar. "What I *do* have is two dead men in South Jersey and another corpse just around the corner! I *do* have one of my people on her back at Gouverneur's who just missed a trip to the morgue! I've got two machine gunners shooting up the night and then walking off free as birds! I've got the man who is somehow tied to *all* of this strolling away from a crime scene, climbing into his car and driving off into the night without anybody noticing him even though I've got seven Keystone Cops tripping all over themselves *in the same fucking vicinity!*"

Van Dyne dropped into his chair, began fumbling with a cigarette and his holder, but then the rage surged again. The cigarette holder went flying across the room and Ronnie heard it split against the wall just before he heard the *boom* of Van Dyne's fist coming down on his desk. *"Jesus!"*

But then it was over. Van Dyne closed his eyes, took a breath regaining himself, and drew erect in his chair, fidgeting with the Hugo Boss tie he'd thought to wear and knot in a natty Windsor even at such a late hour.

"We shouldn't be driving ourselves nuts with this," Big Sid said. "We should dump this on Manhattan South. He's *their* guy! Let *them* clean up after him!"

Van Dyne opened his eyes, nodding, appreciating the point. "He's their guy, but thanks to one of my soft-hearted – and soft-*headed* – cops," a nod at a flinching Ronnie, "his mess is *here*. Need I remind you; Ralph Zinni was found around the corner from *my* house. Teresa Ortiz is one of *my* people." Van Dyne dropped his head, seemed to be mulling something.

It went on long enough that Big Sid finally asked a concerned, "Boss?"

"Wait for me in the muster room," Van Dyne said without looking up. "Go. *Now.*"

The muster room on the first floor was a long, narrow room where each patrol shift gathered for roll call and briefing before going out on their tour. It looked not unlike a schoolroom with a blackboard and a slightly raised dais at one end, a collection of one-armed writing chairs that had seen much better days, and a bulletin board on the back wall covered several layers deep with notices no one read.

It was also – for God knows what reason – one of the few rooms in the stationhouse with heat. The radiators along the window side of the room hissed loudly and incessantly, the panes above them steamed opaque. Within minutes of taking a seat Ronnie was dabbing at the sweat gathering along his upper lip and forehead.

Big Sid did not take a seat. He paced restlessly. "I've worked for that guy a long time, kid. Y'unnerstand? I've never seen the Boss rattled like that. Never."

Ronnie thought the same thing.

"He's not pissed we screwed up," Sid went on.

"That's funny. That's how he sounded to *me*," Ronnie said.

"Well, that's because you're a dumbass, kid. I *know* him. He's pissed we *didn't* screw up. Like with Zinni. He wasn't on me 'cause I made a bad call bouncing Zinni. He was on me 'cause he knows it *wasn't* a bad call. *That's* what's eating at him. We're doing what we're *supposed* to be doing, but the breaks are still all breaking bad." Big Sid frowned, and he patted at the beads forming on his wide forehead with the back of his sleeve. "Something else going on with him."

"Maybe he's edgy because he's still got the flu."

"You think that's it?" Sid walked up to the blackboard, grabbed a chalky eraser. He looked at the eraser, he looked at Ronnie then, with that suddenness with which the big man could surprise him, he hurled the eraser at Ronnie. It wasn't a great shot, but a good one, and detonated in a puff of white powder against Ronnie's shoulder.

"What the hell's with you?" Ronnie said, coughing in a cloud of chalk dust.

"It's not because he's still got the fucking *flu*, ya fucking mental defective!" Sid said.

But further discussion was put aside when Van Dyne announced his presence from the muster room doorway with a, "Problem, gentlemen?"

Whatever Van Dyne had done alone in his office to give himself a psychological tune-up, it had evidently worked. The captain stood straight-backed, strode to the front of the muster room with an energized commanding stride, quickly gauged the heat of the room and stripped off his overcoat, flinging it over one of the desks. He tugged at his vest, shot his French cuffs, grabbed a stubby piece of chalk from the blackboard shelf.

"'An idea is a feat of association,' so sayeth Robert Frost." Van Dyne stood at the center of the blackboard. "My thinking is let's have all the pieces up in one place and see if we can't associate ourselves into some ideas about what's going on. Where to start?" It was rhetorical: Van Dyne had obviously worked all this out in his head before he'd showed up in the doorway. He wrote ZINNI in the center of the blackboard, surrounding it with a chalked oblong. "Let's begin with the luckless Mr. Zinni, since his appearance on the scene – and abrupt departure therefrom – seems to have been what first stirred the pot. Now, do we know anything of a relevant and salient nature about poor Mr. Zinni?" He turned to Big Sid, then to Ronnie, and Ronnie guessed the looks on their faces let Van Dyne know neither was quite sure what constituted "relevant and salient." For himself, Ronnie didn't even know what "salient" meant. Van Dyne tried an interpretation: "Anything about this meatball we should know?"

Big Sid pulled out his notebook and began flipping through pages. "According to BCI, the Organized Crime Task Force has Zinni tagged as a soldier on Willy Stabile's crew. Is that what you mean by relevant and the other thing?"

"That depends," Van Dyne said. "Who is Willy Stabile and why is it of interest that Zinni was one of Willy Stabile's people?"

Big Sid smiled. "Because OC also has Stabile tagged as being one of Tony Boy Maiella's captains. One of his go-to guys, actually."

"Ahhhh." Van Dyne drew a line north from Zinni's oblong, drew a rectangle and wrote inside, STABILE, and then another upward stroke to a larger rectangle and wrote, MAIELLA. "Now, *that's* relevant and salient!" He drew a downward arc, beginning at MAIELLA, swinging wide to the left and then coming back and ending with an arrowhead embedded in ZINNI, then writing across the apogee of the arc, KIERNAN. "And then we have the telegenic Ms. Kiernan whom we know is Maiella's attorney which suggests that whatever Mr. Zinni was doing, he was doing for Maiella."

Now, the two of them – Van Dyne and Big Sid – fell into a duet like the one Ronnie had envied between Big Sid and the Jersey cop MacAlistair at Sal Dell'Acqua's house.

"Tony Boy calls up his most trusted captain," Big Sid said.

"Stabile," Van Dyne said.

"Maiella says, 'Hey, I need somebody reliable to do me a solid.'"

"And much to Mr. Zinni's misfortune—"

"Stabile volunteers Zinni."

"And the fact that Ms. Kiernan presented herself so quickly – and that Mr. Zinni was sent to his reward with equal dispatch – indicates how adamantine Maiella was that nobody have the chance to question Zinni or backtrack him to whomever issued him his orders." Van Dyne paused and studied the connecting lines on the blackboard. "Works so far."

"That APB on Kiernan turn anything?" Big Sid asked.

Van Dyne shook his head. "According to her office, within hours of Mr. Zinni's demise, Ms. Kiernan unexpectedly decided to spend the holidays outside the country, whereabouts unknown."

"I checked with OC on Stabile's whereabouts. He took a powder, too, about the time Zinni showed up tailing the girl. So, he gives Zinni to Tony Boy, then figures it'd be better to be someplace else."

Van Dyne nodded, unsurprised. "So if something untoward happened..."

"He'd be clear of it." Sid took a moment, then, "Tony Boy's gone, too."

Van Dyne wasn't surprised, but the announcement made an impression.

"OC suspects he's still in the City," Sid continued, "but underground."

"They offer an opinion on why?"

"OC thinks maybe internal problems. All the press attention Tony Boy's been getting every time he goes to court isn't making his colleagues happy. It's not just hurting his own business; it's hurting *everybody*'s business. The cockroaches can't raid the fridge when somebody keeps turning on the kitchen light. The only thing OC knows for sure is he's invisible, and, since he hasn't surfaced anywhere, they're guessing he might still be in the area."

Van Dyne's eyes narrowed at the blackboard. "Curiouser and curiouser. Ok, so; what was Zinni doing for Maiella?" Van Dyne drew a horizontal line out of ZINNI to the left and drew the old Roman

153

symbol for the goddess Venus: a circle, then a downstroke crossed by a single line representing a mirror and handle. Ronnie thought it looked almost like a figure from a game of Hangman. "He was following young Ron's Isolde."

Ronnie didn't know what that meant, but he was sure it was a dig and that was enough to bring a brighter flush to cheeks already red from the steamy atmosphere of the muster room.

"Do we know of any connection between Ms. Bracero and Mr. Maiella? Ron, you have a chance to talk with her since the unpleasantness?"

"Some."

"Drugs? Gambling debts? Prostitution?"

Ronnie shook his head.

"Maybe something romantic?"

"She says no. And I believe her."

Big Sid patted his chest, his impression of a love-thrilled heart once again.

"I'm getting real tired of that," Ronnie said.

Big Sid smiled without apology, then turned to Van Dyne. "But I'm inclined to believe her, too. She's got no sheet. If she was into something off the radar, I'm not sure she'd risk bringing Galahad here into her business and maybe have him trip over it. And, with the guns out, it's not in her interest to lie if there *is* a connection."

Van Dyne cast Sid a wise-old-owl look over the top of his glasses. "Sidney, you've been on the job long enough to know there's no end to what people will lie about even when it's in their interest to do otherwise."

"That's true," Big Sid said, "But I'm still with the kid on this."

"What about this place where she works? This palace of the exotic arts?"

Sid flipped through his notebook. "Routine beefs. Some trouble with the Liquor Licensing Authority, some nickel-and-dime tax issues, citations for a minor on the premises, customers getting out of hand... But nothing hinting they might be mobbed up in any way."

"So, if it's not the girl, and it's not the bar, it's got to be..." Van Dyne drew a horizontal line out of the woman's figure connecting it to the Roman symbol for Mars, the God of War: a circle with a spearhead rising up on a diagonal – the shield and spear of the warrior. "What do we know about Detective Meara?"

"I talked to a guy I know down in Manhattan South," Sid said. "Meara's been with the house five, maybe six years. Before that, he's a blank with my guy, but in the time he's been with South, nothing bad on him; good cop, reliable, respectable record. He's got his 20 in." Here, Big Sid held up a finger – an alarm: "He put in his papers a couple of months ago, he comes out next month. But here's the relevant and sentence thing—"

"Salient," Van Dyne said.

"My guy says all along Meara's been saying he was gonna work until his exit date. But a week and a half ago, he puts in for terminal leave. Out of the blue. No explanation. It was close to his exit date, and he's got more than enough accrued time on the books, so they figured what the hell and signed off on it. But what makes it a little stinkier: since then, nobody's heard a peep from him."

"Including Lourdes Bracero," Ronnie said, happy to have some little something to add, only to feel – again – useless as Van Dyne and Big Sid went back into their duet.

"They tail the girl hoping Meara'll surface," Van Dyne said.

"Zinni blows the surveillance," said Big Sid, "so they raise the ante."

"They make a try at the girl, hoping it'll bring Meara out into the open." Van Dyne turned back to the blackboard, appraising. "Not bad, it fits. Except..." And here he drew a big question mark somewhere in the space west of Maiella and north of the God of War. "What's the 'why'?"

The three were quiet. Ronnie stared hard at the board as if maybe just pouring enough eye power into the chalk lines would somehow make them come together in an answer. As he had at Dell'Acqua's house, he felt the need to make some points. "Maybe he's doing some undercover thing for Manhattan South targeting Maiella."

"The guy's a coupla weeks from buying himself a turkey farm," Big Sid said. "That's not a guy you put on a serious deep cover operation."

Ronnie stared harder at the blackboard. He felt a little throb at the break in his nose and sweat crawling down his forehead. "IAB's tagged 29 cops for taking money. What if Meara thought he might be Number 30?"

"The shoo-flies haven't gone into Manhattan South," Big Sid said.

"Yet," Van Dyne said. The captain's eyes darted around the figures on the blackboard, then he finally judged it with a little shake of his head. "Not bad, Ron, but it doesn't quite sit level. A) We don't know Maiella's been the payee in any of these IAB cases; B) Even if he is, there'd be so many buffers around him it's doubtful any of the parties involved would know it's his money; and C) for the same reason, if Maiella is behind the payoffs and Meara knows it, Maiella would be too insulated from the actual operation for Meara to hurt him in court. Maiella'd have no reason to be concerned about him. He hasn't skated free as many times as he has by being an idiot."

"Besides," Big Sid added, "even if it is Maiella, and Meara knows it, and Maiella knows Meara knows, you don't kill a cop. These guys have rules. They may only follow them when it's convenient, but one they almost never break: you don't kill a cop. Kill a cop, the big shit comes down on *everybody*. 35,000 cops want your scalp, plus the feds, plus an army of crusading reporters. The other bosses are *already* pissed with Tony Boy 'cause every time he goes to court he puts light on 'em. Kill a cop and the kind of shitstorm *that'*d set off..." Big Sid shook his head; words wouldn't do it justice. "You don't kill a cop."

"They didn't try to kill a cop," Ronnie said. "Lourdes—"

"His girl, his family, same thing," Van Dyne said. "Untouchable. Taboo."

There was another moment of silence before Sid asked, "How does any of this tie in with Dell'Acqua?"

Van Dyne drew a square off to the east with no connecting lines to the other figures and wrote DELL'ACQUA in the square. "I don't know."

"Maybe it doesn't?" Sid offered.

Van Dyne's head tilted side to side, weighing the possibility, then shrugged it off. "I keep thinking it *has* to. You gentlemen think that was Meara's car down there –"

"Not positive," Sid qualified.

"Granted. But the MO on the two shootings is so identical," Van Dyne pointed at the Venus figure and Dell'Acqua's square, "that if they aren't related, somebody should sue for copyright infringement. And it's within the same, very compact time frame. Maiella, Meara, and Dell'Acqua all drop out of sight within days of each other, Dell'Acqua shows up in South Jersey not long after, Meara – possibly – shows up at Dell'Acqua's, then Zinni shows up following the girl, there's the hit on Dell'Acqua, then the try at the girl with the very same—" Van Dyne froze, transfixed by something invisible on the board. "My, my…" he said, barely aloud, almost to himself. He set the point of his chalk on MAIELLA. "What happens two weeks ago?"

Whatever the invisible thing was, Big Sid could see it. Ronnie saw the big man's eyes widen, then Sid seemed to sink with an unhappy realization. "Shiiiit…"

Frustrated at the invisible thing's invisibility and his own inability to see it, Ronnie blurted out an impatient, "What?"

Sid smiled. "Forgive him, Boss, the only part of the papers he reads is the funnies."

As if talking to an idiot – which was how Ronnie felt – Van Dyne spoke slowly, tapping MAIELLA with his chalk: "Two weeks ago,

Maiella is acquitted from his third trial. That's the igniter. No sooner does he finish his smartass remarks on the courthouse steps for the benefit of the media then he and Meara go underground, and then all the rest of these dominos fall. But there's still one piece missing." His chalk moved back to the floating question mark.

"The 'why'," Big Sid said.

Another musing silence, and while they were quiet and studying the blackboard, something came back to Ronnie, something Van Dyne and Sid had said about the Rules of Engagement between Mob and cop, about what was – even in a world of bodies turning up in dumpsters – unallowable. And then the same way that little bit of white putty in Dell'Acqua's windowsill had tickled at his eye, some other little bit of something tickled at him.

"Ya know…" Ronnie began tentatively.

"What?" Van Dyne quietly demanded. "C'mon, Ron, we're all friends here. And *this* friend has the power of life and death over you."

"I was just thinking…" Ronnie mumbled, still gun-shy.

"Don't hurt anything," Big Sid said.

Van Dyne shushed him.

Maybe it was that crack of Sid's, but Ronnie sat up a little straighter in his desk, spoke more firmly: "What you said before, about Meara not being able to hurt Maiella in court. What if, well, I mean suppose this isn't about going to court?"

"Meaning?" Van Dyne asked.

"I don't know," Ronnie said, flushing. It had all seemed clear in his head, at least for a moment, but he realized he was trying to express a *sense* more than a fact or supposition. "I'm just looking at this, and thinking, I dunno…"

But Sid seemed to understand. "If it's something *personal* between these two, Maiella might feel the rules don't apply. If Tony Boy thinks he's in some *mano a mano* kind of thing, and especially if he's feeling pressed hard enough, y'unnerstand, *cornered*…he might think he's got no choice but to go balls to the wall no matter who it pisses off on which side."

"A vendetta of some sort?" Van Dyne asked. "Over what?"

Sid shrugged. "Fuck if I know, but if you look at it that way…"

Van Dyne turned back to the blackboard and looked at things *just* that way. "I wish it didn't, but that makes a certain amount of sense." He gestured at the isolated square to the right. "What about Dell'Acqua?"

Big Sid shrugged. "All we know is Meara saw him—"

"Probably."

"—and Maiella whacked him."

"Possibly."

"Ya know, there's an ear we use. It's that same guy took over Dell'Acqua's outfit: Juan Teixeira. A couple of the downtown houses use him. He might know something."

"Is he reliable?"

Big Sid looked like he might laugh. "Like a two-dollar watch. A royal bullshit artist and a scumbag, always holds out, talks out both sides of his mouth when he doesn't. Sell his momma for a hot pretzel. But he does hear things."

"Work him. Hard."

"Hey, Captain?" Ronnie asked. "Isn't this something we should alert IAB about?"

Van Dyne tossed his stub of chalk on the blackboard shelf. "They seem busy enough these days."

"We should at least let Organized Crime—"

Van Dyne turned to them, stood ramrod straight, slipped his hands in his trouser pockets. "This is a house matter," he said. "It stays under this roof, it stays off the record. No 'sixes' on this."

Ronnie flinched. The "sixes" were the daily reports they were supposed to fill out when they were on a case.

"You don't talk to IAB," Van Dyne said, "you don't talk to OC, you don't talk to Personnel or Manhattan South, you don't talk to *anybody* else in *this* house, and when you're pitching woo to Meara's girlfriend – which I'd prefer you didn't for the time being – don't bring it up with *her*. Am I clear? Ron?"

"Yessir."

"What about the Jersey cops?" Big Sid asked. "I already asked for those shell casings, and that shoot-'em-up on The Bowery's gonna be all over the morning news. They'll be calling."

"If they call, we are investigating, but have yet to determine any connection between our incident and theirs."

Van Dyne strode out into the room, picked up the eraser Big Sid had thrown at Ronnie, and returned it to the blackboard. "Go home, get a shower – especially The Guacamole Kid – take a quick nap. At the start of business hours, call DMV. Meara's car. Get it all: plates, make, model, color, year, most importantly his *address;* I don't want to go through personnel or his colleagues at Manhattan South. Let's make sure the car fits what the Jersey cops found. Chase down your snitch, squeeze him. I want you two back here before the morning's out." Van Dyne began swinging the eraser in wide arcs, wiping the blackboard clear. "Go forth…and *do*."

After the suffocating heat of the muster room, the cold outside had Ronnie shivering so hard it hurt him to force his mouth to work properly when he said, "It doesn't feel good, Sid. Cutting out IAB, we're not even telling Meara's commander down at South? No sixes? That feels off."

Big Sid looked back up at the station house from where they were standing at the foot of the front steps: the green globe light over the front door with "Police" written on it, flickering with a bad connection; the Doric columns streaked with soot on either side of the front door; a missing window pane filled in with cardboard; *"Oink!*

*Oink"* and *"Kiss my ass!"* daringly spray-painted along the front of the building.

Sid shook his head and began walking along the row of blue-and-whites lined up at the curb toward where their unmarked Buick was parked near the end of the block. "When the Knapp Commission put out their final report," Sid said, "they made a bunch of recommendations. Top one – the *top* one – was all commanders be accountable for what their people do. You a precinct captain? One of your beat cops on the pad for a few bucks? Doesn't matter you didn't know; doesn't matter you never heard anything. *Your* house, *your* man, *you're* responsible."

"You said it, though: Meara's not *ours.*"

"Doesn't matter," Big Sid said, shaking his head. "The Boss is right. The *mess* is *ours.* How much do you know about the captain? What'd you hear up in the One-Nine?"

"He didn't have many fans there."

"Doesn't have many fans *anywhere.* When he was a Detective Third, did a year with Internal Affairs. So good at nailing dirty cops, he was brought on as an investigator for the Knapp Commission. So he goes into the Rat Squad Detective Third, after a year with Knapp comes out a lieutenant. Looked to a lot of people, he bought his gold bar with cop scalps.

"There's people out there, minimum wage security guards at 99 cent stores 'cause the Boss cost 'em their pensions, y'unnerstand. People still in the Department he made look bad, won't mind seeing him take a fall. They smell his blood in the water and the Boss *knows* it. He tries climbing out of the water, they're just waiting to step on his fingers and push him back in."

Big Sid stepped off the curb, reached for his keys to unlock the driver's side, but was stopped by something he saw across the street. "Ah, shit…"

Ronnie saw it, too. He followed Sid across the street to the crumpled figure in the doorway of small coffee shop.

It was a man curled around himself like a cat. In the pale, bleaching light of the streetlamps, Ronnie couldn't quite tell if he was old or just worn out: his whiskered face was weathered, deeply lined, the skin chapped and peeling in places, the area around the mouth sunken in toothlessness. The skin looked bloodless and cold as marble.

Ronnie stayed on the sidewalk while Big Sid knelt over the body. "I can't tell if it's rigor or he's just froze. You recognize this guy? See him hanging around?"

"Nope."

"Me neither."

The old man's clothes were worn, dirty, every hem an unraveling frill. A ruffle of newspapers stuck out the tops of his shoes around skinny, dirt-crusted, sockless ankles. The flat, hard light of the streetlamps made harsh, bottomless shadows in the hollowed cheeks and sunken eye sockets, like a puzzle with pieces missing.

Sid went through the old man's pockets. "No ID. Poor bastard musta been out here all night." The big man grunted to his feet, looked at his watch under the streetlamps and groaned. "Look, kid, go on back to the house and report it."

"Me?"

"You married? Then it's you. I've hardly seen my wife in two days 'cause of you, so it's *you*. Meet me back here at nine."

"*Fongool*," Ronnie said in a burst of steamy breath as he watched Sid take the Buick down the street and around the corner. He started back for the station house, stopped at the front steps, and looked back to where the old man was laying. From there, Ronnie couldn't see him. Invisible.

She didn't turn at the rattle of his key in the lock. When he swung the door open she was standing on the back of the sofa – the bed frame

162

unfolded as usual, but stripped of sheets – using a roll of duct tape to fix flattened cardboard boxes over the shot-out windows. She didn't miss a beat with the tape and cardboard, just a quick turn of her head, a brief acknowledging smile, and back to work.

"Shouldn't the super be doing that?" Meara said, closing the door behind him.

"I'm lucky I got the tape 'n' cardboard from that *pendajo*. Talk to him, he makes it sound like it's my fault. Watch him charge me for the new glass."

"I could talk to him."

"I'll bet you could."

He liked she was wearing his denim jacket although he was damned if he could remember how she'd wound up with it.

"They got somebody out front," she said. "Two of 'em. In a car. Right across the street. Keep an eye on me, I guess."

He nodded. He wasn't surprised.

"They know your car, Jack."

"It's in a lot up in Little Italy," he said, lighting a Pall Mall. "Unless they're searching lot-by-lot for it, they won't see it. I been riding the Six train uptown and back until I figured the crowd had cleared." He dropped heavily into the living room's one chair, with its Rockaway Beach towel slipcover hiding the holes in the upholstery. "I thought they'd probably have somebody on your place. There's an alley on the other side of the block. I came through that way, hopped the fence, through the back door."

"You might wanna change careers. I think you're better at bein' a bad guy than a cop."

"You need help with that?"

"I'm just about done." She affixed one last strip of duct tape then stepped down onto the fold-out bed and from there to the floor. She stood back from the covered windows, studying the result. She shrugged; that was as good as it was going to get. "Ya know what's sad? This place is such a dump this is actually an improvement on the view. You hungry? I'll make you some breakfast." She didn't wait for an answer, disappeared into the kitchen. He heard the clatter of a pan on the stove, heard cracking eggs, butter sizzling in the pan, the slosh of her beating eggs. Scrambled, always scrambled because it was easiest.

"I'm sorry," he called to her.

"For what?"

He heard glass-on-glass now; she was pouring herself a drink. And then the rattle of her vial of Percocets. He gave her a minute to down the pill before he pulled his leaden self out of the chair to sit in one of the two vinyl-and-metal chairs at the bare little table in the kitchen.

She was stirring the eggs around in the frying pan with a fork. She had her own lit Pall Mall between her fingers, and he smiled to himself; probably from his jacket, probably his pack.

"I didn't know... I didn't think it was gonna spill over like this. You know; that it was gonna touch you. Truth is, I wasn't thinking at all. I just... Well..."

She nodded, shrugged. It was done. "I feel bad about that cop, that girl."

"She'll be ok," Meara said. "Really. She wasn't hurt that bad. She'll get some nice sick time, probably get herself a commendation. It'll work out good for her."

"You make it sound like the best career move she coulda made was gettin' shot." She dumped the eggs onto a plate, plopped a couple of slices of white bread next to them. "You want some coffee? It's on the stove; I just gotta heat it up."

He shook his head.

"The other one, the other cop..."

"What other one?" he asked.

She took her drink and sat across from him. "The one come runnin' up here. Maybe you passed him in the hall." She shook her head, realizing she'd forgotten to bring him a fork.

He stubbed his cigarette out on the rim of the plate. "Oh, yeah. What's he? 12?"

She smiled as she set a fork down in front of him. "If that. He's the one come by the bar when we had that problem with the guy sent me to the hospital. I think he's got a crush on me."

"Coo-coo-ca-choo, Mrs. Robinson." He dabbed at the eggs with the bread. They were runny but they were always runny.

"I don't know what that means, but he should find himself a nice girl. He's a nice kid."

"You *are* a nice girl."

"If I was, we wouldn't have a goddamn thing in common, would we?"

"You didn't ask me where I've been."

"When do I ever ask?"

"I thought, maybe this time, under the circumstances..." He saw her eyes flick to the bruised knuckles of his left hand sitting on the table. He let his hand drop into his lap.

"Do I wanna know?"

"Maybe this time you should."

She took a long drag on her cigarette, took as long a time letting out the smoke. "Why?"

"Because by this time next month, I'm out. And we're gone. We're gone and we're never coming back."

"Gone where?"

He pushed the plate away, some eggs and bread still left on it. "Some place always sunny. I want to go so fucking far away they never heard of New York, they don't even know what cops are."

"I don't think they got that kinda place anywhere."

165

"We'll look. I was kind of saying goodbye to somebody. We got a little time…"

She smiled. "You mean if I got anybody to say g'bye to?" Her smile faded, her hand slid across the table, one knuckle rubbed alongside one of his fingers. Her eyes set on the bruises across his knuckles, but she didn't ask about them. "Jack, I got so little holdin' me here, one strong wind and I'm gone." She pulled her hand back, took another of those long drags on her cigarette. "We could go now. Today. I told you; I got no holds."

"Soon. Aren't you gonna eat?"

She drained the last of her drink and held up the empty glass. "I ate. You look tired."

"I *am* tired."

She pulled a pair of tattered quilts from her one closet and threw them over the bare mattress, explaining she'd felt she'd never get all the broken glass out of the sheets and blankets that had been on the bed so she'd thrown them out. She turned out the lights in the apartment, poured herself another drink she left for herself on the milk crate end table, then they climbed under the quilts fully clothed and pulled close together.

It was dark in the apartment with the only windows covered, though the cardboard glowed faintly with the morning sun, and there was a slim frame of amber light around the edges. It was cold. They could hear the wind flutter around the rim of the cardboard in the empty windowsills, whistling past the edges, but together, still dressed, still in their jackets, they were warm enough.

They'd be ok because this wasn't about love and that was a good thing. How many calls had he been on to find some girl with her face banged up like a bruised apple, because the love of her life didn't like that his dinner was cold, or her nagging him why he was always late coming home, or her yelling about how he always managed to have money for beer and OTB and his whore girlfriends but the kids were living on bologna sandwiches? And how many times had he rolled up to some place to find some guy with his head caved in by a skillet or a steak knife pushed up under his ribs because whatever kind of hell he'd been dishing out, the love of his life had finally decided she couldn't take it anymore? And it had always started with, "I love you."

Meara slipped an arm around Lourdes. She pulled closer, instinctively, because with the exhaustion of the night and the booze and the Percocet she was already out. He rubbed his cheek against the springy curls of her hair.

The afternoon talk shows were all about how you built healthy relationships by communicating and sharing. Horseshit. What you had to do was keep your fucking mouth shut and haul your own shit because everybody was already busting a gut hauling *their* shit; they didn't want yours on top of it, the smell was bad enough.

Try coming home to communicate and share about the Pakistani cabbie with a pregnant wife and five kids who got his brains blown out all over his dashboard because he wouldn't hand over the $33 in his kitty to a junkie stick-up man; the NYU coed who got gang-raped and sodomized and dumped in a park barely breathing with her head half caved in by a brick as part of some gang initiation; the 11-year-old molested by the new "uncle" banging her booze-soaked mother. Try sharing that stuff and you could guaran-fucking-tee it wasn't going to form a closer bond between you and the love of your life. She'd forget about all that pledged troth and for-better-or-for-worse crap and run screaming from the room with her hands over her bleeding ears.

Share, don't share, what the fuck was the difference since you wound up the same way either way; on your own, hauling your own shit until you either limped to your pension, curled up with a bottle, or finally said fuck it all and ate your gun.

167

In the little bit of light filtering through and around the cardboard in the windows, he could see rust spots bleeding through God-knows-how-many coats of paint on the patterned tin ceiling.

He didn't share with Lourdes Bracero. And she didn't share with him. When they huddled together under the blankets and she ran her fingertips over the puckered scar on his chest where the bullet had gone in – that little dead spot where the hair didn't grow and which was numb to her touch – she never asked about it and he never volunteered. And when his fingers danced along the crescent-shaped scar on her back – a knife he guessed, thin, narrow blade, probably a switchblade – or the rough, rippled patch on her thigh – an old burn – he never asked and she never volunteered. There was nothing about the freak show either of them could tell the other they didn't already know.

The normally cold apartment was even colder, losing its meager heat through the cardboard-covered windows, and he and Lourdes snuggled closer.

He turned away from the rust-spotted ceiling and closed his eyes.

Teresa Ortiz was a cop, she'd been shot, so she rated a room to herself. Ronnie stood in the doorway, letting his eyes adjust. The blinds were drawn, the only light spilling through the doorway and from the dim, green glow from her vital signs monitor. A cast covered her upper right arm and shoulder, and her crooked arm had been carefully laid on a cushion of pillows. He took a step into the room, looked closer at her mostly shadowed face, thought she was asleep.

He heard a snort from elsewhere in the room. In the shadows along the far wall, slumped in a chair, was a short, potato sack of a woman, her deep-in-exhausted-sleep breathing occasionally lapsing into a purring snore, and just as occasionally into a snort and a gasp which partly roused her until she resettled herself in the chair and sank back into her deeper sleep.

Ronnie sidled by Teresa Ortiz' IV stand to be near the head of her bed. Without the bulk of her vest and uniform and gun belt she looked surprisingly small – dainty, even – under the blanket. Throwing a cloud of 9 mm bullets her way seemed so one-sided and unfair.

He crouched by her head. The soft glow of her monitor fell on her cheek; her face looked smooth in sleep, childishly young. He forgot for a moment how close in age they were as he thought, Jesus, she's just a kid.

And at that, he found his hand softly – feather-light, so as not to wake her – on her hair and he felt a pain – the pain of knowing how much worse the pain *could've* been – over the idea of what might have happened if the Kevlar vest hadn't held, if Meara the rogue cop hadn't pulled Teresa Ortiz out of the line of fire.

That feeling, that pain, welled up in his chest, and then he was bending over her, telling himself he probably shouldn't do this but feeling the need all the same, but then he stopped, his lips hovering over her forehead.

"Ya gonna kiss me or what?"

His head whipped back, and his face suddenly went so hot he wondered the whole room wasn't glowing red.

Her eyes opened, but only partly. She spoke thickly, weakly, from under a dense layer of whatever they'd given her for the pain.

"How ya feeling?" Ronnie asked.

"Wha'ever givin' me 's pretty good."

"Enjoy it. I didn't mean to wake you." He kept his voice down, not wanting to wake the woman sleeping in the chair.

"I been in 'n' out all nigh'. My mama still here?"

The purr of the woman across the room stuttered into another snort and gasp.

"Oh," Teresa Ortiz said. Her eyes slipped closed and her breathing changed, slower, and Ronnie guessed she'd gone under again. He started to turn for the door.

"Where you goin'?"

He turned back. Her eyes were still closed, and he wasn't sure how conscious she was. "I gotta go to work," he said. "I just wanted to stop by and see how you were. The doctors say you'll be fine. Coupla weeks, maybe, and you're back on the job."

"My dinner," she slurred.

"What?"

"You promise' me dinner."

"Soon's you're up and around. I swear."

"Shot inna line a duty. Better make it good."

"We'll shoot the moon."

"Lobster. Steak."

"Whatever you want, Ter."

She was quiet, again, and he warily began to back out of the room.

"You were gonna kiss me."

She still hadn't opened her eyes and Ronnie was beginning to wonder if Teresa Ortiz had any idea what she was saying. Well, he told himself as he bent back over her, she asked. He lowered himself toward her forehead.

"Not there...stupid ass."

As much as she could in her druggy state, she puckered her lips.

Ronnie lightly touched his lips to hers, but even before they'd met, he sensed she'd slipped away again.


Big Sid drove them uptown on Tenth Avenue, then whipped over onto Ninth just a few blocks below the Port Authority Bus Terminal, heading them back south.

"Our boy's in there," Big Sid said, pointing past Ronnie's nose to a narrow tenement on the west side of the avenue, almost sticking him in the eye. "Juan Teixeira. Johnny Texas. His bread and butter, some bookie shops he runs downtown, but he'll wheel and deal whatever'll make him a buck: whores, weed, TVs fell off a truck..."

"Peddling information."

"Wave some green under his nose, he'd rat *himself* out."

"This is a long way uptown. He's pretty far from home, isn't he?"

"You ever hear, 'Don't shit where you eat'? He comes downtown to shit on us, he eats here."

Since before a 19th century cop named Dutch Fred had christened it, Hell's Kitchen had been a rat-infested slum crowded with new immigrants on their way – hopefully – up and out to better things, and where boozers, junkies, hookers, thieves, goons, wannabes and never was's, settled on their way *down* and out.

But now Hell's Kitchen was dying. Since the '60s, developers had been marching south from Lincoln Center with a column of posh condos and hotels, and shoving north from an increasingly trendy Chelsea, and whatever they couldn't renovate into something pricey, they tore down and built over. More recently, the 42nd Street Redevelopment Corporation had been driving west, looking to plow under the grindhouses and porn shops in the heart of the neighborhood. All this tony redeveloping had whittled Hell's Kitchen down to a dozen or so blocks of sagging five- and six-floor walk-ups clustered around the back end of the Port Authority, measled with boarded over windows and "CONDEMNED" notices.

Sid pulled back onto Tenth and into a gas station clotted with Yellow Cabs – it was their only refueling oasis in all of midtown – shoehorned onto the corner of one of those remaining tenement blocks. As Sid maneuvered the Buick into a small bit of open space near the air pump, a swarthy attendant in coveralls and grimy hoodie came running over, yelling at them in God knows what kind of accent that this was no parking lot, to which Sid responded by flashing his badge out the window and telling the pump jockey to mind his own fucking business.

Sid pointed through the windshield across the hollow center of the block to the rear of the tenement on Ninth he'd pointed out to Ronnie.

"That's him," Sid said. "Gimme ten minutes to close the back door case he rabbits, then you walk around front, ring for Sara Grajales."

"Who's Sara Grajales?"

"Skank he shacks up with. Lean on the bell – I'm serious, *lean* on the bell – say you want Teixeira. Be a pain in the ass. I know you know how to do that." Sid reached for the door handle, but then settled back in his seat. "Ever handle a snitch before?"

Ronnie shook his head.

"Johnny Texas is a scumbag on a good day. This Meara guy, every day he's on the loose this mess gets bigger. We don't have time to horse around here, y'unnerstand?"

Ronnie thought he did, then he saw the hard, cold look on Sid's face and realized he didn't...then, with a cold feeling in his stomach, he did.

"How it's gotta be, kid. You don't wanna be around for this, take a walk around the block."

Ronnie thought of that moment back in Van Dyne's office when the captain had looked – for the only time he could remember – vulnerable. "What do you want me to do?" Ronnie asked.

"This dick has to know he's in a box, nobody's throwing him a lifeline. No matter what I say, no matter what I do, look like you could give less of a shit. Y'unnerstand?"

"You're not gonna kill him, are you?"

"Well, let's see how it goes."

After that conversation, it felt good to Ronnie to climb out of the clammy heat of the car into the cleansing cold of the winds whipping through the midtown canyons. He lowered his head against the gusts and crossed over to Ninth, then up to the six-floor walk-up Sid had singled out in the middle of the block between a boarded-over convenience store and a coffee shop being stripped to the bare brick walls by a salvage crew. From the empty and broken windows above him, Ronnie guessed half the apartments were already empty, the landlord doing only the minimum in maintenance to keep the Department of Housing off his back while he waited for the leases of the remaining tenants to expire so he could sell out to developers.

In the phone booth-sized foyer, Ronnie ran a finger along the mailboxes until he found "S Grajales" sloppily written on a piece of masking tape. Ronnie poked the buzzer button below the tape. It took a second poke to get "Who is it?" in a sleepy, heavily Spanish-accented woman's voice through the intercom.

"Police, Ms. Grajales," Ronnie said into the intercom. "We're looking for Juan Teixeira."

"He ain' here so get los'."

Remembering what Big Sid had said about leaning on the button and being a pain in the ass, Ronnie leaned on the buzzer button, kept leaning on it, so hard his index finger hurt.

Señorita Grajales responded with a machine gun-paced mix of shouted and hissed Spanish and English invective delivered so furiously Ronnie could only make out the oft-repeated phrase, "fockin' maricone!"

There was a rap on the front door glass, and he turned to see a beaming Sid holding up what Ronnie assumed to be a Juan Teixeira by his left ear like a proud fisherman holding up a prize-winning trout. "Look what I found!"

Juan Teixeira was small – almost child-sized, Ronnie thought – pipe-cleaner thin, with a puffy, pock-marked face and red-rimmed rat eyes. He was probably Ronnie's age but looked worn in that way someone might if that someone didn't watch what he ate, keep regular hours, or avoid a wide variety of unhealthy recreational substances. He had, evidently, left Señorita Grajales' residence in great haste, throwing a frock-length leather jacket over a stained wife-beater, and pulling a pair of blocky Frye boots over the legs of baggy pajama bottoms. Despite his quick exit, Johnny Texas had managed to hold on to his personal jewelry: a half-dozen gaudy rings spread out on the fingers of both hands, and a gold chain around his neck from which were suspended a small gold crucifix, a small gold engraving of the Holy Family, and a small gold cameo of the Virgin Mary because someone like Johnny Texas never saw the paradox in a completely conscienceless shithead beseeching the Almighty to help him out of a jam.

Ronnie followed Sid as he tugged Johnny Texas up the block by his ear.

"Kid, meet Johnny Texas," Big Sid said.

"How you doing?" Ronnie said.

"Not too bad," Johnny Texas managed to grunt while his face twisted in pain.

"I caught him coming out the back door," Sid said. "Listen to this. Hey, Ja-wan, what were you doing going out the back door?"

"I tol' jou, I's takin' out da garbage."

"Tell my partner what you said when I asked how come you didn't have any garbage with you?"

"I forgot it."

Big Sid laughed and gave Johnny Texas's already fire engine-red ear a yank. "I *love* that! 'I forgot it.' Almost made me piss in my pants! 'I forgot it.'" Big Sid pulled Johnny Texas to a bus kiosk on the next corner.

"Wha' da fock's a matter wit' jou?" Johnny Texas whined. "Dis ain' how we do t'ins!"

"It's how we're doing 't'in's' today, Ja-wan."

There were a few people in the kiosk, bundled up against the cold, their heads buried in a *Daily News* or *National Enquirer* or a copy of *Hollywood Wives*. Some of them had tried to stay out of the wind by standing away from the open sides of the kiosk against one of the plastic walls carrying a poster for *A Chorus Line* on which someone had carefully colored in eyeglasses and neat little Van Dykes with

174

Magic Marker on each of the 17 silver lamé-clad dancers in the triangle formation filling up most of the poster.

A big, over-coated black man jerking a skinny little half-undressed Spanish guy around by his ear couldn't help but catch the notice of the people in the kiosk. Sid dealt with the issue by flashing his badge and a butt-the-fuck-out glare which put the citizens' heads even deeper into their newspapers, paperbacks, or a close study of the vandalized *A Chorus Line* poster.

"Know what this is?" Big Sid asked Johnny Texas, pulling him around the kiosk by his ear.

"'Sa fockin' bus stop, so what?"

"So *this!*" Sid said and jerked on Johnny Texas's ear to bring the little man teetering at the edge of the curb on his booted toes. "You give me your usual bullshit today, I'm gonna pull you over here and throw you under the next fucking bus that comes along. *Tu sabe?*"

Johnny Texas tried to wriggle away from the curb, but every wriggle only brought more pain from the ear clamped between Big Sid's thick fingers. "*Que pasa, hombre?* Dis ain' how is done! Alla time, we sit son place warm, we get a little coffee, eh? We shoot da shit, you slide me sontin cross a table—"

"You mention sliding something across the table, again, and I'm gonna slide a coupla tons General Motors bus across your fucking spine. New rules today, *amigo!*" a declaration Sid punctuated with another jerk on Johnny Texas's tortured ear. "Today, I ask you a question, you gimme straight shit and *only* straight shit or I swear to Christ you're going under the Ninth Avenue express." With that, Big Sid gave Johnny Texas's ear a last twist before pushing the little man away. "*Tu entiendes, amigo?*"

Johnny Texas was still trying to massage the pain out of his ear as he looked from Sid to Ronnie to the commuters with their faces buried in Danielle Steele and "Garfield." When he saw there was evidently going to be no salvation from Ronnie or anyone else, he sagged a bit. *"Yo entiendo."*

Big Sid's face suddenly opened in a broad smile, his thick arm shot around Johnny Texas's shoulders, intended as a friendly embrace though Johnny Texas – and everybody else in the bus kiosk -- flinched when they saw it coming. *"Bueno!"* Big Sid said. "Now we got that settled, we can be friendly! Apologize for disturbing these nice people, *amigo,* and I'll treat you to brunch."

"Wha' da fock is *brunch?"*


Brunch turned out to be beef kebabs bought from a cart parked under the Port Authority bus ramps curling out the rear of the terminal down to the Lincoln Tunnel.

The vendor, a dwarfish guy with bad teeth and a duffer's cap and fingerless gloves, slapped barbecue sauce on the kebabs with a paintbrush, flipped them over on the grill and sprinkled them with salt. Fat and sauce dripped onto the coals with pops and crackles, giving off a sweet, charcoaly smell.

"What kind of meat is that?" Ronnie asked the vendor.

The vendor shrugged and smiled. Ronnie wasn't sure if that meant the vendor didn't understand much English or that he didn't have a clue what was cooking on his little grill.

Across the street from the rear entrance of the terminal was a day shelter for homeless men. There were maybe a dozen milling around the shelter door, looking a lot like the poor bastard Ronnie and Sid had found frozen to death across from the station house. Ronnie didn't like the way these other poor bastards were gathering at the curb sniffing at the kebabs sizzling on the grill, not caring what kind of meat was cooking. He wished Sid had found some other place to eat.

The vendor gave the kebabs a last turn, stuck a thin slice of French bread on the charred tip of each wooden spit and handed them out.

Sid guided them back down Ninth. "Feel better now?" He gave Johnny Texas's belly a friendly pat. "Sittin' all nice and warm down there in your tummy, *amigo?*"

"'S'ok."

"So, you ready to *hablar?*"

"Jou wanna talk, talk."

"Sally Dell'Acqua."

"Joe Blow. We jus' sayin' names or what?"

"Funny guy. I'm talking about what happened to Sally."

"Fockin' shame. Bad enough, den you gotta get croaked in *Yersey?* Dat makes it *worse!*"

"I heard you were upset."

"Jou heard dat?

"I heard you were *so* upset you waited all the way until the morning after Sally got whacked to move on his books."

"Das wha' jou heard?"

"That's what I *know.*"

Johnny Texas made a face. "Yeah, well…"

"Well what?"

"Hey, I feel bad wha' happen a guy, but still…"

"Business is business."

Johnny Texas shrugged philosophically.

"Life goes on."

Johnny Texas shrugged again.

"What was Sally doing all the way down there in Jersey, Ja-wann."

"I dunno. I know sontine he say he wasn' happy."

"Why wasn't he happy?"

"He say t'ins is goin' to shit. 'Look aroun',' he say. He got some Russians movin' into his turf, he say he got some crazy voodoo goat-killin' Haitians movin' in, some crazy fockin' Columbians, all takin' son a his business… He tell me maybe is time to, jou know, retire."

177

"It didn't look like he retired to me, *amigo.* Looked like he lit out and found himself a hole."

Another shrug.

"Why'd Tony Boy have Sally whacked?"

Johnny Texas stopped, his face frozen in mid-chew. "Who said anyt'in 'bout Tony Boy?"

Sid gave Johnny Texas a who-the-fuck-do-you-think-you're-kidding look.

Johnny Texas sighed, shrugged. "I dunno."

It had only been an educated guess on their part that Maiella had been behind Dell'Acqua's killing, but now Sid had baited Johnny Texas – quite nicely, Ronnie had to admit – into confirming that suspicion.

"But Sally was scared," Big Sid said, "That's why he lit out. Right?"

"Well, is true like I say, people movin' on his ground. Sally, he kicks to Tony every week and he don' get nothin' for it, he say he jus' payin' Da Boy's lawyer bills, wha's da fockin' point, *si?* He say Tony so busy goin' to court alla tine he ain' takin' care a business, where's da protection, *tu sabe?* Den, after dat las' time Tony go to court, Tony come out, he disappears, the word is sontin' got Da Boy spooked 'n' maybe is not a good time to be sonbody like Sally.

"Look, jou know how it is. Jou a big earner, jou tight, an *amigo,* Tony Boy say, 'Hey, maybe good time jou take a vacation somewhere where dey don' –. Wha's dat word? Where dey don' send you back?"

"Extradite."

"*Si,* go get a suntan where dey don' exerdite. But jou sonbody low on the pole, sonbody – . Whatchacallit? Jou *'spendable –'*"

"Then you're out in the weeds stuffed in an oil drum." Big Sid started back down the avenue, Johnny Texas close behind, Ronnie bringing up the rear.

"Hey," said Ronnie. "Why'd Dell'Acqua drag his grandfather along with him?"

Johnny Texas tapped his chest. "He sof'. Jou check out his bail tickets; is all got da ol' man's name on 'em. *Su abuelo* only fambly Sally got ever give a shit 'bout 'im. Jou t'in jus' 'cause a guy make book, he ain' got no heart?"

"I wonder," Big Sid said, frowning over his shoulder at Johnny Texas. "What did the cop want with Sally?"

Johnny Texas stopped, again. "Wha' cop?" he said, coughing around a mouthful of kebab meat.

Sid – with that surprising swiftness of his – got an arm around Johnny Texas's shoulders before the little man could step clear. Sid smiled and hugged him a bit too tight for the hug to be considered truly friendly. "The cop who came to talk to you," said Sid, tapping Johnny Texas on the nose with his kebab, leaving behind a little brown spot of barbecue sauce.

"Lotta cops come to talk to me," Johnny Texas said, wiping at his nose and trying to squirm free. "*Jou're* talkin' to me."

"That's right, Ja-wan, I'm talking to you and I'm not hearing what I need to hear, y'unnerstand." Sid squeezed him a little tighter. "We agreed, *amigo,* you were gonna be straight with me. Now, I'm gonna ask one more time, you try to give me another one of these handjobs of yours, I'm gonna push this kebab in your ear 'til it comes out the other side," and Sid tickled Johnny Texas's earlobe with the tip of his kebab spit. "Manhattan South cop, woulda come to you a day, maybe coupla days before poor Sally got clipped."

Sid let Johnny Texas push himself free. Johnny Texas spat the meat out and tossed the kebab toward the street. Ronnie ahemmed to get Johnny Texas's attention and pointed to the "No Littering" sign at the corner.

"Fock off, huh?" was Johnny Texas's response. He turned to Sid who had his eyes closed, his face turned toward the sun, a little smile on his face, as if he was there to enjoy the day. Sid lifted one hand, twitched his finger-tips, signaling, Come on, *amigo,* give it up. Johnny

179

Texas shivered, pulled his leather coat closer around him. "I don' know wha' house he from, I never dealt wit' 'im before."

"Ok."

"He wasn' axin' 'bout Sally."

"What was he 'axing' about?"

"Is like he wanted a in."

"Whaddaya mean, an 'in'? What kind of in? An in to *what?*"

"*Hombre*, jou wanna lot for a fockin' brunch."

"It's the season for giving, *amigo*. Hey, partner, do I hear a bus?"

Ronnie knew his cue. "You got time, it looks like a local."

Johnny Texas made a face. He knew it was a charade, but it was a charade with a point. "He start out axin' 'bout Da Boy."

"Maiella? Why?"

"*Compromiso*, eh? He din' feel like splainin' his um, *que es la palabra*, his *motivations* to me, *tu sabe?* Tony Boy's Tony Boy, da cop's a cop; cats 'n' dogs, wha' jou gotta know? Lemme tell jou, dis guy, dis cop, he almos' big a prick as *jou!* He wan' wha' he wan' 'n' if he don' get it, he say I'm gonna get my ass kicked up 'roun' my ears. Is almos' Christmas, why everybody so fockin' hostile? Wha' happen peace on Eart'?"

"The times we live in, *amigo,* the times we live in." Big Sid pulled the last bit of meat from his kebab and twirled the spit into the curb. "So, this cop wanted some kinda lead on Maiella."

"Wha' I'm gettin' – he don' say, is jus' a vibe I get – is he wan' sonbody maybe he can get to roll, den he gets *dat* guy to roll onna *next* guy, ba-da-da ba-da-da alla way up to Da Boy."

"And you threw him Sally Dell'Acqua."

"Hey, I like da guy but he ain' no blood to me, *tu sabe?* Gets da cop off *my* ass."

"You're a fucking prince, *amigo.*"

Ronnie felt something – as the captain had put it back in the muster room – wasn't sitting quite level.

He heard a *click-click-clicking* noise behind him, turned. About ten feet back, standing in the middle of the sidewalk staring after him was a dog; a nondescript, shorthaired tannish mutt. No collar: a stray. Its bald-patched pelt hung loose from its ribs and jutting hips, the fur around its eyes was stiff and crusty, its few teeth were a dull yellow. The *click-click-click* had been the sound of its untrimmed nails on the sidewalk. It was sniffing at the air, at the trailing scent of Ronnie's kebab. There was something about the dog's desperate-eyed need, which reminded him of the men back at the day shelter. Ronnie tossed the remaining half of his kebab toward the dog.

He needed to talk out the jumble in his head. "Hey, Sid?"

Sid didn't look happy at having his momentum interrupted, gave Ronnie a this-better-be-important glare. *"Compromiso,"* he said to Johnny Texas. "I got to confer with my colleague here for a bit."

"Confer jou ass off," Johnny Texas said.

They took a few steps away from Johnny Texas, showing him their backs.

"Something's not right," Ronnie said.

"Like?"

Ronnie fidgeted, unsure.

*"Like?"* Sid pushed.

"This clown sent Meara after Dell'Acqua because he knew Dell'Acqua belonged to Maiella, right?"

"Skip to the good part, kid, and there better be a good part."

"This guy moved on Dell'Acqua's operation even before the killing made it on TV."

"Sometimes the grapevine's faster than *Eyewitness News.*"

"He knew Dell'Acqua belonged to Maiella. That means Dell'Acqua's books belonged to Maiella; that means that was Maiella money. Johnny here *knows* that."

Big Sid shook his head and Ronnie got the feeling the big man was either going to walk away in exasperation...or punch him in the nose.

181

"Sid, where does a guy like this get off making that kind of move against Tony Boy Maiella's turf? He's gotta know Maiella's not gonna stand for it. Unless he's got some kind of green light, right?"

And now Big Sid was no longer fidgety and impatient. His large, black face clouded with processing, assessment. He looked back to where Johnny Texas was stepping from one foot in an ice-cold boot to the other.

"Hey, *hombre*, could we finish, huh?" Johnny Texas said, his hands shoved deep in his jacket pockets. "My *cojones* is ice coobs!"

Now that Ronnie was talking it out, other pieces seemed to quickly jell. "Even saying he's got the ok, would Maiella give those books over to an outsider?"

"No way. So either he brought this shit-bird in…"

"Or he was *always* in."

"Which fills in a lot of holes."

"And what happens if he sends Meara down there, but Meara comes up dry? Meara's gonna come back, right? And pissed? And even if Meara *does* get what he wants out of Dell'Acqua, that points him at Maiella, and then *Maiella's* pissed with this guy. Either way, it's bad news for your *amigo* here. If I was in those Frye boots, I woulda been outta town on a rocket five minutes after I talked to Meara."

"Unless you knew Meara wasn't coming back." Big Sid looked down at Ronnie and he gave a slight, impressed nod. "I'm not sure I won't have to take it back tomorrow, kid, but I'm starting to think you're worth keeping around. Maybe. Sometimes."

Big Sid turned back to Johnny Texas with a wide smile, but it was a smile that had Johnny Texas leaning back, figuring whatever was coming was going to be bad.

Sid dabbed at some sticky spots of barbecue sauce at the corner of his mouth with a finger, reached out and wiped it on the front of Johnny Texas's leather jacket. "You got a hearing problem, *amigo*."

Johnny Texas was frowning down at the brown streak on his jacket. "This shit better come out, *pendajo.*"

"'Cause at the top, I told you you gotta be straight with me, and it turns out you haven't been completely forthcoming."

"For-wha'?"

"Honest," Ronnie said.

"Like wha' didn' I tell jou?"

Big Sid smiled conspiratorially, made a big show of looking this way and that to make sure no one else was listening, leaned his head close to Johnny Texas's and said, almost in a giggle, "You didn't tell me you set the cop up for a hit."

Ronnie saw Johnny Texas's eyes go wide, saw his head twitch, his mouth work, before he finally realized the best thing to do was run.

But by then Sid had already painfully vise-gripped one of his huge hands on the back of Johnny Texas's neck and slammed the little man's face against the rough brick face of one of Ninth Avenue's tenements.

"I didn' kill *nobody!*" Johnny Texas managed to get out as Sid's hand continued to grind his face against the front of the building.

"You little wormy shit!" Big Sid hissed into Johnny Texas's ear. "You didn't tell me you knew Sally belonged to Tony Boy because *you* belong to Tony Boy!"

"I tol' jou *zackly* wha' jou ax me!"

"This guy's a regular Richard fucking Nixon," Big Sid said to Ronnie. "'I didn't lie; I just didn't tell you everything.'" Sid put more pressure on Johnny Texas's head. "You fingered Sally for the cop; then you set the cop up for Tony Boy! And for being a stand-up member of the firm, Tony Boy gave you Sally's operation."

Sid grabbed Johnny Texas by the shoulder, whipped him around and slammed his back against the wall. Ronnie winced at the mushy-sounding *thunk* of the back of Johnny Texas's head bouncing off the bricks.

"Jou outta jou fockin' mind?" Johnny Texas said. "Jou gonna pull dis shit wit' da whole fockin' worl' watchin'?"

"That's how pissed I am with you right now, *amigo!*" Big Sid said, grabbing a fistful of Johnny Texas's leather jacket and bouncing him off the tenement wall a second time. "You set up a *cop?* For what? To pick up a couple more bookie shops? For that, I don't give a rat's ass the whole fucking world watches me put you through this fucking wall!"

Ronnie believed him. Big Sid's face was shining with sweat despite the freezing winds on Ninth Avenue, so twisted in fury Ronnie wouldn't have been surprised if Sid suddenly lunged forward, clamped his teeth on Johnny Texas bobbing Adam's apple and tore his throat out.

Johnny Texas saw that look, too. *"Oye, cuidado, chico!"* Johnny Texas desperately called to Ronnie. "Jou don' step up 'n' pull dis fat fock off, jou gonna go down wit' him when I make my beef!"

Ronnie kept remembering Big Sid's instruction to look unfazed no matter what he saw or heard, but he hadn't counted on those frightened, gaping faces pointing his way from cars passing by and in the few inhabited windows in the buildings on either side of the avenue. Ronnie'd never felt so naked…or so wrong.

"You think *he's* gonna help you?" Big Sid said to Johnny Texas, grinning maliciously. "Five spics gang-raped his momma when he was a kid. Only thing he wants is take you in the back seat of my car with a tire iron! He's done, you're gonna look like a bad banana, y'unnerstand?" Big Sid bounced Johnny Texas off the building again.

Johnny Texas yelped, rubbed at the back of his head. His face twisted in a mix of fear and anger when he saw his hand smeared with blood. *"Moy loco!"*

"You don't know *how moy loco!*" Big Sid said coldly, then his hand slipped up around Johnny Texas's throat and began to squeeze, lifting a gagging Johnny Texas up on his toes.

"Hey," Ronnie said. He was trying to keep his voice even, but it sounded like a squeak to him. "I don't want to spoil your fun, but maybe you should get him to talk *before* you put him through the wall. What do you think?"

Big Sid blinked, as if he was just waking up. He let go of Johnny Texas's throat, stepped back. He wiped a sleeve along his sweaty forehead, took deep breaths as if he'd finished a long, hard run.

The threat of imminent doom now removed; Johnny Texas allowed himself the luxury of outrage. "Jou psycho fock!" He ran a tongue along his front teeth. "I t'in jou chip my fockin' toot'!"

"You're lucky I didn't chip your fucking skull," Big Sid said. He nodded at Ronnie. "C'mon, let's go. Only true thing this prick told us is it's cold."

Ronnie followed Sid down the street, leaving a puzzled Johnny Texas behind. But then Sid stopped – so suddenly, Ronnie almost walked into him – and turned back to Johnny Texas with a delighted smirk.

"You don't even know how much shit you're in, do you, you dumb spic?"

"Wha' da fock jou –"

"You're in so deep you couldn't dig yourself out with a steam shovel!" Sid chuckled. "You wanted to move up? Congratulations, *amigo*, you made it! You graduated to the big time!"

"Jou jus' fockin' wit' me now!" Johnny Texas said, but the bluster was all show.

"Sally and the cop, you mental defective!" Big Sid cackled. "That's a pair of Murder Ones! *Dos!*"

"I didn' kill—"

"Doesn't matter you didn't pull the trigger, ass-wipe! Nobody's gonna cry over Sally getting clipped, but the DA's gonna tear your ass up over setting up a cop!"

"What do they call that?" Ronnie asked. "Accessory? Complicity? Conspiracy?"

"They call it being *fucked!*" Sid gloated. "And you know something? That's not the worst of this dipshit's problems." Sid leaned in close to Johnny Texas, penning him against the tenement again. "Let me tell you something didn't make the news, *amigo*. Those guys your boss sent down to Jersey *missed!*"

It was Johnny Texas's turn to grin. "Now I *know* jou fockin' wit' me! I saw it on da news Sally—"

"Oh, yeah, Sally, that poor bastard was so ventilated, looked like a spaghetti strainer. The *cop, stupido!* He's *alive!* Worse for you: he's back in town!"

Johnny Texas's face went slack. *"Que?"*

"And if I got any kind of read on this guy, I figure he's gonna be wanting to talk to you about what happened at Sally's."

Ronnie could see it in Johnny Texas's slumping figure, his dropping jaw. The little man was beginning to understand what Big Sid was cackling about: how deep deep *deep* in the shit he was.

Big Sid laughed. "You went for the hat trick, *amigo!* Because once The Boy hears the cop is back in town, he's gonna figure the same thing; the cop is gonna be talking to you, and he's gonna start worrying about that big yap of yours."

"No, no, no!" Johnny Texas said, though he didn't really believe it. "I did righ' by Tony Boy! Like jou said: I'm a stand-up—"

"You're a rat-fucker and Tony Boy knows it," Sid said. "You sold out Sally, you sold out the cop, it's not gonna be hard for The Boy to think you'll sell him out, too. You're gonna have the DA going after you with 20-to-life, the cop's gonna want to put a .38 in your ear, and Tony Boy's reserving a spot for you out in the weeds! You're fucked in all three holes, *amigo! Adios!*" and he nodded at Ronnie to follow him down the sidewalk.

"Where jou goin'?" Johnny Texas called after them.

Sid turned, back-pedaling down the sidewalk as he called to Johnny Texas: "Done with you! See ya, wouldn't wanna be ya!"

Johnny Texas stood there for a second, seemingly dazed. "Wai' wai wai'," he called after them, weakly, it was all still sinking in, and then a rather grim mental picture of his rather grim future jelled and he bolted ahead of them, trying to block Big Sid – "Wai' wai' wai'!" – but Sid pushed on by.

"You dug your grave, now crawl down in it," Big Sid said.

"Dis ain' righ'!" Johnny Texas pleaded. "Jou gotta do sontin for me!"

"I'll piss on your grave. How's that?"

"C'mon, *hombre*, less talk! Tell me wha' jou wan'! Ax me whatever! I'll be straight, I swear! But jou gotta bring me in! Jou gotta make da protections for me!"

Sid continued to brush by. "I don't gotta do shit."

"*Jesu Cristo, hombre!* I give up wha'ever jou wan'!" Johnny Texas looked close to crying.

Big Sid stopped, studied the shaking figure in front of him. He paced in a contemplative little circle.

Ronnie heard the tinkle of a shop doorbell, caught a whiff of sawdust and blood. He saw they were standing in front of some kind of butcher shop. He didn't know what kind: the signage wasn't English, it wasn't even in Arabic letters. Hanging in the window from a meat hook through its ankles was a large rabbit, still in its downy white fur, its pink eyes open.

"What do you think?" Big Sid asked Ronnie, having stopped his pacing. "Let this turd twist in the wind or what?"

Johnny Texas turned his wet, pleading eyes to Ronnie.

Ronnie looked down at his sneakers, shrugged. "You're the boss."

"Don't fuck with me anymore," Big Sid warned Johnny Texas.

"Jou help me out, I swear to Chris' I make dis good for jou!"

187

"The cop went to Sally looking for a name," Big Sid said. "He was after the next guy up, the guy Sally kicked to. You kick to the same guy, *si?*"

"*Si.*"

"Name."

"Guy come 'roun' every week," Johnny Texas said. "Big guy, a bonebreaker, *tu sabe?* Jou don' got a fat envelope every week, he goin' home wit' jour finger in his pocket. But I ain' got a name."

Big Sid sighed disgustedly. "That's what you're gonna give me? A guy you don't know his name?"

"No, wai', will jou hol' on a sec? But da firs' tine, when jou firs' open up, is *another* guy. He da one lay it out for jou, tell jou jou better kick in every week or *phhhht* to da weeds. Him I know. Das a name, jou work book for Tony Boy, jou know it. Name's Malloi."

"Tony Boy has a mick running his books for him?"

"No, it jus' *soun'* like a mick, but he spell it some kinda wop way. I don' know why he do it like dat. Why jou t'in he do it like dat?"

"I'll ask his mother when I see her. Where do I find him?"

"I hear he got a place jus' over da river in Yersey, but das all I know."

"'A place over in Jersey?' That's it?"

"*Que?* Jou t'in da guy has me over for dinner? C'mon, all dose fockin' files jou got down Police Plaza, jou prolly got paper on dis guy, *tu sabe?*"

Sid nodded at Ronnie to follow as he walked past Johnny Texas.

"*Oye!*" Johnny Texas called running after them. "Where jou' goin'? Jou gotta bring me in!"

"I gotta talk to people first, I gotta set it up."

"Fock you gotta set it up! Jou told me—"

Big Sid froze Johnny Texas with a .50 caliber index finger aimed at the little man's nose. "Gimme grief and you don't get *shit!* For now, go back to your whore, pull the shades, lock the door. Don't go out until you hear from me." Big Sid took a step closer, fixed Johnny Texas with an unblinking eye. "If I hear you took out the garbage and forgot to come back, I swear to Christ I'll rat you out so loud to *both* sides, you'll have *everybody* on your ass from Girl Scouts to every two-bit hood, hype and hooker looking to collect a bounty from The Boy, *entiendes?*"

"*Si.*"

"Now fuck off. I'll be in touch."

Ronnie stood with Big Sid as they watched Johnny Texas cross Ninth Avenue. Johnny Texas's head was so filled with worries about a vindictive Jack Meara and a preemptive Tony Boy Maiella and a crusading District Attorney that he didn't have any attention left for the traffic whizzing by him, the horns honking at him, the cabbies yelling at him to wake the fuck up and watch where he was going.

Big Sid laughed. "Lookit! This dick's so rattled he might not make it cross the street."

"I thought you were gonna lose it there for a second," Ronnie said.

"I *did* lose it there for a second. Prick like that, it's easy."

"Why *didn't* you bust him?" Ronnie asked. "We at least had him for accessory to murder."

Big Sid nodded at Ronnie to follow him down the avenue. "We didn't have him for shit, kid. We *know* what he did, but we don't have diddley to prove it. Soon's he calms down enough to think straight, he's gonna figure that out."

"So you were bullshitting him about the DA and Meara and—"

"About the DA, yeah. About Meara and Tony Boy?" Big Sid shook his head. "Between the two of them, I'll be surprised if this scumbag lives out the week."

"You promised him protection."

"This guy set up a cop, kid." He stopped and turned to Ronnie. "Got a problem with that?"

"I don't know," Ronnie said.

"Well, you digest it a bit and get back to me."

"That should be it," Big Sid said as they came out of the Lincoln Tunnel. The big man twisted around in his seat to look up out the passenger window at the high-rise sitting atop the steep bluffs climbing up to Union City. "Now you just gotta get us up there."

Which, Ronnie thought, was going to be a hell of a lot easier said than done.

Big Sid had used a pay phone at the Tenth Avenue gas station to call Police Plaza. Juan Teixeira had been right: BCI did have a sheet on Lorenzo Malloi who, under the name Lawrence Malloy, was living across the Hudson in Union City in a pricey condo supposedly owned by a non-existent Mrs. Malloy. Big Sid had Ronnie drive them across the river on the assumption that since Ronnie was from Jersey he could be expected to find any address anywhere in the state; an assumption that, as Ronnie zigged and zagged through the funhouse maze of narrow Union City streets, proved to be utterly baseless.

"Ya know, *I* coulda got us this lost," Big Sid said.

At one time, Union City had been "The Embroidery Capital of the US." Ronnie knew this because there was a bragging sign in bold letters posted near the exit ramp into Union City stating as much. But, whenever that had been, it must've been some time ago because the sign was old and faded, and Union City had the same weary, tired look all the other northern Jersey factory towns had now that the factories were dead.

Eventually, they did find The Riverview Condominiums, its ten stories and cantilevered multilevel garage perched at the very edge of the cliffs overlooking the flats running past the edge of the Palisades to the Hudson and down into Hoboken. The building was curved, the peak of the bow angled east and down the river to give the maximum number of residents a view of the Hudson from midtown Manhattan all the way to the narrows.

They pulled into the garage where Sid directed Ronnie to an empty handicapped parking space close to the ramp. As Sid rooted around in the trunk for an "NYPD – OFFICIAL BUSINESS" sign to leave in the car window, Ronnie drifted to the open side of the garage facing east.

The Jersey side of the Hudson, as a working waterfront, had expired long ago, was marked now only by the skeletal fingers of derelict and burned-out piers jutting into the whitecaps and spume of the wind-whipped water. The same wind brought Ronnie the lulling aroma of the Maxwell House plant further downriver in Hoboken. The breakfasty smell wearily reminded him of how long it had been since he'd had a full night's sleep. On the other side of the wide blue-gray band of the Hudson were the spires and piles of concrete and steel and glass of midtown Manhattan, windows here and there flaring and fading as they caught the sun's changing angle.

Sid was standing beside him, taking a deep pull on the coffee smell from the Maxwell House plant. "Jesus, I could use a cup of that."

"When I was a kid, we took a bus ride from Cape May to see the Ice Capades at the old Garden," Ronnie said. "That was the first time I saw New York. I remember looking across the river, I saw all those humongous buildings, I couldn't believe how big they were. I was a kid. I didn't know what an island was. I thought an island floated on the water. I asked my father, 'How come it doesn't sink?'"

"I ask myself that all the time," Big Sid said.

They walked up the garage ramp and around to the main entrance where a pudgy, blotchy-faced doorman sitting behind a podium desk shared the foyer with an artificial silver Christmas tree decorated with red silk balls and an electric menorah. The doorman wore a braided peaked cap and was stuffed into an epauletted jacket dripping more braid, closed with a double row of straining buttons. The doorman seemed to be under the misbegotten impression all that braid empowered him with some kind of authority, and he haughtily refused to allow Big Sid and Ronnie to pass or even admit Lawrence

Malloy lived there. "We got a policy," he said from behind his podium desk, ending the pronouncement with a sniff.

"Listen, General, I got a policy, too," Big Sid said and badged the doorman.

The doorman stopped his snotty sniffing as he eyed Sid's tin, then leaned over his podium desk, now very much one-working-stiff-confiding-to-another. "Look, I'm not trying to be a pain in the neck," he said, "but if I let you in and there's a beef, I could maybe lose my job."

Big Sid nodded compassionately then said, "If *I* beef, you will *definitely* lose your job."

"Seventh floor, unit 709, just to your left coming out of the elevator."

As the doorman buzzed them through, Sid stopped in the inner doorway, leaned back toward the doorman. "If I find out somebody tried to fatten up their Christmas envelope by calling ahead and letting Mr. Malloy know we're coming, me and that somebody are going to have a talk."

Ronnie followed Big Sid across the marbled lobby on a band of plush red carpet, past *faux* Grecian urns and flower vases on pedestals. The elevator was paneled with gold-flecked mirrors and had the same plush red carpet. The elevator Muzak dripped an instrumental version of *Hey, Jude* so snoozy it could've put a crystal meth freak to sleep.

"I don't even *like* the Beatles," Big Sid said, "that's white boy crap. But *Jesus,* that's a shame."

"You gonna bounce this guy off the walls, Sid?"

"Would that bother you?"

"I'm just asking."

"You more comfortable if I took a different approach?"

"I wouldn't mind."

The elevator door opened and there was more red carpet, more gold-flecked mirrors on the corridor walls, more urns and flower vases. They stopped at 709, a choice location just off the peak of the building's curve on the river view side.

"I'm gonna sit and talk with him," Big Sid said. "I want you moving."

"Moving?"

"Wander around. Look at stuff. Touch things. Ask any stupid-ass question comes into your head. Do they allow pets? Where do you get your hair cut?"

"What the hell is that supposed to do?"

"I want him off balance. Maybe he'll slip, maybe he won't lie as good."

"This works?"

"We'll find out. I thought you might like it better than me bouncing him off the walls." He nodded at Ronnie to knock on the door.

Ronnie knocked; he tried the doorbell then he knocked again.

"Don 't you know how to do a cop knock, kid?"

"A what?"

Sid pushed Ronnie aside and pounded on the door with his fist. "Yo, Malloi! Let's go! Open up!"

Ronnie flushed when he heard one or two other doors on the corridor open a crack, just long enough for someone to take a quick peek before closing their doors again. Ronnie heard the rattle of door chains after the doors closed.

Sid gave another cop knock then stabbed the doorbell a few times. "C'mon, Malloi, need to talk to you."

"*Who* wants to talk to me?" The voice sounded scratchy, groggy.

"I think we woke him up," Ronnie said.

Sid looked at his watch. "He's living a good life. It's the police, Malloi. Just need to ask you a few questions."

"How the hell did you get up here? Who was on the door? That little fat fuck? I swear to Christ I'm gonna kill that—"

"Coupla questions and we're gone, Malloi."

There was a pause, then, "Hold your ID up in front of the peephole." Sid did so then the door opened a crack, still on its chain. "Let me see that." Sid passed his badge cover through the gap. "How about you? Where's yours?" Ronnie followed suit. A moment, then the leather covers were pushed out the gap and flopped on the floor and the door closed.

"Dick," Sid muttered as he picked up his badge. "Malloi!"

"Those are New York!" Malloi called back. "Hope they reimburse you for the tolls. Have a nice ride back."

"C'mon, Malloi, we just need to talk to you for a few minutes."

"Talk to the wall."

"I'm trying to do this the nice way, but if I gotta talk to you through the door, I will. Now, that means the neighbors are gonna hear everything I got to say to you…*Lorenzo.*"

Another moment, then the chain rattled, and the door swung open. "This is harassment, ya know," Malloi said letting them in.

Big Sid shrugged.

"You're a prick."

"Not the first time I heard that today," Sid said. "Probably won't be the last."

They stepped into a living room as big as Ronnie's apartment. There were sliding glass doors to a balcony offering a panoramic view of the Manhattan skyline from the needle of the Empire State Building down to the double exclamation points of the twin towers of the World Trade Center. Through an archway Ronnie could see not a dining *area* but a full dining *room*. A hallway led off to other no doubt equally spacious rooms.

It was all done up in a striking if hardly hospitable black-and-white scheme: black leather sofas and chairs, deep pile white rug, black lacquer and smoked glass and chrome furniture, canvases on the white walls of black lines and blobs on fields of white, and white lines and blobs on fields of black.

The striking impression all that starkness was supposed to make was substantially mitigated by the appearance of someone having unloaded a garbage truck in the room. Glasses and beer bottles were everywhere, there were drink stains on the rug along with ground-in crumbs and pieces of food, trays of leftover hors d'oeuvres were piled on any open space not already occupied by stacked plates of half-eaten food. Ravaged steam trays were lined up on a sideboard in the dining room, their Sterno cans burned out and black. The whole place smelled like a damp ashtray.

"Any survivors?" Sid asked.

Lorenzo Malloi ignored him, carelessly pushed a few plates out of a leather chair onto the floor and plopped down. Malloi, wearing a silk kimono – and nothing else, apparently – the same eye-burning red color as its owner's eyes, reminded Ronnie of cartoons he'd seen where a turtle had lost its shell: short, deathly pale, a shapeless middle and disproportionately short, stubby limbs. Malloi even had the flat-topped, beak-nosed head of a turtle whose appearance he'd unsuccessfully tried to improve with some obvious dental work and an even more obvious toupee too dark and full to belong on that wizened little middle-aged head.

"Mind if I sit?" Sid said.

"Actually, I do," Malloi said, letting his knees flop carelessly open. Ronnie guessed that was Malloi's way of saying – literally – kiss my ass.

"Thanks," Sid said, pushed some stacked trays to the side and settled in at one end of a sofa, across a littered black lacquer coffee table from Malloi. "Helluva blowout you had here," Sid observed.

"Christmas party," Malloi yawned. "For friends. Which was why you weren't invited."

"Nothing but comedians today," Sid said to Ronnie, giving him a barely perceptible nod to remind him what he needed to be doing.

"You got some view here," Ronnie said over by the sliding doors. "I'll bet you could see all the way down to the Statue of Liberty and the narrows if Hoboken wasn't in the way."

"I'll have to get Hoboken to move, then," Malloi said, yawning again, rubbing his red, tired eyes. He gave Ronnie an up-and-down look. "They bounce so many cops over there they're hiring midgets now?"

"Be nice to the kid, Larry," Sid said. "You mind if I call you Larry?"

"Yes."

"So, Larry, where's the hostess?"

"The what?"

"You know: your *wife*. She *is* the deed-holder on this palace, isn't she?"

"Out of town. Visiting relatives."

"Yeah? Where's that?"

"Boston."

"No kidding. I got family up in Boston. I go up there all the time, y'unnerstand. What part of Boston? I'll bet I know it."

Lorenzo Malloi smiled an ok-that's-one-for-you smile, and Sid smiled back an I-*know*-that's-one-for-me.

Ronnie poked at a tray still carrying a few crackers smeared with a gray paste. Ronnie picked up one of the crackers, took a whiff of the paste and made a face. "Hey, what is this stuff? People eat this? It looks like the stuff they use to put up wallpaper."

Malloi craned around at Ronnie. "That's pâté, dumbass. I don't figure you'd know that. You're probably more a Ritz and Cheez Whiz kinda guy."

"Why you got to talk to him like that?" Sid said. "He's a curious kid."

"You shouldn't leave food out like this," Ronnie said. "You'll get cockroaches."

"This building doesn't have cockroaches."

"They got you, don't they?" Sid said.

Malloi smiled sourly. "So you're a comedian, too?"

"Not in your league," Sid said. He flicked the rim of a champagne flute on the coffee table with his fingertip and a soft crystalline *ting* hung in the stale ashy air for a moment. Sid smiled appreciatively. "Bookmaking must pay pretty good these days."

"What bookmaking? Whaddayou talking about? I'm a legitimate businessman."

"Boy, it didn't take us long to get to that," Sid said. "What's your legitimate business, Larry?"

"I own a carwash."

Sid made a show of looking around the room, impressed. "Jesus, Larry, how many cars you gotta wash to pay for this?"

"*I* don't wash them," Malloi huffed. "I have people who do that for me. I actually own more than one."

"Still. We're in the wrong business," Sid called to Ronnie.

"I'm learning that," Ronnie said.

Malloi shifted in his seat, there was a wet, smacking sound as his bare bottom moved around on the leather upholstery. "What is it you want?" he said impatiently. "If there's a problem with the deed, that's between me, I mean, my *wife* and the management company."

"You didn't actually read these, did you?" Ronnie was poking along a shelf of books in a chrome and glass wall unit. It was a dazzlingly eclectic collection: novels, histories, textbooks, some in languages Ronnie didn't recognize. The only thing they all had in common was they had the kind of old, cloth covers which looked distinguished on a bookshelf.

"Course he didn't!" Big Sid chuckled. "The only thing this guy's ever read is a racing form! Decorators buy 'em by the yard to fill up the shelves. Isn't that right, Larry?"

"You said you had some questions," Malloi said, annoyed. "Or are you just hanging out to run up overtime?"

"Look, Larry, I don't give the slightest shit about you and your hinky deed or your non-existent wife or filling up your bookshelves to hide you being a moron."

"Hey!" Malloi bristled.

"You heard about Sally Dell'Acqua?"

"I think I know that name. Something I heard on the news. Some kind of accident or something?"

"I wouldn't exactly call it an accident, y'unnerstand."

Ronnie lifted one of the steam tray lids, gave a look to the stale remains of whatever had been in it, let the lid drop with a clang. "Looks like something died in there."

"What's that guy doing?" Malloi asked Sid. "What're you doing in there?" he called to Ronnie.

"Looking," Ronnie said.

"Don't."

Big Sid cleared his throat to regain Malloi's attention. "Those two torpedoes your boss sent down to Sally's—"

"Whoa! Whoa! Whoa!" Malloi said, holding up a hand. "First off, I'm my own boss. I own my—"

"Yeah, carwashes."

"That's right! And I don't know what you mean about torpedoes and all that."

"Ok, Larry," Big Sid said, nodding. "Let's say we got a complaint."

"A complaint? What kind of complaint?"

"From one of the customers at your carwash. Seems two of the guys who work at your carwash didn't wash a car they were supposed to wash."

Malloi was still sprawled in his chair but something went through him like a barely felt electric shock.

"I guess those boys at the carwash didn't tell you about that," Sid said. "Otherwise you wouldn't be in such a Christmas party mood. Well, I can understand that, right? Who wants to tick the boss off right

198

before you get your Christmas bonus? But, see, here's the thing, Larry. Guy who owns that car? He's back in New York and he's not happy about what happened – I'm sorry," a chuckle, "what *didn't* happen. I mean to his car. At your carwash. I got a feeling this guy's gonna want to lodge a complaint with you. *Personally.*"

Malloi sank a little deeper into his chair, his head moving this way and that before it began shaking in a mix of disbelief and confusion.

"Hey, who's this Mantiovanni guy?" Ronnie was poking through shelves of albums by a stereo rack system. "Jesus, how many records did this guy make?"

"What the fuck is with this guy?" Malloi said peevishly, nodding at Ronnie. "Is he some kind of ree-tard or something?"

"I told you, leave the kid alone," Sid said. "So he's a little simple. Be nice."

Malloi's confusion gave way to wariness and he sat up in his chair, his eyes narrowing at Sid. "What's this got to do with you?"

"Well, Larry, I'm here to do you a favor, y'unnerstand."

"A favor? Do *me* a favor?"

Malloi turned at the clatter of Ronnie shifting dirty dishes around on the dining room table. "Man, I feel bad for your maid."

"Would you just find a place and park yourself?" Malloi snapped. To Sid: "Would you tell the ree-tard to sit his ass down?"

"We want to stop this guy from coming to you with his complaint," Sid said.

"And why would you want to do that?"

"I'm a nice guy, spirit of the season, who gives a shit why? I'm saving you an ass-beating, Larry."

Which Ronnie didn't think was the best possible tack. "Let's just say it's not going to do anybody any good if this guy comes to you with his complaint," he said, earning himself a frown from Sid.

"And how would you make this thing not happen?" Malloi asked.

Sid leaned back in the sofa. "We hadn't really thought it out that far." He waved a hand at Ronnie, a gesture of as-long-as-you-opened-your-mouth-finish-it.

Ronnie thought a moment. "I guess we could put a couple of men on you, and if this guy shows—"

Malloi made a face. "You want to hang a couple your guys on me, interfering with my business—"

"You mean your carwash business?" Sid said.

"— embarrassing me in front of my neighbors—"

Sid laughed. "I doubt your neighbors think as well of you as *you* think they do."

"We're trying to help you here, Mr. Malloi," Ronnie said.

"Bullshit!" Malloi snapped back. "You're trying to bust my balls is what you're trying to do! Put a couple guys on my ass—"

Ronnie was about to protest, make another plea, but Big Sid suddenly stood and waved at him to let it go. "Forget it, kid. If this is the way this mental defective wants to play it, fuck 'im." Sid pulled a business card from his wallet and flicked it into the mess on the coffee table. "My number's on there, genius. Case you grow half a brain, y'unnerstand. Or for after this guy shoves your head so far up your own ass you look like a pretzel." Sid nodded at Ronnie to follow him to the door. Before they left, Sid turned toward Malloi, brooding in his chair across the room. "Personally, Larry, I hope you stay dumb."

In the elevator on the way down, Sid leaned tiredly against the mirrored walls of the elevator, let his eyes close.

"You didn't really try that hard to convince him to cooperate," Ronnie said.

Sid smiled. "You're wrong kid. I didn't try at *all!*"


From his place at the table in the dark kitchen, Meara could hear Lourdes Bracero stirring on the sofa bed, moving sporadically until she realized she wouldn't be falling back asleep. He heard her swing her feet to the floor, than a phlegmy smoker's cough she soothed with the drink she'd left on the milk crate end table. Then, the *phhht* of a striking match, a brief flare of light from the other room, that first, deep drag on a cigarette, then letting out breath in something as much a sigh as an exhalation.

"You here?" Her voice was still raspy. She coughed again.

"In here," he called. "C'mon. I've got lunch."

She shuffled to the kitchen carrying her drink, backlit by the feeble light bleeding through the cardboard over the front windows, smiling at the pizza box on the table from the doorway.

"Is that Ray's?" she said, nodding at the pizza box, "or Famous Ray's? I don't like Ray's."

It was an old New York pizza connoisseurs' argument over which was the better chain, which he had never understood. He shrugged and smiled. "Same shit to me."

"That's 'cause you got no class," she said, and dropped into the seat across from him. She didn't turn on the kitchen light, but that was fine with him. "You went out?"

"They delivered. You should dig into that. It's still warm."

"That makes one of us," she said, pulling his denim jacket close around her, shuddering. "Jesus, I can't seem to get my blood going."

He set a pot of water on the stove to boil, went back into the front room, came back with his bombardier jacket and laid it across her shoulders. "Eat," he said. The blue flame from the stove gave him just enough light to find a mug in one of the cabinets, her hot cocoa mix in another.

"How long you been up?" she said through a mouthful of pizza.

"I don't know. A while. You scheduled to work tonight?"

"I go on at six." She took another sighing pull on her cigarette. "I'm not sure I feel like goin' in."

The water was boiling now. Meara poured her a cupful, stirred in the cocoa mix. He went into the near-empty refrigerator, found a pint of milk, sniffed at the spout to make sure it was good, mixed a dab into the cocoa to thicken it. "Keep everything normal. If you're scheduled to work, work. Your babysitters outside'll probably stick with you when you leave which'll make things easier for me."

"Make what easier?"

He set the mug of cocoa down by her. "It's easier for me to get in and out of here without being seen than my place, even when they're sitting outside. What I'm thinking is, after dark, if I can, I'm going to get into my place, pick up some stuff, and then stay here. If that's ok. Then, when it's time to go…we just go."

He couldn't make out the features of her face, just the tired hanging of her head. The red tip of her cigarette floated up, pulsed as she took another drag, and for a moment he saw her eyes in the red glow staring vacantly into the darkness. "Stay here? Sure. Yeah." She ate some more of the pizza, then tossed the half-finished slice back into the box. "I'll have some more later. Sometimes it tastes good cold."

"When I was a kid, if I got up before my mom and dad, sometimes I'd have leftover pizza for breakfast. My mother thought it was disgusting but my dad did the same thing. He used to call it an Italian breakfast pastry. He said that was how you could tell it was a good pizza; if it still tasted good the next day cold for breakfast."

She let out a little amused huff, nodded in recognition. "My mama called 'em Italian breakfast tamales." She resettled in her seat, tipped a little from her drink into the hot cocoa, swirled the mug around, mixing the liquor in, took a sip. "I keep meaning to get real marshmallows," and something made her smile about that. "You sure you need to go back?'

"There's some stuff I need."

"You can't buy what you need?"

"There's the money."

"I got money."

"How much? How far will it get us?"

She took another sip of her laced cocoa, let her head sag against the wall. "I'm just worried, you go back—"

He extended a leg under the table, rubbed the toe of his boot along her calf. "If it looks bad, I'll turn around and come back."

She turned to him, he saw her shoulders rise and fall, heard the whisper of a breath, like she was ready to say something...but then let it go.

"You want to ask me – again – for us to just go," he said. "Now."

"I wasn't going to."

"But you want to. I've been sitting here thinking about it. I keep telling myself that would be the smart move, leave now."

"But you won't. That's what I expect from somebody don't know the difference between Ray's and Famous Ray's."

They each forced a smile over that.

He'd been sitting there however long, alone in the dark, pondering just that point: why he wasn't making the smart move, why he hadn't made a smart move in weeks. It had been all movement and moves, stimulus/response, not a lot of introspection. But he'd sat there in the lightless kitchen working it out in his head in a way he could explain because she deserved that. "Part of it..." He stopped, wondering if it would sound stupid. "Part of it is if I don't do this, it's gonna hang over me the rest of my life."

"A man's gotta do what a man's gotta do."

Which *did* make it sound stupid because that was pretty much what he'd said. "I guess," he said lamely. "Thing is, I can't shake it, I'm not *gonna* shake it, I *know* that. I don't want to be dragging this around with us. When we go, we're leaving here clean. Everything's finished. No ties, nothing owed to anybody...but us."

After a moment, he could see the dim outline of her head nodding. Even if she didn't agree, she understood. "You said *part* of it." She took a deep drink from the cocoa mug.

"It's too late," he said flatly. "This is the kind of thing, once you start it, you gotta take it all the way to the finish. Things have been done and there's no taking 'em back. Even if I wanted to walk away now, I couldn't because people would come after us."

"Cops?"

"I'm not worried about *them.*"

"Oh." She took a last pull on her cigarette, finished her cocoa then sat quietly for a moment as if she was adding sums in her head, finally nodding with an answer. After a bit: "When did you say you were going?"

He felt her fingers fumble across the table in the dark finding his. "Sometime after dark."

With her other hand, poked at her half-eaten pizza slice in the box, like she was considering maybe picking it up again.

"Who you fooling?" he said. "Ray's, Famous Ray's; *you* can't tell the difference."

She shrugged. "I never said I had class either. Look who I hang out with."


Big Sid was snoring like a bulldog by the time Ronnie nosed the car to the curb back at the station house, his big head parked against the passenger window. He woke up Sid, and the two of them trudged lead-footed to the house, met Berman and Berberick outside on the front stairs, the two of them just coming through the double doors heading out on a call.

"Well, well, well," Berberick said, "Look who it is! Snow Black and one of his dwarfs."

"I'm not in the mood for you," Sid growled at Berberick, and then told Berman, "You better warn him I'm not in the mood for him. The Boss in?"

"And waiting," Berman said, cautioning.

"Yeah, see if you two douches can get 'im even *more* pissed," Berberick said, "'cause that makes a great day for *all* of us!"

Berman winced in a way signifying there was, sadly, something to what Berberick was saying. "He wants to know if either of you two have a watch, if you know how to tell time, so on and so forth, comments of that nature. Also, you had call-backs from DMV and Ballistics. I took the info down. It's on your desk."

"Thanks," Sid said.

"You been in the office this shift?"

"In and out this morning."

"So you don't know? About Cutler."

"He call in sick, again?"

"The pussy quit," Berberick cackled.

"He was waiting for Van Dyne when the captain came in this morning," Berman said. "Turned in his shield, his piece, a copy of a resignation letter he'd already dropped off at Personnel."

"Pussy," Berberick said.

Berman took a patient breath. "Go wait in the car, Berbs."

"I'm not your dog, *Sperm*-man," Berberick said.

"If you were, they'd make us put you down!" Big Sid said. "Fuck it, they think the same thing about you anyways!" and Sid detonated, lunging for Berberick with one hand while he grabbed for his holster with the other.

"*Jesus!*" Berman said, trying to get between them, pushing Berberick clear.

"*Jesus!*" Berberick said, flailing away at Sid with his short, stocky arms.

Ronnie didn't say anything, couldn't believe Sid was serious about going for his gun, but tried grabbing the big man's gun arm anyway because he wasn't 100% positive.

Berman finally managed to open some space between Sid and Berberick.

Sid stepped back, gulping air. "I *told* you!" he said to Berman, "I got no patience for this prick's bullshit today!"

This time, when Berman told him to go wait in the fucking car, Berberick didn't beef or hesitate, said something about them all being out of their crazy fucking minds and sped off down the street to one of the unmarked Buicks.

Berman shook his head over Berberick. "Insane. Cutler quits, but this guy we still have."

Sid had calmed down some. "So it's over? With Cutler?"

Berman shrugged. "Personnel told the captain to hold onto the letter for a few days in case Cutler changes his mind…but I don't think he will."

"Did he say why he was quitting?" Ronnie asked.

Berman looked at Sid with a nod toward Ronnie. "He really *is* young, isn't he?"

"Still wears diapers," Sid said as Ronnie followed him into the station.

As Ronnie trailed Sid upstairs to the squad room, he asked Sid if he had any idea why Cutler might've quit.

"What're you, nuts?" Sid said. "I *never* have a question when somebody quits. My question is why anybody fucking *stays.*"

"But neither Teixeira nor Malloi had any idea as to what might've lit the fire under Meara about going after Maiella?"

"Boss!" Big Sid said urgently, bracing himself in the corner between the seat and the passenger door. "Boss! That cab's not moving! Boss, he's letting people out! *Boss! Jesus—*"

The Buick swerved sharply left, then even more sharply right.

"*—Christ!*"

Ronnie, sitting in the back seat, heard the tires chirp, saw a bike messenger's God-save-me-please face flash past his window. Like a kid watching a horror movie, Ronnie turned his head away, half-closed his eyes so he could close them faster if he saw they were about to plow into something…or something was about to plow into them.

Back at the station, as soon as Big Sid had told the captain about the call from the DMV, Van Dyne had forgotten about dressing them down for obviously ignoring his instruction to be back before the morning was out, grabbed his coat, and roughly herded them out of his office, down the stairs and back to their car where he took the wheel.

"I was saying," Van Dyne continued, unperturbed by the close-calls with the cab or the bike messenger.

Big Sid, however, was still shaking his head over both almost-collisions. "Maybe it's as simple as Teixeira said: Good Guy versus Bad Guy."

Van Dyne shook his head. "There's got to be more to it than that. The lengths these two are going to? *Has* to be more."

Van Dyne threaded the car through First Avenue traffic apparently feeling any application of the brakes was a sign of weakness.

Big Sid – wincing at the brush-bys, honking horns and middle fingers raised in their direction – moved on to the call from Ballistics. "Four shootings in the last three years. Not just the same MO, but the same two weapons. According to Organized Crime, each one of those hits seemed to be about solving a problem for Tony Boy: a turf war, a suspected rat, that kind of thing. One of the weapons used last night matches one of the weapons used in those previous four hits. We should have those ballistics samples from Jersey this afternoon. I'll bet you lunch those Jersey guns match those four earlier hits, and the one that got away at Dell'Acqua's also matches up with the try on the girl."

"These guys seem like pros," Ronnie said. "I thought that was a rule with pros: get rid of the gun."

"This is a signature," Van Dyne explained.

"It's like a trademark, y'unnerstand," Big Sid said. "Tony Boy *wants* people to know this was his work. It's like him saying, '*This* is what happens when you fuck with *me!*'"

With another chirp of the tires, Van Dyne pulled off First and into the parking lots of Stuyvesant Town. He found Meara's building, rolled into a slot giving them a view of the entry foyer. Van Dyne and Sid shifted around in their seats, making themselves comfortable, then sat quietly for some time.

Whatever it was they were waiting for wasn't readily apparent to Ronnie and after a few minutes he softly asked, "I don't want to seem stupid—"

"Too late," Big Sid said.

Ronnie ignored him. "Can I ask what we're waiting for?"

"A way in," Van Dyne said.

"Why don't we just buzz the super?"

"We don't know how tight Meara is with the super," Big Sid explained. "If he's in there, maybe the super warns him we're coming. If he's not in there, maybe the super tells him, 'Ya know, you had visitors today.'"

"Until I have a better idea of what's going on," Van Dyne said, "I want to stay as invisible to him as he's been to us." Van Dyne studied Ronnie in the rear-view mirror for a second. "Weren't you supposed to get a haircut?"

They sat for a few more minutes.

"I may need you to work the weekend," Van Dyne said to Sid.

"I was supposed to be off Christmas."

"I'm short. Again. You heard about Cutler?"

"Berman told me."

"It doesn't surprise me," Van Dyne said. "Cutler always struck me as a very sharp young man."

"He's smarter than *me*," Big Sid said. "*He'll* be home for Christmas. If *any* of us had half a brain, we'd *all* buy a turkey farm upstate."

Van Dyne sat up in his seat. "Ahh. Here we go. Perfect."

Ronnie followed Van Dyne's eye-line to a young black woman pushing a baby stroller along the walk toward Meara's building, her baby so swaddled in blankets against the cold it looked like a ball of laundry.

When Van Dyne started to climb out of the car, Ronnie moved to follow, but Big Sid motioned him to stay put and to keep his eyes on Van Dyne.

It was about timing. Van Dyne had to pace himself, never looking anything more than casual, to enter the entry foyer only after the young mom had unlocked the inner foyer door but while she was still trying to wrestle her carriage through the doorway. Her guard would be down; she wouldn't be thinking mugger, purse-snatcher or any such thing, not of a middle-aged white guy in a Burberry coat looking like he'd stepped off the cover of *GQ*. And then, while this kindly, dapper businessman type offered to help her with her carriage, and went on about how cute her baby was – even if he could only see the kid's eyes through the blankets and snow suit and woolen cap – she would only half-notice Big Sid and Ronnie – also very casual, very matter of fact, very "Oh, hey, let me help you with that" – following her and her stroller and the helpful businessman through the door and to the elevator.

This elevator, Ronnie couldn't help but notice, didn't have Muzak or plush red carpeting or gold-flecked mirrors. It jerked along like it might stop any second, "Paco is a fagg!" and "Candy sux – apt 444!!!" were markered on the walls, and it smelled a little bit like pee.

Van Dyne kept up the baby-flattering chat with the mom for three floors, helped her wrangle the stroller out of the elevator and gave her a farewell smile and wave as she headed down the corridor. As soon as the elevator doors slid closed, Van Dyne's smile died, his waving hand dropped to his side, and he seemed to sag with exhaustion.

"Quite a charmer when you put your mind to it, Boss," Sid said. "Should go into politics. Shake hands, kiss babies..."

"You should shut up," Van Dyne said, wiping at his nose with a tissue.

They got off at Meara's floor, found his door, took a glance up and down the hall to make sure it was empty. Van Dyne asked for Ronnie's parka. The captain folded the parka into a square, cushy pillow, set it on the floor in front of Meara's door and used it for a kneeling pad.

"Why didn't you use Sid's coat?"

"Sid's coat? That's a *nice* coat."

Van Dyne reached inside his coat for a small, leather pouch; something like a manicure kit. But instead of nail clippers and files and the like, tucked inside were small, slender, polished steel blades and needles. Van Dyne studied the two locks on Meara's door, started trying different implements in the keyhole for the dead bolt.

Through one of the doors down the hall they could hear Jose Feliciano singing "Feliz Navidad"...over and over and over.

"Damn, I hate that song," Big Sid said. "Even more than Muzak Beatles." Then, after a bit, "I know it shouldn't, but it bothers me a respected precinct commander should have a set of those. It bothers me even more he knows how to use them."

"Don't let it worry you," Van Dyne said as he fiddled a blade and two needles into the lock for the dead bolt. "I'm not that respected. Here, grab that one at the top and help me turn this." The dead bolt clunked open and Van Dyne started on the keyhole in the doorknob.

"Can we do this?" Ronnie asked.

"I *am* doing this," Van Dyne said.

"I mean...is this, you know...*legal?*"

"I'm afraid a discussion of the relevant Constitutional issues will have to wait for another time," Van Dyne said. There was a click from the lock and the door swung open. "For now, the point is academic."

They quickly stepped inside and closed the door behind them.

Ronnie was immediately struck by the barrenness of Meara's apartment. It reminded him of bunkers he'd seen on cable documentaries about World War II.

"You two check the bedroom and bathroom," Van Dyne said. "I'll take the living room and kitchen."

"What're we looking for?" Ronnie asked.

"We'll know when we find it," Van Dyne said.

In the bedroom, Sid motioned Ronnie to take the closet.

Sid went for the dresser and methodically worked his way through the drawers. He'd pull each one, set it on the unmade bed, carefully go through its contents, examine the outside of the drawer to make sure nothing had been affixed there, then go down on his knee to feel around inside the drawer slot.

"Shit," Sid sighed.

"You find something?"

"No. It's that fucking song. I can't get it outta my head, irritating the piss outta me. And it reminded me I still got Christmas shopping to do, now *that's* irritating the piss outta me!"

Ronnie opened the bedroom's one closet and got hit again with that same, heavy, depressed feeling he'd had when he'd first stepped into Meara's apartment and for the same reason: there wasn't much there. One light sport jacket (for warm weather, Ronnie guessed), one dark sport jacket (for the colder months), a couple pairs of matching slacks. There were a few dress shirts, worn around the cuffs and collar, a few ties in not much better shape. There was one set of uniform blues, still in the plastic from the last time it had gone out to the cleaners. On the breast was the green/white/blue bar of a Meritorious Police Duty medal, and a second MPD medal with a green star in the white field for Exceptional Merit. Next to the blues was one of the old Department-issued winter coats that weren't used anymore; the kind with a double row of buttons running up to a high collar. Ronnie had heard the veterans talk about them in the locker room; they used to call wearing one being "in the bag," and said when you were in the bag you went downhill twice as fast as you went uphill because the coats were so damned heavy.

He stopped for a moment, turned for another look at the bedroom: the bed, a night table, the dresser. That was it. "Jesus."

"Song pissing you off, too?"

Ronnie was surprised; he hadn't realized he'd said it out loud. "I was just thinking…"

"Why do I always get a chill when you say that?"

"I mean, Jeez, look at this place. 20 years in the Department and this is all he's got?"

"You *really* want to get depressed? Go home with Berman, toilet he lives in in The Bronx. 27 years in. See what you got left after two divorces. Poor fucker *can't* retire; he'd starve."

On the floor of the closet were a pair of uniform shoes, a pair of loafers, a pair of coming-apart canvas sneakers. Ronnie poked inside the shoes.

There was one shelf across the top of the closet: some gloves, a scarf, a dusty uniform cap to go with the set of blues, the shield on its peak overdue for polishing. Meara's uniform duty belt, the leather cracked and so old it had the texture of felt, with his .38 service revolver buckled into the holster. Ronnie showed the gun to Sid, Sid showed it to Van Dyne.

"That goes with us," Van Dyne said. "If we can't find him, at least we can pull one of his fangs."

There were three shoeboxes on the shelf.

Ronnie took down the first one, set it on the bed. It was filled with bank statements, check stubs and registers, and the like. Ronnie found a passbook for a savings account, leafed through a few pages. "Hey, Sid!" He held up the account book. "This guy's got almost seven grand in the bank!"

Sid came over for a look, studied the pages closely. "You back to thinking payoffs?"

Ronnie shrugged, trying to look noncommittal...but he *was* thinking payoffs.

"Look at the dates of the deposits, kid. Like clockwork every two weeks."

"That's what made me think—"

"Look *hard* at those dates, kid. Those are paydays."

"Oh. Still, seven thousand bucks—"

"He's single, hasn't bought a new car since Henry Ford, and he lives like a fucking monk. If I didn't have a wife, a daughter in college and a mortgage, I'd be living like King Farouk."

Still, Sid showed Van Dyne the bankbook. Van Dyne kept it with the holster: "Cut him off from his money, maybe we can starve him into the open."

Ronnie set the second shoebox down on the bed and opened it. The box was filled with photographs. There were the big rectangles of 35 mm shots, curled black-and-whites with a little pull-tab from old Polaroid Instamatics, the garish color of the 1950s and early 1960s. There were pictures of parties and backyard barbecues, pictures of children and old men and women, pictures of people just *being* – sitting around a dinner table, a game of cards, together on the stoop of one those narrow houses you saw squeezed together in the working class neighborhoods of Queens or Brooklyn. It was the record of a life.

There were several recurring faces and after sifting through a few pictures Ronnie began to put together a face with the DMV descrip of Jack Meara. Not bad looking, but not exceptional, someone who wouldn't stand out in a crowd. He seemed to have been a guy who wasn't reluctant to horse around for the camera, to plant sloppy smooches on the two older people Ronnie took to be his mom and dad.

There was a photo taken in a cramped kitchen, a "CONGRATULATIONS!!!!" banner hanging overhead, and a young –

as young as Ronnie – Jack Meara in a crisp, new-looking set of blues. He had one arm around his father, and his other arm was actually holding the squealing little figure of his mother off the floor. It didn't say it anywhere in the picture but Ronnie knew; the pride in the faces of the parents, the "CONGRATULATIONS!!!!" banner, the exuberance of the young man in the middle, those razor-creased new blues; that was the day Meara had graduated from the Police Academy.

Ronnie remembered the snapshots his mom had taken of his own graduation, the party with family afterward. We all look the same that day, he thought, we come out and think we're going to fix the world.

There was another recurring face: a girl. Pretty in a mousey sort of way. The way she kept appearing in the stack of photos, the way Meara looked at her, kidded with her...she was no date, no casual acquaintance. And sure enough, deeper into the box, there were pictures of her – still just a girl – and young Meara (probably around the same time he'd been in the Academy) with him in a tux, she in a simple wedding dress in a park standing under a pink-flowered tree in one of those sappy, moony pictures wedding photographers seemed obligated to make new couples take. The same two people splashing in the surf on a crowded Coney Island beach; posing alongside a beast of a sparkling white Chrysler (newly bought, Ronnie guessed); perched on the same car under a "WELCOME TO LAKE GEORGE" sign.

He sifted through the box looking for pictures of Lourdes Bracero. There were none, and that's what made him notice there were no pictures taken after a certain point; at least none that had been kept. Time had stopped in the shoebox not long after those two happy people had dripped young love into each other's eyes under a tree full of pink blossoms.

Ronnie gently put the lid back on the box. He looked around the sparse bedroom, at Sid rummaging through the dresser, wondering how you went from the smiling times and pink blossoms he'd seen in the shoebox to this.

He turned to the last shoebox, a large square one, the kind used for boots. He opened it and said, "Oh."

He said it in a certain kind of way which made Sid curious, made him come over to see what was in the box holding Ronnie so transfixed.

Then Sid, too, said, "Oh." And then, "Boss? Come see this."

The shoebox was filled to the rim with papers. On top was an article clipped from a newspaper. There was a picture of a heavy-set middle-aged man in a very nice overcoat with a mane of white hair as well-coiffed as Van Dyne's. He was on the steps of the courthouse down on Centre Street. And he was smiling. Across the top of the article were the excited italics of *The Daily News* shouting, *"'Teflon Tony' Walks – Again!"* The subhead read, *"Third Strike for DA v Reputed Mob Boss."*

Then Van Dyne was standing with them. He blinked his eyes – still red and watery with the flu – to clear them, slipped on his reading glasses and took up the clipping. There were other newspaper stories just below: stories on the acquittal from other papers, editorials on why the trial had gone the way it did. Still further: articles covering every stage of the trial from *"DA Gains Indictment Against 'Teflon Tony,'"* to *"Mob Boss Trial Starts Today"* to *"Jury Hears Closing Arguments in Maiella Case."*

"So," Sid said, "all this – " and he waved at the shoebox " – is him following Tony Boy's trial?"

Van Dyne dug deeper into the box. "No. This goes back years. And it's not just about Maiella."

Mixed in with newspaper clippings were Xeroxes of detectives' notes, copies of NYPD records, Department of Corrections records, parole records, still more articles. Some were yellowed with age, brittle like parchment.

"Not just him," Van Dyne said and held up another newspaper clipping: "'Suspected associate of reputed gangland leader Anthony

215

'Tony Boy' Maiella...'" Another story: "'Allegedly connected to mob boss Tony Boy Maiella...'" And another: "'Long thought by police to have ties to organized crime and particularly mobster Anthony Maiella...'"

"He's been mapping out Tony Boy's whole organization," Big Sid said. "For years."

"This stuff roughly seems to follow a reverse chronology," Van Dyne observed, "most recent to oldest. So, if we're going to get to the bottom of this, I surmise we need to get to the *bottom*." He covered the box, held the lid in place with one hand, put his other underneath – "Like so" – and neatly flipped the box over on its lid. Carefully, he shimmied the box clear, leaving the contents in a neat, upended pile on the bed. *"Voila!"* He reached for the face-down top sheet – an aged piece of newsprint – but he hesitated for a second, his fingers flexing. "'What mighty contests rise from trivial things,'" the captain murmured, like a prayer kept to himself. Then he turned the paper over and laid it back on the stack.

There were headshots of two cops: the newspaper had used their official ID pictures. Ronnie recognized one of them immediately; an unsmiling version of the face that, in the other shoebox, had been one big grin on the Academy's graduation day. Over the pictures of the two young officers ran the headline: *Rookie Cops Felled in West Side Shootout,"* and then underneath, the subhead, *"One Dead, One Critical, Gunman Escapes."*

The captain picked up the clipping and began to read:

"'Two newly-minted NYPD patrolmen were gunned down in a West Side tenement early this morning...yadda yadda yadda...pronounced dead at the scene was PO Raymond T. McInerney, 25, of Rego Park...yadda yadda...wife and two children...yadda yadda..." Van Dyne paused, then silently read ahead, sighed and nodded his head with understanding. "'Critically wounded was PO John H. Meara, 26...'"

"What was the date?" Big Sid asked and took the clipping from Van Dyne. "He's retiring next month?" Sid did some quick math. "Would've still been a probie. Jesus, barely know how to write out a parking citation and you take a bullet? *I* woulda put in my papers right then! But what's the connection to Maiella?"

"'Gunman escapes,'" Van Dyne quoted.

"You think –"

Van Dyne didn't let Sid finish. He scooped all the papers back into the box. "Let's go."

Sid started to put the dresser drawers back in place.

"Leave it," Van Dyne said. "Leave everything the way it is. I *want* this sonofabitch to know we were here. Maybe if he knows we're on to all this, that'll be enough to scare him into a cease-and-desist."

"You think so?" Sid said doubtfully.

"No." The captain stopped in the living room to pick up Meara's holstered pistol. "But I can hope."


"They had him," Big Sid said.

"And they lost him," Van Dyne said.

Sid and the captain were sitting in the front seat of the Buick, still parked in front of Meara's building. They were going through papers from the shoebox on the seat between them.

Sid held up a sheet of paper for Ronnie slouching, bored, and feeling left out in the back seat. The paper was some kind of form. "Arrest report," Sid explained. "You never saw one of these, huh, kid? I don't even remember how long ago they stopped using these."

"How come the parts they filled in are so blurry?"

Big Sid chuckled. "Carbon paper. Maybe you read about it in history books." He pointed to a box on the form labeled "Subject Name." Even typed in smeary blue letters, Ronnie recognized the name of Maiella, A.J. "Meara picked him out of a photo array. That's how they got him."

Van Dyne sucked meditatively on a tooth. "It wasn't enough. According to these memos between the DA's office and Meara's precinct commander, the DA had reason to think Meara's ID was too iffy to hold up at trial. There were no other witnesses, no physical evidence... They couldn't hold him."

"So that's what all this is about?" Ronnie asked. "Meara's been hunting Maiella for the last 20 years?"

"No," Van Dyne said. "Not hunting. Sidney's colleague at Manhattan South said Meara's played by the rules up until now. I don't think he's been hunting Maiella. I think he's been keeping track of him."

"And he waits 20 years to do something about it?"

"A little less than 19, actually," Van Dyne said. He set the memos from the District Attorney's office back in the box, reached inside his coat for his case of Paris Opals. He struck a match, lit one of the slim, dark cigarettes, took a few puffs, made a wry face and dropped it out the car window. "Not the same." He pointed over his shoulder at Ronnie: "That's your fault."

Van Dyne ran his fingers through his thick hair, careful not to disturb it too much. "I'm loathe to play armchair psychologist, but think of it, Junior. Maiella kills one cop, puts our man in the hospital. And he walks. Meara IDs him, but he still walks. 19 years Meara's keeping an eye on him, waiting for him to get – to borrow a word from Booth Tarkington – his 'comeuppance.' And it never happens. Quite the contrary." Van Dyne poked around in the box of paper: "Maiella comes up through the ranks. He makes boss. He gets arrested, sometimes he even gets indicted, sometimes he even winds up in court...but each time he walks. All that time, Meara's waiting for the scales to even out...and they never do."

"So, this last acquittal with Maiella," Ronnie said, "that's like some kinda last straw?"

"I suppose that's the nub of it," Van Dyne said. "Everybody has their fault lines. Hit them just right, keep hitting them, tap-tap-tap for 20 years...*crack.*"

"Now do we call IAB?" Ronnie asked.

Van Dyne continued looking through the papers as if he'd heard nothing.

"I know it's not exactly PPP," Sid said, "but I'm still for holding our nose, turning the other way, let this crazy fucker do whatever he wants to do."

"As tempting as that may be, Sidney, and putting aside the various legal and Departmental issues that would consequently arise, I keep remembering that one of my people is in the hospital because of this guy, and that he almost got his girlfriend killed. Collateral damage, Sidney. In the movies, Dirty Harry never misses. Things don't always work out so neatly in real life."

"Here they are," Sid said. He was pointing to a Buick like theirs which had rolled into the parking lot. He waved at them to pull up alongside.

The Buick slid up on Van Dyne's side of the car, the windows went down. Ronnie recognized the two guys in the car as patrolmen from the house, only they were dressed in their street clothes. The black cop in the passenger seat was Horn, and the white guy at the wheel with the permanent five o'clock shadow was Moffie.

Van Dyne pointed to the building behind them. "That is the subject structure. You are to keep the entrance of the subject structure under observation. You are looking for a John – or Jack – Meara." Van Dyne gave them a description. "He is a police officer. If you see him, you are to approach with caution, confirm his identification, request he surrender his weapon, and thereafter escort him back to the station. If I am not there, have me notified and hold him until I get there. In the interim, you are not to allow him contact with anyone else: nobody at his station house, nobody at our house, not his PBA lawyer, *nobody*, do you understand? You hold him incommunicado until I get there."

Moffie and Horn looked at each other. Nothing about that smelled good to them.

"Uh, Captain?" asked Horn, raising his hand a bit as if he was in class. "What if he doesn't want to go with us? Or give us his gun? Or –"

"You are to use any means necessary to gain his full compliance," Van Dyne said icily. "*Any* means. Am I understood?"

They didn't understand, not really, but past Van Dyne's ear they could see Big Sid miming giving someone a sharp rap on the head with a baton. *That* they understood and nodded their affirmations to Van Dyne.

The captain reached for the ignition. "You'll be relieved when I can find enough warm bodies to relieve you," he said as the engine coughed and settled into a rough idle. "I'd truly appreciate it if you two manage not to fuck this up."


Ronnie staggered into his apartment, gave the door a push behind him as he passed hoping it would close but not really caring if it didn't. He took a few steps and fell face down on his futon, still in his parka, still in his shoes.

There hadn't been anything more to do after they'd left Stuyvesant Town, but hope Meara surfaced either at Lourdes Bracero's place or his own apartment and the respective surveillance team picked him up when he did. Back at the stationhouse, Van Dyne had retreated to his office with the shoebox, intending to sift through it in the thin hope there might be some kind of lead in all that stuff, and had told Ronnie and Big Sid to go home to – finally – get some rest.

Almost as soon as his face hit the scratchy upholstery of the futon cushion, Ronnie's phone rang. He was of half a mind to let his answering machine take it, but he worried it might be news of a fresh development so he reached down to the floor for the phone, fumbled the receiver out of the cradle and parked it close to his face. "Umph."

"This is your *mother!*"

"You gotta be fucking kidding me."

"*What* did you say to me?" she honked. "*What* did you say to your *mother? That's* the kind of language you use on the *phone* these days?"

"Sorry, Mom, I thought you were somebody else."

"Like who? Who would you talk to like that?"

"Did you want something, Mom?"

"Where've you been?" I've been calling you all week—"

"I've been working."

"All day and all night? I've been calling you all hours!"

"I *know*," he said.

"Don't get smart. I'm still your *mother.*"

A siren wailed in the street below. Ronnie pulled himself up, looked out the window. Traffic had snarled somewhere down the block and an ambulance was jammed in front of his building.

"What's all that noise?" his mother asked.

He slid back down onto the futon. "Nothing."

"That doesn't sound like nothing. That sounds like a siren."

"It's just an ambulance, Mom."

"It sounds like it's in your living room! Are you all right?"

"Fine. Hunky dory. Did you want something?"

"The same thing I've been calling about all week! Are you coming home for Christmas? Your cousins are coming, the aunts from Toms River—"

"I—"

"—everybody's asking—"

"I have to work, Mom."

"On Christmas?"

"I don't think I'll be able to get time off until after New Year's. We're short-handed."

"Because of that *mess*, right? That *mess* with all those policemen taking money! *You're* not part of that *mess*, are you?"

"No, Mom."

"Are you sure?"

"I think I'd know."

"I think you'd *lie* to me if you were. You *better* lie if you are because I'll come after you with a wooden spoon if you're doing something you're not supposed to!"

"I—"

"Everybody's going to be sitting around the table eating turkey and lasagna – your Aunt Jo's bringing her lasagna, you know how you like her lasagna…"

"I—"

"… wondering why you can't take a lousy three-hour drive to spend Christmas with your family."

"I gotta *work!* What do you want from me?"

"Don't get snippy with *me!* You don't get snippy with your *mother!* What're you going to do for Christmas? Just sit there by yourself?"

"I know some people, we'll do something. Maybe I'll even get a tree."

"You don't have a tree? It's almost Christmas, you don't have a tree? Your cousin Andrew's a *bum,* the only thing he spends money on is cigarettes and beer, and even *he* has a tree!"

"Mom—"

"I didn't want you to be a policeman, you know."

"I know, you're always—"

"Not even *here!* But *especially* not up *there!* With all that *mess!* You could've gone to Monmouth County, got a degree in whatever it is your cousin Russell does where you *don't* have to carry a gun—"

"Ma, I gotta go."

"—just like your father, no talking to you—"

"Ma, I gotta *go!* There's somebody at the door."

"Who? Who's at the door?"

"I don't know! That's why I gotta get off the phone so I can answer the damn door!"

"Watch your mouth with me! I think you're just saying that to get off the phone!"

"I *really* gotta go, Mom."

She didn't say anything for a few seconds, and Ronnie felt something soft in that silence. Then, quietly, "Are you sure you're all right?"

"I'm fine, Mom."

"You don't sound fine."

"Just tired. Long day. I gotta go."

"Behave."

He fumbled the receiver back into its cradle. The ambulance outside had worked its way clear, its siren a fading echo. It was quiet and still in the apartment, and for once he was uncomfortable with that. He flipped the hood of his parka over his head, closed his eyes, and one breath later he was asleep – for what seemed like just minutes before he felt a soft but nonetheless irritating series of pokes in his back.

"Ronnie, like, what're you *doing?*"

"Mom, would you *please* let it *go?*"

It finally soaked through the parka hood over his head as well as several layers of grogginess that the voice Ronnie was hearing was not that of a honking, irritated middle-aged mother, but the sing-songy whine of a much younger if no less irritating female. "Tamela?"

She looked like something out of a Madonna video: white denim jacket so brief it was practically a vest with shoulder pads sticking out so far they looked like diving boards, glitter-spattered pink T-shirt, some kind of black knicker-like tights, frilly tops of a kid's lacey ankle socks sticking out the top of black canvas sneakers, fingerless black leather gloves. There was whore-red gloss on her lips, some sparkly stuff painted on her eyelids. She'd bleached her hair a frighteningly unnatural blonde-almost-white – which hardly blended with her Asian features – and had somehow affixed a piece of wide, filmy red ribbon to the short, blindingly light spikes of her hair.

"How'd you get in?" Ronnie groaned.

"Your door was open which is, like, incredibly *crazed* to do in New York." She was looking at the casserole dish she'd brought over days before, still sitting on Ronnie's little stove. "You didn't eat my casserole?"

Ronnie struggled to sit upright. He didn't know how long he'd been asleep, but it hadn't been enough. He tried to focus his eyes out the window: it was dark. "I meant to, really," he said, "it looked terrific, but I've hardly been home, Tam. I've been working."

She nodded, put on the kind of brave smile people do who are used to getting their feelings hurt. She dropped on the futon next to him. "Like, why aren't you ready?"

"For...?"

"The *party*, Ronnie! Don't you remember? This guy from my school? A *party? Christmas* party? You promised you'd come?"

Ronnie had a dim memory of Tamela saying something to him about a party when she'd brought the casserole over, but damned if he remembered expressing any kind of interest. But now he felt bad over the uneaten casserole and Tamela having gone to all the trouble of ruining her hair for the occasion. He nodded resignedly, said something about getting into a fresh shirt and throwing some water on his face.

"Actually," she said, "not to be, like, *rude?* But maybe you should take a shower? 'Cause it is, like, a *party?*" She wrinkled her little button nose a bit. "'Cause, not to be, like, *rude?* But you *are* kinda *ripe.*"

Ronnie lifted an arm and took a sniff. He *was* kind of ripe.

"We have time," Tamela said. "It's not, like, one of those parties where there's, like, you know, a special *time* you have to be there.

People're gonna be in and out all night. It's gonna be *crazed* like that!" which seemed to appeal to her.

Ronnie gave another resigned nod, hauled himself to his feet letting his parka slide off and shuffled off toward the bathroom.

Tamela leaned back on the futon, a bit to one side, something cat-like in her pose. "Want me to scrub your back?"

"Thanks, no, I can scrub my own back," he said through a yawn.

"Sure?"

He pulled off his sweatshirt and gently threw it at her, landing it on her head. "If you ever want to get out of here and make it to your party, behave."

Her little nose wrinkled again over the sweatshirt. "Ew, *Ronnie!* When *was* the last time you had a shower?"

Ronnie stood in the bathroom doorway a second, considering the question. "Damned if I remember."


Stake-out duty requires an almost Zen-like ability to maintain one's focus – maybe for hours, maybe days, maybe even months – on absolutely nothing, waiting/hoping/eventually praying something – *anything* – will happen to break the boredom. This makes it a hard pull even for veteran cops.

Officers Moffie and Horn had 13 years on the force between them, but this had been as patrolmen. Stake-out duty had not been one of their typical activities. Consequently, about an hour after Van Dyne had left them at Stuyvesant Town, the excitement of being – even if only for the day – upgraded to plainclothes work had worn off and their minds began to wander.

Officer Moffie's eyes kept drifting from the front door of the subject structure to watch young women coming home from work. He was married, but not a fanatic about it, and it was a favorite thing of his to watch young women in long coats, looking for the coat to flap open in

225

the hope that underneath they would be wearing a short skirt and he'd get a glimpse of stockinged thigh.

But then the daylight faded, and all the young women were home. Lights came on in the building, warm yellow lamps, cold blue TVs.

Officer Moffie shifted and fidgeted in his seat. His fingers and toes were cold. He started the engine and cranked up the heater. "I'm either sweatin' or freezin' in here," Moffie muttered as he finagled with the heater controls. "There's no way to make this, like, just *nice.*"

Officer Horn was flipping through a copy of *The New York Post,* holding it up to the window, trying to read it by the parking lot lamps. "Hey, lookit this," Officer Horn said, holding his newspaper over for Officer Moffie to get a look.

"I can't see it," Officer Moffie said. "What is it?"

"They had another case of that thing. Out in Staten Island."

*"What* thing?"

"That thing eats your skin."

"What? Leprosy?"

"No, dummy. What is it?" Officer Horn held the newspaper up to the light. "'Streptococcal group A,'" he read. "Takes the flesh right off ya." Officer Horn studied the photograph accompanying the story. "Oof. They shouldn't show pictures of that stuff in the papers."

"The guy die?"

"Woman. I dunno." Officer Horn squinted at the paper. "Nah. I bet that puts a crimp in her love life, though."

"I thought it was only leprosy did that."

"Well, see, this doesn't always eat your flesh, it says here, this strepto-whatever. Sometimes it's like the flu, except, man, you get that, you're gone in *hours.* Zip."

"No shit?"

"No shit." They sat quietly for a while, then Officer Moffie said, "I had an uncle worked the One-20-Two out on Staten Island. Told me they *did* used to have lepers out there."

"No shit? On Staten Island? They had a *leper* thing out there? Whatcha call it? A leper colony?"

"Well, no, not like a leper *colony*. It wasn't like in *Ben-Hur* or anything. It was some kinda *hospital,* a regular hospital, like a sanitarium or something. And they don't like to call it leprosy. Gets people all shkeived out."

"Well, yeah."

"It's Something Disease. I forget. I used to know it. Somebody's name, prolly the guy who discovered it or something. Something Disease."

"Out on Staten Island? It's still there?"

"Folded up years ago, my uncle said."

"So where'd they go?"

"Who?"

"The *lepers,* man!"

"How the hell do I know?"

"You think some of 'em are still around?"

"I dunno! This is *years* ago my uncle's talking about."

"Jesus," Officer Horn said and looked again at the picture in the paper showing the results of a streptococcal group A infection. "Isn't that contagious? Leprosy's contagious, isn't it?"

"I know 'cause *I'm* a Something Disease specialist."

"Is *this* stuff contagious?" Officer Horn shook the newspaper to indicate he meant streptococcal group A.

"Wazzit say?"

"I can't see. Bleah. I may never eat in a salad bar again. Find a finger in the Bac-O-Bits from one of these Something Disease guys."

The parking lot flashed through with a bright, white light and on the tail of the flash came a sharp *BOOM* thudding into their chests followed by the clatter and tinkle of debris and glass hitting the parking lot pavement.

The suddenness of it had left them both frozen, then they each found their breath, found themselves gasping. Even before they looked out the windshield, they both knew which windows were blown out, and both sensed – without quite knowing how – that they had screwed up.

Officer Moffie finally found the nerve to look upwards to find what he knew he'd find where he knew he'd find it: six floors up, a pair of glassless windows filled with smoke.

"Fuck me," he said.


Ronnie had not been in New York long before he'd learned all that crap about how The City never slept was just that: crap. If it was late enough, and the mercury had dropped far enough, parts of The City were dead as cemeteries. Oh, there were islands out there in the dark where things jumped until the sun came up, punk clubs like the Mudd Club, the Roxy, Danceteria, a bunch of others springing up like mushrooms the last few years in old storefronts and warehouses and piers. There were titty bars, queer bars, galleries more about all-night wine-and-weed parties than art. But between those isles of noise and light were vast stretches with nothing on the street but a few bums wrapped in filthy scavenged blankets, huddled in doorways, or trying to stay warm on subway grates.

Ronnie was in one of the dead spots, far enough uptown even Broadway was dark and dead. The street belonged to tank-like Checker cabs which wouldn't stop on the assumption anyone out this late was likely trouble. There was an occasional hansom cab with a well-dressed couple bundled together under a blanket in the rear seat, the driver up on his – or her – bench, slumped inside a heavy coat and piled scarf, top hat pulled low, the sway-backed horse clopping down the street, tired head bobbing, muzzle crusted with frost, body steaming in the cold.

The party was crammed into a loft close to the Hudson; too many people, too much smoke – legal and illegal – too much blaring stereo. Ronnie quickly lost Tamela in a group dressed like her. He felt out of place in his white linen shirt and his "good" jeans, the ones with a crease.

He found a sheltered corner behind a refrigerator, holed up with a Michelob and a paper plate of deviled eggs. Around the corner of the fridge he could hear a conversation between what must be an actor and an actress:

"I knew you were working!" the actor effused.

"Really?" the actress said.

"Oh, yes! I could tell!"

"Really? *Really?* How could you tell?"

"Oh, it shows!"

*"Really?"*

"Oh, yes! In your face! You look so *alive!"*

The tide of people in the loft swept the actor and actress away. Another pair washed up. One was saying how she hadn't cried so much since The Beatles had broken up.

"*I* didn't cry," her companion declared. "I kept hoping that nut who shot Lennon would escape and get the other three."

Ronnie tried to move out of his corner but was blocked by two young men hovering over the stereo, going through the rack of albums.

"What're you looking for?" one asked.

"A waltz would be nice."

"A waltz? Tell me you're kidding!"

"Don't you ever feel like a good waltz? Don't you ever say, 'Today's a great day for a waltz!'? C'mon, don't tell me that Strauss guy doesn't make your nuts jump!"

Ronnie started back to his cubbyhole by the fridge.

"And that's when I heard; he's got the sickness."

229

"Jesus. That's almost everybody I know who was on the island last summer!"

"Everybody who was at the house."

"You're sure?"

"That's what I heard. Big purple spot and everything."

As soon as Ronnie got himself back into his cubby, the actor and the actress washed back up. She was screaming to be heard over the other partiers and whatever was blaring out of the stereo speakers.

"No subtext, he tells me!" she said. "I go up to this guy, this other character whom I'm not even supposed to *know*, and I just blurt out, 'Why don't you fuck me you big black buck!' And he tells me there's no *subtext?*"

Ronnie had made enough ground that he could look down Broadway and see the lights of Times Square. That *was* a part of The City that never slept. Even at two in the morning, the Square was still glowing.

It was the garish gleam of a cheap circus coming from the cold, ugly lights of late-night arcades, porn shops, all-night grindhouses. There was another glow, further down at the southern edge of the Square, by the base of the Times Tower, at the intersection with 42nd Street – The Deuce. Ronnie could see a cab burning, and a crowd was drawing around.

"I'm hot," the girl said after she nuzzled her way into his cubby by the fridge, apparently enjoying the close quarters. She had a rough, handsome face, a throaty voice. She was slim, athletic-looking, and evidently not too interested in preliminaries. "I said I'm *hot*."

He offered her a sip of his beer.

"I don't mean hot like that. I mean…*hot*."

"Oh."

"Think you could help me out?"

"Excuse me?"

"You know..."

"Now? *Now?*"

"You with somebody?"

Ronnie looked around the crowded room but didn't see Tamela. "Well, uh—"

"Then there's no problem." She took him by the hand with a firm grip and led him out into the hall.

Ronnie stopped at the top of Times Square, trying to plot a course across. Most of the sidewalks were blocked by construction. Bulldozers and cranes were eating into the few remaining old buildings or had already begun erecting skeletons of dark steel to build new glass-faced towers like the ones which had already begun walling in the Square.

He cut across the traffic islands in the middle of the Square, walking across the metal grills covering the transformers which never stopped humming and kept the glittery billboards and noisy arcades and porn theater marquees lit.

Ronnie wondered if anybody was still in the burning cab.

It had felt good to get out of the crowded loft when the girl had pulled him into the hall. It was empty and cool there, and – aside from the stereo bleeding through the wall, telling him to Wang Chung tonight – relatively quiet. The girl led him up a narrow, unlit stairwell to the roof. In the shadows her hands began roaming all over him. She clamped her mouth on his and her tongue shot deep.

Ronnie gasped for breath. "Look, why don't we hop a train to my place—"

"I can't wait." Her hand went to his crotch. Her face turned disappointed. "Your heart isn't in this."

"Give it a minute."

They went back to kissing and clutching. Her hands worked on enthusing him – quite adeptly, as it turned out – but every time his hands reached for her so Ronnie could return the favor, she gently batted them away. Finally, he got a hand between her slim, muscled thighs, reached up to where her legs came together, and, where there shouldn't have been a bulge…there was a bulge.

Ronnie retracted his tongue from her mouth and backed against the stairwell wall.

"Can't blame me for trying," she – or he – said (Ronnie wasn't sure of the proper pronoun). "Sure, you're not interested?"

Ronnie nodded dumbly, forced a polite but weak smile. He rubbed the sore back of his head where it had rebounded off the wall.

"No hard feelings?"

He shook his head, doing a poor job of looking unfazed.

"Go back and enjoy the party." He – or she – laughed and gave him a peck on the cheek. She – or he – started down the stairs, then stopped at the hallway and looked back up to him. "You know, you should consider yourself flattered."

The fire in the taxicab was dying. The bright, yellow shell of the Checker was blackened, smoke still rolled out the windows, the panes of which had burst from the heat. The smoke had the sick smell of burning rubber, gasoline, and vinyl, giving the air a greasy, sticky feel.

Ronnie tried to skirt the crowd gathering around the fire, occasionally stopping to go up on tiptoe to see what was happening.

"Hey, man. Hey, *man!*"

Ronnie came down off his toes, found a black man standing in front of him in a ragged pea coat and unraveling watch cap.

"Hey, man," he said, "I know 's col', man, 'n' I don' wanna hassle you or nuffin', but mebbe ya gots some change, some loose change or somethin', righ'? I mean, like, I know 's 'n' imposition-like,"n' I'm sorry, man, but if ya gots *anythin'*…"

Ronnie looked at the uremic eyes, the gap-toothed smile. He took in the sneakers stuffed with old newspapers. Ronnie dug into his pocket and handed over some change without counting it.

"Oh, hey, man, thanks a lot! Really! I *really* 'preciates it!"

Ronnie nodded, but the guy didn't go away. The beggar looked at the change in his hand, then back to Ronnie.

"This all ya got?"

Ronnie pushed past him.

"This *all* ya *got?*" the beggar called after him.

Ronnie made it past the expanding fringe of the crowd to 42$^{nd}$ Street. The smoke from the cab was drifting slowly down 42$^{nd}$, wrapping around grindhouse marquees carrying titles like *Driller Killer* and *Taboo American Style*, past the blinking lights of porno arcades with neon-lit names like The Blackjack and The Naked Eye.

The crowd around the cab flexed. People on the inside, afraid of the fire, pushed back; people on the outside pushed forward for a better look.

The din hammered at Ronnie's head. There was shouting and hollering, and boom boxes moving through the crowd with their overcranked speakers blaring out music in a half-dozen different languages and styles. There were rap Christmas carols, salsa Christmas carols, rock Christmas carols, all of them in overmodulating fuzz. Pushers moved through the crowd like vendors at a ball game: "Coke, smoke, coke, smoke, free toot! You don' like, you don' hafta buy!" Traffic was backing up on 42$^{nd}$. Horns honked; people climbed on top of their cars to see the fire.

Then came the sirens.

The Midtown beat cops were already there, and blue-and-whites were bringing more. They were trying to herd the crowd out of the way to make a hole for the wailing pumper from the 43$^{rd}$ Street firehouse.

In the street in front of Ronnie, an impatient U-Haul edged out of the stopped traffic and tried to U-turn. The truck swung too wide; the front wheels jumped the far curb. One fender clipped a "No Parking – Bus Stop" sign. The top of the cargo box crunched into a movie marquee announcing a Vanessa del Rio triple-X retrospective and the plastic marquee letters clattered to the sidewalk.

The theater bouncer came running out of the lobby carrying a Louisville Slugger. He cursed the truck driver and banged on the door of the cab with the baseball bat. The two guys in the truck cab spat back Spanish obscenities as the driver tried to restart the stalled truck. A pair of Midtown cops ran in to break up the discussion before it got physical.

Ronnie turned west on 42nd, away from the fire. He stopped short to avoid colliding with an old man coming out of a small candy-and-cigarettes kiosk jammed between a porno shop and a grindhouse showing *Piranha.* The old man was carrying a dead mouse – still in the Victor trap that had almost cut it in half – in a dustpan to the curb.

Ronnie turned the other way, hurrying for the corner subway entrance leading down into Times Square Station, hoping he wouldn't have to wait long for a train, and taking some comfort – which he rarely did – in the fact that he had a gun on his hip.


This time Ronnie remembered to hook the chain on his door, throw the bolt and set the anti-burglar bar hoping all that would at least slow Tamela down. Heading for the futon to recreate his headfirst dive into fully-clothed sleep from earlier in the evening, he tossed a sad glance at the still unassembled pieces of his Sopwith Camel model on the coffee table, trying to remember when last he'd worked on it, then turned back to the futon and was ready to take his fall, when he noticed his answering machine on the floor blinking with six messages.

His mother – or even Tamela – wasn't *that* big a pain in the ass. He dropped on to the floor next to the phone but before he could replay the messages, the phone rang. He quickly scooped it up.

"Pete?"

"There's nobody named Pete here," Ronnie said.

"Is he coming back soon?"

"There's no Pete. Nobody named Pete lives here."

"Are you sure?"

"Positive."

"Your name's not Pete?"

"Not even close."

"Oh." A pause, then, "Well, what're *you* doing now?"

"I'm getting ready to go to bed."

"Ah, bed. That's a nice place to be. Can I ask you a question? Are you gay?"

Jesus, Ronnie thought, am I giving off some kind of *scent* or something tonight? "Nope."

"You sure?"

"Look, buddy, I'm a cop."

"So?"

Ronnie hung up. All that noise up in Times Square, the cold, the exhaustion... The break in his nose was throbbing, the pain spiderwebbing up into his forehead.

The phone rang again. He picked it up, irritated. "Listen, pal, if you don't want to get your ass busted—"

"What the fuck is your problem?"

"Sid?"

"I been calling all night. Where you been?"

"What's the matter?"

"You better get down here, kid. Right away."

"Down where?"

"Meara's place. This thing just went really, really bad."

It was a 15-minute crosstown jog along empty streets for Ronnie from his place in the Village to Stuyvesant Town. He could see the parking lot boiling with flashes of colored lights when he was still more than a block away, like a Christmas display in garish primary tones: red, blue, and yellow.

But there was nothing festive about the lot. The yellow flashes were from Con Ed trucks, the red from the ambulances and fire trucks, the blue from police cruisers and the blockhouse shape of the Bomb Squad's rig, all of them clustered around the entrance to Meara's building. There were a couple of uniforms stretching crime scene tape on the bare ground below Meara's blown-out windows to keep people off the broken glass and debris there, conferring knots of cops and firemen, firemen and the guys from Con Ed.

Ronnie looked up; even this late the building was alive, it seemed like all the buildings in Stuyvesant Town were alive, apartment lights on, people in bathrobes at the windows, staring, gawking. He saw the glass-less windows of Meara's apartment six floors up, wisps of smoke drifting out to be caught and spun by the wind, the silhouette of helmeted firemen inside against the sweep of flashlights.

He was moving toward the building unaware of his moving legs, indifferent to the bite of the cold on his face. His face was burning though, the headache he'd had back at his place now grown into some white-hot blinding thing and he had to squint to keep the charred squares of Meara's windows in focus.

Somebody was talking to him, a familiar voice, but he couldn't place it – Big Sid? Sergeant Troupe? – tugging at his sleeve, trying to slow him, stop him.

Fragments of the monologue drifted into focus "…first thought maybe a gas explosion…some people shook up but thank God nobody else hurt…waiting for Con Ed to cut everything, make sure it's safe…you better stay here."

The tug on his sleeve became a firm clamp.

236

A stretcher was being wheeled out the front doors of the building toward a nearby ambulance.

"Even one of the EMTs got sick," the voice told him.

Ronnie shook the hand on his arm loose, felt himself moving, again, faster, toward the stretcher.

It wasn't right, the shape wasn't right. Even under the red-mottled sheet tucked – thankfully – tightly in place around the body he could tell it wasn't right, it was lopsided, like a drawing by a kid who doesn't know how to make both sides equal.

He reached for where the sheet was wrapped around the uneven ovoid that should've been the head, soaked through red.

Somebody yelling at him, that voice, again, saying how bad an idea that was...

And they were right.

A micro-memory, context-less, flashed on him – a few days before, Berman: "...raspberry jam."

Then there was blackness and he felt himself falling; and then not even that.

# four: ghosts

*Close the door, put out the light*

*You know they won't be home tonight*

*The snow falls hard and don't you know?*

*The winds of Thor are blowing cold.*

John Paul Jones, Jimmy Page, Robert Plant, "No Quarter"

Lourdes Bracero didn't say anything for a long while. She sat hunched over in her one, marshy chair, deep inside the oversized denim jacket which had belonged to Jack Meara, her arms around herself, eyes on the thin rug. Ronnie didn't know if he should touch her, stand there, leave.

She abruptly stood, went into the small bathroom closing the door behind her. She threw up, and when she was done, he heard her drop the toilet seat down, and then the cover. She was sitting on the lid, he guessed. Then he heard the crying.

He took a step toward the bathroom, then thought, no, stayed there in the small, cold front room, dark behind the cardboard-covered windows. Around the edges of the cardboard he could see the gray of early morning.

His head still hurt, though it was bearable now, and there was another pain from the bump at the back of his head from when he'd passed out in the Stuyvesant Town parking lot. And he was tired; he felt it come up on him, suddenly and completely as he was standing there. He wanted to sit on the unfolded, unmade sofa bed but something about that seemed improper.

After a bit, he heard the bathroom sink run, then the door opened. Her eyes were red, she was shaking. She walked unsteadily the few steps to the chair and dropped back into its shapeless cushions. "Jesus, I'm cold."

Ronnie slipped off his parka and put it around her shoulders.

"Be a good kid, Blue, I got a bottle in a cabinet over the sink, ok?"

"You think that's a good idea?" He looked at his watch. "It's not even—"

"I think it's a great idea."

"I could make you a cup of coffee. Maybe that hot chocolate of yours."

"My man's dead, Blue. You think hot chocolate's gonna do it for me?"

He went into the kitchen, found a bottle of J & B where she told him it'd be. He poured a small dose into a water glass, then ran the sink water as quietly as he could so she wouldn't hear him cutting the booze. He brought her the drink. "But no pills, ok?"

She took a sip, smiled up at him, an I-know-what-you-did smile over the diluted drink.

"Do you want me to go?" he asked.

She shook her head. "You can make yourself some coffee if you want."

"I'm good."

"You better sit down, Blue, 'cause you look ready to fall down."

He sat on the edge of the foldout bed. It still didn't feel right.

She took another draw on her glass. "They sent you?"

"No. I just thought, well…"

"Somebody had to tell me, right? 'Cause, see, you're not the wife, so *they* don't tell you. I don't get a cop coming to me with the, uh, whatchacallit? The cop priest?"

"The chaplain."

"I don't get that 'cause I'm not his wife." She took another sip of her drink. "But what could a priest tell me to make it all right?" She thought a moment, then, "Do they tell his ex?"

"I don't know. I don't know how that works."

"Somebody should tell her." She drained the glass, pulled herself out of the chair with a grunt and weaved into the kitchen. He heard her pour another drink, no sound of running water after. A small, tinny-sounding radio in the kitchen flicked on. She cruised through the channels, found some FM rock station. Traffic doing "Dear Mr. Fantasy." She reappeared in the kitchen doorway. "You like this? White boy stuff? When you was in college, you'd sit around with the black lights on, talk all serious, smoke your mara-ja-wanna…" She closed her eyes, swayed slightly back and forth to the slow, smoky whirl of the music, took a pull on her glass. "Ah, 's not too bad."

*Dear Mr. Fantasy, play us a tune...Something to make us all happy...*

She stopped moving, finished off the glass, set it down on the kitchen table. She turned to him, held out a hand. "C'mere, Blue."

He hesitated, unsure.

Her fingers beckoned him. "C'mere."

When he drew close, she took his hands in hers, pulled his arms around her. "You dance?"

"Not really," he said.

She pulled close to him, laid her head between the side of his head and his shoulder. Her arms went around him. They rocked from one foot to the other in a rhythm that had nothing to do with the music.

*... Do anything to take us out of this gloom...*

She felt good there, a nice fit against him, making him feel warm in the cold apartment.

But it still wasn't right. He opened some space between them but she pulled close again.

She stepped away, took him by one hand and led him to the foldout bed.

He held back.

She smiled. "'S'ok, Blue. Just lay down with me. Just hold me."

She slipped off his parka and the denim jacket and climbed under the quilt, holding it up to bring him in.

His throat tightened as he slid in under the quilt and he felt a pang of pity when he saw there were no sheets.

She turned her back to him, nestled herself tightly against his chest, pulled his arm around her, snuggled still closer, the denim across her buttocks tight against his groin.

He tried to squirm a little space between their middles, but she didn't let him. She breathed and he could feel her back expand against his chest, filling the space inside his arm. Her hair was in his face, smelling of cigarette smoke from her last shift at the bar. She turned slightly, there was the dark skin of her cheek, the olive smoothness

243

broken here and there by the odd-shaped little wounds of long-ago acne, then lower, a blue vein pulsing in her neck.

She turned inside his arm, facing him. She set a hand on his cheek. He was surprised how rough the skin on her hand felt. She moved her head forward, her lips brushed his, feather light. "At least one person in this world should get what they want." She moved away, reached under the blankets, he heard the jingle of a loosened belt buckle, then she kicked her jeans out from under the quilt.

Ronnie lay there for a minute, again feeling none of it was right.

"This isn't gonna happen with these in the way," she said, tugging at the waist of his jeans.

He wasn't as adept as she was. He had to sit on the side of the bed, kick off his sneakers and wriggle out of his jeans. The awkwardness of it made him feel silly. He could feel his face redden, even as his bare legs pimpled from the cold air in the room. He didn't want to turn and have her see that as embarrassed – and ashamed – as he felt, part of him certainly wasn't feeling embarrassed or ashamed.

"'S'ok," she said, softly, taking him by the shoulder and helping him back under the quilt. She reached down between his legs. Her hand was cold on him as she put one leg over his hip and guided him into her.

When it was over, she turned and again fitted her back against her chest, her rear against his middle, pulling his arm back around her. Her breathing became relaxed and shallow, he felt her body go slack under his arm, her head loll slightly.

When he could be certain she was deep asleep, he carefully slid out from under the quilt, tip-toed to the bathroom. He peed, washed himself in the sink, then went back to the front room and, quietly as he could, pulled his pants back on. He sat in the chair, watched the quilt rise and fall with her breathing. His head still hurt and he wondered just what kind of asshole he was.

The phone rang. He didn't want it to wake her up, scooped up the receiver before the second ring. "Hello?" he whispered into the mouthpiece.

"Hey, kid."

"Sid? How'd you know—"

"Because I'm starting to understand what kind of animal you are. I *knew* you'd be there. I can't decide if I'm impressed or disgusted with you. Jesus, kid, you couldn't wait a day?"

"Did you want something?"

"I decided: I'm disgusted."

"Sid—"

"Put your dick away and meet me at Meara's place soon's you can."

Ronnie set the receiver softly back in the cradle, found Lourdes looking at him from the sofa bed. She'd gotten her cigarettes out of her jacket on the floor, had one lit.

"I was trying not to wake you," he said.

She wiped at something in her eye. She had a strange, closed look on her face. "You should go, Blue."

He nodded, pulled on his sneakers, picked his parka off the floor and started for the door. He stopped, wanting to say something, do something that would somehow make it all feel right.

As always, she read him easily. "Don't worry about it, Blue. You're still a good guy."

He smiled a thanks but left not believing her.

Meara's apartment still looked like a WWII bunker, only now one belonging to the losing side. The sofa had been thrown across the room, the part Ronnie guessed was closest to the blast having gone through a woodchipper. The TV was against a far wall, a candidate for those boxes of jumbled junk the electronics shops on Canal sold to tinkerers for a couple of bucks. The blank white walls were blackened, scratched and pitted. The metal front door had been blown off its hinges and lay inside the apartment just to the left of the doorway, punched into a shallow bowl. The shiny black splatter of dried blood almost completely covering Meara's front door looked like it had been shot through a fan. About two feet to the right of the door, a little below knee level, a head-sized hole had been blown through the cinderblock wall into the hallway, and the metal frame on that side of the doorway had been blown clear of the jamb and twisted like a crueller.

The small apartment was crowded. There were two Fire Department guys camped out in the kitchen, a fire watch left behind to make sure there were no after-fires; since Stuy Town was in his precinct, there were two dicks Ronnie recognized from the night shift at his own house poking around plus a uniform on the door to keep gawkers away; three guys attached to the Bomb Squad rig he'd seen in front of the building digging things out of the walls; and a CSU team whose boss kept yelling there were too many fucking mo-mos clomping around and the crime scene wasn't going to be worth shit unless they all got the hell out.

And Big Sid was there. He helped Ronnie step around the black pools in the doorway and past the twisted doorframe. Sid waved over one of the Bomb Squad guys, a beetle-browed cigar-chomper named Yelavich. "Sarge, do me a favor, enlighten my young colleague?"

Yelavich pointed to where his people were digging little bits of something out of the walls. "We're finding two kinds of metal fragments that don't look to be debris. I'm not gonna be sure until we can do a good lab exam, but the heavy ones look like steel. Shrapnel. A grenade."

"A *hand* grenade?" Ronnie asked incredulously.

"No, a *foot* grenade." Yelavich rolled his cigar from one side of his mouth to the other as his heavy brows crunched into an intolerant frown. "Yes, a *hand* grenade. The lighter metal fragments, well, it's *really* hard to eyeball 'em, they've been blown to shit, but I'm betting aluminum or tin, probably tin."

"Tell him why tin," Sid said.

"Soup can," Yelavich said. "I used to see this in Nam a lot 'cause it was simple, something even a retarded VC could put together." He pointed to the hole in the front wall. "This is your point of detonation. You take a soup can," and here, Yelavich mimed holding a soup can, "and you tape it to the wall," which he also mimed. "You put it down here, off to the side and low, way out of the eye-line of anybody coming through the door. You take a grenade, put it in the soup can, pull the pin. The can's too tight a fit for the spoon to release -- "

"Spoon?"

Yelavich looked from Ronnie to Big Sid. "Where'd you get this guy?" he asked Sid.

"Box of Crackerjacks. I was hoping for a whistle."

Yelavich rolled his cigar back to the other side of his mouth. "C'mon, son, you've seen a grenade in war movies, right? The spoon is that long thingie goes down the side. The grenade won't arm unless that's released." Yelavich continued his mime performance: "You take something to use for a tripwire, tie it around the grenade and run it behind the door. When the vic comes through the door, the door pushes on the tripwire, the wire pulls the grenade out the soup can, the spoon releases, and—"

"Boom," Big Sid concluded.

"We're just lucky nobody else was in the hall when this went off," Yelavich said. "My kids play hockey in the halls where I live," and the mental image made him shudder.

Sid thanked Yelavich who went to argue with the CSU team leader about who was the better of the two teams to be digging for bomb parts.

"Without making a big deal and drawing attention," Sid quietly said to Ronnie, "have a close look at that door. Don't touch it," he warned. "A lot of that blood is still damp. Ok, what do you see?"

"It's pretty banged up."

Ronnie could almost *hear* Big Sid rolling his eyes. "Well, yeah. That's to be expected. You know: *hand grenade!*" Sid took a patient breath. "Walk yourself through it. You come home, standing at your door…"

"I open the door and go in."

"Jesus, you make my head hurt. What do you do? Stand in front of your door, go, 'Open Sesame'?"

"Oh, well, yeah, I have to unlock—" Ronnie looked to the two locks on the door. The keyholes were empty, yet the dead bolt was in the open position.

Before Ronnie could blurt out anything like "Eureka!", Sid was saying goodbye over his shoulder to all the arguing cops in the apartment as he shoved Ronnie out into the hallway and pulled him toward the elevator. "Got a car downstairs," Sid said and wouldn't let Ronnie talk until the elevator doors closed behind them.

"Could the blast maybe have shaken up the locks— "

"I asked Yelavich," Sid said. "He's not sure what it would take to jolt a locked lock into unlocking. That's something he's gotta test. But the key should be in there. Even if the outside part got sheared off by the explosion, the blade should still be in the keyhole. That got me thinking, I called the morgue. They found keys embedded in the vic's right leg, right about here." Sid patted the upper part of his right thigh.

"Holy shit," Ronnie said. "His keys were still in his pocket."

The long room had no windows, was cold and smelled of formaldehyde. The floors and lower part of the walls were tile, the upper part was plaster covered with a sickly green paint. Two rows of stainless-steel tables ran the length of the room. Each table was crossed with an X of gutters running to a drain in the middle. Morgue techs were getting some of the tables ready for the first work of the morning, wheeling in bodies from the storage room and setting them on the steel tables. Until the work started, the bodies would remain covered by sheets except for the feet, allowing the techs to read their respective identifying toe tags.

There was a radio somewhere, and the Motels' "Only the Lonely" echoed blurrily around the room.

One table had already been working when Ronnie and Sid had shown up. Sid was with them now, at the far end of one row, hovering around the assistant medical examiner and his two techs in surgical greens, pointing at this, mumbling a question about that.

Ronnie had kept to himself at the opposite end of the room, his back to the rows of steel tables. He wondered if one of the covered bodies was the old guy he and Sid had found frozen to death across from the station house the other night.

Then Sid was coming toward him, carrying two stacked rubber basins in his rubber-gloved hands. He set the basins down on the open table nearest Ronnie.

"This look familiar? You don't have gloves, don't touch anything. They're still waiting for this stuff to dry out." Sid picked up what was left of a frock-length leather jacket, which had been draped over the top basin. There wasn't much left of the right side – closest to the blast, Ronnie assumed – and it was a trick for Sid to find a place to hold it without the shredded fabric coming apart in his fingers. But the left side, even with all the dark splotches of blood, Ronnie immediately recognized.

Sid laid the jacket down on the table, careful not to smear the still-tacky bloodstains, and turned to the first basin. "How about these?" Sid held up a more-or-less pair of boots. Similar to the jacket, the right boot was so mangled the only part recognizable was the thick sole and blocky wooden heel, but the left one was relatively intact. Again, Ronnie knew what he was looking at right away: a pair of Fryes.

Sid put the boots back in the basin, then pushed the second basin toward Ronnie. Scattered around the bottom, each in its own individual plastic evidence bag, were a half-dozen rings. Some were twisted like pretzels, dark with crusted blood. Ronnie poked among the bags, found, along with the rings and also bagged separately, an engraving of the Holy Family, a twisted crucifix, a cameo of the Virgin Mary neatly folded in two, all about the size you'd expect hanging from a neck chain.

Sid pointed to the three medallions. "Those they dug out of his chest."

"Juan Teixeira," Ronnie said.

Sid nodded. "I had 'em pull his card. There's enough of his left hand to get decent prints, but as far as I'm concerned, that's just confirmation."

"What tipped you?"

"The body didn't look right to me when the EMTs brought it down."

"How the hell could it look right? You know: *hand grenade.*"

"Even with all the *yech,* didn't look right for size, weight, not for our guy. Then I saw the locks on the door… It all started looking wrong."

A phone rang on the other side of the autopsy room. Then, "Hey, Leland!" one of the techs called. "For you!"

Big Sid hit the blinking light on the phone extension on the wall nearby, picked up the receiver. "Leland…You have her there now?...Ok, just hold her in the box 'til I get there." He hung up and began to reassemble the pile of basins. "I've got them holding Sara Grajales at the station."

"Who?"

Sid shook his head. "You know, my grandma has a canary remembers tricks better than you and he's got a brain the size of an orange pit. You were leaning on her doorbell yesterday morning. Dumbass."

"Teixeira's girlfriend?"

"Let's call her that to be nice." Sid picked up the basins. "I gotta bring this stuff back."

As Ronnie waited for Sid, he heard the whirring sound of a motor at the far table, the gurgle of body fluids being sucked down the drain. He decided to wait outside.

The station house had two interrogation rooms on the second floor. They were small rooms, just enough space for a little table, a chair on each side, and barely enough room to get by around them. The walls and ceiling were covered with acoustic tiles. The ceiling tiles grew new, brown water stains every time it rained or snowed.

Each interrogation room had a one-way mirror set in a wall, and the mirrors looked out from the observation room, which wasn't so much a room as a narrow corridor squeezed between the two interrogation rooms. It was stuffy and always smelled like old socks.

Ronnie was in the observation room. Sitting across the table from him in Interrogation 2, hunched over in her chair, trying to keep her hands warm between clenched knees, was Sara Grajales. She and Juan Teixeira could've passed for brother and sister: she had the same spindly, toneless shape, the same haggard-looking face, the same way of burning through a young body twice as fast other people.

It was a little after nine and she looked like she'd been dragged out of bed. Ronnie had a feeling she was the type that no matter what time of day you caught her, you'd be dragging her out of bed. She had barely pulled a comb through her stiff orangey hair and had under-dressed terribly for the weather: holed jeans, sandals without socks, and a pink denim jacket with Bedazzled curlicues. Under the jacket she was wearing only a T-shirt and, evidently, no bra, although she didn't have the body to make that a point of interest.

Big Sid came through the interrogation room door carrying two cups of coffee, set one down in front of Grajales. He reached into his pocket and dumped a handful of blue Equal packets on the table in front of her.

"You wanted it light, right?" Sid said, his voice crackling through the small intercom speaker in the observation room. He squeezed into the chair on Ronnie's side, his back to the mirror. "Good and hot, that should help warm you up. We didn't have the other thing, Sweet 'n' Low, but we had those," he said meaning the Equals. "I hope that's ok."

She shrugged. "I'm tryin' to watch myself," she said and dumped three Equal packets into her coffee. She took a sip from the cup. "Jesus, jour coffee sucks."

"Sorry about that," Sid said. "We've been having a problem with our water."

The problem with the water, Ronnie thought, was no one ever used it to clean the pot.

"Jou know, a cup a sucky coffee don' make us no friends," Sara Grajales said. "Dat was pretty shitty what jou do to Juan, tellin' 'im all dat shit 'bout da DA comin' after 'im 'n' all dat, jus' tryin' to fock wit 'im." She said some other things which, from the snarly look on her face, must have been equally uncomplimentary and accusatory, but the intercom speaker crackled with shorts and her voice went in and out: "...son *pendajo* like jou come roustin' us...never bother nobody...all jou do is give grief 'n' make sucky coffee..."

Ronnie banged on the intercom a couple of times to clear up the sound. When he looked up, Big Sid and Sara Grajales were both staring at the one-way mirror, wondering what all the thumping was about.

Sid turned back to the woman. "I think Juan misunderstood me, Ms. Grajales. Just trying to make him aware the kind of bad spot he was getting himself into. May have had some miscommunication on what I was saying about the DA and criminal charges, y'unnerstand, but he knew I wasn't just blowing air when I told him he had other problems to worry about. Last night, when he figured out he was clear with the DA, still scared, wasn't he? Knew he still had worries, didn't he? *Big* worries?"

She shrugged, not willing to give ground. "Prolly jus' more cop bullshit."

"He went out last night, you haven't seen him since, right? That's not more cop bullshit."

"Da fock jou care?"

"Ms. Grajales, Juan has been working with me for quite a while. Gives me information, I help him with this and that. You know how it works; you didn't just get here from Kansas. I'm not gonna b.s. you, make out we're friends or anything, but because of that information, Juan is very important to me. He's in trouble, I'll help. But I need to know what's going on."

There was just enough truth to it to make sense which helped cover up the fact that most of it *was* cop bullshit. Sara Grajales chewed on her lower lip with teeth crying out for a visit to a miracle-working orthodontist. She nodded: go ahead.

"Somebody called last night," Sid said, "or stopped by…"

"Phone call," she said.

"You know who it was?"

"How da fock *I* know? Is *his* phone call!"

"Could you tell if Juan knew the person?"

"Oh, yeah, he knew who it was right away."

"What was the conversation about? What was Juan saying?"

She took a sip of her coffee, curled a lip over the taste then frowned with concentration. "Well, like he say stuff like, 'Hey, I'm sorry, 's not my fault, I didn' know nothin' 'bout it, sorry, sorry, sorry.' Dat's da tin I 'member mos' is him sayin' 'I'm sorry' a lot 'n' whatever it was he was sorry 'bout he didn' know nothin' 'bout it."

"He was afraid?"

"Oh, yeah, he pick up da phone, he hear da voice, he look like he gonna shit right there!"

"Never mentioned the other guy's name, never said who it was?"

Sara Grajales shook her head. She took another sip of her coffee. "What jou make dis wit? Jou stir dis wit a dirty stick or sontin?" She emptied another pack of Equal into her cup.

"So, Juan was scared, talking to this guy, then what?"

"Well, den d'other guy, he musta ast 'im to do sontin, Juan say, 'Si, I can do dat,' but he still scared, he say, 'How dis gonna work?' 'n' d'other guy say sontin 'n' Juan get all like—" Sara Grajales flashed an are-you-fucking-*crazy* face "— 'n' he tell d'other guy, he say, '*Oye,* I go ou'side, I show my face, I'm a dead man!' Den d'other guy say sontin, 'n' I can tell Juan don' know is good or bad, he's t'innin' 'bout it, den he say ok 'n' he go out."

"You mean he left the apartment."

"Da's what I mean I say he go out. Maybe jou don' drink so much a dis sucky coffee jour brain work better."

"Maybe. What time was this?"

"I dunno. 'S not like I check a fockin' clock alla time."

"What were you doing? Were you watching TV? What was on?"

"Oh, well, yeah, *que es,* wit' da good-lookin' guy, dat *Magnum* show."

"So he left between eight and nine. Didn't say where he was going?"

"Juan never say where he go. He got all kindsa business, he don' talk dat stuff wit me."

"Say when he'd be back?"

She shook her head. "He jus' say not to go out, don' answer da phone or opena door for nobody but him." She studied Sid for a moment through her bleary, prematurely aged eyes. "Sontin awready happena Juan, *si?* Jou *know* sontin."

Sid looked her in the eye, took her little hand with its gnawed-down nails between his bear paws, and said in a soft, sincere voice, "No, Ms. Grajales, I don't know if anything's happened to Juan. But I promise you, I'm going to try to find him before something does."

Sid turned her over to a uniform to drive her home and came into the observation room. "Jesus, it stinks in here. Why don't you take a shower once in a while, kid?"

"It always smells like that in here."

"Suuuure. By the way, nice touch, hammering on the wall. Made her feel real relaxed, not worried about anybody listening in. Smooth."

"Are you ever going to tell her what happened to her boyfriend?"

Big Sid took a sip of his coffee. He made a face. "She's right about this horse piss. Fuck it, she'll figure it out soon enough. She's no virgin, she knows what she was shacked up with. Not good enough for you? Tell you what. Can probably still catch her before she leaves, *you* can explain to her how her scumbag boyfriend got himself blown up because he tried to set a cop up for a hit. Sure she'll be very comforted by that. Now: we done with Be Kind to Skanks Day?

"Here's how I'm seeing this," Big Sid said. "Soon's Larry Malloi closed the door on us yesterday, he's on the horn to whoever, next guy up the chain, y'unnerstand. 'Tell Tony Boy, thing was supposed to happen in Jersey? Didn't happen. Cop's still above ground, he's back in The City on the hunt.'"

"So Tony Boy puts out the order; 'Take care of this guy.'"

"Only he's got the same problem *we* got: nobody knows where the fuck this guy is. So, he does something a little like what we did."

"His people booby-trap Meara's apartment hoping he'll show up there sooner or later."

"Which he does."

"Moffie and Horn were watching the door. They didn't see Meara go in."

"Does it even fucking *matter?* Lotta ways into that place, kid. Boss only had troops on the front door. So maybe Meara spotted Moffie and Horn, went in another way. Maybe he's the overly cautious type, *always* goes in another way. Maybe – shock of shocks – Moffie and Horn fucked up. Point is, he goes in, sees the door's wired—" Sid saw the question on Ronnie's face. "How the fuck I know how? He's Super Cop, got x-ray vision. *Again:* does it really fucking *matter?* Point is, he *did.*" Impatiently: "*Anyway,* he sees a chance to get everybody off his back, buy some running room, as a bonus, get a little payback for what happened down at Sally Dell'Acqua's place."

"He calls Juan Teixeira."

Sid nodded. "Like any good cop, Meara knows these shitheads always think they're smarter than they are, gets Johnny Texas believing he's bought his line about not having anything to do with what happened at Dell'Acqua's, 'I didn't know it was gonna be a hit blah blah blah.' 'Yeah, ok, whatever you say.' Then Meara lays it on just as thick: 'You're still on my shit list. Want to square yourself with me? I need a favor, something, whatever. Come over my place, we'll work it out.' Juan's still hinky, Meara says something like, 'Hey, I'm not gonna try anything in my own place, not with coupla hunnerd citizens around.' Whatever; he spins it good enough, Ja-wann wants to believe it bad enough, so he bites."

"'C'mon over, I'll leave the door open for you.'"

"*Adios,* Johnny Texas. Witnesses put the explosion a little after nine; it fits."

"But Meara had to know once the ME did the post –"

"Course he knew," Sid said. "But if I hadn't bumped Ja-wann to the head of the line, could've been coupla days before he got his turn on the table."

"Jesus, Sid. *Jesus!* Now we have *got* to get the captain to go to IAB. That's *murder!*"

"Really?"

"And, like the Bomb Squad guy said, what if some citizen had been walking by when that grenade went off?"

Sid nodded his head gravely, drained his coffee and set the empty cup on the sill of the one-way, pursed his lips in an exaggerated presentation of giving the matter serious thought. "Ok, for the moment, forget the what-if's, we'll put aside whether or not *anybody* gives two shits about Johnny Texas. Here's the thing, y'unnerstand. We go to IAB, you know who winds up with their balls in a vise? You, me, the Boss, that's who."

"How do you figure that?"

"What do we have?"

"Sid, he set Teixeira up."

Sid waved that away. "What do we *have?* Can you prove Meara knew about the grenade? That he's even been anywhere near his apartment in *days?* Can you prove Meara made the call to Johnny Texas? Hell, without Johnny Texas to say so, you can't prove these two jamokes even *knew* each other!"

"If we put it together with everything else—"

"Like?"

"We can put Meara's car at Sally Dell'Acqua's."

"Without an ID on the plates, all you've got is a could be/maybe ID on the car. Put that in front of the shoo-flies and I can guaran-fucking-tee you Meara's PBA lawyer is gonna be there telling them how many *other* old tanks just like it are still on the road. And you can bet your left nut he'll find more than a few. And even if you *could* put him at Dell'Acqua's, what does that get you? No proof he was there when the hit went down, only prints on the gun took out that shooter belong to Dell'Acqua."

"Teresa Ortiz can put Meara in Lourdes Bracero's place the night—"

"So what? Gets a reprimand for leaving the scene and a handshake for saving her life. But he didn't *do* anything, not anything *criminal.*"

"What about all that stuff we pulled out of his apartment—"

"So he keeps a scrapbook on the guy he thinks shot him 20 years ago. Weird, ok, maybe even a little creepy, but it doesn't *prove* anything! You want to know what they *can* prove? When you go to them, tell them how we know all this stuff, what they *can* prove is you, me, and the Boss are guilty of breaking and entering into Meara's apartment to conduct a warrantless search – *that's* what they *can* prove! And then it's, 'Merry Christmas, hope you enjoy your suspension!'"

Ronnie wished there was a chair in the observation room; his legs were feeling weak. The small, stuffy room was feeling smaller and stuffier. "Where does this come out, Sid?"

"I dunno, kid, but no place good."

"So, what do we do next?"

The observation room phone extension rang, Sid held up a finger to Ronnie to hold on to that last thought as he hit the blinking button for the live line and answered the phone. "Interrogation, Leland…" Sid listened for a moment, then his face sagged, his eyes closed, pained. "You gotta be fucking kidding me. Tell me you are shitting me. *Please* tell me you are shitting me!" Sid kept nodding at what he was hearing, looking more pained all the time. "When was this?" He checked his watch, shook his head. "Ok, ok, where's the Boss?... Man, I hope he brought his Preparation H because that's not gonna be fun…No, I'll deal with it. If he gets back before I do, tell him I'll touch base this afternoon and I have the kid with me."

Sid hung up the phone and put both hands over his face. "Kid, if you stay on this job any length of time, do yourself a favor and don't give a shit about anybody else. Not even your CO, y'unnerstand. Especially if he's going off the rails. Just watch out for your own ass."

"What happened to the captain?"

Sid dropped his hands and nodded at the phone. "That was Berman. Says soon's the Boss came in this morning he got called downtown for a meeting with the Chief of D's, somebody from the commissioner's office, somebody from the DA. That's not gonna be good."

"They can't know about all this Meara stuff, can they?"

"I don't see how they could. I'm guessing they're just kinda pissed this precinct has turned into little Beirut last coupla days."

"Something happened."

"Something happened," Sid said with a glum, deep nod. "You were asking what our next move is? Our next move is back to Jersey."

"Malloi," Ronnie guessed. "Meara."

Sid nodded. "Sometime the wee hours this morning, Meara busted into Malloi's place, tuned him up a bit. Malloi's in the hospital, the local cops want to know why they found my business card in his condo. Kinda wondering the same thing myself." He shook his head then glared at Ronnie. "You know how between those times when you're really smart you get those attacks of the stupids? I'm thinking they must be contagious, kid, and you're giving them to *me!*"

Lieutenant Ernesto Matos of the Union City Police Department was a head shorter than Big Sid, but built like a vault door: wide, thick, hard enough to roller skate on. The lieutenant's dark, olive complexion had taken on an unpleasant reddish-purple undertone which went with his being mightily pissed off, enough so that even the constant shushing from the nurses at the nurses' station didn't have much effect other than to have the lieutenant reflexively swish his hand at them every few seconds like he was shooing away flies, almost knocking over the little plastic Christmas tree they'd set up on the counter.

Matos wasn't quite yelling, but, for a hospital, he was disturbingly loud, going on and on at Big Sid about what kind of fucking *cowboys* were they growing on the other side of the Hudson who came *marauding* over here to Jersey, kicking in *doors* in the middle of the night to beat the *crap* out of people. Oh, hey, it wasn't like they were rubes over here, they *knew* Lawrence Malloy was really Lorenzo Malloi, but still, this was *unacceptable*, even if the vic was a Mob *scumbag*. Maybe this kind of rubber hose shit was ok on the other side of the river since it seemed like all *kinds* of shit was ok on the other side of the river, but *here* on *Ernie Matos'* turf on *his* shift they still believed in stuff like jurisdiction and cooperative protocols and *God* help Sid and Boo-Boo here (meaning Ronnie) if this had *anything* to do with that IAB corruption sweep that was all over the news, and so on and so forth.

Sid stood there and quietly took it, his face switching between being pissed off himself – since Sid was not someone who normally took that kind of verbal barrage complacently – and embarrassed because while Matos was off base on some of his specific suppositions, the gist was on the money enough that Sid couldn't really argue the issue.

Ronnie was on the other side of the nurses' station talking with the doctor on call who had treated Malloi. He was youngish, with a Burt Reynolds mustache, a mullet, and a USA for Africa T-shirt. Ronnie was looking over Malloi's chart. He understood "contusion" and Malloi seemed to have a couple of them around his head and ribs, but not much else. Except…

"What's this thing?" Ronnie asked the doctor. He read, "'Fracture of the proxy-something pha-something of the fifth digit.'"

"Proximal phalanx of the fifth digit," said Dr. Mullet. He held up his right hand and flexed his littler finger. "Broken pinkie."

"Guy's got a broken pinkie?"

"Snapped like a twig."

"You know, Doctor, I'm not quite sure I understand everything I'm reading here, but this doesn't look like it was much of a beating."

Dr. Mullet gave Ronnie a patient smile. "I don't know how *you* measure that kind of thing, but *I* wouldn't have wanted to go through it."

"What I'm asking is if there's any reason Mr. Malloi can't leave the hospital?"

"Well, there were, as you can see, a few blows to the head," and Dr. Mullet pointed to another part of the chart Ronnie didn't understand. "Any time you deal with impacts to the head, you want to be cautious, and the usual protocol is to hold the patient overnight for observation to make sure—"

"Not to interrupt, Doctor, but let me put it another way. Forget about being cautious and liabilities and all that stuff. If this guy wanted to, is there anything physically wrong with him that could keep him from walking out of here?"

"He'd be very uncomfortable—"

Ronnie twirled an impatient finger to push the doc quickly to the bottom line.

"—but there's nothing wrong with him you couldn't treat with an ice pack and a few aspirin. Which is what we're doing now."

Ronnie waved at Sid to join him. Sid apologized to Matos for stepping away, assuring him he could resume his ass-reaming momentarily. Ronnie found a small, windowless room not far from the nurses' station marked "Family Conference." There were some pastoral paintings on the wall, their frames draped with gold and silver garland in the spirit of the season, a comfy sofa and a few comfy chairs, an end table with a lamp and a Gideon Bible. This was where the doctors brought family members to give them bad news, like maybe it was time to pull the plug on poor old granny. Ronnie closed the door behind Sid and showed him Malloi's medical chart.

"You've seen more of these than I have," Ronnie said, "so you probably understand all the medical junk better than me."

"What's this fracture of a what-the-fuck—"

"Meara broke Malloi's pinkie."

"A pinkie?" The more of the chart Sid studied, the more puzzled his face became.

"Meara works him over until Malloi gives up what Meara wants. To me, this looks like Malloi gave it up pretty damn quick."

Sid frowned at the chart. *Really* damn quick."

"Yesterday, when you had them pull Malloi's sheet to find out where he lived, what'd you find out about him?"

"He's been with Tony Boy too long to cave after getting a little ruffled like this. I've seen guys day late on their shylock payments take more of a beating."

"Something's not kosher, Sid."

Sid handed back the chart and smiled. "Where the hell did *you* learn a word like 'kosher'?"

"Berman taught me. Look, Sid, remember yesterday with Teixeira? We were wondering why, if he'd bullshitted Meara, he would've stuck around to get his ass kicked when Meara came back? And if he *had* given him the straight dope—"

"He'd have to worry about Tony Boy coming after him for ratting."

"I talked to the doc. There's no reason Malloi can't walk out of here right now."

Big Sid's broad shoulders rose and fell with a long breath. "It's another set-up. And when it goes down, Malloi can say, 'I had nothing to do with it, I was nowhere near it when it happened, I've got all these doctors and nurses and even cops to testify as to my whereabouts.'" Sid considered a moment, shrugged prosaically. "Well, I wouldn't worry about Meara, kid. He's dodged more bullets than Arafat. If *we* figured out it's a set-up, so did he."

"What do you think we should do?"

Sid ran one hand tiredly across his bristly pate and yawned. "I'm of two minds, y'unnerstand. One of 'em is we do what I've wanted to do ever since this mess started; it's none of our business, dump it in someone else's lap, like Lieutenant Hissy Fit out there. Tell him, 'It's *your* jurisdiction, it's *your* problem,' then go home, I can put up my Christmas tree."

"You said you were of *two* minds."

Sid smiled grimly. "Not to say *shit* to *anybody*, go home and put up my Christmas tree. Let Meara keep doing what he's doing. He ends up putting one in Tony Boy's ear, not exactly a *bad* thing, y'unnerstand."

"And what happens if some poor slob citizen gets caught in the crossfire?"

The big man's smile faded; that was a part of the equation he was trying not to think about. "I'm thinking you have a third choice I'm probably not going to like."

"Probably not. I'm thinking *we* take him—"

"*Jesus*, kid!" Sid put his head in his hands and looked torn between laughing and popping Ronnie a good one on the nose.

"Hear me out, Sid! I'm thinking about what you said back at the house, about the spot you, me, and the captain are in. If we could just this once get ahead of Meara—"

"'Cause we been so good at that so far."

"—and take him quietly—"

"Machine guns and grenades, yeah, sure, *always* quiet around this fucker."

"—then that's *gotta* be good for us, for the captain, even for The Department!"

Sid shook his head, more disbelieving than disapproving. He walked that little ruminative circle of his. It being a small room, it was a small circle, but he didn't need to walk it long. "Ya know, kid, it's not like I don't think you care about my welfare, the Boss's, that I question your concern for the image of the New York City Police

Department in these trying times..." He started wagging a finger at Ronnie's face: "More I think about what you're saying, more I think you're full of shit."

Ronnie felt his face growing hot.

"You boinked this guy's girlfriend when you thought he was dead," Sid said, "you find out he's alive, you feel bad about it. Figure you owe him something. Or her. Or both of them. Or *some* goddamn thing."

Ronnie turned away and looked at one of the pictures on the wall. It was mostly oranges and yellows, a view of either a setting or rising sun through the reeds of an expanse of marshland. It made Ronnie think of dawn across the salt marshes down in South Jersey and right then he wished that's where he was. He rubbed at the throbbing pain at the break in his nose.

"You turned your head when you knew there were cops taking money. You had your reasons. I got mine for this."

Ronnie waited, braced himself for a verbal blast, a conk on the head, either of which he felt he deserved. But there was nothing. Then, "Good shot, kid. *Cheap*...but good. Ok. But *you're* the one has to sell it to the Big Tamale out there." Sid reached for the door to wave Matos over, paused with his hand on the doorknob. "Ya know, kid, I liked you better when you were stupid. You were nicer."

Matos hadn't calmed down any. "You don't *beckon* me like I'm your fucking *pet!*"

Sid nodded an apology as he closed the door behind Matos then pointed the lieutenant to Ronnie seated in one of the comfy chairs across from the comfy sofa. "Young fella has something he wants to discuss. Might want to have a seat."

Matos didn't sit.

Ronnie nervously cleared his throat. "Lieutenant, nobody's saying you shouldn't be pissed—"

"You're goddamn *right* I should be pissed!"

Big Sid gave Matos a give-the-kid-a-chance look, and Matos reined his temper in, nodded at Ronnie to go ahead.

"This has nothing to do with any of the problems you've been reading about in the papers that we've been having on our side of the river," Ronnie said. "Trust me on that."

"Oh, yeah, well *sure!*" Matos said. "Half your fucking *department's* under investigation for being on the pad, but otherwise you're all honorable guys so I should take your *word!*"

Sid – thankfully – stepped in. "Lieutenant, did Malloi identify the cop worked him over? Other than he had a New York shield?"

"You mean a name? No."

"Malloi *knows* who it was. He's holding back a lot more from you than that name. He's playing you, Lieutenant; you're part of his alibi."

"Alibi? For what?"

"He's setting the cop up for a hit."

Matos blinked a few times, like he hadn't heard it quite right – or wished he hadn't – then sat down on the sofa across from Ronnie. He wasn't ready to stop being angry, and he was more than ready to suspect maybe this was all some kind of tactic to defuse him when he should *still* be angry. "Bullshit."

"I'll bet your bars," countered Sid, "you dump the LUDs on Malloi's phone from last night, you're gonna find he made another phone call *before* he called 911. I don't know to who, and I'll double that bet that number's already disconnected, but it was to confer and get the ball rolling on setting up the cop."

Matos sat back on the sofa, still wary. "So what's the deal with this cop?"

"Kind of the opposite of what you've been thinking," Ronnie said. "Up until a few weeks ago, this was a good cop. Good record. Decorated."

"Up until a few weeks ago," Matos said.

"He's got it into his head to go after somebody. A Bad Guy. Somebody big."

"How big?"

"You know Malloi, you know his connections, you can do the math. It looks like this cop's thinking the only way he's gonna be able to do it—"

"Is go Dirty Harry."

Ronnie nodded. "He's got himself in a pretty big hole doing it. We're trying to keep him from digging it any deeper."

Matos looked from Ronnie to Big Sid and back to Ronnie, studying them. "This cop must be a pretty close friend of yours."

"Never met him," Ronnie said. "We're just trying to keep a good cop from jamming himself up. And we're asking another cop to help us."

At which Matos flamed, again, shooting to his feet. "You're gonna throw that Brotherhood of the Badge *bullshit* up at me? Screw *that!* You're not talking about fixing a coupla *traffic* tickets, ya know!"

"Actually," Sid said, very calmly, "I don't think the kid's asking you to *do* anything. He's asking is you to *not* do anything."

"We want the chance to take him," Ronnie said, "bring him back to our side of the river, let our department deal with him."

"And besides him being a member of the fraternity," Matos said, "I should do this because…?"

"Because," Sid said, "right now, without us, you're probably gonna have a couple bodies in your backyard before the day is out… One of 'em'll be the cop. We can help you avoid that situation."

Which gave Matos something to think about, and he sat back down on the sofa. "Who's the cop? Who's he after?"

"I give you names and you'll act on 'em," Ronnie said. "You'll *have* to. But if I don't…"

"Kind of like what I don't know won't hurt me…except for maybe getting me suspended, demoted, maybe even cost me my job."

"Something like that," Sid said.

Matos stared down at his knees a good, long while. Then he looked up at Ronnie. "What exactly are you asking for?"

"Your man on Malloi's room," Ronnie said, "he goes to the can for five minutes."

"And while he's in the can...?"

Sid wagged a warning finger. "What you don't know..."

"No rough stuff," Matos warned.

"No rough stuff," Sid said.

"That it?"

Sid thought of something Ronnie hadn't: "Keep Malloi on ice. A coupla hours. Can't be able to warn anybody we're on to the set-up."

"How the hell am I supposed to do that?"

"Hold him as a material witness."

"Material witness to *what?*"

"To his getting the crap beat out of him. Or call it protective custody; you're worried whoever whomped on him might come back."

Matos looked at him skeptically. "You really think that's gonna hold up?"

"Only gotta hold up a coupla hours."

"If anything breaks bad," Ronnie said, "we'll take complete responsibility."

Matos looked from Ronnie to Bid Sid. Big Sid pointed him back to Ronnie: "*He'll* take complete responsibility."

Matos studied his knees again. He had the look of someone who knew he was going to be unhappy with whatever choice he made. After a bit, the lieutenant put his hands on his knees and pushed himself to his feet with a grunt and a long, tired exhalation. He shook his head over himself: "I gotta be outta my fucking mind."

Big Sid set a sympathetic hand on Matos' shoulder. "Ya know, Lieutenant, I been saying same thing to myself least once every day this week."

"Jethuth Chritht, *you* two?" Lorenzo Malloi sat abruptly up in his hospital bed and couldn't have looked any unhappier than if Dr. Mullet had come in to tell him he had prostate cancer. He'd been watching *The $25,000 Pyramid.* Jack Klugman was feeding clues to a middle-aged lady with a slow drawl and a helmet of heavily lacquered red hair.

Malloi had a semi-private room to himself with as nice a view of Hoboken rooftops as St. Mary's could provide. He had one ice pack balanced on his toupee-less pate, was holding another one against the swollen left side of his face. He was wearing a pair of salmon-pink silk pajamas and a lot of bruises. Besides the aforementioned face swelling, there was a nasty-looking purple welt across his forehead like he'd had his head slammed against something, and a puffy and blackened left eye. Behind split and bloated lips too tender to close completely -- where yesterday Ronnie had seen a few thousand dollars worth of caps – were two rows of gray stubs, ergo the lisp. And, of course, there was that right pinky encased in gauze and splints.

Big Sid smiled, moved toward the window and pulled the blinds on the rows of Hoboken walk-ups as Ronnie drew a chair up next to Malloi's bed. "Heard you were ailing," Sid said. "Wanted to come by, pay our respects."

With the pinky splints in the way, Malloi awkwardly picked up the call button for the nurses' station and started mashing it with his thumb. "Get the fuck outta here! I don't have to talk to you guyth! I'm gonna have the copth throw you out on your atheth!"

"Don't think so, Larry," Sid said. "You better let me have that. Just gonna sprain your thumb with this thing and you got enough problems." He took the call button from Malloi's hand and set it on the night table, then moved to the door and threw the bolt. Malloi started to fidget, wincing as if he already anticipated someone finishing the beating Meara had started a few hours before.

"Not smart," Big Sid said, "not that I'm surprised. Didn't talk to us last time, now you got a mouth full of stumps. Know something? This is gonna be a distraction." Big Sid meant the TV. He took Malloi's remote from his lap, turned to the TV. "Like this show? Never get a chance to see it. Damn, look at that! Dick Clark looks just like he did when he was doing *American Bandstand!* How's he do that?"

"Pencils," Jack Klugman was saying. "Pens...chalk...crayons..." Desperate, he started to repeat himself, evidently thinking if he was more emphatic, the lady with the helmet hair would figure it out: *"Pencils...PENS..."*

Sid shook his head. "Jesus, broad's gotta be some kind of mental defective. It's, What Are Things You Write With, dumbass!" He switched off the TV, put the remote on the night table by the call button.

"We know what you did," Ronnie said to Malloi.

"What're you talking –"

"You set Meara up to get hit."

"You guyth don't give up!" Malloi waved his hands like he could shoo them away. "I run a coupla car washeth—"

*"Again* that bullshit?" Big Sid said. He turned to Ronnie: *"You* talk to him, he's already making me want to slap the rest of his teeth loose." Sid went around to the other side of the dividing curtain, stretched out on the other hospital bed and turned on the TV for the other bed.

"We wasted an awful lot of time yesterday," Ronnie said to Malloi, "and if we'd talked straight, good chance neither one of us would be here right now. I don't like to be rude, not even to someone like you, but my partner's right: you're not being smart. He tells me gambling's been your business a long time, so it surprises me you're making such a bad bet."

Malloi had been pretending not to listen until that last bit when Ronnie could see a what-the-fuck-does-*that*-mean? look wrinkle up Malloi's turtle face.

Ronnie smiled. "Your guys tried to take Meara out at Sally Dell'Acqua's, and what happened? They miss and one of *your* guys gets taken out. They missed *again* when they tried for his girlfriend, and then there was that firecracker last night. What happened? *Again*, they miss, *again* one of yours winds up in the morgue, and *you* get used for a punching bag. You guys are oh-for-three against this guy, and you're betting against him *again?*"

"Things You Make With Apples!" Sid called out from the other side of the curtain. "I want to know where this broad's from, if they're all mental defectives like her, I want to make sure I never go there."

Ronnie leaned close to Lorenzo Malloi. "And when it goes bad, you *know* he'll come looking for payback."

Big Sid pulled the curtain aside. "Look what happened to Johnny Texas. Man, there wasn't enough left of him to fill a paper bag."

"And when those cops outside your door hear what you did – I'm sorry, *tried* to do – to another cop?" Ronnie went on, "I don't think they're gonna have a problem being distracted when he tip-toes into this room to settle up."

Sid chuckled. "Meara won't have any trouble finding you, Lar, because *this* is where you're gonna be: right here in this room! Lieutenant Matos hasn't gotten around to telling you yet, he's decided to keep you in protective custody. Worried you might get your ass beat again. Nice man, dontcha think?"

Under the mottled bruises, Malloi was going pale. "You can't do that."

"It's *done*, Larry!" Sid gloated. "Oops, gotta go. Commercial's over." He pulled the curtain closed again.

Malloi turned to Ronnie. "You can't threaten me like thith!"

"*I'm* not threatening you. *Nobody* here is threatening you. In fact, I'm trying to keep you from winding up like Johnny Texas." Ronnie rubbed his eyes; they were itchy and burned from lack of sleep. "Look, we don't want you, we don't want the guy you sent Meara to, we don't even want Maiella. We just want the cop."

Sid turned off the other TV and the curtain between the beds shot open. "Thought you had to take some kind of test to get on these shows! I'm like a fucking *genius* next to this broad! *I* should get on this show! Could use 25 grand!"

Sid swung his legs over the side of the bed, yawned and stretched. "Speaking of morons, Larry, use that pinhead God gave you. You got a chance here to get in good with the other bosses. They can't be happy, this feud between your guy and our guy. This hit goes down – no matter how it comes out – gonna make things worse, now the Jersey cops are gonna get dragged in… You want to be on the wrong side of that? Go to them, to the bosses, say you knew how they felt, knew this was a bad beat, blah blah blah, that's why you pulled the plug on it. Make you Employee of the Month."

"We just want the cop," Ronnie said.

Malloi slid the ice pack on top of his head to the other side of his face so he had his head sandwiched between the two, soothing packs. He closed his eyes, blew a breath through his swollen lips – which apparently hurt quite a bit -- then settled back on his pillow. For a moment, he reminded Ronnie of Matos just a few minutes earlier; that same sense that his choices came down to shitty and shittier. "Thith thuckth," he said.


A soft rap on the window glass over his head. "Hey, hon? Wakey-wakey." Meara stirred from his sleep, instinctively reaching for the pistol in the pocket of his bombardier jacket, then he remembered. He unwrapped himself from the grease-spattered quilt he'd gotten from his trunk, eased himself up, his back stiff from the New Yorker's rear seat, and also not a little bit from the bone-gnawing cold.

"You with us, hon?"

He shivered and rubbed his eyes open. He didn't know her, but there was something vaguely familiar about her. Fortyish, not a great blonde dye job, packed just a tad too tight into a pink polyester waitress' uniform. Maybe she was just familiar because all waitresses had that same tired, fading look.

He could see a little better now. The sun was up, but not making much of a show of it. The sky was overcast, everything was gray. Except for the waitress's sunshine yellow hair and stoplight lipstick.

"You told the kid on the night shift to wake you up at eight," the waitress said. "What he didn't tell you before he took your five bucks is he goes off-shift at six. He left me a note. He didn't leave me any of the money." Meara remembered the zitty kid working the counter at the all-night diner. He'd flashed the kid his badge, dished up some bullshit about being on a job and had given him a fin to let him pull the car out of sight around back to catch some sleep.

"What do I owe you?" Meara said in an early morning croak, the words wavering as his jaw quivered with the chill.

She smiled. "Why don't you come inside, hon. You must be freezing." Which was true.

He went to the men's room, peed, ran cold water over his face. He saw his pale, unshaven, sagging face in the mirror and thought, Well, after all, you did die last night.

The waitress had a cup of coffee waiting for him at the counter. He smiled a thanks, took a sip. It felt good going down.

"Black, no sugar, right? I remember." She saw the puzzled look on his face. "You don't remember me?" She pointed to one of the booths by the front windows. "The other night. The night it rained? You were sitting right there. For hours, it felt like. I musta poured you a gallon a coffee. That much caffeine in you, I figured you'd be awake until New Year's."

"It doesn't affect me like that. I don't know why. Sometimes I wish it did."

"You should eat something, hon. You look like death warmed over."

"Toast."

"That's it? Toast?"

"Butter."

"Oh, well, *butter!*"

Meara squinted at his watch. Around eight. He'd been asleep a little more than four hours.

The waitress was back with his toast and a little paper cup of jelly on the side. "I threw in the jelly," she said. "Go to town."

He asked if he could get some ice tied up in a towel. When she came back, he set the bundle down on the swollen, bruised knuckles of his right hand. "I took a fall," he said. She hadn't asked but he could tell she was wondering.

"The kid you gave the money to; he said you said you're a cop. He said you're working."

"Well, sorta."

She looked at his haggard face, his scraped knuckles. "I hope your OT is better than mine, hon."

The morning crowd was starting to filter in and he was glad it drew her off. He smiled at the scrapes on his knuckles, even at the dull ache when he flexed his fingers. He remembered that shocked, surprised, totally what-the-*fuck* look on Malloi's face at the sight of his shattered caps plopped on that deep-pile white carpeting of his in a dark glob of phlegm and blood. Meara flexed his fingers, again, and thought, Jesus, just for that one look alone it was worth a 20-year wait.

With the coffee in him, chewing on the crunchy, butter-soaked toast, his senses started coming back into focus and he was feeling pretty good about where things sat.

When he'd felt that delicious tiny *snap* of Malloi's little finger in his hands and Malloi had started to spill, Meara had known something was wrong.

Malloi had given him the name Joe Rocco – Joey Rocks. He's the next guy up the ladder, Malloi had said. Not far from here, he'd said, maybe ten minutes, over in Weehawken. Malloi'd given him the street address. He'd given him directions. "He's probably there right now." He'll be in bed, Malloi said, you'll catch him asleep.

And that was the problem. Malloi had said too goddamn much too goddamn fast.

Meara had driven down from the heights of Union City and picked up Park Avenue in Weehawken, the broad boulevard that was the city's main artery. Except for Park, Weehawken – like most of the old cities along the Jersey waterfront – was a maze of narrow, almost alley-like one-way streets lined with old, small two- and three-family homes packed cheek-to-cheek.

Joey Rocks lived on a three block-long street running from Park steeply uphill to Bergenline Avenue, the store-lined main drag in Union City. When Meara had gotten to Joey Rocks' street, he hadn't driven up. Joey Rocks, he knew, was not the next man up the ladder. Joey Rocks was waiting for him, looking for him, probably sitting in his living room in the dark with his nine mm Smith & Wesson submachine gun sitting in his lap.

Meara had parked at the foot of the street, gotten a pair of low-powered binoculars out of his trunk and walked a few doors up the block, staying in the shadows. He'd looked at the number on the nearest house, did a calculation on which place belonged to Joey Rocks and sighted in the binoculars.

It was the only new house on the block, and, judging by the one mailbox, the only single-family house as well. Stairs led up to the entry door on the second floor, the rest of the ground floor given over to a one-car garage. Sliding glass doors and a balcony over the garage, more glass doors, and another balcony on the second floor. The curtains were pulled and dark across both glass doors.

Meara had walked around to the other side of the block, found the house sharing a backyard fence with Joey Rocks'. He'd walked quietly up to the house after checking to make sure all the windows were dark and there was no "Beware of Dog" sign anywhere, hopped the locked gate into a narrow alley leading to a small concrete square of a yard. He'd stayed in the shadows of the alley, ran his glasses over the back of Joey Rocks' house. Curtains pulled across every window, no lights, no movement. The rear door, he guessed, was out of sight, below the rim of the fence. The fence was new: metal looking like white-painted wood, high for privacy and topped with barbed wire to insure it.

That was good. Joey Rocks wanted to keep people out, but it also meant if he rabbited, there was no easy way out the back for him.

But then Meara had known Joey Rocks wasn't going to rabbit. Joey Rocks was waiting, he and his nine mm buzz saw.

In that case, Meara had told himself, let him fucking wait.

He'd climbed back into his car, drove the few blocks to a ramp down to Route 3 and headed for the 24-hour diner he remembered from the night he'd come back from south Jersey. By the time he'd gotten there and paid Zit-Face five bucks to let him catch some z's out back, Meara'd sketched out a plan in his head, and the biggest part of the plan was—

Let the fucker wait.

Lorenzo Malloi was nothing more than a glorified bookie; he didn't have the juice to authorize *any* hit let alone a hit on a cop. That order *had* to come straight from Tony Boy. That meant Joey Rocks had either dealt directly with Maiella or somebody close to him. Joey Rocks may not have been the next man up the ladder, but he was just as good. Maybe better.

He guessed – no, he *knew* – Malloi had made a call to start the ball rolling as soon as his door had closed behind Meara. And as soon as Joey Rocks had gotten his call, he would've thrown some water on his face, got some clothes on, parked himself by a window where he could watch the street, his submachine gun in his hands, and waited to see that big New Yorker come up the hill squeezing between the two files of cars parked nose-to-tail along the narrow street.

When the car didn't come when it should have, Joey Rocks would've still waited. Maybe the cop got lost, he'd have thought. Maybe something had held him up. So he'd have kept waiting and still the car hadn't come.

Joey Rocks would have to wait afraid that when he stopped waiting, when he put the Smith & Wesson Model 76 back where he kept it hidden, *that* was when the cop would hit. He wouldn't be able to nap, he'd even be afraid to take a leak worried he'd be in the middle of a piss when the front door came down.

So, Meara figured, let the fucker wait. Let him wait while I get some rest. Let him wait while I get some hot coffee in me, have a little something to eat, get myself together. Let him wait, let him get tired, edgy, hungry, impatient. Let him sweat. Let him have to hold a piss.

But that wasn't Meara's only reason for waiting. Joey Rocks was surrounded by civilians. Both sides of his house, across the street, behind his house, all close by, piled on top of each other. It was probably why the sonofabitch had picked the place, knowing nobody – not the cops, not other hoods – would try fireworks with that many citizens around.

Meara wanted to wait until the go-to-work crowd had gone to work. He guessed a downscale neighborhood like this would still have a lot of stay-at-home moms and their kids, but at least *some* civilians would be out of the way, and the cold would keep the rest inside. Not a great situation, not even a good situation, but better. He knew that, more often than not, better is all you can hope for.


It was a little after ten when Meara turned the New Yorker into Joey Rocks' street, goosing the gas a little to send it up the slope. The wide, old car nearly dammed the street; if he didn't thread between the parked cars just so, he was going to take a half-dozen side view mirrors up the hill with him.

At Joey Rocks' place, he pulled the car to the curb, parking across the base of the short driveway, and killed the engine. He sat for a minute behind the wheel, his hands around the .38 in his lap, listening to the cooling engine tick-tick-tick. He looked from the front door of Joey Rocks' place to the glass doors over the garage, then the glass doors behind the top floor balcony. The drawn curtains didn't move, but in the gray daylight he could now see there was a slight gap in the curtains; just big enough for someone to see through to the street while standing far enough back in the unlit room to stay invisible.

He suddenly felt tired, heavy in the seat, not wanting to move. Not from too little sleep. From too much...of everything. It felt like he'd done this 100 times before and that made him tired.

He took a breath, shook off the heaviness, and with a grunt opened his door and stepped out onto the driveway. He held the .38 out of sight, behind him, as he walked across the apron of the driveway to the stairs, moving slowly, the idea being to make himself an irresistible target.

But, at the same time, he knew Joey Rocks wouldn't bite.

Sally Dell'Acqua's. The try at Lourdes. Joey Rocks may have missed both times, but he hadn't played either of them dumb, and the smart move was to wait until Meara was in close, no-running-room close, can't-miss close.

Still keeping his .38 out of sight, Meara slowly climbed the stairs, giving himself time to study the landing above him, flick an eye to the balcony curtains looking for movement, for a shadow beyond the gap.

Then he was at the door, standing close, his nose almost against the dark-stained wood, because that close Joey Rocks would have to show himself to get a decent angle on him from the glass balcony doors.

Meara took a deep breath, looked up at the slate gray sky. He felt aches in his joints, tasted a dampness in the air. Snow's coming, he thought. Maybe not today, but it was coming.

He stepped over the railing along the side of the landing, holding himself on his toes on the thin ledge over the driveway, still hugging the wall close to the door. He held the cold iron of the railing with his left hand while he reached across with the .38 in his right and placed the muzzle against the doorbell near the left side of the front door.

And then he pushed the doorbell.

From inside the house he heard a muted chime, the kind of high, hanging note that signaled it was the beginning of a series of chimes.

But he didn't hear the other chimes. The first one hadn't even faded when the door erupted in splinters, from inside: the same staccato *rrrriiiippp* that had sprayed pieces of Sally Dell'Acqua all over his living room wall.

Meara held on to the railing, turned his face to the wall, away from the flying bits of wood, while the door not a couple inches from head continued to shred, seemed like it would never stop…

Until it stopped.

Screams from somewhere on the block. Broken glass hitting the sidewalk across the street.

Car engine. From the garage. Revving.

Meara jumped down into the driveway. His stiff knees buckled, he went down.

Engine in the garage screaming now.

Meara staggered to his feet, back-pedaling clear of the door—

A big bull of a black Cadillac El Dorado, tires smoking/shrieking on the cement, erupting rearward through the closed garage door, an explosion of wood and metal and glass—

Meara still kicking back toward the stairs, the vaulting car *just* clipping him with the rear quarter panel, a sudden explosion of pain from his ribs and leg and he started to go down—

Then another explosion of metal on metal, a spray of red taillight glass as the El Dorado buried its tail in the New Yorker blocking the foot of the driveway.

Meara, on the ground against the stairs, getting his pistol up, pointed at the broad-shouldered silhouette behind the wheel, sending off a shot. The soft-nosed bullet grazed the heavy, raked windshield and winged off. Shattering glass somewhere. A fresh scream.

Meara pulled himself to his feet. The pain in his side kept him from straightening, from drawing a full breath. He felt sweat on his face, wiped at it with the back of his hand, came away with blood, not sweat, all those flying shards from the Caddy bursting through the garage door...

The El Dorado had shoved the New Yorker out into the street where both cars sat log jammed. Joey Rocks – even through the smoked glass of the Caddy's windshield, Meara could see where that big, no-necked pile of fat and muscle had gotten its name – was still trying to shake off the shock of the collision.

Meara held his breath so as not to provoke the pain in his side, raised his pistol again, took careful aim, and put two bullets through the dark glass.


"All units, all units, we have multiple 911 reports of shots fired..."

The radio dispatcher gave the street name. It was the same street name Ronnie and Big Sid had gotten from Lorenzo Malloi.

"Shit," Sid sighed.

Ronnie thought the same thing.

But whatever they thought, their training and their time on The Job kicked in and they reacted automatically. A fellow officer was down – one of their own – even if whatever was going down was probably his own fault, so Sid punched the gas while Ronnie reached out the window to stick a blue flasher on the Buick's roof.

And all of it was the wrong move. It was the wrong move because they were away from home and they didn't know the ground. They were cannonballing up Park Avenue from Hoboken, couldn't get a read on the sirens that seemed to be coming from everywhere over the noise of their own roaring engine. Up ahead, a white van blocked the left lane at the juncture of a V intersection. Sid spun the wheel right and left to swerve around the right side of the van, rocketing blind into the intersection and it was only then he saw the flashers of a Weehawken P.D. cruiser shooting down the other side of the V.

Ronnie heard a scream – maybe it was him, maybe Sid, maybe both of them, maybe it was just the locked tires skidding across the asphalt, maybe all of it wrapped up in that wailing siren which suddenly sounded like it was in the car with them.

And then there was nothing.

# five: apogee

*My body's aching and my time is at hand*
James Taylor, "Fire and Rain"

"Take it easy with those stitches. Bad boy, do you hear me?"

She sounded far off, garbled like she was talking underwater, but if he concentrated, Ronnie could make out what she was saying. "Hm."

"I don't want you doing anything that might stretch them. Don't play around with them, don't scratch them. They'll open right up."

"Hm."

Ronnie was lying on the exam table cradling his right arm across his chest, morosely studying the gauze wrapped around most of his forearm and part of his hand. His field of vision was crimped by another swath of gauze covering much of the right side of his face, nipping at the corner of his eye. The bandages and stitches itched, and the more he was told not to scratch them, the more they seemed to itch. She had told him he must be imagining things because the local anesthetic hadn't worn off yet. In his head or not, those stitches itched like hell.

The doctor was a small, trim middle-aged woman, lost in baggy ER scrubs, with a wide, handsome Philippino face, a little bit of an accent, and a nice walk. The fact that –as bad shape as he was in – he'd still noticed her walk made Ronnie wonder if Sid wasn't right; that he had some kind of sickness.

"Can you sit up?"

Ronnie tried, but whatever they had given him for the pain weighed on him like a few tons of lead. "Mmm-mm."

"Don't be a sissy." She helped him up. His head went spinning and for a few moments, heavy as they were, the painkillers and anesthetic stopped working and his arm and the side of his face lit up.

She held up a small pill bottle of amber plastic in front of his unobstructed eye. Ronnie still couldn't focus on it. "These are for when you leave. This is for the pain. Two every four hours. *No more!* And no alcohol as long as you're on them. They're for pain, not for play."

Ronnie nodded, just slightly because that was all he could manage without sending his head spinning, again.

"If they don't do the job, *don't* take any more, and *don't* take anything else with them. No home-style prescriptions, understand? It bothers you, try an ice pack." She shoved the bottle into his good hand, and then held up another pill bottle. "This is an anti-spasmodic for your back and neck." She shoved the second bottle in his hand. "If you feel yourself tightening up again, take them. Apply heat. Maybe take a hot bath. If you do, keep your stitches dry. Understand?"

"Right. Cold on the face. Heat on the back. Take a bath. Keep dry." At least that's how it sounded in his head. His lips felt only half-attached to his face and it came out sounding something like, "Hmph, o mnaface, heaonack, hayabah, hee die."

She shoved a third bottle at him, and Ronnie fumbled to hold them all in his one unwrapped hand. "Antibiotics. Eat before you take them. Two with every meal and two before you go to bed."

"O mnaface, heaonack, abah, eee."

"With what we pumped into you, once we get you into a bed you'll sleep through the night. When you go home, sleep as much as you can. Loaf for a few days. I don't want you moving around too much. No smoking for the first 24—"

"I don shmo—"

"—and *what did I tell you?*" She grabbed his good, bottle-filled hand where it had started to fidget with the gauze on his arm and planted it firmly back in his lap.

"I *said* not to fool with that, didn't I? Bad boy! Isn't that what I said?"

Ronnie nodded. He noticed for the first time the thin scattering of dark spots across the front of her scrubs. "Zat fom me?"

She pushed his pointing finger away. "If it itches, let it itch. You better get used to the idea you're going to be uncomfortable for a while, so don't be a cry-baby about it."

"Knock knock." Van Dyne stepped through the curtains of the ER treatment cubicle. Ronnie's vision hadn't quite cleared, but he recognized the voice, even with its influenza nasality. The captain was carrying what looked like a pair of plastic shopping bags in one hand. Ronnie's drug-addled mind careened off a cliff into a nice fantasy and he thought it was nice the nice captain had brought nice gifts.

"Doctor Barangan?"

The doctor nodded at Ronnie. "This belong to you?"

"I'm afraid so," Van Dyne said. "What kind of shape is it in?"

"He's damned lucky he didn't lose that eye. An inch to the left..."

She stood by Ronnie like a tour guide pointing out places of interest, describing the multiple contusions along the right side of his body, particularly a good case of bruised ribs, strain – and possible tearing – of the muscles in his back and neck.

"Whiplash," Van Dyne interpreted.

"For lack of a less insurable word." Then she went on about the stitches in his face and arm. "Both wounds are pretty deep, enough so that I have a concern about possible nerve damage. We won't be able to get a clear picture of what's going on until the swelling goes down. Even without that, once those stitches come out, he's probably looking at restricted mobility in the hand. If there's been no major damage to the nerves, that would be something we could probably address with physical therapy. As for his face, without remedial surgery he's going to have a hell of a scar. You should consider sending him and his friend around to schools illustrating the dangers of not wearing seatbelts." She tugged on Ronnie's ear. "You *weren't* wearing your seatbelts, were you, you bad boys?"

"Where *is* his friend?"

Doctor Barangan slipped out between the curtains. Van Dyne beckoned at Ronnie to follow.

Ronnie slid gingerly off the table. As soon as he unsteadily got to his feet, he could feel the numbness recede, again, the flash of pain in his face, his arm, and, now that he was upright, in what seemed to be most of his body. He felt dizzy, he felt nauseous, and he felt Van Dyne staring impatiently at him. He swallowed the nausea and shuffled off after the captain.

They went behind another set of drawn curtains where an ER nurse was just helping Big Sid – with a lot of grunting effort – sit up on the exam table. Sid saw Van Dyne and his eyes went to the floor. The nurse helped settle Sid's heavily plastered right wrist inside a sling.

Barangan picked up a metal binder with Sid's chart from the work stand by the table. "Well, aside from the obvious – a pretty nasty snap of the wrist – there's *that* beauty." She pointed to an ugly, purple welt running clear across Sid's forehead. "And, if he was in the mood to hear it, I'd lecture him on his blood pressure, cholesterol count, blood sugar and *this*..." At which point she poked Sid's mid-body roll with the edge of the binder.

"Can they travel?" Van Dyne asked.

"With concussive head injuries, I'd prefer to hold them overnight for observation."

"What would be your second preference?"

"They're not going anywhere without signing a release."

"Oh, they'll sign."

"In that case, either their own doctors or a departmental physician should give them a look-over tomorrow to make sure they're still breathing."

"I'm sure the boys would prefer that to staying here overnight. Wouldn't you boys prefer that to staying here overnight?"

Ronnie and Big Sid each made a shruggy nod and grunt.

Barangan left to get the forms and Van Dyne gave Sid's nurse a stare giving her the idea she should follow.

Van Dyne set the plastic bags on the exam table. "Your personal effects," he explained. He reached into each bag, pulled out their badge covers and holstered pistols, slipped them into the pockets of his Burbury coat. "You won't be needing these for a while."

Big Sid winced with a pain greater than the one in his broken wrist. "How long?"

"30 days, 90 days, maybe the rest of your miserable fucking lives." Van Dyne found a box of tissues on the worktable, grabbed a few and blew his nose. "It hasn't been decided yet. I think they're researching the worst, possible thing they can do to you short of standing you in front of a firing squad. I believe the word 'flaying' was bandied about." Van Dyne rubbed his eyes. There was a sag to his shoulders Ronnie didn't remember having seen before.

"My phone's been going like an alarm clock all morning," the captain said. "The borough commander, IAB, the Chief of D's, the commissioner, the city attorney, the DA, the borough president, the Deputy Mayor's office, the *Mayor's* office... Then there's the calls from *this* side of the river, that ball-buster what's-his-name, Matos, he started in on me before I even got out of the parking lot..."

"It was my call," Ronnie said, though it came out like, "I wa m all."

"What?"

Ronnie tried to reach through the deadening drugs and carefully form the words: "My call. My re-spon-si-bi-li-ty."

"Well, that's very noble of you, Junior, but let me explain something to you. *You don't have responsibility!*" Van Dyne didn't shout, but there was such an acidic drip to his voice it stung more than if he had. "You're a *kid*, a *child!* You are *expected* to be stupid! That's why we put children like you with seasoned veterans; to keep you from doing stupid things. Isn't that right, Sidney? We put children like this with mature, experienced police officers who can counsel them against doing stupid things?" Van Dyne closed his eyes, pained. "Everybody thought we were corrupt; not *inept!* But thanks to you two..." He blew his nose a second time into his wad of tissues, tossed it at a waste basket. He missed. *"Fuck!"* This time, he shouted.

Then Barangan was back with the release forms. She handed a pen to Ronnie but it hurt for him to get his fingers around it.

"I may have to use my other hand," Ronnie said.

"Sign it," Van Dyne said, "if you have to hold the pen in your fucking teeth."

Big Sid was slouched on his end of the Buick's rear seat, his eyes fixed on the cast on his wrist. When the car caught a pothole or a bump, Sid would wince, and as soon as the pain subsided, he'd turn to Ronnie at the other end of the seat with a look which made Ronnie want to climb down the space between the seat and the door to hide.

"Sid..." It came out, "Shid..."

"You say one fucking word to me and I'm gonna use this cast to pound your head into pudding. Y'unnerstand?" Sid turned away, staring out the window at the tiles of the Lincoln Tunnel blurring by.

Ronnie sagged in his seat. The good stuff they'd given him at the hospital was starting to fade and he could feel stinging twinges in his arm and face.

Up front, Sergeant Troupe was at the wheel while Van Dyne sat slouched against the passenger door. For the first time, Ronnie noticed the captain's hair didn't have its usual newscaster's sweep. It hung loose, matted. It looked grayer than he remembered.

They came up out of the tunnel into midtown, near the ramps that curled up into the Port Authority terminal. Ronnie asked Troupe to pull over.

He wasn't aware of falling as he tried to climb out, just suddenly Van Dyne and Troupe helping him up, propping him against the side of the car.

"Get back in the car," Troupe said. "We'll take you home."

Ronnie managed a slow nod of his head, forced his legs to steady up under him. The wind howling down Tenth Avenue tasted like soot and it had an edge which stirred the faint burning sensation he could feel under his stitches, but he didn't want to be back in the car with Sid and the captain. Maybe he said something else, he wasn't sure, thought he heard Troupe saying something which sounded pleading, then Van Dyne saying dismissively, "He wants to go, let him go." Then the car was gone and Ronnie was alone at the curb.

He walked, his head unsure where, but his feet seemed to know the route. There was the urinal smell of a subway station then he was sitting in a near-empty subway car rumbling downtown. The rocking of the train stoked that unwanted feeling in his face and arm still further and he hoped he could get home and knock himself out with the pills the ER doc had given him before the shot from the hospital wore off completely.

Someone tapped his shoulder. Ronnie looked up at a large black man in a fraying plaid coat. The man had a childish, toothless grin and smelled unhealthy. Ronnie reached out for the white slip of paper the black man held out to him. He squinted at the poor Xerox of poor typing:

*This is a fact.*

*My name is Louis Brown. While boxing it was accidental since then I became deaf mute and was practically blind. I recently has my vision returned to me. I would like to help me reach my goals to become a movie actor. I always like to entertain people. My enjoyment is to make people laugh and smile. Will you please donate 25 cent in order to gain this goal?*

*Thank you.*

Ronnie handed the Xerox back to the man and looked up at his good-natured grin. Ronnie enunciated his words carefully. This time they came out precise and clear which was good because on the off chance the beggar's note had the slightest bit of truth in it, Ronnie didn't want there to be any mistake about what he was saying which was, "Fuck off."

Meara woke but didn't open his eyes. He'd been drifting in and out all day behind his closed eyes, partly from shock, partly from the pain meds, partly from just feeling so...fucking...*empty*. From whatever reason, for all those reasons, it had been enough – along with the mother-hen doctors with their "He's in no shape to answer questions!" – to keep the Jersey cops off him for the day.

He let his eyes open a little. It was a double room, but he had it to himself. It was dark except for a low headboard light over the room's other bed. There was a uniformed cop stretched out on the bed watching the wall-mounted TV. He could hear Johnny Carson thanking the night's guests. The shades over the window were drawn but around the edges he could see the icy glow of streetlights. He closed his eyes, listened hard, found the hospital sunk in a late-night sleepy stillness. He heard the cop in the other bed yawn.

Meara opened his eyes, tried to focus, get a study on the cop: 30s, a little soft in the middle, bored shitless with a third-shift glaze in his eyes.

Meara tried to shift in his bed, felt his right wrist handcuffed to the bedrail, a swollen stiffness in his right leg, a feeling like a giant hand holding him around the middle, making it hard – making it *hurt* – to take anything but a shallow breath.

"You awake?" The cop was out of the bed, now, on his feet, immediately wary.

Meara grunted. "Gotta pee."

"Now?" The cop was standing back, his right-hand hovering around his holster.

"I been in this bed all damn day. Yeah, now. You don't have to uncuff me. There's a bedpan in the can."

The cop came back with the stainless-steel bedpan. Even though it was empty, he held it away from his body, his nose wrinkled up unhappily.

"I'm gonna lift up," Meara said, "you slide it under."

"*You* slide it under."

"I can't. I only got one hand free."

290

Meara grabbed hold of the bedrails and pulled himself to a seated position. Pain – bad enough to take his breath away – exploded in his side and in his right leg. He almost let himself fall back down.

"That looked like it stung," the cop said.

"Busted ribs," Meara grunted out. He waited for the pain to ebb some then he told the cop he'd hold himself up on the bedrails while he slipped the bedpan underneath. It brought another detonation of pain, he couldn't see straight for all the flashes and glittering pinwheels going off in his eyes. "I shoulda just peed on myself," Meara said.

"Then you get the nurse to clean you up. That's not bad."

"You seen the nurses here? *You're* prettier."

They shared a chuckle, but the stabs from his side and his leg cut Meara's short.

"That's it," he gasped after a minute. "It even hurts to pee. You ready?" Meara meant for the cop to pull the bedpan out while he held himself up again.

"What am I supposed to do with it?"

"Just pour it out in the can. Or leave it in there for the nurse."

The cop nodded, reached under Meara to put his hands on the steel seat. "Ready."

Meara steeled himself, started to pick himself up, the cop started to slide the bedpan out, Meara gasped a painful "Shit," and started to lose his grip, falling toward the cop.

The cop was worried about the pan spilling on him which was the wrong place for his attention to be, and which was why he didn't know Meara's free hand was coming at him until it punched him in the throat.

The cop clutched at his neck, trying to draw a breath that wouldn't come, his knees started to buckle, but Meara's free hand grabbed him by the front of his uniform shirt and pulled him across the bed. The cop knew what Meara was after, tried to cover his holster with his gun hand, but with no air he didn't have the strength and Meara easily got to the pistol and laid it down across the back of the cop's neck, at the base of his skull, interrupting the flow of tiny electronic impulses that kept the cop upright and walking and talking.

The cop went slack across Meara's lap and the pain in his right leg from the weight of the cop was nearly blinding. Meara kicked the throbbing leg free from under the body, then he sat there trying to catch his breath. The effort to fight off the fireworks and pinwheels to make his move and carry through under the struggling cop had left him in not much better shape than the man lying across his bed.

When all the throbbing and flashing lights in his eyes had subsided enough where he could see and breathe as well as his cracked ribs would allow, he checked the cop to make sure he was still breathing (he was), then went through his pockets for the key to the handcuffs. He got himself uncuffed, kicked the cop clear with his one good leg. He picked up the hem of his gown to look at his other leg. There was a red-stained gauze bandage where he'd watched the doctors drain almost a cup of blood out of a hematoma taking up half the space between his knee and his hip.

He stripped off the cop's uniform and shoes and using the cuffs from the bed and the pair from the cop's duty belt, handcuffed him face down to the bed. He tore some strips from the sheets of the other bed for a blindfold and gag.

The cop's uniform pants were baggy and long on him, and the sleeves of the shirt didn't cover his wrists, and the shoes swam a bit on his feet, but it would all do. He strapped on the duty belt, put the .38 back in its holster.

In the bathroom, he ran cold water in the sink, threw it on his face, saw himself in the mirror over the sink: Band-Aids here and there covering the larger cuts, the smaller ones stained with mercurochrome. Beyond the cuts... *Jesus, you look old. Jesus, I feel old.*

There was a wallet in the pants pocket. He flipped it open and there was a photo of a younger version of the cop on the bed hugging a plain, smiling girl who looked like she was just out of high school. *I had a picture like that once.* He took the 40-odd dollars in cash out of the wallet, tossed the empty leather sheath on the bed, grabbed the cop's cap and jacket from where they'd been left on the other bed and stepped out into the hall.

The hall was empty, he couldn't see anybody at the nurses' station some yards away but could hear them talking quietly to each other. He eased the room door closed quietly behind him, stepped across the hall to an emergency exit and headed down the stairs, holding tightly to the railing to keep the pressure off his leg.

He found the cop's cruiser parked in a visitor's space for the ER. As he pulled away from the hospital, he could see from the Union City heights across the dark Jersey side of the river, across the wide, black band of the Hudson, to The City where a scattering of lights up and down the length of Manhattan still glittered, standing out like sharp, pointed stars in the winter night. The red and green and white Christmas colors of the Empire State Building floated high above the rest, under a soft reddish-green halo reflected in the thick blanket of low clouds above. He rolled his window down and the air tasted refreshingly, stirringly cold.

For a moment, the pain washed away, and he felt at home alone in the night.

Guielmo "Willy the Whale" Stabile stepped back from the urinal in the cramped diner's bathroom, reached under the vested bulge of his stomach and fumbled around looking for his zipper. This is where prosperity gets you, he thought; you can't see your feet. 30 years ago, when he'd first been coming up, he'd been so lean and mean they used to call him "Willy the Whip." Now? Willy the Whale. Not to his face, of course, but still... He finally managed to get his zipper up, washed his hands and went back out into the dining room.

The twins, home from college, were sitting together on one side of a booth by the front windows across from their mother. He took a moment before he headed for the booth.

Both girls had their mother's dark coloring and angled looks. The sharp planes of their faces just missed coming together in a handsome whole, thrown off by their single genetic inheritance from their father; his disproportionately grand, gracelessly designed proboscis. "This is *your* fault," Josephine would say, pointing at her nose then pointing at him before going into a long nag about how – since it *was* his fault – he should put out the money for rhinoplasty since "'ya know, ya kinda *owe* it to us!"

Josephine was now staring moodily out the window, but then she was always staring moodily at something. Carmela – who also had a penchant for moody staring – was staring unhappily at her plate. Willy Stabile didn't know why his daughters were so unhappy; they had omelets in front of them. At his place, next to his wife, was a plate with two slices of dry wheat toast, a small grapefruit juice, and a saucer carrying a cup of hot water and a packet of Sanka. In front of his wife was a stack of pancakes.

"Where are my eggs?"

"You don't need eggs," his wife said.

"I don't care what I *need*. I *want* eggs." He was aware he was probably doing little for his argument with the way he had to squeeze and wheeze his way into the booth next to her.

"Tell your blood pressure how much you want eggs," she said. "Tell your arteries."

He bit down on the scratchy, tasteless, unbuttered wheat toast. "Foo." He busied himself mixing his Sanka.

"I don't know if you've noticed," his wife said and nodded at his daughters.

294

"I'm trying not to," he said. "All right. *Che cosa c'è?*"

Carmela poked at her omelet with her fork and shrugged.

Josephine rolled her eyes.

He turned to his wife. "See? I asked. Happy?"

"See, Mom?" Josephine snapped, like she'd been waiting for the chance to pounce. "He always gets sarcastic. I *told* you he'd be sarcastic."

"Eat," he said, meaning, "Shut up."

"I'm not hungry," Carmela mumbled.

"Then why did you order all that?"

"I didn't," she grumped. "She did," and nodded curtly at her mother.

"She doesn't eat," his wife said. "She's getting skinny."

"That's because she's anorexic," Josephine snorted.

Carmela pinched her sister under the table.

Her sister retaliated by miming sticking her finger down her throat and vomiting.

"E-*nough!*" he declared. "The girl doesn't want to eat, then she doesn't want to eat." He reached across the table for her plate. "But I'm not going to have them throw out an entire plate of perfectly good—"

"Don't you *dare!*" his wife said. "You eat what's in front of you."

He sighed and took another bite of his toast. "Foo."

Unprovoked, Josephine said, "This is *so*—" and not finding a suitable word made a noise that was part huff, part sigh, with a little martyr's moan at the end.

"What's so unfair, baby?" His wife was giving her pancakes a fresh coat of syrup.

He looked at her heavily glazed pancakes, he looked at his cardboardy toast, and threw it down on his plate.

"First you drag us out of school, then you drag us down to Florida, then you drag us back here, then you take us to this dump—"

"There was no food in the house," Willy Stabile explained.

"Eight *thousand* places to eat and we have to come *here."*

"Your father and I have been coming to this place—"

Josephine did her eye-rolling thing. "Yes, Mother, we know, ever since you two blah blah blah."

"You don't talk to your mother like that," he said firmly.

"The family should be together on Christmas," his wife said.

"We didn't get pulled out of school because of Christmas," Carmela said with an edge and a sharp eye at her father. "'Business,' right, Daddy?"

He made a threatening motion at his daughter with his teaspoon but before he could tell her to shut her goddamn mouth about things she thought she knew but didn't, Josephine was at it again: "I've got a *life,* Mom!" she protested. "I've got *friends,* you know?"

It was Carmela's turn to snort. "C'mon, Jo, even your friends can't stand you!"

Josephine pinched Carmela. Carmela pinched back.

"Psycho!" Josephine said.

"Bitch!" Carmela said.

It wasn't omelets and pancakes that were going to give him a heart attack, Willy Stabile thought. It was his goddamn family.

There is a narrowing, rocky spur marking the eastern end of the Palisades. On the spur are a half-dozen residential blocks. In Weehawken, this is where the money lives.

Unlike the rest of working-class, traffic-clotted Weehawken, here, on the spur, the narrow streets are smooth, they're quiet enough for kids to bicycle and play ball and almost never have to worry about a car coming along. Ground is precious on the spur, so the houses snuggle close. The yards and lawns are small. The houses are not. Paradoxically, the further out on the spur one drives and the less ground there is, the bigger the houses get, particularly those overlooking the riverfront with an unobstructed view of the Manhattan skyline. Near the end of the spur, the ground narrows to a single street, a *cul-de-sac* lined with the biggest and most expensive homes in the neighborhood, in Weehawken. This was where Willy Stabile's family lived.

It was a wide, two-story place faced with white brick and was supposed to give the impression – but didn't – of an Italian villa. There was a spurting fountain on the small front lawn, pillars of more white brick anchoring the wrought iron fence and electric gate across the driveway.

It had not been easy for Willy Stabile to negotiate the turns through this tight, insular little neighborhood funneling down to his single street. The Lincoln was big, and his own girth forced him to steer by keeping his hands low on the wheel and feeding it right and left past his belly. At each turn, the Lincoln swung wide, like an aircraft carrier.

"Jesus, Dad,!" Josephine had mocked. "If you just weren't so *big!*"

They had been sulking since they'd left the diner. He wished they'd go back to sulking.

"Tell me again how you want eggs," his wife said.

He hit the remote control tucked in the sun visor and the gates to his driveway swung open. He tried to turn into the driveway, but his turn was too wide, and he had to back out and straighten the Lincoln before he could thread between the brick gateposts. "Don't anybody say a goddamn word!" he warned them all as he slipped into reverse.

In the driveway, he stopped at the flagstone walk leading from the drive to the front door.

"Are you going to need this car?" he asked his wife.

"I was thinking of taking them over to say Merry Christmas at Aunt Terry's—"

"Oh, Jesus, Mom, not Aunt Terry!" fumed Josephine. "She's half *dead!* It's like going to a funeral every time we go over there!"

His wife smiled tolerantly. "You can put this one away. I'll take mine. We'll pick up some groceries on the way home. But I want to change first."

His daughters followed his wife, their heels click-clacking on the walk as they argued about who *had* to go where, and who *should* go where, and so on, and why didn't Daddy have to get dragged on these excruciating visitations, and so on.

He pulled the Lincoln down the driveway to the two-car garage in back. It was a tight fit past his wife's Buick which she had left in the drive because she'd never quite gotten the knack of getting it into the garage. He reached up to his visor for the garage door remote.

The garage door rolled up and he eased the Lincoln smoothly through, putting the nose snug against the back of the garage then killed the engine. There wasn't much clearance to open the car door on his side, and it was an effort to squeeze himself through the narrow opening. Half-way out the door, he wondered if he might've gotten himself stuck, started considering it might be easier to slide back into the car and crawl over to the passenger's side.

And then, at that point, his mind was cleared of thoughts about the car and how to get out and what pains in the ass his daughters were growing up to be. Instead, he was wholly focused on the icy cold steel tube which had burrowed itself into the bulging back of his neck.

"Don't even breathe."

Instinctively, he began to turn to see who was behind him. The steel against his neck nudged him not to do so.

He heard the car's back door open. "Now; we slide in together."

They did. The back door closed.

"Close your door, Willy. Lock 'em. All of 'em. And shut the garage door."

He did.

The gun barrel rested along the roll of fat spilling over the collar of his coat. The steel was cold enough to burn. The Sanka churned in his stomach.

"Relax, Willy. No reason this can't go easy."

"What do you want?"

"Your guy."

"My guy?"

"The Boy."

"I don't know—" which even as he said it he knew was something he'd pay for.

The pistol slammed into his right ear and his head rocked against the driver's side window. He clutched his ear, stinging with cold and pain.

"Listen, mister, if you want money—"

The pistol crashed down again, this time on the gloved knuckles of the hand he had cupped around his swelling ear.

The gun came back but not to his neck. It settled against the back of his skull.

"Oh." He felt warmth in his crotch and smelled piss. For the moment, he was glad he hadn't had much for breakfast.

The man behind him sniffed at the air. "Jesus, Willy, is that you? I guess you been off the front lines too long. You spook too easy. Look, Willy, your head's not gonna hold up near as well as this gun. But I don't feel like spending all morning pounding your head into Jello, much fun as that would be. You're a businessman, Willy. I'm gonna make you a proposition. A smart proposition. A smart business proposition for a guy who's smart about business."

"A proposition?"

"You know this war The Boy's been on has been a big mistake. *Big* mistake. You're outfit's *gotta* be getting heat from the other bosses. It's been bad for your business, it's been bad for *their* business. You let him go on like this and he's going to drag you and the whole operation down the shitter with him. You don't want that, do you Willy? You know the other bosses don't want that. But, you give him to me, Willy, and they're gonna *thank* you. His seat'll be open at the table, they're gonna think you deserve to take it, and then everybody can go back to making money. This guy's a cancer for you; cut him out. Because if you don't, after I'm done with you, I'm going into your house where your wife and girls are. Now—" The pistol muzzle pushed hard against the back of his skull, he could feel the hammer being thumbed back, the cylinder moving into place. "—one more time, Willy. For the *last* time."

Ronnie was in and out for…it could've been hours, days. When the pain meds thinned out enough for the sharp, burning sensations in his face and arm to stir him, he reached for the pill bottle on his coffee table, downed a pill – or maybe two – with tepid water from the glass also on the table, and collapsed back on the futon cushion. He didn't look to see what time it was, if the prescribed period between dosages had elapsed yet. He had his own prescription: he hurt, he took a pill.

He woke, it seemed dark. Night? Or were the shades pulled? Did it really fucking matter? A day passed, two, ten, did it really fucking matter? He downed a pill.

The phone rang, he knocked the receiver off the cradle and left it on the floor and took a pill. The door buzzer buzzed, a knock, somebody calling to him – Tamela? A voice in his head? – he took a pill and slipped off to where he couldn't hear it, where it was dark and dreamless and where not giving a damn seemed just fine.

He was shaking. No, he was being shaken.

"Junior?"

He couldn't get his eyes open, whole body didn't want to move. He heard the rattle of his pill bottle.

"How many of these have you taken?"

He knew he could force his eyes open, but he didn't want to, he wanted to slip back off, but that annoying shake, again, and it was starting to spark things in his face and arm. He made a noise, something like an angry grunt, to chase whoever it was away.

Then he was being pulled up, propped up against the back of the futon. His face and arm felt, heavy, rigid, swollen.

"Let's go, Ron. I'm not going away."

Ronnie managed to crack one eye, the one clear of gauze.

Captain Van Dyne was standing over him. "Are you back?"

Ronnie made a small, unsure motion of his head. Even that hurt.

"I'll make you some coffee," Van Dyne said. "Do you have coffee?"

Ronnie made a lazy wave of his hand to the shelf over the stove.

"Instant," Van Dyne said, finding the jar. "Barbaric."

Ronnie heard Van Dyne rattle around the stove, water run in the sink, the clatter of a sauce-pan on the stove. He had both eyes open, now, though not quite focused. Van Dyne was turning something around in his hands. Ronnie squinted, finally managed to clear his vision somewhat. It was the engine assembly from the Sopwith Camel model still unfinished and cluttering up his coffee table.

"I used to make these when I was a kid," Van Dyne said. "This was always the hardest part: the engine. All those little –"

"Would you put that down?" Ronnie croaked.

Van Dyne nodded and set the assembly back on the table. "My pardon." He turned back to the stove, poured a mug of hot water from the saucepan, stirred in the instant coffee. "Milk? Yes, you'd take milk." He rummaged around in the little refrigerator, splashed some milk in the coffee and set it down on the coffee table, then readjusted the placement, making a show of moving it quite clear of the half-finished model biplane.

Ronnie picked up the mug in his unbandaged hand, took a sip. The hot coffee seemed to slide all through him, he could feel himself start to come more fully awake, and when that sensation reached his face and arm he knew that wasn't going to be a good thing.

The mug pulled at his good hand, too heavy, started to shake and splash. Van Dyne stepped up and rescued the mug, setting it back on the table. Ronnie reached for the pill bottle. Gone. Looked up, saw it in Van Dyne's hands.

"Not yet," the captain said. "I need you to hear something."

"How'd you get in here?"

Van Dyne smiled, reached inside his coat and flashed his leather picklock case. "You didn't answer the phone, you didn't answer your buzzer. And I need to talk to you." He rattled the few pills left in the bottle. "I need you to be able to hear it."

Ronnie squinted at the gray light around the pulled shades. He tried to remember: hadn't it been dark at one point? "Is it still Friday?"

"Saturday. The 24th. Christmas Eve."

"You got something to say…"

"Some decisions have been made and I thought you should know them. I didn't want you tortured by suspense over the holidays." Van Dyne was rattling around the kitchen area, again. Ronnie heard him in the fridge, the crack and clatter of an ice tray. "Well, I'm out. I get to keep my pension, but effective two weeks from now, I'm a civilian."

Ronnie felt his face redden, and that made the stitches sting. "I'm sorry."

"Oh, I believe you," Van Dyne said. "But that hardly helps, does it? Here, try this." Van Dyne had made an ice pack from Ronnie's one dishtowel and cubes from the tray. "You and Sidney are on 30-day suspensions. Sidney will be demoted. They may even break him back into uniform; that hasn't been decided yet. You're to be spared that, but only because you're already so far down in the ranks they can't break you down any further…except to bounce you off the force…which has been considered and isn't completely off the table. If you are allowed to stay on the job, the upside is you'll have quite a few years to prove yourself all over again and make the Department forget these early year embarrassments of yours. Sidney won't have that luxury. Wherever they put him is where he'll likely stay for as long as he remains with the Department."

Ronnie felt a new pain, something inside, and he knew there was no pill for it.

"Have some more of your coffee," Van Dyne said. "I want your head clear. Do you need help?"

Ronnie shook his head and managed to get the cup to his lips and back to the table without a problem. He could see Van Dyne more clearly now, even in the dull gray light seeping through the shades. The captain was wearing the same clothes he'd been wearing yesterday, looked like maybe he'd slept in them. He was unshaven, slumped. It was like watching an Olympian athlete being eaten up by cancer. Ronnie felt that pain inside, again.

Van Dyne reached around in his jacket and pulled out his cigarette case. "Do you have an ashtray?"

"I don't let people smoke in here."

"Ashtray."

"Use whatever you can find."

Van Dyne poked around the kitchen area, looked through the motley collection of glasses on a shelf over the sink. Something made him give out an amused, "Huh!" and he set a small glass down on the stove near him, lit one of his sleek Opals. He flicked the ash into the glass and even though Ronnie couldn't see it quite clearly, he recognized the shape: a Welch's Jelly Flintstone glass. He'd had it since...forever.

"There's other news," Van Dyne went on, "from across the river."

For the first time, Ronnie felt alert. "Meara."

"Sometime during the wee hours of the morning, he escaped from the hospital in Union City. He took the uniform, the weapon, and the police cruiser belonging to his guard. Not to be nasty about it, but it's gratifying to see our New Jersey colleagues do their part in contributing to what may be the biggest series of fuck-ups in the history of organized policing. They found the cruiser next door in Weekhawken. Meara had, evidently, stripped the patches and shields off the uniform; they found them in the car, along with his guard's duty belt. He still has the service revolver and spare ammunition."

"Weehawken?"

"Within walking distance of the residence of William Stabile. Remember him?"

Ronnie frowned. Something familiar…

"Ralph Zinni – Do you remember *him*? I expect not; you don't look like you're recalling all that much just now. He was the hood who'd been following Lourdes Bracero and wound up in a dumpster. He belonged to Stabile. I believe Sidney described Stabile as Anthony Maiella's 'go-to guy'."

Van Dyne took a long drag on his cigarette, flicked another length of ash into the Flintstone glass. Ronnie didn't like the ash in his Flintstone glass, and he didn't like the smell of Van Dyne's Paris Opals in his apartment.

"The man Meara went after yesterday – Joseph Rocco – also has ties to Maiella's organization, suspected of being one of his top enforcers. Meara had shot him and the immediate assumption was that was how Rocco died. But when they laid Rocco out on the table, they found fractures of the hyoid bone and thyroid cartilage." Van Dyne smiled when he saw the words only brought a confused frown from Ronnie. "He'd been strangled. Not all at once. My working theory is Meara shot him to immobilize him. Then he sat with him – that's where they found Meara, in the car next to Rocco – threatened to finish him off—" here Van Dyne illustrated by putting his free hand around his own throat, squeezing and releasing, squeezing and releasing,

" – unless Rocco gave him something. Which, I think, Rocco did."

"Then Meara killed him anyway."

Van Dyne shrugged: of course.

"And you think Rocco gave him Stabile?"

"They found a Lincoln Continental registered to Stabile's wife abandoned along the Jersey waterfront, not far from the Hoboken Terminal. The odd thing about that is Mr. and Mrs. Stabile were still at home. Stabile won't explain why his wife's car was off on its own. In fact, he refuses to speak to the police at all. The working theory for the Jersey cops at this point is they think Meara hopped a bus or train at the terminal and he's running. They think that because putting some miles behind him would be the smart, sane thing for Meara to do. Tell me, Junior; you've been chasing him all week. You must have a sense of the man by now. Is that what *you* think?" The captain said it teasingly; he already knew the answer.

"He'd have to be crazy to come back into town." Ronnie said.

"Yes," Van Dyne said, "he would have to be." Something seemed to tug at Van Dyne from the inside, then, he nodded slightly, agreeing with it. "'From hell's heart I stab at thee; for hate's sake, I spit my last breath at thee.'"

Ronnie shook his head.

"He's like Ahab," the captain said. "He's come too far and it's cost him too much to stop now; not when he's this close. He'll ride this train right to the end."

Ronnie sank deep in his futon cushion. It made a sad, inevitable sense.

"But it presents you, young man, with the opportunity to begin your long process of redemption and rehabilitation."

Which, to Ronnie, was as confusing as all that hell's heart stuff.

"Meara will go to the girl," Van Dyne said.

"How do you know?"

"When he runs, he'll need money. He has no ID, no access to his bank, just the few dollars he took off the Jersey cop. And, I think he'd come back for her anyway."

"'Cause he loves her?"

"Because she's all he's got left."

Which Ronnie thought also made a sad, inevitable sense. "What do you want from me?"

"Talk to her. She knows you. Any of us talks to her, she'll close down. She might not for you. I doubt he's told her where he's going to finish this thing, but he will have told her how and where they'll meet up afterward."

Ronnie's head started to throb; not from his stitches. That place across the bridge of his nose. "She won't talk to me. Not about this. She won't give him up."

"You won't know until you try. You've done a lot of damage, Ron. To me, Sidney, the Department, and certainly to yourself. Frankly, I think you *owe* us a try. I think you owe *me*. Don't you?"

"If I do this, can you do something for Sid?"

Van Dyne smiled caustically. "You think you're in a position to negotiate?" Then, a considering shrug. "The demotion is a given. But, possibly something can be done to shorten the suspensions for both of you." The captain stubbed his Opal out in the Flintstone glass, reached into his pocket, stepped across the room and set Ronnie's badge and holstered pistol on the coffee table next to the unfinished model. "So. Do you want to be a cop, again, Junior?"

They stepped into the hall, Ronnie turned to lock the door.

"Ronnie?" It was Tamela standing in her doorway. She saw the gauze, her eyes dropped to the torn, bloody sleeve of his parka, and her smile disappeared immediately, she moved back a step into her apartment. All that gauze and blood spooked her, and he could tell she was ashamed of herself, ashamed she couldn't bring her eyes up to it.

She slowly closed her door, he heard her turn up the music she'd been listening to. As he followed Van Dyne down the hall, R.E.M. came through her door and echoed off the plaster walls of the hallway:

*It's the end of the world as we know it*
*It's the end of the world as we know it*
*And I feel fine…*


"Why don't you just use a pencil?" Murillo asked.

"The idea is not to make any mistakes," Berman said.

"But you *always* make mistakes."

"Yes, but the *idea* is that if I ever do get through it without making any mistakes, I can say, 'Look, I did *The New York Times* crossword puzzle in ink with no mistakes.'"

Murillo made a sour sucking noise around a tooth. "That'd do it for you? You could die happy, then?"

"Satisfied and complete."

"Because you filled out the crossword puzzle in *The New York Times* in ink?"

"With no mistakes."

"And you'll be happy with that?"

"I love being the only person in the stationhouse who knows a five-letter word for offering an opinion is 'opine.'"

Murillo shook his head and re-settled in the front seat of the car. He had a high-cheeked, slant-eyed Aztec face, and was almost scarecrow lean, although in the stationhouse locker room it was clear what little meat he carried was all muscle: slim but sinewy arms and legs, washboard abs, a set of lats so pronounced it was said if he could flap them he'd fly away. His suits – not expensive but well-chosen – hung on him beautifully, like on a model. He looked even more like a model sitting next to Berman slouched behind the wheel. Berman looked like someone sticking his head out of a pile of rumpled clothes from a second-hand store.

The air in the car was getting stale and the windows were starting to mist. Murillo cracked his window a bit.

"That's cold," Berman grunted, still studying the crossword propped on the steering wheel through his reading glasses.

"I'm suffocating. My nose gets stuffy. I'm still not over this flu thing."

"You have a cold. You don't have the flu."

Murillo made a protesting grunt but rolled the window up anyway. He took his eyes off Lourdes Bracero's building and looked along the street behind them for no particular reason other than to break the visual monotony and stretch his back a little. He heard a vertebra crack. "I don't want to be doing all the watching here while you spend your time trying to die happy."

"I am well able to attend to my proper duties while doing this," Berman said. "I have great peripheral vision and enormous powers of concentration."

"What you have is enormous powers of bullshit."

"Well, yes, that, too. Have another croissant. Try the chocolate."

"I don't like chocolate," Murillo said, pondering the croissants lined up belly-to-back in the box between them. "Chocolate for breakfast. That doesn't sound right."

"Try it. I'm telling you, you'll like it."

"I'm still getting over this flu thing. I can't taste anything anyway."

"You don't have the flu."

Murillo pulled a squeeze bottle of Dristan from his coat pocket and gave each nostril a squirt.

"The captain; *he* has the flu," Berman said. "Try the chocolate. Just the one."

Murillo did. "Hey, you know, that's not too bad! These things are pretty fattening, though, right? I can just *feel* the butter bleeding out of this thing when I take a bite."

"Feed a cold."

"But this is the flu."

"You don't have the flu. How's the coffee? I picked that out. I thought you'd like it. Bavarian vanilla cream."

"Not bad. Now what was that thing you were saying before? About me and Sylvie? You were saying I should make up?"

"I said no such thing."

"Then what *were* you saying?"

"I was saying that before you go out *there,* you better think about whether or not you really want to break up."

"You're saying I should make up just so I don't have to be single again?"

"No."

"That's what it *sounds* like you're saying."

"I'm just saying you should really think about it."

"Is it that bad out there?"

"It's that bad."

"And I should listen to you because you're twice divorced. You're an expert on relationships is why you're twice divorced."

"I'm an expert on how bad it is out there."

"You'd take back one of your divorces?"

"No, but I'm telling you it's rough and before you go out there, think about whether or not these problems are as bad as you think they are."

"Were *your* problems as bad as you thought they were?"

"Worse."

"It's not the problems, man. It's that I didn't *do* anything!"

"I've been there. We've *all* been there."

"If I didn't do anything, why should I be the one to make up?"

"Then don't."

"But she's going to blame me anyway!"

"Probably."

"Like the other day. I mean, the alarm goes off, I barely have my eyes open and she goes, 'You forgot today is my birthday, didn't you?'

I'm not even awake, yet, I go, 'Hm?' And she goes, 'I *knew* it!' And I'm thinking, 'Jesus, I didn't even remember today was Tuesday!'"

"I know."

"And then *that* kicks off a whole *line* of shit—"

"I'm just saying you don't want to be out there if you can help it."

"You're seeing somebody, right? Do you go through this with her?"

"I'm trying to finish this puzzle."

"What's the matter? You want to talk about *my* situation but—"

"Doing these things is supposed to be good for your mind."

"Where'd you hear that?"

"I forget. Oh-oh."

Berman had not been bullshitting about his exceptional peripheral vision. He'd caught a glimpse of Van Dyne behind the wheel of an unmarked Buick pulling into the street behind them. Berman ditched his newspaper on the floor and slipped off his reading glasses as Van Dyne's car pulled up alongside. Berman rolled down his window bringing him face-to-ragged-face with Ronnie slouched down in the passenger seat, propped against the door. "Tough day yesterday?" Berman asked. "I don't suppose you'd care for a croissant, Captain? I've got a nice assortment here."

"Fuck the croissants," Van Dyne said. "Say something relevant."

"Unless she's gone out another way, she's still in there," Murillo said, punctuating his report with another double-blast of Dristan.

"I checked with the other posts," Van Dyne said. "She hasn't been to the bar or her bank today. She *must* still be in there." He turned to Ronnie, Ronnie looked back at him, and climbed stiffly out of the car.

He stood for a second between the two cars, shuddered and cupped his bandaged face as a gust of icy-tasting wind puffed down the street. He let out a soft, long, "Yeahhhh..." and started down the street toward the stoop of Lourdes Bracero's building.

"That," Berman pronounced, "is not a happy chappy."

"You think he's unhappy now?" Van Dyne said, "Wait'll you see how he looks when he comes back."

The window in the foyer door was still cardboarded over from the night Ronnie had put his elbow through it. This time, Ronnie had a key; Lourdes Bracero had given them a set of keys, which had passed from surveillance team to team since the night of the shooting as a just-in-case.

He had to stop on the stairs to her floor. His side was hurting and he felt dizzy. He wished he'd brought those lovely little pills of his with him. He also wished he'd told Captain Van Dyne to fuck off and had crawled back into his med-induced semi-coma until this whole mess blew over. He closed his eyes, took a minute to steady himself, then grabbed the railing and hauled himself up to her floor.

At her door, he had the key out, but stopped himself. It felt...invasive. He raised his hand to knock, and as his fingers curled into a fist, the stinging pull of the stitches suggested he might want to consider using the other hand. But even then, his upraised good hand hung in the air and he couldn't make it move against the door.

It came to him, then, that he wasn't hurting or dizzy because he was cut and banged up (although that sure as hell didn't help). It was because he didn't want to be in front of that door, or go into that apartment, or have this talk with Lourdes Bracero. He wasn't quite sure why, but like a kid afraid of a dark basement, he might not know what was down there, but he was goddamn sure it was a place he didn't want to go to.

He made himself stand erect and knock. Some shuffling inside, he knocked again.

"Who is it?"

"Ronnie."

"Just a second."

And that was all it took for him to know why he didn't want to be there, what it was he'd been afraid of, so afraid it made him sick and dizzy and stirred up the pain in his wounds.

It was that she'd lie.

And she had.

He was pissed, then, he could feel the anger come up in him and burn in the gash in his face and arm. In a second, he had the key in the lock, was coming through the door. She had the chain on, but it didn't take much of a shove for the old wood of the sill to splinter and split and the anchor of the chain fly free.

Lourdes Bracero was on the other side of the room from him, on the other side of the open sofa bed, her body in that last bit of settling that tells you you'd just missed seeing what she didn't want you to see.

"What the hell's with you?" Lourdes asked.

He came around to her side of the bed, pushed by her. She had hurriedly pulled the quilt down to cover the suitcase sticking slightly out from under the bed, stuffed and unclosed. He pushed the suitcase clear of the bed with his foot. "Taking a vacation? Well, I can understand that. You've been through a couple of hard days. Been hard for all of us. I wouldn't mind a vacation either. Where is he, Lou?"

She turned away. She was wearing that denim jacket. Meara's denim jacket. She fished a nearly empty pack of cigarettes out of the pocket, lit herself one.

He felt tired. He sat on the edge of the fold-out bed. "Did you know he was still alive when we…"

"Fucked?"

He flinched at the word.

She sat at the little kitchen table, shaking her head over him. "What? You thought, hey, he's dead, I'm just gonna fall for you? I felt bad for you, Blue. It was a pity fuck. I'm sorry, does that hurt your feelings? You want to put more on it than it was, that's your problem.

I'm sorry you got your heart broke, but don't think I'm givin' him up 'cause I tossed you one."

He wanted to hit her then. Wasn't sure why he didn't. He was on his feet, holding up his bandaged arm, pointing to his bandaged face. "Do you see this? Look at it! This is because of *him!* Sid, the other cop who put his life on the line for you that night? He's home, suspended, almost got himself killed yesterday...because of *him!* You forget Teresa Ortiz in the hospital? You forget why that whole thing happened? That *you* almost got *killed* because of *him?*"

She tiredly let out a stream of blue smoke. "I can't afford to care about that stuff, Blue."

"Look at this!" and he held up his arm again. *"Look at this!"*

"Don't start comparin' scars with me, chico," she said coldly, "'cause you're gonna lose."

"Whatcha say, Lourdes." It was a deep voice, coming up from way low in the mountain-sized Latino standing in the door with a baseball bat in his hands, his pint-sized wife/girlfriend/whatever fearfully peeping around his elbow. "Gotta problem here?"

Ronnie flashed him his shield. "Only if you want to make one, big boy! And if you're thinking about it, there's three more of me downstairs, so step off, ok, pal?"

The Latino was looking past Ronnie, toward Lourdes, and she must have given him the ok nod because he reluctantly backed away, shepherded his woman back into their apartment across the hall. Ronnie heard them throw the dead bolt and slip on the chain.

Ronnie closed the apartment door. The dizziness came back, and his head was pounding so bad he could hardly see. He found himself with his head against the door, holding him up.

"Why can't you just let us go? You're making a big show, Blue, but if you were ever serious 'bout feelin' anything for me...let us go." He felt her hand lightly on his shoulder.

He wasn't dizzy anymore. He turned, felt his face twisting, straining against the stitches. "You're gonna try to play me like that?"

She stepped back, shucked the jacket to the floor, started unbuttoning her blouse. "Ok, then, Blue, what'll it take? You want another one? It's ok with me 'cause that's all it was, just a fuck to help pass a bad time."

He didn't realize he'd slapped her, things had gone black for a second, and when the blackness cleared she was sprawled across the bed, the mark of his hand glowing on her face, and his hand – the torn, crippled hand – burned like napalm going off all along the gash, all the way up his arm. He was trembling. Not from the pain. Not from the fear of what he'd done. From trying to keep himself from bringing that burning, searing hand down on her again and again.

She saw it in him, but it didn't frighten her. There was just a sad, pitying smile. "Happy birthday, Blue. You're growin' up."

He turned away from her because it was the only way to keep himself from going at her again. He faced the windows, still covered with their flimsy sheets of cardboard, fluttering with the cold wind howling up and down her street, a cold wind he could feel whistle around the edges and chill the room. "If we know where he's gonna be, we have a chance to take him quiet. Otherwise, more people are gonna get hurt. You may not give a shit about that, but if that happens, sooner or later one of the people who gets hurt'll be him. It's your choice, Lou: you want to visit him at Riker's? Or the cemetery?"

"Oh, yeah," he heard her sigh behind him. "All grown up."


Ronnie pushed her into the back seat of Berman and Murillo's car. "Take her back to the house," he told Berman. "Hold her until this is over. No calls, no visitors, no nothing! You understand?"

Berman blinked at the whip-snap tone, but he nodded a yes.

Ronnie climbed into Van Dyne's car, closed his eyes against the near-blinding pain in his head, tried to massage it away with his good hand.

"Well?" Van Dyne asked.

"He didn't tell her what he was going to do or where it was going to happen. He told her he'd meet up with her after."

"Where?"

"Port Authority Bus Terminal."

"When?"

"He wasn't sure. He told her to get her hands on as much money as she could on the way, get there by 2:30 and wait. He'd find her."

Van Dyne started the car. "I can drop you off at your place on the way."

Ronnie shook his head. "Like you said, Captain. Come too far and it's cost too much."

"How's your head?"

"Full."

The booth was against the front windows of the Times Square Howard Johnson's. Meara squirmed on the green vinyl of the seat trying to find a comfortable position, but between the pain in his ribs and his throbbing leg, there didn't seem to be one.

Out in the square, tourists and knots of families headed uptown for the Christmas show at Radio City, or to gawk at toys only an Arab sheik could afford at F.A.O. Schwartz. There were last-minute gift-shoppers loaded down with shopping bags and boxes in foil wraps and bows.

This is how it is, he thought, how it always is. You watch them through glass, like an aquarium. Even when there is no glass and you're in with them, it's like the glass is still there, you're never one of them, you're apart. They go uptown to see the tree and the light angels and the ice skaters at Rockefeller Center, but you're watching the crowd for pickpockets. They go downtown to look at the *Miracle on 34th Street* dioramas in Macy's windows, but you have your eye out for snatch-and-grabbers eyeballing fat pocketbooks. When they come out of Radio City bubbling about the Rockettes, and the sun is going down and the pools of shadow grow, you watch for the wolf packs in the dark, the muggers, the shithead hoods, the twitchy junkies and alkies, the delusional psychos. Cop's eyes, that what the hair-bags call them, those restless eyes.

The waitress brought him his coffee and set it down next to the bottle of aspirin he'd picked up at a pharmacy as he'd limped his way uptown from the PATH station. He took four pills, washed them down with his coffee, checked the clock on the wall behind the counter: 1:30. Stabile had said he'd set up the meet for around two.

Meara took another swig of his coffee, scooped up his aspirin, left a dollar on the table and pulled himself out of the booth. As the blood rushed down into his leg, the pain throbbed fresh, his leg almost buckled, and for a moment his vision went gray and the Howard Johnson's swam around him. He could feel something warm trickling down his thigh; he was bleeding through the bandage.

He limped outside, and the cold winds whirling around Times Square helped freshen him. He crossed the plaza toward Seventh Avenue, heading uptown. At the north end of Times Square, tucked in the narrow angle formed by the intersection of Broadway and Seventh, was a wedge-shaped block running between 48th and 49th Streets. About halfway up the Seventh Avenue side of the block, on the west side of the street, was the Frisco Theater.

The Frisco was a porn shrine. The theater had debuted the two movies which had made porn something for more than the perv-in-an-overcoat crowd – *Deep Throat* and *The Devil in Miss Jones* – back in the early 1970s and had never stopped running them: 24 hours a day, seven days a week, running head-to-tail, year after year. It didn't make it into the Zagat's guide, but the Frisco had become something of a tourist attraction for the straights who thought going to see two dozen-year-old porn flicks at a grubby little box of a grindhouse was an exhilarating step on the wild side.

But it was Christmas Eve and the straights were off seeing the sights, buying gifts, and heading home to light their trees. Today, the Frisco was a haven for dozing drunks, crashing junkies, and anybody else who needed a warm, dry place and could afford the $2.99 ticket price. They were scattered among the creaking seats of cracked vinyl on either side of the single aisle, each keeping as much space around himself as possible.

Meara found a seat against the back wall, just a few seats off the aisle. He slipped the cop's pistol out of his belt and tucked it in his jacket pocket, his hand tight around the grip.

The small screen was pitted, the ancient print of *Deep Throat* – probably the same print the Frisco had been running since 1973 – skipped and blipped as the projector choked on a parade of splices.

On the screen, trying to squint through his blurry vision, like poring through a gray fog, Meara didn't think Harry Reems and his walrus mustache looked much like any doctor he had ever met. Dr. Reems had just diagnosed non-orgasmic Linda Lovelace's problem: her clit was in her throat. Linda was understandably upset. "How'd *you* like it if your balls were in your ear?"

Dr. Reems brightened at the prospect. "Then I could hear myself coming!"

Well, Meara thought, they hadn't been paying $2.99 all those years for the dialogue.

A hooker worked the aisle, walking up and down the length of the theater with the regularity and listlessness of a watchman. She was black and junkie thin in tight jeans, knee-high spike-heeled boots, and an Army surplus Eisenhower jacket. When she passed someone on an aisle seat, she held out a long, bony finger and trailed it along their neck, through their hair, over their ear, like a trawler running out a

317

line. A taker could follow her to the shit-smelling men's room downstairs. But the crowd today was thin…and broke.

The double doors at the back of the auditorium swung open and closed, close enough Meara could actually feel a little puff of musty Frisco air on his face as they moved. A man stood just inside the door, waiting for his eyes to adjust to the gloom. He didn't look like the other men in the theater. He wore a long overcoat, something fine. Camel's hair, I'll bet, Meara judged. He wore a wide-brimmed fedora pulled low, and the bottom part of his face was covered with a long, dark-colored scarf. The angle was bad; Meara couldn't see the face.

The man in the overcoat started slowly down the aisle, still unsure of his way in the weak light spilling from the screen. He stopped by one of the front rows, leaned over the seats peering into the murk trying to see if the row was empty. Satisfied, he sidled down the row, sitting far from the aisle, almost against the bare cinderblock wall, far from anyone.

Meara flexed his fingers around the grip of the pistol in his jacket pocket, but he didn't move. Wait. Give him a few minutes to settle in.

He watched as the man undid his scarf, slouched a bit in his seat. The man did not remove his hat.

Meara stood, gave himself a moment for his leg to steady up under him, for the fog in his head to thin, at least a little. The pain was there, in his leg, but it didn't pull at him now, it was just background music. He drew the pistol; in the dark, no one would see it held at his side. He moved down the aisle, found the man's row and started along the rank of seats.

The man heard him, turned. The feeble light spill from the screen didn't do much for the fog Meara couldn't quite shake, but he sensed more than saw an annoyed look on the man, and the look turn to discomfort, then worry as he saw Meara wasn't stopping but moving closer, dropping into the seat next to him. He stood to move but Meara grabbed him by his fine coat – and he could feel it in his fingers, it was a fine coat – and pulled him down back into his seat.

"Hey!"

Meara poked the muzzle of his .38 into the man's ribs. Hard. "Sh." He thought it was comical the way the man's mouth dropped, and his eyes went wide, his next word frozen in his throat. Meara almost laughed out loud.

The man made a sudden blind, desperate attempt to fly out of his seat. Meara speared the .38 deep into the man's ribs, a hard-enough jab to make him gasp, and he dropped back onto the cracked, rotting vinyl.

It was too dark to see the man in the overcoat clearly; it would've meant Meara turning in a way which would only have started the hot poker in his ribs jabbing. But he could see the flickering light of the screen dance in the man's dark eyes. Wide, wild, shining eyes. 20 years and the face may have changed, but not those eyes. Oh, filled with fear instead of that cold, hardness that had stared down the stairway at him, but they hadn't changed, he could even make them out through the fog. Meara's finger flexed around the trigger…

Not yet. *Not yet.* Because it *had* been 20 years.

Meara could see the man trembling, hear his puppy-like breathing. He wondered if fear was driving the other man's blood through his ears with the same deafening surf roar he heard in his own. Through that roar, he heard the voices on the screen. Whatever was going on, this was what the people were paying their $2.99 for. Meara waited for the grunts and cries on the screen to peak.

The man in the long, fine coat also sensed that was what Meara was waiting for. He closed his eyes, shut them tightly, expectantly. "Look," he started to say.

"Merry fucking Christmas."

Even with the muzzle of the pistol jammed deep into the folds of the coat, the shot sneaked out and through the sounds of Linda

Lovelace coming. Meara heard seats creak all around the theater as people jumped.

The man in the coat shuddered as the bullet passed through him and cracked into the cinderblock wall. His eyes screwed closed even tighter, then shot open, wide, and panicked. He tried to stand, pulled himself partly out of his seat. Meara heard liquid spill onto the floor. The man's legs buckled, and he collapsed into his seat.

Meara sat with him. The roaring in his ears was gone. The theater felt dark and cold. He could smell the powder-burned fibers of the man's fine coat, hear flakes of cinderblock quietly tap on the floor. The man's seat creaked as his body settled heavier into the cushion, his breath growing short, feeble. Little slaps of something liquid on the bare concrete floor.

And still Meara sat with him, watching the man's body melt inside his fine overcoat, those eyes – one-time hard, killing – growing misted, then dull. The space around their seats grew darker, colder, emptier.

Then the man was still, and it was over.

Meara stood, feeling suddenly tired, *exhausted,* too dulled even to feel his sundry pains. He shuffled to the aisle, dimly aware of the people around the theater standing, gawking.

Then he was in the aisle and there were two men standing just inside the auditorium door. Meara felt his heart accelerate, punch against his chest. The fog thinned and he could see clearly. Too clearly.

They, too, wore fine overcoats. The one – blocky, bulging inside his leather coat – would be the bodyguard.

The other – I'll bet that's camel hair, Meara thought – he knew. He'd never seen him in person, but he knew the face – even in the shadowy light from the screen – from the news photos, the mug shots, the TV. He had a shoebox back at his apartment filled with pictures of him. Anthony "Tony Boy" Maiella.

And Maiella seemed to know him, too. *"Shit!"* he blurted and turned for the door.

The bodyguard did what bodyguards do: he pushed Maiella behind him, through the door, as he stepped forward, his right hand reaching inside his coat.

But Meara already had his pistol at his side, still smoking, and he had it up, was squeezing the trigger even before he'd gotten a steady bead on the bodyguard, just kept banging away, couldn't really see as the muzzle flash blinded him in the dark theater.

Then he was stepping over the body slumped against the doors, charging out into the lobby, could hear the pasty-faced old woman at the snack bar screaming into the phone for the police.

*Pop-pop-pop,* from outside, on the street.

He was outside, damp cold, gray light, still blinking trying to clear the muzzle flashes out of his eyes. Murmur of a crowd, a woman's scream. They were up at the 49th Street corner. Through their legs, a body sprawled in the gutter.

Not thinking, just moving, he turned away, south, tucking the pistol in his jacket pocket as he turned the corner at 48th and began heading west.

For now, he didn't think about the man he'd left in the seat at the Frisco, or the man he'd left slumped against the auditorium doors, or the man lying in the gutter at 49th Street.

All he could think was how much his leg hurt and that it had gotten awfully fucking cold.

# six: coal

*They said there'll be snow at Christmas*

*They said there'll be peace on Earth*

*Hallelujah Noël be it Heaven or Hell*

*The Christmas you get you deserve.*

Greg Lake, "I Believe in Father Christmas"

Ronnie was slouched in the center of an uncomfortable wooden bench by the front desk of the PATH Police offices in the Port Authority Bus Terminal. To his right, handcuffed to one arm of the bench, was a black guy, hair skyrocketing out from his head in Rastafarian tendrils, legs splayed, eyes half-closed in a look of beatific semi-comatosity. To Ronnie's left, cuffed to the other arm of the bench, was a white guy, young, head bobbing, eyes flitting about, feet tapping, free hand drumming incessantly on the seat, singing to himself in a low, thrumming mumble. Both the Rasta and the white guy were dirty and unshaven, and they looked like they'd – and, no doubt they had – been living in their ragged, filth-stiffened clothes.

They also smelled, to the point of making Ronnie nauseous, and it wasn't helping his queasies that the vibrations coming up through the bench from the drummer were spurring the pounding in his head to pound harder, making him feel dizzy and thusly even *more* nauseous. "Hey!" Ronnie snapped at the drummer, "Keith Moon, give it a fucking rest!"

"Rest what?" The drummer's head was bouncing like a ping-pong ball.

The Rasta smiled at that, shook his dreadlocks, and chuckled to himself.

Van Dyne was standing in the doorway to the office of the terminal watch commander, shaking the watch commander's hand, saying something like, "Well, you seem to have it covered," then something else – Ronnie found it hard to concentrate on anything with the pounding in his head, the fire in his arm, the whirl-a-gig going in his stomach. Then Van Dyne was standing over him, nodding at Ronnie to follow him out into the terminal.

"Hey," The Rasta called to him. "You be careful out dere, mon."

"Friend of yours?" Van Dyne asked Ronnie.

The Rasta shrugged. "Jus' t'inkin' *ever'body* should be careful out dere."

The PATH Police office was tucked away in a quiet ground floor corner of the terminal's South Wing, off behind the escalators leading up to the mezzanine, away from the shops girdling the main concourse and the murmuring flow of people heading upstairs to the bus gates.

"How're you holding up?" Van Dyne asked walking briskly toward the escalators.

"Barely," Ronnie said, struggling to keep up on his rubbery legs. "What're we doing?"

"The PA cops are on a rabbit drive, sweeping each floor. They've alerted the TA cops who have men on the subway accesses if he tries to go underground. Midtown's sending troops to cover the street exits."

"Jesus, why don't they call the FBI in while they're at it?"

"Do you need help?" Van Dyne was talking about getting on the escalator.

Ronnie squinted his one gauze-free eye, focusing on the parade of corrugated steps coming up out of the floor, and followed the captain onto the escalator.

"They won't find him," Van Dyne said. "They have a description, but *we* know what he looks like. We've got a better chance of spotting him."

"Didn't you just tell that PATH guy something like you were leaving it to him?"

"I lied. Watch your step."

They stepped off the escalator, Van Dyne pulled Ronnie out of the way of tourists and Christmas shoppers.

"Look at me, Ron. Listen to me. I don't want the Port Authority or the TA or Midtown or anyone else to get him. I want him. Do you understand? *I* want him."

Ronnie nodded.

"You said you wanted to take this to the end," Van Dyne said.

"I'm still here, Captain."

"He'll see they're looking for him. He'll go to the bus levels; it's his only chance to get out. I'll take the gates here; you take the North Terminal."

"If I see him—"

"Don't try to take him. Call in."

"I don't have a radio."

"Use the passenger assistance phones. Ask them to page Mr. Johnson. Ask them to say for Mr. Johnson to meet his party at wherever you're at. Then stay put until I find you."

"What about the PATH cops—"

"You call *me*, Ron, do you understand? Only *me*."

Ronnie nodded, then watched Van Dyne disappear into the crowds of people hurrying to get home.

They're all going home, Meara thought. *Home...*

He was leaning against the railing of the South Terminal mezzanine where he could look down on the main concourse through the giant, sequined snowflakes hanging from the ceiling. The Muzak pumping through the terminal was running through what seemed like every Christmas song ever written, from "Jingle Bells" to "Jingle Bell Rock."

Below, on the concourse, a family: mom, dad, three kids, all boys, all swinging little flashlights on red lanyards he recognized as Ice Capades souvenirs. The mom was slapping the boys across the back of their heads. "It's gonna go flying, it's gonna hit someone, and then what? Hm? And *then* what?"

Passing just under him, middle-aged man loaded down with bags, yelling to his wife carrying her own load. "We're going to miss the bus!"

"Well, *help* me!"

"What do you want me to do? Carry something in my teeth? I told you not to wear heels! I *told* you not to wear heels!"

They were pissy now, but then they'd be home, and hubby'd turn Channel Nine to the Yule Log and hand wifey a drink and rub her feet and it'd be ok.

They'd all be ok because they'd be home.

Christmas Eve, the tree was up, the colored lights would come on, and after the kids went to sleep the gifts would come out of hiding and the dads would be up until daybreak trying to assemble the big stuff according to directions that didn't make sense in any of their six languages. The moms would think it was funny as hell, and the dads would get snarly – "You *really* want to help? Go away!" – but it'd be fine in the morning when the kids were kicking up a blizzard of wrapping paper.

Maybe they'd be at midnight mass. Maybe somewhere in all the priestly droning, the meaning of the day would touch someone, fingers would intertwine, heads would bend toward each other. There in God's home.

*Home.*

Even in his head, it sounded like a purr. Everybody Meara saw passing by below him – the shoppers, the tourists, the show-goers, the young couples, the old couples, the families – were on their way home. *Except me. Except me and Lourdes.* There was no *home* for them.

Somebody else isn't going home today. That guy in the Frisco.

Jesus, how does it go that bad? Fuck it. *Fuck it!* Not the time, he told himself. Focus on the moves you have to make. Focus on getting out. Why'd that guy have to be there? Today of all days, some upscale straight needs a cheap jolly? Why the fuck hadn't he been home? *Why the fuck didn't you go home?*

Not the time. *Not the time.*

He plucked at his pants leg where it was sticking to the gauze. Shit, now he was bleeding through the pants.

He squinted around, looking for a clock. He knew there was one out there on the concourse somewhere, but his vision was a bit blurred. Just tired. He could feel the pants leg – more of it, now – sticking, but he kept telling himself, It's fine, you're just tired.

Where the fuck was she? God, he hoped she'd brought her Percocets. He could barely draw a breath without feeling that fist in his side against the cracked ribs; take a step without fire shooting up his leg.

He had his 20 years in. 20 years, and what he had was a stolen cop's uniform, about 40 bucks in his pocket he'd taken from the cop, bleeding out a hole in his leg, and a set of cracked ribs. And a dead citizen back there in the Frisco.

And no place to go. Except out.

*Not the fucking time!*

He shifted on his leg, spiked the pain to drive the thought out of his head.

*Where the fuck is she?*

He felt a little dizzy, the sparkle of the ceiling lights on the sequined snowflakes hurt his eyes and he closed them. He heard a screech of tires, opened his eyes, could see up the concourse and out the glass doors running across the front of the terminal along Eighth Avenue. Three police cruisers from Midtown at the curb. They emptied out, the cops gathered around a sergeant, the sergeant pointing this way and that, then, like a football team breaking out of a huddle, they scattered left and right covering the doors.

He squinted down at the concourse, his eyes fell on two Port Authority cops hurriedly crossing the floor, followed them to where they joined three more PATH cops at the information desk near the escalators. One of them was a sergeant, too. Another huddle, more pointing, another break, and scatter.

He was awake, now, alert, not dizzy anymore. There was a row of payphones nearby, he limped over to them, had a receiver in his hand, was fishing around in the stolen cop jacket for change thinking, Gotta tell her before she leaves, gotta warn her—

He hung up the phone.

She'd sold him out.

They'd run her down, squeezed her, she'd talked. Of course, she'd talked.

He was disappointed. But not mad. How could he be mad? Sometimes the only way you avoided being a victim was to be a perp. And she already had enough scars.

So add that to the score. 20 years, 40 bucks. Cracked ribs, hole in your leg. No home. And alone.

Ok, sister, well that's ok, that's fine, 'cause you just made things easier for me. That much less weight to drag.

He passed through the 41st Street crossover into the North Terminal mezzanine. Opened just a few years ago, the North Wing was more open, airier than the 1950-built South Terminal. From the mezzanine he could see the Eighth Avenue and 42nd Street entrances: Midtown cruisers on the street, PATH cops working the floor, another pair heading for the up escalator.

He tightened his fist around the grip of the pistol in his jacket pocket and headed for the escalator under the sign, "This Way to Buses." Like the rest of the North Terminal, the bus level was open and bright, a wide square surrounded by the heavy glass doors of the gates keeping out the noise and exhaust fumes from the bus circuit. By each door was a board listing departure times and stops. Stops didn't matter to him as long as it was across the Hudson. He looked for a short line to a bus already idling, ready to go. He offered 20 dollars to anyone willing to forego their ticket and take a later bus.

Then he was aboard, spreading across a pair of seats toward the back trying to ease the pressure on his leg, his ribs. There didn't seem to be any such position.

A bulky gray-templed sort in heavy overcoat squeezed in beside Meara. Meara wormed up against the window. Squeezed in like that, his pains spiked, he could feel the sweat on his forehead. It got more cramped when the man beside him opened up his *Wall Street Journal.*

"Do you mind?" Meara grunted, fidgeting to get the message across, but the tubby fuck only reshifted in his seat, finally settled taking up just as much room as before.

The bus' seats filled, then standees begin to fill the aisle.

Two young girls with jangling bracelets and cockatoo hair hung over Meara's row.

"What was his name?" the blonde girl asked.

"Oh, he had one of those stupid little southern names," the girl with black-streaked-with-purple hair said through a mouth full of snapping gum. "Cody, Coby, Kerry…"

"Was that his first or last name?"

"First."

"What was his last name?"

"Anti-Semite."

The other girl laughed. When she laughed it sounded like someone strangling a chicken.

"Yeah, that was it," the dark-haired girl said. "Cody Anti-Semite. I don't remember his *real* last name, but that's how I remember him: Cody Anti-Semite."

Meara was wondering when the bus would move. The seats were all filled. The aisle was filled. But the bus didn't move.

"What's that on your leg?" Tubby sitting next to him said.

"I spilled something," Meara mumbled.

Tubby finally noticed the man next to him; the sweat, the scabs on his face, looked back at the spreading stain on his pants' leg. "Are you all right?"

Meara forced a smile and nodded. "I'll feel better when we're moving."

Meara had a window seat but he couldn't see much. The buses were parked nose-in to their gates, and the buses on either side of his blocked his view. He couldn't see out the front either; the standees were in the way. He tried to turn, see out toward the bus circuit where the arriving buses circled looking for their gates, the departing buses circled toward the ramps leading down to the Lincoln Tunnel. It hurt to turn like that, enough to bring tears to his eyes.

What hurt more was seeing there was nothing moving out on the bus circuit. The buses on either side of him were filled, and they weren't moving either. And through their crowds of standees he could make out the buses further out had filled as well but hadn't left. None of the buses were leaving.

The passengers started to grumble, sigh.

"Maybe there's an accident in the tunnel."

"Christ, I hope not. I used that as an excuse twice last week. Now watch: that's the truth for a change and she won't believe me when I get home."

Some passengers made nasty comments to the bus driver. The driver made nasty comments to the dispatcher standing at the boarding gate.

Meara strained to hear the shouted conversation: "What can I tell you?" the dispatcher said helplessly. "We're still on a hold."

At the front of the bus, where people could see, the grumbling turned to curious murmurings, the passengers craning this way and that for a look out the windows, bubbling up the words "cops...police..." They were turning to the bus on their left. Meara turned with them, saw two PATH cops on the bus. They'd emptied out the standees then one stood at the bus door while the other walked the aisle, studying each passenger.

Meara's right hand flexed around the grip of his pistol.

The PATH cops climbed off the bus, the standees were loaded back on, the dispatcher gave the driver the signal to pull out.

Then the dispatcher signaled to Meara's driver. The doors of the bus hissed open, the dispatcher's apologetic voice asking the standees to file off, just for a minute, this wouldn't take long, the quicker they were about it the faster everybody'd be on their way home.

Meara looked at the small metal plate under his window. On the plate: "PUSH AT BOTTOM FOR EMERGENCY EXIT."

One PATH cop was a red-haired young woman. She stood on the steps by the front door of the bus, her eyes on the passengers, her right hand resting on the butt of her pistol.

Her partner was a young, stocky black guy. He stood at the head of the aisle, scanned the first couple seat rows, took a few steps, scanned the next few rows, then a few more steps...

Please be a fuck-up.

But the black cop wasn't. His eyes ran by Meara, moved on...then swung back...and held on him.

Meara moved like a snapped spring, his left hand shoving out the bottom of the window even as he was rising in his seat, bringing the .38 out, up, no time to aim, just point and shoot and hope to catch the cop in the vest, firing as soon as the muzzle cleared the heads of the passengers sitting in front of him.

The black cop saw him coming up, watched him saucer-eyed, reaching for his own pistol, knowing he'd never pull it in time, Meara saw that face over his front sight – I know the feeling, brother! – before it disappeared in the flash.

Meara didn't wait to see if he'd hit the cop, he already had the bottom part of the window popped free and bent his head down and tumbled out. His legs buckled as he hit the bus deck, a wave of blinding, breath-stealing pain engulfing him. He pulled himself up on the side of the bus, fighting to get to his feet, sure if he went down flat he'd never get up again. He could barely see, hardly hear, everything was about him hurting, but his legs were moving in a lopsided gallop, pushing him blindly away from the bus, the gates, out onto the bus deck, his only clear thought: *away.*

Oncoming bus, could pick out the blaring engine bearing down, a nasal horn sounding an alarm, he stumbled out of the way, limped alongside the bus as it passed, keeping it between himself and the passenger terminal. In only a few steps, he was falling behind, then red lights flashed in his eyes, the bus' brake lights coming on as it slowed to make a turn.

Meara forced himself to stand straight, pulled a deep breath as much as it lit up his damaged ribs to do it, used that pain to drive him the few, springing steps he needed to catch up, get a foot on the rear bumper, reach up and get his fingers in the grating of the air conditioning unit overhanging the rear window. His eyes and nose burned with exhaust fumes, the strain on his side so much he screamed, and it was lost in the loud growl of diesel engines.

The bus made another turn and it was too much for him, he lost his footing, his fingers loosened and he was airborne and when he hit the concrete deck, he fell through a hole into blissfully insensate blackness.

At the top of the escalator to the North Terminal bus level was a young man with one leg and the shakes. He asked Ronnie for money.

"Gimme a fucking break," Ronnie said. He looked around the open space of the North Terminal bus level and said it again, this time to himself: "Gimme a fucking break."

Each terminal covered a city block. There were 85 gates in the two terminals. During the commuter rush, 100 buses an hour headed out of the building. Even if there was only half that now, how the hell did the captain think they were going to cover them all? Plus the shops, the food joints, the bathrooms, the bars, the bowling alley in the south building?

"Gimme a fucking *break!*"

He felt lightheaded, found some seats along a wall. His nose flinched at a smell, a pile of rags squeezed between the seats and a support column moved. The pile of rags was a filthy, tattered quilt and someone was asleep under there. Ronnie moved to another set of seats.

The terminal speakers were giving up a Muzak-ized version of "Feliz Navidad." Ronnie thought if Sid were there, he'd probably shoot out one of the speakers.

There were PATH cops working their way along the gates to his left, another group working along his right. Yeah, he'd talked big to the captain about carrying this out to the end, but there was nothing left to do. Midtown had the doors covered, the PATH cops were working the terminal floors and the gates.

Jesus, his head hurt.

And somewhere under that hurt, something tickled at him. He rubbed at his forehead, if only the ache would fall off a bit, let his head clear...a thought *just* under there, out of reach...

Meara would have to see them coming. If he was on one of the floors, even on a bus, a guy that sharp would *have* to see them working their way toward him. And when he did, he wasn't going to just wait for the end to happen, not him, not Meara, not a guy like *that*.

But no place for him to go. All the ins and outs of the terminal were covered, the buses were covered. The doors were covered, fire exits, entrances to the subways, loading bays...every way in and out had men on it...except the "door" the buses used to get in and out.

His head still didn't feel right, but he got to his feet, headed for the passenger gate closest to him, passed between the buses nosed-in at the gates and out onto the bus circuit. The buses waiting their turn to be searched had been standing at the gates for some time now, ignoring the warning signs around the terminal about running their engines while parked so they could keep their ventilation systems running. Despite the open sides of the bus deck, the air was foul with the smell of gas and oil and the heavy sting of bus exhaust. He spat to get the taste out of his mouth. It was cold out there, he pulled deep inside his torn parka as he walked the circuit around the terminal, through the archway leading into the South Terminal bus deck, heading for the ramps running down to the Lincoln Tunnel.

There were no cops at the ramps.

He heard an engine closing, a horn tooted and he hugged the cinderblock wall by the archway as a wall of grime-streaked metal roared around the corner of the terminal, passed by him, leaving him coughing in a cloud of bluish fumes.

His attention had been on the bus, making sure it cleared him as it passed, so what he saw, off to one side, he saw only out the corner of his gauze-bordered eye, a passing shadow...something falling from the back of the bus.

Then it was not so black, and he could feel the pain, again, and the cold, feel the chill blowing through the open sides of the bus deck. He wanted to lay there. Forever. Leave his eyes closed and slip back into that numbing inky pool. But they'd never let him sleep. Sooner, later, they'd be coming.

It seared his ribs for him to roll over on his stomach, moving his right hand out across the grease-slicked floor, feeling for it, then curling around the grip of his pistol, pulling it in toward him, hugging it close to his heart. He opened his eyes. He was in the shadows by the cinderblock wall framing the archway into the South Terminal, a space littered with dusty traffic cones, oil drums, splintered traffic blockades, all kinds of rusted, rotted junk, and he had swirled into that backwater, too.

He pulled himself up along the rough surface of the cinderblock. Out past the shadows, the light washing across the outer edges of the bus deck from outside was a colorless gray. Fifty feet across the bus circuit, against the strobe lights hung around the outside of the terminal, a man's silhouette, growing larger, nearer, where the face should be an odd-sized square of white...

Ronnie saw it – whatever had fallen from the back of the bus – as a heap of rags on the floor among the other terminal detritus. But the heap moved, rose to take the shape of a man.

In the shadows by the wall, it was no more than a shadow itself, the head wreathed in breath vapor. The figure took a step...toward him. And another, until it stood half-visible in the gray wash of light from outside. The pale light glinted in the squinting, unfocused eyes, in the cross-hatching of black blood trails across the face from the reopened wounds from yesterday and the new ones from the fall.

Ronnie saw the pistol the shadow man held at his side.

He fumbled his own pistol from its holster, his bandaged hand fitting clumsily around the crescent of the grip. Maybe it was the wound, or all that goddamn gauze, or that he'd never held his weapon on anything but a paper target, but the pistol felt big, heavy and awkward in his hand. He thumbed back the hammer as he raised the pistol, sighting past the edge of the gauze by his right eye to the front sight to the two glinting eyes floating before him in the half-light.

Those eyes cleared, focused. No fear in them. No defiance. Just...acceptance.

Ronnie held his pistol outstretched a long time, hours, years, his fingers tense around the grip and trigger, the muscles in his hand winding so tight the sutures in his hand began to open, blood soaked through the gauze, steamed in the cold air, dripped to the floor with soft little pats. His hand filled with blood and now the gun felt warm and comfortable there.

*Pat-pat-pat...*

The only thing keeping him from dropping the hammer was knowing even if he emptied the gun, it wouldn't be enough, even a 100 times over it wouldn't be enough...

*Pat-pat-pat...*

For the second time that day, he stood at the precipice, the dark abyss pulling at him, and he remembered the red brand of his hand on Lourdes Bracero's face…

He looked into those now sharp eyes fixing him and he thought, No, you go in that hole, you go alone. Ronnie carefully lowered the hammer on his pistol, let the weapon drop to his side.

The sharp look in front of him softened into puzzlement…then…sadness.

Ronnie looked away, didn't watch Jack Meara turn for the archway into the South Terminal, step out into the light from the strobes washing through…

The hard, block walls of the bus deck turned the dull pop of the pistol into the crack and roar of lightning and thunder. The bullet caught Meara high in the back, must've hit bone because he spun completely around before he fell with his face on the oil-splattered floor. The body heaved once, as if taking a last, preparatory breath, then eased into slackness, a last geyser of breath vapor, and it looked again as Ronnie had found it; a heap of rags.

Van Dyne was standing over the body, his nickel-plated Chief's Special in his hand, held at arm's length still sighted on the form on the floor. The captain stood over the body, nudged Meara's pistol out of his clenched fingers with the toe of his shining Florsheim, then knelt beside the body to feel for the carotid with his free hand. The captain nodded with finality, holstered his pistol as he picked up Meara's weapon and dropped it into his coat pocket. He stood, dusted off the knee of his sharply creased slacks.

Ronnie heard footsteps, dozens, saw a crowd of uniforms running toward them from both terminals.

Van Dyne started toward them, holding his badge high over his head so they'd know he was a cop.

Ronnie leaned against the parapet of the bus deck, closed his eyes, let the cold wind wrap around him. The traffic three stories below was muted, the air this high sweet and clear. He felt little damp dabs of snowflakes on his face. Somewhere the clang of a bell, softened by the falling snow, a Santa Claus collecting for the poor.

"How's your hand?"

He opened his eyes but didn't look at Van Dyne against the wall next to him. The gray sky had deepened in shade, the flakes had been fluttering down for some time, enough for the people below filing into the terminal to leave an ever-changing pattern of dark footprints in the thin carpet of white. Off to the left, 42nd Street was filling with a lava lamp glow of red and gold neon from the grindhouse marquees. Echoing around in the canyons of the city he could hear sirens.

He had his forearms parked on the parapet. Van Dyne must have noticed the spreading bleed-through blot on the bandage on his hand.

"You should have somebody look at that," Van Dyne said.

Ronnie shrugged.

"So," the captain said.

"So."

"It looks like Stabile set Maiella up for Meara. A porn theater over in Times Square. I guess his people were as fed up with this mess as we were. Problem is, Meara shot the wrong man. A civilian."

*Jesus. Even with him dead, it still gets worse and worse.* He heard the flick of the captain's lighter, caught a whiff of one of his Opals.

"Meara still managed to get his wish. Maiella's dead."

Ronnie turned to the captain, peeping out from around the gauze on his face, not quite sure he'd heard right.

Van Dyne smiled ruefully and blew a thin stream of blue smoke out into the fluttering snow. Ronnie remembered something from when he was a kid, from school or an old movie, about the old Greeks and how when they sacrificed something – a goat, a chicken – they would burn it on an altar and the smoke would carry it up to the gods.

"They had a couple of their own people waiting outside the theater in case Meara missed. He did. They didn't."

*Worse and worse.*

"I could charge the girl," Van Dyne said. "Aiding and abetting. Obstruction. If you want."

Ronnie shook his head and looked back out over the street, looked up at the white flakes materializing out of the darkening sky.

He heard Van Dyne sigh. "'For there is nothing either good or bad but thinking makes it so.'"

Ronnie took a deep, lung-cleansing breath of the cold, wet air, then turned to Van Dyne, holding out his holstered pistol and badge cover in his bandaged hand.

"Maybe this isn't the time to make that kind of decision," the captain said.

"It's the best time."

The captain frowned down at the pistol and badge, then took them and dropped them in his coat pocket. "I'll hold on to them for a while."

"You can hold on to them until the next ice age," Ronnie said. "I'm done."

"You should go home, Ron."

He started to cross the bus circuit. In the archway between the terminals, EMTs were lashing down a filled body bag to a stretcher, the rear door of their rig open and waiting while PATH cops directed a parade of buses past them, their windows filled with gawking faces.

"Ron?" The captain was standing against the parapet, silhouetted against the glow of the street, the iridescent flakes of snow. "Go *home.*"

Ronnie stepped outside the North Terminal doors on Eighth Avenue. The snow was falling thickly, now. The Midtown units were gone, replaced by a waiting line of Yellow Cabs. A young college type stood by the terminal doors, running fingers in fingerless gloves up

and down a recorder, tooting out a shivering *Jesu: Joy of Man's Desiring.*
An upended duffer's cap sat at his feet, in it some change, a few dollar
bills, a gum wrapper. The air was filled with the smells of pretzels and
roasting chestnuts, pralines and grilling kebabs, boiling hot dogs from
Sabrettes carts on the sidewalk around the terminal. Across the street,
against the fence of a parking lot, a row of slapped-together shoeshine
stands stood abandoned, the bootblacks clustered around a low fire in
a trash barrel trying to keep their hands warm. Not far from them, at
the corner of 42nd, a fat black lady in a white cape was screaming at
passersby through a bullhorn: "If you die tonight, would you go to
Heaven or Hell? 'All have sinned,' the Book says, and the wages of sin
is death and damnation! Satan's work is all a-*round* you, *pulling* at you,
*dragging* you into the *pit!* Into the *fire!* The Book says, 'Believe in Lord
Jesus Christ, and thou shalt be *saved!*'" Some people threw gum
wrappers at her, too.

And beyond her, off somewhere in the city, sirens, and clanging
bells for the poor.

He tuned them all out: the sirens, the fat lady in the white cape, the
honking car and bus horns, the cabbies cursing at the pedestrians who
wouldn't clear the crosswalk even after the light had changed, the
commingled smells from the food carts.

Ronnie closed his eyes, held his face up to feel the light, wet kisses
of the snow on his face. He took a deep pull of the cold air, opened his
eyes, and started down Eighth, toward Penn Station, and a train
headed south for home.

## ACKNOWLEDGMENTS

A writer may sit at the keyboard alone, but behind his/her chair are those who help and support.

I not only had the honor of calling the late, great NYPD detective Sonny Grosso a friend, but what I learned from him over the years about what it meant to be a policeman on the streets of New York is immeasurable. Thank you, Sonny (and his significant other, Chrissy Krauss, who kept the gears of the Sonny machine oiled and moving).

I have lost count of the books that have provided me with some understanding of both the procedural and human sides of policework, but have neve come across one better at illustrating the worldview of the American city cop than Adam Plantinga's *400 Things Cops Know: Street-Smart Lessons from a Veteran Patrolman.*

And, as always, my great gratitude to the ladies of my household who put up with the workings of the crazy old man in the basement.

Bill Mesce, Jr. is an award-winning author and playwright as well as a screenwriter. He is an adjunct instructor at several colleges in his native New Jersey.

Printed in Great Britain
by Amazon